WI...

"This pursuit novel roc... ...t
to stay alive and face... ...-
other. Fascinating seco... ...r
own books. Here's hoping the talented Bast will oblige."
—*Romantic Times*

"*Witch Heart* is a welcomed addition to the series, and readers who love Ms. Bast's books will not be disappointed."
—*Romance Junkies*

WITCH BLOOD

"Any paranormal fan will be guaranteed a Top Pick read. Anya has provided it all in this hot new paranormal series. You get great suspense, vivid characters, and a world that just pops off the pages . . . Not to be missed."
—*Night Owl Romance Reviews*

"Gritty danger and red-hot sensuality make this book and series smoking!"
—*Romantic Times*

WITCH FIRE

"Deliciously sexy and intriguingly original."
—*New York Times* bestselling author Angela Knight

"Sizzling suspense and sexy magick are sure to propel this hot new series onto the charts. Bast is a talent to watch, and her magickal world is one to revisit."
—*Romantic Times*

continued . . .

WITCH FURY

ANYA BAST

BERKLEY SENSATION, NEW YORK

THE BERKLEY PUBLISHING GROUP
Published by the Penguin Group
Penguin Group (USA) Inc.
375 Hudson Street, New York, New York 10014, USA

Penguin Group (Canada), 90 Eglinton Avenue East, Suite 700, Toronto, Ontario M4P 2Y3, Canada
(a division of Pearson Penguin Canada Inc.)
Penguin Books Ltd., 80 Strand, London WC2R 0RL, England
Penguin Group Ireland, 25 St. Stephen's Green, Dublin 2, Ireland (a division of Penguin Books Ltd.)
Penguin Group (Australia), 250 Camberwell Road, Camberwell, Victoria 3124, Australia
(a division of Pearson Australia Group Pty. Ltd.)
Penguin Books India Pvt. Ltd., 11 Community Centre, Panchsheel Park, New Delhi—110 017, India
Penguin Group (NZ), 67 Apollo Drive, Rosedale, North Shore 0632, New Zealand
(a division of Pearson New Zealand Ltd.)
Penguin Books (South Africa) (Pty.) Ltd., 24 Sturdee Avenue, Rosebank, Johannesburg 2196,
South Africa

Penguin Books Ltd., Registered Offices: 80 Strand, London WC2R 0RL, England

This is a work of fiction. Names, characters, places, and incidents either are the product of the author's imagination or are used fictitiously, and any resemblance to actual persons, living or dead, business establishments, events, or locales is entirely coincidental. The publisher does not have any control over and does not assume any responsibility for author or third-party websites or their content.

WITCH FURY

A Berkley Sensation Book / published by arrangement with the author

PRINTING HISTORY
Berkley Sensation mass-market edition / June 2009

Copyright © 2009 by Anya Bast.
Excerpt from *Wicked Enchantment* copyright © 2009 by Anya Bast.
Cover art by Tony Mauro.
Cover design by Rita Frangie.
Interior text design by Laura K. Corless.

ISBN: 978-0-425-22869-2

BERKLEY® SENSATION
Berkley Sensation Books are published by The Berkley Publishing Group,
a division of Penguin Group (USA) Inc.,
375 Hudson Street, New York, New York 10014.
BERKLEY® SENSATION and the "B" design are trademarks of Penguin Group (USA) Inc.

PRINTED IN THE UNITED STATES OF AMERICA

10 9 8 7 6 5 4 3 2 1

For Pete G.
who used to share his poetry with me.
You'll never be forgotten.

Acknowledgments

Thanks to the Sixth and Main Coffeehouse where I spent many hours working on this book . . . up until I figured out they had free Internet.

ONE

Sarafina might've been named for the angels, but she'd always known one day she'd end up in hell. Her mother had told her that a hundred times while she'd been growing up. She just never figured it would be while she was still breathing. But here she was—broke, dumped, and grief-stricken. It couldn't get any worse.

Her fingers white and shaking, she released the yellow rose she held and let it fall onto Rosemary's casket. It came to rest on the polished poplar top, followed by many more roses released by those around her. Yellow roses had been Rosemary's favorite. *They match your hair, buttercup.* That's what Rosemary had always said, holding one of the flowers up to Sarafina's nose.

Sarafina had scraped together every last cent for that shiny coffin. She hadn't been able to afford it. The funeral had almost beggared her. However, her foster mother had deserved the best. And since Rosemary had never had what she deserved in life, Sarafina had made sure she'd had it in death. The only problem was that now Sarafina had ninety-five dollars left in her bank account and rent had been due last week. She'd make it through, though, she always did.

She couldn't cry. It was like all the tears were caught up inside her, stoppered tight. It would be good if she could. It would relieve this awful pressure in her chest. Sometimes crying was like bleeding, it helped cleanse a wound. That's what Rosemary had always said.

"Bye, Rosemary," she whispered.

Reverend Evans droned on, but Sarafina hardly heard him. She barely noticed the others around her, either, all of Rosemary's friends who'd come to say their farewells. They clasped her hands after the funeral was over, squeezed her shoulder, and offered condolences. Her foster mother had had lots of friends.

If Sarafina had still lived here in Bowling Green, she knew she'd have half a million sympathy casseroles on her doorstep by now. As it was, she was headed back to Chicago right after the funeral. Back home.

She couldn't wait.

Still in a daze, she turned away from the grave and came face-to-face with Nick. His dark brown eyes regarded her solemnly from the handsome face she'd known for years. "You're not fit to drive seven hours today, Sarafina. Stay the night and head out in the morning. You can crash at my place."

A smile flickered over her mouth. "Oh, really? Amanda said that would be all right?"

She and Nick had been sweethearts during high school. Although that fire had long since flickered out and faded to friendship, Sarafina had lost her virginity to Nick. She strongly suspected his wife, Amanda, didn't want her on their couch.

Robin, another friend from childhood, came to stand near Nick. "If you don't want to stay with him, you can stay with me." She tilted her blond head to the side in a gesture Sarafina knew meant she was concerned.

Sarafina couldn't swing a cat in Bowling Green and not hit someone from her past. As soon as she'd arrived, she'd been beset by old friends—and other people. Those *other people* were why she wanted to leave so badly. Like, now.

Whispers.

In Bowling Green there were whispers wherever she went. *Hey, that's the girl who . . . Isn't that the daughter of the woman who . . .* She was a walking freak show. Even fifteen years after it had happened, people still recognized her. High school had been hell.

She leaned forward and hugged Nick, then Robin. "You-all are sweet to offer, but I have to go into the office tomorrow. I can't miss any more work than I have already." She had a funeral to pay off.

Nick shifted and frowned. "They don't give you grief leave?"

Damn it. Caught right in the middle of her subterfuge.

"Yes, a few days." She pressed her lips together. "It's just that—I don't want to . . ."

Understanding came over his face. "Oh."

Sarafina relaxed. "Yeah."

"It's too bad, but I get it, Sarafina," Robin said, her brown eyes sad.

"I'm glad you both understand. The other reason why I don't want to stay is because I don't want to wallow, you know? I need to stay busy, get my mind on something else. If I don't do that, it'll be worse. The grief, I mean."

If she lost her momentum now and allowed herself to be mired in the loss of the only true mother she'd ever known, Sarafina knew she'd just dissolve.

"This fall I'll come to visit." The words popped out before Sarafina realized it. She'd wanted to appease Robin, but they both knew her words were a lie. Sarafina only came back here when she absolutely had to.

"Will you, really?" asked Robin suspiciously.

"I-I promise to think about it."

Robin patted her back. "Will you at least call when you get home? I'm going to worry about you all day."

Sarafina nodded. "I will." She paused, swallowing hard. God, she wished she could cry.

It wasn't that she wanted to leave her friends. Sarafina loved them, as she'd loved Rosemary, but the town itself held too many bad memories. Once she'd turned eighteen she'd saved up her money, bought a car, and had driven away. Spending time here now, just breathing the air, it made her feel suffocated.

"Why didn't Alex come with you, anyway?" Nick asked.

Sarafina looked down at her toes. *Ugh.* "Alex and I broke up."

"What? When?" Robin exclaimed.

"About a week before Rosemary died. It just wasn't working out." Alex had dumped her, actually.

"I'm so sorry, sweetie," said Robin, cupping her shoulder.

Sarafina probably should've broken up with Alex first, a long time ago. Selfishly, she hadn't wanted to be alone. She'd been *afraid* to be alone, to be perfectly honest. Because of that fear she'd stayed with him long after the fire had gone out, up until Alex had decided to give the relationship the axe. He'd done them both a favor. It'd been like pulling a dying plant out by its roots. It was a relief not to have to watch the leaves wilt anymore.

"Honestly, I don't miss him much. I do miss you guys, though," she finished, her voice breaking.

Robin hugged her again, making Sarafina let out a small sob. "Well, then, come back," Robin whispered.

Sarafina shook her head and held on to her friend for another long moment. "I can't."

Robin drew back and smiled sadly. "I know."

Sarafina turned and walked away, toward her rusty Honda Accord. "I'll phone you when I get home," she called over her shoulder. That was, if her telephone service hadn't been shut off.

Robin and Nick stood at Rosemary's grave, waving.

She might be penniless and on the verge of bankruptcy, she might have no family left, and she might be newly dumped, but at least she had good friends. There was always a spot of light in the dark if you looked for it.

The Accord started with a little hitch that made her heart pound.

"God, please, no," she whispered. The last place on Earth she wanted to get stranded was Bowling Green, Kentucky. "If you're going to have trouble, do it far from here, okay?" she crooned at the vehicle. "Or better yet, don't do it at all. My bank account can't take it."

Holding her breath, she guided the car away from the curb and out of the cemetery. She'd take the long way back to the highway, avoiding the subdivision where she'd grown up. It was a pretty drive from here to Louisville, full of hills, gorgeous exposed rock walls, and green trees. Kentucky was a beautiful state, but Sarafina couldn't wait to get back to Chicago, where the scent of car exhaust filled her nose and the honking and voices of humanity constantly filled her ears. Where no one knew her on sight. No one knew her bizarre family history.

Where there were no whispers.

As she drove, a swell of memory assaulted her. Images her brain was able to suppress in Chicago reared their nasty heads here, so near her childhood home. In her mind a memory of her mother flickered. The middle-aged redhead stood on the lawn of their home brandishing a grilling fork, insane words pouring from her lips. Flames and the scent of burning . . .

Sarafina lunged for the radio and found a good station that played loud hard rock music. She opened the window of her car and threw herself into the song, singing the lyrics out loud. She wouldn't allow her mind to go back there, she just couldn't.

Instead, she thought of Grosset, her Pomeranian. She'd left him with her neighbor for the trip south and couldn't wait to see him again. Sarafina smiled. See? Life wasn't so bad. She had friends, a job, and most importantly, she had the love of a good dog.

Then there was that guy who kept asking her for a date. His name was Brian. No . . . Bradley. Cute, too. He was a UPS guy, came into the office every afternoon and sought her out specifically to sign for the deliveries. What was it about UPS guys? He flirted with her every day, cajoling her to go to dinner with him. It was flattering. She'd been turning him down because of Alex, but now she was free. Maybe the next time he asked, she'd say yes.

She rolled into a northern Chicago suburb in the early evening and parked in front of the beautiful eighteenth-century home where her apartment was located. It was only a few blocks from her office downtown, though she always took the EL in to avoid parking problems.

Stopping the car at the curb, she turned off the engine and stared up at the beautiful, huge windows. Sarafina loved this place. The neighborhood was quiet and older, the street lined with stately old trees. Hopefully, her landlord would give her an extension on the rent. Most likely he would. After all, this would be the first time she'd ever been late.

She knocked on her downstairs neighbor's door and Brandy, a college girl, answered. "Grosset? Oh, he's already at your place. Your boyfriend came and picked him up. He's cute!" she squealed, then said, "Your boyfriend, I mean. Grosset's cute, too, though. Ta!" and closed the door in Sarafina's face.

Boyfriend? God, she hoped Alex wasn't having second thoughts. She stared at the closed door for a moment, anxiety making her stomach muscles tighten. Then she stalked up the stairs to her apartment, her mind whirling about what she would say to him. Now that he was gone, she wanted him to stay that way.

Her apartment door squeaked open and she started down the hallway, hearing someone cough in the living room. "Alex, listen—"

She stopped short and her keys clattered to the floor. Shock held her immobile as she stared at Stefan Faucheux standing in her living room . . . holding her dog. Her mind stuttered.

Stefan Faucheux?

Everyone knew who he was. The rich playboy and CEO of Duskoff International had been the media's darling for a long time. He was everything they loved—handsome, interesting, intelligent, and monied. Then one day he'd disappeared. For a year the world had wondered where he'd gone. Foul play had been suspected and investigations undergone. All the entertainment shows had been atwitter with the mystery.

Then suddenly, six months ago he'd simply popped back into existence, taking up where he'd left off as if he'd never been gone. He'd been traveling, he'd explained. Mostly he'd been in Costa Rica surfing. No one had been able to find him because he hadn't wanted to be found. If you had enough money, Sarafina guessed, you could do that—just disappear without a trace. Personally, she wouldn't know.

Most people thought it had simply been a publicity stunt. Maybe they were right. Stefan seemed to like attention.

Right now he really wanted hers.

The bigger question was why? Why was he standing in her living room?

"Wha—" She started and then snapped her mouth closed as Bradley stepped out from her small hallway and stood next to Stefan.

What the hell were the UPS guy and Stefan Faucheux doing in her apartment?

Stefan inclined his head. "Sarafina Connell, it's a pleasure. I think you've already met my associate." He took a step toward her while Grosset panted and smiled a happy doggie smile at her. "We tried this the easy way, but you were more resistant than most to Bradley's charms. Women normally just swoon right at his feet, boyfriend or not, making our job so much easier."

"What's going on? What are you—"

"Since Bradley couldn't get you alone, I'm afraid we'll have to do it the less pleasant way. Trust me, we're doing you a favor." He clucked. "Data entry, Sarafina? You're wasting yourself. We'll make the most of your skills where we're taking you. I just wish your initiation could have been nicer."

That was a threat. Stefan Faucheux had just threatened her in her own living room, and he was holding her dog!

Sarafina opened her mouth to scream when someone grabbed her from behind, a big meaty hand clamping down hard over her lips. A needle bit deep into her hip and a thick drowsiness closed over her. Her knees buckled and someone lifted her. Her head lolled to the side, unconsciousness beckoning her in a slow wave.

Stefan tilted his head to the side and petted Grosset's silky head, while the Pomeranian panted happily. "Now we have you and your little dog, too."

TWO

Apparently, things *could* get worse. Extremely worse. Had she considered yesterday to be hellish? Yesterday had been a walk down a lane filled with daisies. Today she wasn't sure if she was even still alive.

Sarafina opened sleep-heavy eyes with colossal effort and watched two men make their way around the small room where they'd locked her up. She must still be alive since not even the drugs they'd given her could dull the sharp panic cutting up her throat or the slam of her beating heart. This was her worst nightmare. She was a ball of terror imprisoned in a body too heavy to move.

Alive in a dead body.

She'd been drifting in and out of consciousness for over twenty-four hours . . . she guessed. Just when the drugged lethargy began to ease from her muscles, someone came in and shot her back up again. The time had passed as if she lived in a lucid dream, her consciousness scrabbling against the padded container it was locked within.

As the men left the room and shut the door behind them, her eyelids grew heavy again. Sarafina struggled to keep them open, fought to stay conscious, but she was no match for the drugs wending their way through her veins.

When Sarafina woke next, the first thing she noticed was the absence of the heaviness in her limbs. She could move! Her fear was also gone, replaced by an all-consuming rage.

The second thing she noticed was a man sitting in a chair in the corner of the room, his face hidden by shadow. Creepy.

She bolted upright and addressed the most pressing matter at hand. "Where's my dog? I swear to God if you did anything to Grosset, I will—"

"Please, your dog is fine," came the dulcet voice of Stefan Faucheux, his French accent still audible even though he'd spent most of his life in the United States. He stood and smiled, spreading his manicured hands. "What do you take me for, a monster?" His full lips twisted and he gave a one-shouldered shrug. "Okay, so I'm a monster, but not one that hurts children or animals."

"Where is he?"

"He's safe, I assure you, sleeping on a doggie bed in my room. I will bring him to you after we've talked."

Sarafina pushed off the bed and went for the door. "Talk? No way. I'm getting my dog and leaving this place right now."

The door was locked, of course. She used both hands to twist the unyielding knob and when that didn't work, she hit and kicked the solid oak, yelling at it until she was hoarse.

Stefan stood in the center of the room, watching her with a patient expression on his face. Like she was a two-year-old throwing a tantrum and he was waiting for her to realize the futility of her temper.

Stymied by the door, she whirled and spotted a window. Ignoring Stefan, she stalked to it, pushing aside the heavy burgundy drapes. They appeared to be in a farmhouse in the middle of absolutely nowhere. Cornfields spread out in every direction she could see. The room they'd put her in was on the second floor and there was no convenient tree or trestle beyond the pane of glass. Not that Stefan would have let her get that far, anyway. Not that she would've tried it without Grosset.

She picked up a tacky porcelain figurine of a milkmaid from the table near the window, turned, and threw it at Stefan. He raised his hand and it burst into a ball of white-hot fire before it reached him, falling to the carpet and smoldering there.

She stared. "What the—"

"You have questions."

She jerked her gaze up from the melting piece of kitsch. "Questions? Yes, I have questions. What the . . ." She knew her eyes were just about saucer-sized.

"I can call fire, Sarafina." He smiled. "I play devil to your angel, yes? Although, as you will soon see, we're not that unalike."

Her stomach clenched. Calling fire. *Fire?* It had to be some kind of a trick. God! She had a headache. "You're playing some kind of sick and twisted game with me because you know about my mother. You saw the news articles or the TV show, and now you're doing this for kicks."

Stefan shook his head. "This has nothing to do with your mother, Sarafina. Not directly, anyway. It's not a game we're playing here."

She swallowed hard against her dry throat and mouth, a result of the drugs, she was sure. "What's going on? What do you want from me? *What was that crap you pumped through my body?*"

"We want to help you realize your potential, Sarafina. Nothing dark or sinister. We simply want to tell you who you are. Like many of our kind, you've slipped through the cracks of your heritage."

Sarafina turned to face him. "What are you talking about? Tell me who I am? I know that already. Anyway, if you're going to try and convert me to some cause, why not just ask me out for a nice cup of coffee? You have to resort to kidnapping?"

"If we had asked you for coffee and revealed this truth, you would have caused quite a scene and probably called the police. That's why we don't do it that way." He held out a hand. "We hope you'll forgive the kidnapping, Sarafina, once all is revealed."

She shook her head. "I want to go home. I want my dog and I want—"

"Data entry, Sarafina? No self-respecting fire witch would ever work in such a mundane field. What are you thinking? I can make your life so much more meaningful. I can provide a way for you to make lots of money so you can live the life you were meant to live."

The words *fire* and *witch* in the sentence made her vision dim. Her knees went weak and she caught herself on the back of a chair. "What did you say?"

"Don't pretend ignorance, Sarafina. Even if you don't know, you *know*."

She studied him. "The only thing I know is that you're crazy, as bat-shit crazy as my mother was."

Stefan smiled and took a step toward her. "Your mother *was* crazy, Sarafina. I'm sorry about that. I'm sorry your father went AWOL, too, because he would have raised you correctly. As it happened, your mother, your only living blood relative, went insane and torched herself before she could teach you anything. That's a pity for you."

Her mother, a highly religious woman, had raised Sarafina alone in a modest middle-class subdivision just west of Bowling Green. Every Sunday her mother had dragged her to church to cleanse the wickedness from Sarafina's soul. Every day her mother had told her she was sinner, a tool of Satan. For a while Sarafina had even believed her.

Sarafina's mother had said hell would be Sarafina's punishment for being a witch, her watery light blue eyes narrowed in accusation. She'd pointed a thin index finger and declared, *Thou shalt not suffer a witch to live!*

Nearly every single day her mother berated her, up until the time she'd gone straight past crazy and over the cliff of truly insane. After that her mother's berating days had come to a fiery end and Sarafina had collected a whole shiny new set of nightmares . . . and a foster mother.

Stefan's smile turned predatory. "As it turns out, it's an advantage for us, though."

"What's an advantage?" Her mind whirled. She couldn't track what Stefan was talking about. He made absolutely no sense. It was like talking to her mother at the height of her illness. Sarafina would've said she was on *Candid Camera* or something if the whole situation hadn't been so bizarre and threatening. *Candid Camera* did light and funny, not dangerous and crazy.

"That you're a fire witch, of course. A powerful, untrained, completely oblivious, and vulnerable fire witch." He smiled. "Ours for the taking, if we can convince you to work with us."

"W-witch?"

"I know it's hard to believe. I can imagine what you're thinking given your past and all the things I know you grew up with. It must be hard to comprehend that even though your mother was quite insane, she was also . . . right."

Sarafina shook her head. "This is nuts. This is—" She cut off her sentence, her breath coming faster and faster in an impending panic attack. She whirled, looking again for a way out even though she knew there was none.

"We don't have much time, so I'll prove it to you." Stefan stalked to her, knelt, and forced open her palm.

Power—that's the only word she could use to describe it—poured from her chest, right between her breasts. It bloomed bigger and bigger until she couldn't hold it anymore. It was hot, stinging her to the point of pain. Her head snapped back and something within her swelled in response. It became larger and larger until it exploded from the center of her.

Stefan stepped away and fire—*fire!*—streamed in an arc from the center of her body to land in a pool of white-hot intensity in the middle of the floor.

The stream ended in a tingling rush that made blood roar through her head. Her eyes wide and her heart pounding, she stared at the charred carpet of the room and marveled in the euphoric sensation of the power that Stefan had forced her to wield.

"Oh, my God!" she gasped, staring. The rug crackled.

"Ah, *there* you are. I knew you were in there somewhere." Stefan stared at her for a long moment, a strange smile on his mouth. Then he left the room, clicking the lock closed on the door behind him.

Sarafina stared at the singed spot on the floor until long after it had grown cold and black, until her shoulders hunched and her muscles were stony with stress. She stayed that way until the door opened again and the scrabbling of nails sounded on the floor. Doggie yelps of joy filled her ears. She broke from her imitation of a statue to scoop Grosset into her arms.

Nuzzling the Pomeranian's soft fur she sank down onto the floor and held him close, trying to absorb the massive shift her reality had just taken.

* * *

THEO PINCHED THE BRIDGE OF HIS NOSE. "LET'S JUST go in." Damn all the planning and waiting to hell and back. He wanted action.

"I agree with Theo. We don't have time to waste," said Jack McAllister.

Jack looked a little sick. Of course, Jack had just sent his only daughter north to protect her against the swelling magickal storm. If Theo had a two-year-old daughter who was a coveted air witch, he'd probably be feeling sick right now, too. Eva, the child, had gone to a secret location with several of the trusted Coven, including Helen, an earth witch of limited power who was the unofficial Coven nanny.

Thomas Monahan paced away from the elemental witches gathered around his desk, his face pensive.

"We don't know yet what's going on," said Claire in her quiet and strong voice. "However, the Duskoff have proven time and again they aren't to be trusted, isn't that right? Therefore, the Coven would be well within our rights to raid them. Anyway, it's not like they'd call the non-magickal police force in to combat us."

Thomas Monahan never did anything the rash way—well, not normally, anyway—but all the signs lately were pointing to something afoot, something dark and bloody. With the Duskoff that was usually the case. And there was ample evidence to suspect the Duskoff, a cabal of warlocks, were behind it. Warlocks were witches gone bad, who'd betrayed the Coven's rede of *harm ye none* and used their supernatural abilities for their own gain—for money and power.

Lately, there had been a rash of witches outside the Coven who'd gone missing—weaker, younger ones and more powerful ones who'd been alienated from their birthright somehow and were easy pickings.

They'd managed to take an air witch, too. Emily Parker, a witch of low ability, had been snatched from her home near Boston about three months ago and hadn't been heard from since. All Emily could do was send and receive faint messages via the air. She had no real power to call, couldn't pick objects up or send her consciousness out to travel from her body.

Hell, she was so low level the Duskoff probably wouldn't even want to sacrifice her in a demon circle. That's how the warlocks brought *Atrika* through from Eudae. The strength of the sacrificed witches mattered, and poor Emily had only a breath of power. No one could guess why they'd snatched her.

The Duskoff didn't only count on greed alone to fill their ranks. Kidnapping was how the Duskoff recruited some of their members; they got them young and seduced them to their side. If seduction didn't work, they broke them, twisted them, molded them. They were like the military at times, breaking down a witch completely and stripping away all that was, building them back up in the image of a warlock.

Theo knew the process all too well.

Judging from the recent frenzy of kidnappings and inductions, it seemed as if the Duskoff were preparing for something and were becoming desperate, like they were building an army and were running out of time. These days the warlocks were taking risky chances, kidnapping witches who were older and would be hard to break and remold.

The Coven had a lead on a house about an hour's drive from Chicago where the Duskoff were holding some of the unfortunate witches. Raiding it might yield some answers.

Theo turned and stared at Thomas's back. The head witch stood at the end of the room, staring out the huge picture window that looked out over part of the Coven grounds. "Thomas, it's time. Claire has taught us how to more effectively wield our magick. This will provide us with a great chance to show the dirty warlocks everything we've learned."

Claire was a different breed of witch. Raised on Eudae. By a trick of fate, she'd spent most of her life as handmaiden to a *Ytrayi* demon who'd twisted her magick little by little. She'd been born to the power of earth, but now she was the only witch anyone knew of who could draw on all four elements whenever she chose.

A year and a half ago, he, Claire, and Adam Tyrell had battled two *Atrika* demons—not to be confused with the other three demon breeds who were like fluffy bunnies in comparison—for her freedom. They'd won the battle and Adam had won the girl. These days Claire and Adam were deeply in love, and Claire served as the Coven's professor of elemental magick.

Thomas said nothing for a moment, then turned toward them. "We raid the farmhouse tomorrow morning. We'll take them by surprise and retrieve anyone they've got captive."

Theo's fists curled involuntarily. Getting out anyone who'd been taken; *yeah*, he wanted that job.

Thomas nodded at him, as if he knew exactly what was on his mind. "Theo, you'll be charge of taking back the kidnapped. Mira will head up a team to try and glean any additional information."

That meant securing warlocks and making them talk. Also a good job.

"What will you be doing?" Jack asked.

"Once we break the wards, Micah and I will have an errand of our own." Thomas looked at them each in turn and it was clear he had no plans to elaborate. "That's it. You got what you wanted. Claire, I need to talk to you. Everyone else can leave."

Dismissed. Claire had to stay after school. Adam gave her a wink and filed out of the room with the rest of them.

Theo headed to his apartment. He'd lived at the Coven since he'd been eighteen, when he'd gone to work here, and had one of the bigger quarters in the house. It was part of his compensation package. Really, he probably didn't get paid enough, considering he'd risked his life in the line of duty on more than one occasion, but Theo couldn't imagine living any other way.

He entered his living room, which was strewn with the detritus of bachelorhood—jeans slung over the back of his couch, shoes lying by the coffee table. Dishes stacked on the counter in the spacious kitchen, tumbled together with cooking equipment.

The kitchen was why he'd wanted this particular apartment. Earth witches had to cook up their spells and charms. They were a breed apart from the other elements that way, having no power seat in the center of them like air, fire, and water witches. Earth witches deliberately placed and stored power on their bodies. Some of them, like Theo, did it via magickally infused tattoos. He also stored it in his hair, which fell below his shoulders.

Theo inked other earth witches in the Coven, too. His equipment lay on a card table in a corner of the living room. He glanced at the clutter and rubbed his chin. Yeah, he really needed to hire someone to come in and clean.

He pulled his shirt off, let it land beside his discarded jeans, and headed to his workout room. The impending raid had his blood pressure and anticipation up. It coursed through his body, making him tingle with energy. He needed to burn some of it off.

The punching bag hung in the center of the large room, weights and workout equipment scattered around the edges. Not having much of a social life, work was Theo's primary focus. To do what he did—hunt down warlocks and bring them into Gribben, the prison on the Coven grounds—he needed to be in excellent shape. His workout room was where Theo spent most of his time, maybe rivaled by the kitchen.

Theo was all about giving the Duskoff payback. He lived for it.

After taping up his hands, he went straight for the bag and started in, hitting it with satisfying thuds that reverberated up his arms and through his shoulders. Punch, punch, roundhouse kick. Soon his whole world became the impact of his body against the bag, drowning out the clamor in his mind and bleaching the memories that haunted him to a shadow of their former selves. Working out was his meditation, bringing him to a place outside his head, clearing his mind and giving him peace just for a little while.

When he'd been seventeen, he'd been kidnapped by the Duskoff. He was a run-of-the-mill earth witch, a dime a dozen, but he was strong—stronger than average. The Duskoff had viewed him as vulnerable because of his youth and because his family situation had been bad. His status as an at-risk earth witch had earned him a one-way ticket into the bowels of Duskoff International. When seduction hadn't worked, they'd gone for physical torture.

Perhaps if Theo had been weaker of mind, emotion, or spirit, it might have worked. He'd been young enough to be broken down and remolded into an image of their choosing. After all, he'd been looking for a home, a family, somewhere to belong. But Theo had *known* he didn't belong to the Duskoff, known it down to his very fiber.

He'd fought them every inch of the way, a thing that had only made them more intent on breaking him. Eventually, once his torturers had figured out they weren't going to win, they'd used him as a toy. Then their treatment of him had come from pure sadistic ire—hatred of him and his resilience, his rejection of what the Duskoff stood for.

By the time the Coven had come in on a raid just like the one they were about to conduct, Theo had had broken limbs and organ damage. He'd almost died.

But he hadn't, and when he'd recovered the Coven had garnered his undying loyalty. They'd also become the family he'd never had.

Scars marked his torso as a result of the ordeal, trailed down his arms and legs. They'd been made by a whip and a very sharp knife. Theo could still clearly remember the man who'd made the cuts, his greasy face shining in the wan light of the building's basement. Years later Theo had looked into that face again, right before he'd dragged his ass to Gribben. Being in Gribben, a place that magickally neutered all witches, was worse than death.

Otherwise he'd have killed him.

Ink covered a lot of Theo's body now, playing counterpoint to the scars. The tats weren't there to cover them, but to celebrate them. The black tribal marks twisted alongside his scars, swirled around and dovetailed them. Theo wore his scars like badges of honor.

He always would.

Theo hit the bag hard enough to send it sailing into the wall behind it.

He was looking forward to tomorrow.

THREE

❧

"WHO WAS THE MAN WHO CAME INTO MY ROOM last night? Big guy, glowing red eyes." The words came out surprisingly calm considering the fact that Sarafina's stomach wobbled like a mountain of Jell-O. Perhaps the last few days had numbed her to strange and bloodcurdling events.

During the second night of her kidnapping, a man had entered her room while she'd been sleeping. She'd awoken to see him looming over her bed, studying her in the dark with eerie red-colored eyes.

Yes, *red* eyes.

It was too much. Too weird. Far too creepy. All of this was one step beyond what her rational mind could take.

She'd snatched Grosset close to her and screamed. The man had simply smiled, melted into the shadows, and left the room. Actually, it had seemed as though he'd *disappeared*, but that was impossible.

After that she'd wedged a chair under the doorknob and been wide awake until morning. Today she was exhausted, past her weird threshold and annoyed as hell.

Stefan's jaw locked for a moment and his expression looked pinched. "Calm down, Sarafina, I'm certain he was only curious about you. I will give Bai a stern talking to and it won't happen again."

She crossed her arms over her chest. "You'll give Bai of the *red eyes* a stern talking to? Do monsterlike men with red eyes accept it when you talk *sternly* to them, Stefan? Do they obey you?" Sarcasm drenched her words. "I want out of here now. I *demand* to be set free."

Stefan chuckled like she was cute, which ratcheted her blood pressure into the stratosphere. "Have you had some time to think?"

"I don't want to think. I just want to go." She moved toward the door, Grosset at her heels.

Fire puffed into existence two feet in front of her. She gasped at the intense heat and coughed when smoke filled the air. "I suggest you sit down, Sarafina." All the chuckle was gone from Stefan's voice now.

Defeated, she sank into a wing-backed chair across from Stefan. Grosset jumped into her lap and bared his teeth at the man across the room. At least the little dog was finally figuring out the score.

It had been just yesterday when her world had been tipped on its axis and shaken like a bone between Grosset's teeth. They'd given her the rest of that first day alone to absorb the information. Yesterday evening Bradley had come to her and again she was shown the magick she held within her. Bradley had done it in a much gentler way, no yanking it from the center of her the way Stefan had.

She'd learned how to pull threads of her power and perform tasks with them, like lighting candles and producing puffs of fire. She could do everything Stefan could do, but she knew all too well he outmatched her in the power and experience department.

She stroked Grosset's head. "I would need a lifetime to get used to the idea that magick and witches are real."

Stefan shifted in his seat. "I find that hard to believe considering your younger years. You must have had some clue."

"The only clue I had was the one that told me my mother was insane," she snapped.

"You never once entertained the notion that all those times your mother called you a witch she might be telling the truth?"

Sarafina tipped her head to the side. "What the hell is wrong with you? Of course not."

Stefan's faint smile faded. He leaned forward. "Most witches worth a damn can feel it somewhere deep inside."

She flinched. How could it be that the comment actually

hurt? She didn't care about being a witch "worth a damn," did she? At this point she barely believed she hadn't gone insane herself.

Irritation swept through her. "Look, you told me what I need to know, showed me beyond a shadow of a doubt my true nature, now it's time for me to go. I have a life, you know? I have a job I need to get back to, bills to pay, friends who—"

"You're not cut out for data entry, Sarafina." He shook his head. "Fire witches don't work in cubicles or fetch coffee for their bosses. Stay here with us so that we can show you your true potential, so you can harness your birthright and get all that is due you."

Due her? Apparently, she lacked the sense of entitlement that this man had decided she should have.

Sarafina looked down at Grosset. "Look, I'm grateful that you"—her mouth snapped shut as she searched for the right wording—"unlocked this unexpected part of me, but I don't owe you anything, and I don't think the world owes me anything, either. You're lucky I don't call the cops on you-all." She would, of course, but it was no help telling him that. Holding Grosset close to her chest, she stood. "I really am leaving now."

Stefan stood, his handsome, pleasant face overcome with storm clouds. "You're not going anywhere. You do *owe* us, Sarafina. Don't make us do this the hard way."

Yeah, she'd been afraid he'd say something like that.

Her anger flared. In response, that seed of hot magick buried in the center of her chest pulsed with newfound power. Sarafina knew Stefan was a fire witch, one far more skilled than she was at wielding the element as a weapon. Newly born, so to speak, she had no chance against him.

But there was no way she was staying here, and no way she was going down without swinging. She set Grosset to the floor so he wouldn't be hurt.

Unbidden and largely untutored, raw fire magick bubbled up from her, streaming down the backs of her arms.

Stefan stiffened, sensing the swell of her magick. The air suddenly smelled hot as the witch in front of her allowed his own power to rise. Apparently, it was high noon and they were headed for a showdown.

Shouting came from beyond the room. Stefan turned his head and Sarafina took the distraction as an opportunity.

She fumbled for a moment, wondering what the hell she should do next, when an uncontrolled burst of flames exploded from her. It felt like she'd fired a cannon and hadn't aimed well. It went wide, toward the door of the room.

The door burst inward, ripped from the hinges at the same time the uncontrolled blast of fire hit it. Sarafina screamed in surprise, stepped backward, tripped, and fell on her ass.

For a hazy, confused moment she thought her magick had exploded the door. Then she focused past the smoke and saw the dark outline of a man—tall, muscular build, long dark hair, grim expression on his face.

The man glanced at her for the barest of moments. His long hair blew around his face from the force of the magickal battle behind him. His eyes were hard and dark. In his brutal expression lay control and power. Knowledge—deep and wide. Sarafina noticed all that about him in a second and it took her breath away.

What new nightmare was this man?

The newcomer turned and deflected an aggressive attack from Stefan. The room exploded into chaos. Two men barreled through the door after the intruder. Instead of using magick to defend himself, he punched one in the face, grabbed him by his shirt front, and threw him into the second. Then he whirled to once again face Stefan.

The scent of white-hot fire and dark, rich earth filled her nose as furniture slid across the floor and slammed into the walls. The floor itself rippled. It was like a battle of supernatural titans.

Sarafina clutched Grosset to her chest and crawled behind an overturned table, holding her trembling dog close and wishing like hell this was all some really strange dream fueled by her grief. Any second now she'd wake up and shake her head over it, tell herself she'd never eat cold enchiladas before bed again.

But this was no dream.

Shouting, cursing. Explosions. Fire crackling. Growing hotter and nearer until thick bursts of earth extinguished the flare-ups.

Silence.

Footsteps pounded through the rest of the house. Shouting in the distance. In the room where Sarafina and Grosset hid behind the overturned table there was no sound. Nothing.

Maybe the intruders—whoever they were—had forgotten about her. Maybe the hulking man in the doorway had gone away. Maybe this was her chance to get out of here.

Moving slowly, she peeked around the edge of the table and saw only a smoldering fire in a trash can over in the corner of the room. Smoke wafted through the air. She inched out a little more, straining to hear any other sounds from inside the house. She didn't know who the party crashers were and wanted to avoid them. With her luck they were worse than Stefan and his ilk.

Movement. The swirl of a long black duster.

The man was still there. Peeking out, she watched him circle the room, languid, lethal. His muscular body seemed tense with the desire to kill something, didn't really matter what. The man turned toward her and she ducked back behind the table and closed her eyes, praying he'd pass her by.

"Warlock."

A hand grasped her collar and lifted her straight up. Sarafina screamed and Grosset exploded in a flurry of Pomeranian rage. He snapped and growled at the man who'd trapped her in his big, sweaty, meaty hands—hands big enough to snap her neck in two seconds flat, she noted with unease.

"Tell your dog to chill." The words came out gravelly, like they were forced from an infrequently used set of vocal cords. His grim expression grew even darker, his eyebrows coming together in the middle and the lines around his mouth deepening.

If she'd met this man on the street, she'd turn and walk the other way out of sheer instinct for self-preservation.

And she was currently caught in his powerful hands.

She stood trembling with fear, pulling as far away from

him as his grip on her shirt would allow. "G-Grosset, baby, it's okay. S-shhh. S'okay, baby."

Grosset could scent her fear and hear the tremor in her voice. He wasn't a stupid dog and knew when his mistress was lying. The crazy dust mop only yapped louder. Pomeranians had no sense of size. He thought he was a Rottweiler.

The man growled and yanked her forward. "You're coming with me, warlock. You were all cozy in here with Faucheux. That means you're special, and you've got tales to tell."

Warlock? What the hell? What was a warlock? Wasn't a warlock a male witch? Couldn't he fucking see she had boobs? Her mind spun. She'd just gotten used to the idea of witches. Now there were warlocks? "Listen, I'm not—"

He shook her once. That was enough. Her brain rattled in her skull and she snapped her mouth closed. "Quiet," he snarled.

The man yanked her out of the room and Grosset followed, sinking his teeth into the man's pant leg. God, she was afraid the hulk would kick him, kill him, but all he did was drag him along with him as though the small dog wasn't even there.

Sarafina gasped at the state of the house. It was like a battlefield. Men and women lay motionless on the floor, draped over chairs and tables. Some groaned and moaned, nursing injuries. Others went to each of the fallen, inspecting wounds and trussing some up like prisoners.

The whole place smelled like magick. Now that she knew what magick smelled like, she could pick out the individual elements. Together, it all burned her nose with a harsh, bitter bite.

The man pulling her through the house stopped for no one, talked to no one, helped no one. Her panic grew with every step she took. There was no way she was leaving with this man.

Once they hit the outdoor air and sunshine blessedly bathed her face, burning away the stink from the magickal battle within, she bolted. Pulling away from him with a sudden jerk, she scooped up Grosset and cleared the front steps in a single leap, hitting the grass running.

She'd been on the track team in high school and apparently she hadn't forgotten anything. A cornfield surrounded the house and she made for it, intending to hide among the autumn stalks.

The man bellowed behind her—a roar of displeasure that chilled her blood. She forced her feet to move faster. A bolt of power moved the earth at her heels and she yelped, plunging into the cornfield. Holding Grosset firmly to her, the dry stalks slapped her face and arms as she plowed through them.

Sarafina darted to the right and then slowed, moving carefully now to avoid breaking the late season stalks and leaving a clear trail for him to follow. Weaving in and out and back and forth as quickly as she dared, she got lost in the field.

But she knew he was right behind her; she could feel his presence.

Something behind her boomed and the rich scent of overturned earth filled the air. The very ground behind her furrowed in a ridge, following the path she'd taken through the field like a heat-seeking missile.

Sarafina didn't have time to think, to breathe, to do anything. The ground shook beneath her, parted, and she went straight down into it, screaming. Grosset jumped from her arms and landed near her, barking like a furry wild thing.

She lay on her belly, spitting out dirt when his big hands closed around her waist. He swung her up and set her on her feet. She was covered in earth and exploded bits of cornstalk. It smeared her face and clothes, caught in her hair, and was ground into her palms. Grosset was barking his little Pomeranian head off.

The man's heart-stopping glower swung from her to the dog and he took a step toward her pet.

Sarafina jumped into his path, blocking his way to Grosset, and put a hand to the man's chest. It was like touching a boulder—just as hard and just as cold. "Get away from him!"

He simply reached out, grasped her by the shoulders, and moved her to the side. Then he scooped the dog into his hands. Grosset—to Sarafina's surprise—didn't bite him. Of course, Grosset didn't have the best taste in men. He'd proved that by allowing Stefan Faucheux to coddle him.

The man didn't say anything, he only took her by the upper arm and gave her a look that said: *you can't get away from me.*

Yeah, okay, she understood.

He pulled her through the stalks toward the house.

"Theo," a man called when they emerged from the field and into the house's front yard. A blond man with short spikey hair and a crooked nose jogged toward them. "We're taking all the warlocks we round up to Gribben."

Theo—the hulk—shook her a little. Anger made her jaw lock and her body stiffen. "This one was having a close tête-à-tête with Stefan. She needs to be interrogated."

Oh, great, interrogation. Fun.

The blond man looked her up and down and frowned. "Are you okay?"

"*Marvy.*"

"We're not the monsters here."

"Could've fooled me." She spat the words.

The blond man turned his gaze back to Theo, ignoring her pointedly, and jerked his head toward her. "She's a charmer."

"Yeah. Any sign of the air witch?"

Crooked nose man shook his head. "No luck. They've got her hidden away good. Not even Mira or Claire can hear a peep."

"Fuck."

"Yeah. You can take this one back in the van. I'll see you at the Coven." He turned and strode back to the house, where a pretty woman with long, curly dark hair waited for him on the porch.

Theo yanked her forward and she jerked away from him and snapped, "Stop touching me. Touch me again in this lifetime, and I swear to God I'll sear the flesh from your bones."

Not that she knew how to sear the flesh from someone's bones, but, wow, it sounded impressive.

"Don't run."

"I won't run, genius." She looked pointedly at Grosset. "You're holding my dog hostage."

FOUR

➤

STILL COVERED IN DIRT THE WAY A WARLOCK SHOULD
be, the woman flounced down onto a cream-colored chair in
one of the Coven's common areas, crossed her arms over her
chest, and glared at him.

Her dog jumped into her lap and settled down, looking
up at him with beady black eyes, unaware that Theo was
inches away from strangling his human.

Grime streaked the woman's long blond hair and her
light blue eyes gave him the gaze of death from a filthy face.
One long leg moved incessantly in her agitation. Too bad
she was a warlock; she was pretty. But she definitely had the
temper to go with her element.

"What's your name?"

Her full lips compressed and she looked away.

"Tell me now or tell me later, but you'll like it better if you
tell me now."

Her gaze snapped to his face. "Don't threaten me." Her
chin rose. "I can call fire."

"And I can call earth. You know that because you're wearing it. Don't play with me. Earth trumps fire. I can counter
anything you throw at me. Don't make empty threats." He
bared his teeth. "*I* don't."

Carefully and slowly, she unclenched her teeth. "My
name is Sarafina Connell."

"Before I throw your warlock ass in Gribben, Sarafina
Connell, tell me what you and Stefan were talking about
when I came in."

She drew a breath and looked away from him. Her fingers

found dog fur and stroked. "He was telling me I was his prisoner. That I owed him for showing me I was a witch and I had to stay there with them and do—" She broke off. The breath hissed between her teeth. "Whatever it is they want me to do. I don't know. I had the feeling that if I pressed the matter my safety would be in question."

Theo considered her for a moment before drawing the obvious conclusion. "You're going to play the part of an abductee to avoid Gribben, is that your plan? It won't work with me. I know better than that. Stefan wouldn't be playing footsie with a kidnapped witch."

Her head snapped around. "*I am an abductee!* Twice! First Stefan Faucheux appears in my living room, then you take me from him. God, I'm so *sick* of this whole thing!"

She stood and paced the room, leaving dirt marks on the carpet as she went. Her dog leapt from her arms and watched her. She muttered to herself as she walked back and forth. "I was minding my own business, living my life. I come home from a trip to find Stefan Faucheux has broken into my apartment. Two seconds later, I'm out cold. I wake up in a strange place, surrounded by strange people—*kidnapped*. They pull this . . . this *ball of fire* out from the center of my chest and teach me how to use it." She stopped short and the silence stretched like a piece of taffy. "They told me my mother wasn't half as crazy everyone thought she was," she finished softly.

Theo blinked, staring at her back. If she was acting, she should get an Oscar. And maybe that meant she wasn't really acting. *Maybe.*

"The Duskoff have been taking many vulnerable witches lately," he said finally. "Older witches, too."

She whirled. "Who are you calling old, buddy?"

"For the Duskoff, over eighteen is old. Normally, they don't try and recruit any older than that."

"Recruit me? That's what they were trying to do?" She made a scoffing sound. "Man, they suck at it."

He sighed and rubbed his face. The fight at the farmhouse had been brutal and he was tired and drained. Either she was telling the truth and he'd mistreated her, or she was a great actress with something to hide.

Stefan Faucheux didn't deal with just any witch. Only those highest in the hierarchy held court with him. It seemed unlikely he'd be giving this kind of specialized attention to a recent abductee. Stefan didn't get his hands dirty, that's what the underlings were for.

So, what to do about this woman while he decided if she was a victim or a villain?

His mind flicked through possibilities. He could hand her over to Claire and Adam for the night, or maybe Isabelle, but they were all busy with the real abductees and dealing with the warlocks at Gribben that they'd managed to round up and bring in. Anyway, he didn't trust anyone but himself to keep an eye on her.

But did he really want to bring a possible fire warlock into his abode for the night? That was a little like volunteering to sleep with a black mamba, wasn't it?

"Just let me go home," Sarafina said in a low, quiet voice. Her shoulders slumped. "That's all I want. I just need for this nightmare to end."

He sighed and rolled his eyes toward the ceiling. "Come with me." He turned and walked to the door, the dog trotting at his heels.

Sarafina followed. "You're letting me go?"

He scoffed. "Hell, no."

"Then where are we going?"

"My room. Let you take a shower, eat, then sleep. We'll sort this out in the morning."

Silence.

He stopped and turned to see she'd halted in the middle of the corridor. Hip cocked. Toe tapping. "I'm not sleeping in your room."

"You don't have a choice, princess. Anyway, I'm not attracted to you. Get over yourself." He turned on his heel and continued on.

To his gratification, the dog panted along right beside him, ensuring she'd follow. Fuck, he should've grabbed the stupid dog first thing.

* * *

HE PUT A PLATE WITH A PEANUT BUTTER AND JELLY sandwich down in front of her. Theo, apparently, wasn't exactly a gourmet chef, or any kind of chef. Her stomach growled, anyway, and she fought not to fall on it like a starving dog.

Speaking of dogs, Grosset was digging into a bowl of SPAM, the only thing Theo could find in his kitchen for him.

She'd taken a shower and dressed in his clothes, a pair of sweatpants and a sweatshirt about five sizes too big. Scrubbed clean, she picked at the crust of her sandwich and eyed him. He leaned against the counter, partially blocking a tangle of dirty cooking pots, bowls, and wooden spoons. All of them smelled of herbs, not of food. Spell-stirring? Did witches do that in real life just like in the movies?

He was lean, but thickly muscled. When she'd been showering, he'd changed into a pair a faded jeans and a tight long-sleeved black shirt that showed every ridge and valley to intimidating perfection. At the cuffs and neckline, black tribal tattoos writhed on his dark skin, stretching up his throat with power-filled tendrils. Sarafina could feel the pulse and beat of his magickal strength even across the room. As she watched him, he crossed his arms over his chest and glowered at her.

And that was his intention, of course—to bully her. If this man enjoyed anything in life—and Sarafina had her doubts on that score—it was menacing people.

"Eat," he barked in a low voice.

"It's not poisoned, is it?"

He rolled his eyes, leaned forward, grabbed one half of the sandwich, and took a bite. While he chewed and swallowed, he threw the bitten sandwich back onto the plate. Sarafina stared at it, lip curled.

"See? Not poisoned." He growled. This man always growled. It was just a natural part of his voice.

Avoiding the contaminated half, she took a bite and closed her eyes. God, when a person hadn't eaten for a day and a half PB&J tasted like just about the best thing in the whole world.

"What's your dog's name?"

Well, at least he'd turned somewhat talkative. He hadn't

said much at all since they'd walked the corridor. Once in the apartment, he'd mostly just shoved things at her and grunted.

"Grosset," she answered around a mouthful.

"Why Grosset?"

She shrugged and took another bite. "That's just his name. That's what the Humane Society said it was."

"He looks like a tribble."

"He's not a tribble, he's a Pomeranian!"

"Whatever you say." He grunted again and pushed off the counter. "I'm going to bed. Take the couch."

"What if Grosset has to pee?"

Theo stopped in the doorway and spoke without turning around. "You're not getting out of my place tonight, not for nothing."

She sighed and shrugged a shoulder even though he couldn't see the gesture. "Dogs have to pee. You can't stop nature." She paused. "You're not very good with people, are you?"

He stood for a moment, shoulders hunched, his body going tight. Then he scooped Grosset up mid-SPAM bite and stalked out of the apartment. Sarafina smiled a little, knowing she'd just annoyed the hell out of him. That gave her a little thrill of satisfaction. Maybe now she had a nice short-term goal. Short-term since she planned to get out of here just as fast as she could.

He was good-looking in a way that would make most women's mouths water. Tall, ripped, handsome, virile, and mysterious as all get-out.

Too bad his personality left so much to be desired.

She finished the half of her sandwich Theo hadn't bitten and went into the living room. The first thing she did was try the door. It was locked with a dead bolt and there wasn't a key in sight. Not that she'd leave without Grosset, anyway. Theo had found her Achilles' heel right there.

Sarafina turned and surveyed her surroundings. Discarded clothes lay over the couch, the floor, and the card table in the corner. Loose herbs scattered the coffee table and the carpet. It was pretty clear that Theo wasn't much of a housekeeper to go along with not being much of a cook.

From the looks of this man's apartment, he didn't receive many visitors and Sarafina highly doubted he had any kind of a steady girlfriend, either. Of course, given his disposition, that wasn't much of a surprise.

Sarafina was the outgoing type and she had lots of friends who stopped by at all hours of the day and evening. Just because of that, she kept her place picked up. Of course, she also cleaned while she was depressed or stressed, which meant that lately her apartment had been pretty much spotless.

Right now her fingers itched to find a dustpan, but no way was she doing this guy any favors.

The thought of her friends made a small jolt of panic go through her. They were probably concerned about where she was. She wondered if they'd contacted the police yet.

Biting her lower lip and suddenly in full-on worry, she picked the clothes up off the couch without even thinking about it and cleared the coffee table. Before she knew it, she'd cleaned the whole room, piling Theo's clothes onto his bed.

God, what did the man do, just shed his clothes as soon as he walked through the door? Did he prefer to hang out in his place nude all the time? A vivid image of him naked popped into her head and made her mouth go dry.

"That's enough of *that*," she scolded herself under her breath and grabbed a blanket and pillow from the linen closet and threw them onto the couch.

The door opened and Theo came through, Grosset trotting at his heels. Sarafina realized with a start that she hadn't worried for a moment about her dog in Theo's care. She'd trusted him not to hurt her beloved pet.

That didn't mean she liked the man, though.

Ignoring his presence, she settled down on the couch and pulled the blanket over her. Grosset jumped up to lay beside her.

Theo lingered in the doorway for a long moment. "Okay?"

"Okay?" She twisted around to look at him. "Okay about what? Okay that I was kidnapped by a darling of society and had my witch powers activated? Or okay that some big untalkative guy is holding me captive in his apartment and making me sleep on his couch after he gave me a mud bath earlier in the day?" She blinked. "Which life-altering event are you asking me if I'm okay about?"

He shifted and his expression grew stormy . . . well, storm*ier*, anyway. "You cleaned."

"Wow, your powers of observation leave nothing to be desired, do they?" She flopped onto her side so she wouldn't have to look at him.

"Do you have enough blankets?"

"I'm fine. Can you please stop talking to me now?"

"My pleasure. I'm going to bed." He started to walk toward the hallway.

"Wait!" She turned to face him. "Look, big guy, do me a favor. Forget the not-talking thing. Sit down with me and pretend you actually don't think I'm a warlock. Tell me where I am, what warlocks are, why they're bad, and all that stuff."

"I won't play games with you." The words came out in an especially low growl.

"I don't want to play a game, I just want information."

"Bullshit. You want to play me for a fool." His voice rose. "You want the pleasure of having me sit there and tell you things you already know so you can laugh at me."

Damn it. "That was a lot of words." She compressed her lips into a thin line. "Did saying all that give you a headache?"

"I—"

"Never mind." She turned back and rolled her eyes. "Forget I asked."

"I already have." He turned and left the room.

FIVE

❦

MICAH LAID A MANILA FILE FOLDER ON THE TABLE
in front of Theo. "Sarafina Connell. We found files on some
of the kidnapped witches and hers was among them." Micah
and Isabelle had been put in charge of sorting out the abducted witches they'd recovered from the farmhouse the day
before.

Theo stared at the file folder. "She could be lying about
her name." He still believed Sarafina was a warlock. She had
to be. Every instinct he had screamed she was dangerous, no
matter the pretty package she came in.

The Coven archivist and all-around geek snapped the file
open. There, paper-clipped to a sheaf of papers, was a photo
of Sarafina. It had been taken while she'd been sitting at a
Starbucks. She was talking with a good-looking man about
her age. Her head was tipped back on a laugh, her long blond
hair curling around her shoulders and falling down her back.
One hand gripped a paper coffee cup, her slim arm resting
on the tabletop near the man's.

"That your woman?"

Theo nodded.

Micah flopped down in the chair opposite him and pushed
one hand through his shaggy brown hair. "Then she's an
abducted witch and she's been telling you the truth, Theo."

Fuck. He picked up the file folder and began reading the
information on her. "It doesn't make sense."

"It doesn't make sense, I agree," said Isabelle from across
the room. She sat on the edge of her husband's desk, one
long leg swinging, foot encased in a red sandal. "Why was

Stefan meeting with this woman, this *one* abductee? What makes her so special?"

"There's nothing out of the ordinary in her file," Micah answered. "Both her parents were fire witches. Her father left when she was just a baby, leaving her to be raised by her very religious mother. We're talking born-again Christian, here—fire, brimstone, and big tent revivals. There's no way to know the mother's story, but as near as I can piece together, being a witch sent her right off the deep end. Sarafina's mom is famous in Bowling Green because one day when Sarafina was eight, her mother chased her out of their house screaming at her for being a witch, then burst into flames halfway down the block in one of their neighbor's backyards."

"Oh, wow," murmured Isabelle. "Her power killed her. Maybe she didn't even know how to wield it. Maybe it just exploded out of her when her emotions ran high."

"Yeah, I tracked down all the old news stories on it. It freaked out everyone in town. It's still studied by parapsychologists as one of the most well-documented cases of spontaneous combustion on record. They did a fucking *Unanswered Mysteries* segment on it."

"Poor woman," said Isabelle softly. "Her name makes sense, if her mother was really religious. Does Sarafina play off the—"

"Seraphim," Micah interrupted her. "The highest-ranking angels of heaven according to Jewish scripture." He paused and twisted his lips. "It also means burning one."

Isabelle's jaw dropped. "Tell me you looked that up and didn't just know it off the top of your head."

They continued talking to each other, but Theo didn't listen. At the back of the file folder were several more photos of Sarafina. In one she held the hand of the man from the coffee shop, probably her boyfriend. The warlocks seemed to have watched her for quite some time before they'd snatched her. Gods, she really did look like an angel with all her long pale hair, creamy skin, and light blue eyes.

Theo looked up from her photos. "After her mother died what happened to her?"

"She didn't have any extended family to take her, so she

went into foster care. She went to a couple of different families before finding one woman whom she stayed with until she was of age. They were very close. In fact, she'd just come home from burying her foster mother when Stefan snatched her."

Theo gazed down at Sarafina's smiling face. In all the photos she was laughing and smiling, yet she'd had such tragedy in her life.

"Bastard," said Isabelle under her breath. "So Sarafina probably didn't know what the hell she was until Stefan showed her. Sounds like her mother didn't accept her power, then offed herself accidentally when Sarafina was just a child. There were no other blood relatives and the father disappeared when she was just a baby. Sarafina's foster mother was a non-magickal, right?"

Micah nodded.

Isabelle pushed off the desk and walked toward them, her expression thoughtful. "So she's one of the few out there who made it to adulthood without knowing who they truly are."

It happened sometimes, witches slipping through the cracks, though it was uncommon. The only one Theo knew personally was Mira McAllister. Her parents had been air witches sacrificed in a demon circle by William Crane, Stefan's father and once the head of the Duskoff. Mira's aunt had raised her with strict instructions from Mira's parents to keep her witchiness a secret. All that had changed once the Duskoff got wind of her status as a rare and powerful air witch. They'd wanted to sacrifice her in a demon circle, but had ended up with more than they'd bargained for.

Theo looked back down at the pictures. "She's strong. You can feel it radiating off her in waves. It's uncontrolled, but the intensity is there."

"I know what you're thinking," Micah answered. "You're thinking that's why Stefan seemed to be paying extra attention to her, because she's kicking powerful." He shook his shaggy head. "I don't think that's the reason why."

"I don't know." He shook his head. "Judging from her mother combusting like she did, she had to be really powerful, too."

"There are lots of powerful fire witches in the world," Micah answered. "It doesn't mean His Majesty, Stefan Faucheux, would want to spend personal time with them. I'll do some more digging and see what I can come up with."

"In the meantime, let her go. Send her to me, Theo," said Isabelle. "I'll smooth things over with her a little and then send her home."

He turned and glared at her. "What makes you think I can't smooth things over with her?"

She made a scoffing sound. "Uh-huh. No offense, but you lack skill in the diplomacy department. Better send her to me. I can only imagine how you've treated her. I heard all about the run through the cornfield. In hindsight that was pretty brutal, wasn't it? She probably hates your guts."

Theo thought back to the conversation he'd had with Sarafina the night before. How she'd asked him to tell her about the world she'd fallen into and how he'd rebuffed her. Isabelle's words hit him in the solar plexus. Sarafina almost certainly did hate him.

He glanced down at the file folder. "Probably."

"Okay. We're agreed. Un-abracadabra the earth wards on your door and send her down to me, poor woman."

Theo rose, holding the file. "I'll go get her."

He left the room and headed to his apartment. He should be happy to be free of the woman and her yapping little dog, but tension had settled in the pit of his stomach instead. Perhaps it was because he still sensed that Sarafina—never mind the fact she was named for a kind of angel—was dangerous. Theo didn't like the idea of releasing her. Or perhaps it was because she was, in fact, an innocent and he'd treated her so brutally. Hell, she'd been abducted just like he'd been. Maybe guilt was the reason for the tension in his gut.

He entered the apartment and found her lying on her stomach across the couch, reading one of his spell books. She'd folded the blanket and set it on the end of the couch, on top of the pillow.

Sensing something was different, he glanced around. The room was spotless. It looked like she'd even taken a dust rag to the bookshelves. A glance into the kitchen revealed the same level of cleanliness.

Damn, that was the first time he'd seen the countertops in months. His best spell pot gleamed on the stove. It looked like she'd polished it to within an inch of its life.

She glanced up at him with an annoyed look on her face and then returned to giving the book her complete attention. Grosset seemed happy to see him, at least. He bounced like a dust mop on crack at Theo's feet, small pink tongue hanging out.

Sarafina's hair spilled loose down her back, silky white blond against the black of the T-shirt she'd pilfered from him that morning. Her nose, long and slightly snubbed at the end, was buried deeply in the spell book, but Theo had a feeling it was all just for show. As he watched, she puckered her full lips a little and turned a page. One bare foot jiggled with irritation, toenails painted light pink. He tried really hard not to notice the luscious shape of her smooth calves where the hem of the sweatpants she wore had ridden up.

The woman really did look and act innocent, but Theo suspected that was all a show, too. Even though he wasn't crazy about the thought of having her as a houseguest, he wished he could keep her here a little longer, long enough to ferret out her mysteries. Maybe it was better he playact now and try to make amends. If she liked him better, it would be easier for him to keep an eye on her once she left the Coven.

He stooped to pet Grosset, then rose and walked to the center of the room. "They've been able to sort out the people rescued from the farmhouse and there's proof that you were abducted." He paused a moment, hating having to admit he'd been wrong . . . maybe. "You're not a warlock."

"No kidding." She closed the book with a thump. "I was falsely accused. I told you so."

"I know. I'm . . . sorry."

Her lips twisted and she tilted her head to the side. "Do the syllables of the words *I'm sorry* taste bad? You're grimacing."

He ignored the comment. "You and I got off on the wrong foot—"

"You think?" She sat up, put the spell book on the coffee table, then leaned back with her arms crossed over her chest. "Normally, I love being buried alive."

"Look, I'm sorry, all right? Sorry for everything. I was really rude to you last night and I feel bad about it, so if there's anything you want me to tell you about—"

"Everything." She uncrossed her arms and leaned toward him, her blue eyes suddenly bright. "I feel like I've been transported to a foreign country and I don't know the language or any of the customs. I feel like I've found a missing part of myself, a part that's completely familiar to me, and yet totally alien at the same time."

He rolled his eyes. Gods, were they going to have to talk about their emotions? He'd rather stab himself in the eye.

"Plus—" She snapped her mouth shut. Her hands were clenched in her lap and had gone totally white. "It pisses me off that I'm admitting this to you, but I'm grieving right now." She practically snarled the words. "Not that you care."

His heart softened a bit. *Damn it.* "I heard. It's unfortunate all this is happening to you at once."

"Yes, I think that's why I feel extra . . . lost. If you could give me a compass, I'd appreciate it."

He leaned forward, bracing a hand near her shoulder on the couch, and pulled a book from the shelf behind her head, bringing his body uncomfortably close to hers. She smelled good. He'd noticed it yesterday, even under the scent of the dirt he'd tried to drown her in. It was her perfume, maybe, or the shampoo she used. Her soap? Whatever it was, it was subtle and seemingly an integral part of her. His gaze caught hers and he noticed her eyes were a little shiny. A beautiful blue . . . and filled with just the lightest sheen of tears.

Theo drew back, book in hand. He hoped she didn't cry. *Oh, Gods.* The last thing he needed on his hands was a blubbering female. What the hell did you do with a weeping woman?

After tossing the book into her lap, he eased down into the chair behind him, a safe distance away from her. The dog jumped into his lap immediately. Theo stared down into Grosset's furry, panting face and tried not to curl his lip.

Sarafina looked down at the red hardcover book in her hands. "What's this?"

"That's all we know about what we are. Micah, our scholar and the cousin of the head of the Coven, compiled it and had it bound for the members of the Coven. It's our history, as much as we know."

She picked up the thick volume and turned it over in her hands, a thoughtful look on her face.

"Take it home, read it, and then ask me any questions you have." Hopefully, that would ensure they have contact after she left this apartment, so he could keep his eye on her.

"Answer one for me right now?"

"Shoot."

Her face tightened. Theo recognized fear when he saw it. "Do witches have red eyes?"

He stilled, a nasty icy jolt going through him. "There's only one thing I know of that has red eyes and they're not witches."

"What are they?"

"Where did you see someone like that?"

"At the farmhouse. He woke me up in the middle of the night and nearly made me soil the mattress. He didn't hurt me, but everything about him was threatening." She paused. "And he was big, almost unnaturally so. When I asked Stefan about the creature, Stefan never told me what he was, only that he was curious about me."

Theo ran his hand over his jaw and looked away from her. Demon. Probably an *Atrika* demon. What the hell was an *Atrika* doing Earthside . . . again? He sighed, weariness bubbling up from the depths of him. Gods, he did not want to have to deal with *Atrika* again. "It wasn't a man."

"Okay." Pause. "Not a man. So what did I wake up to in the middle of the night, Theo?"

"My guess is a demon." He let her absorb that for a moment. Theo had grown up with this stuff, she hadn't. He could only guess how shocking it was. "They call themselves *daaeman* and they come from a place called Eudae. It's all in the book."

"I just can't . . ." She trailed off, putting a hand to her forehead. "I think I need a drink."

"I'm sorry." Her body was trembling slightly and her face had gone pale. "There's a bottle of Scotch in the kitchen, if you're serious about needing that drink. Look, I'll give you a minute. I need to make a phone call."

"Sure."

He got up and went into his bedroom, pulling his cell out of his pocket. He punched the speed dial for Thomas. "Yeah, we got another *Atrika*."

Silence.

"Did you hear me? The woman I thought was a warlock, but isn't, says she saw one at the farmhouse."

"Fuck."

"I just thought you should know right away, man."

"Tell me everything she saw."

Theo told him what Sarafina had said.

"Okay." Thomas's voice was heavy and a little tired sounding. "Somehow, some way Stefan's allied with the *Atrika*. That's the implication. It's nothing we didn't already suspect might somehow happen."

"Our worst nightmare."

"Pretty much." Thomas exhaled slowly. "Micah and Isabelle have determined Sarafina is no threat, right?"

"Yeah, we're sending her home."

"Let's keep an eye on her, though."

"I'm already on it, boss."

Theo hung up the phone and returned to the living room where Sarafina still sat on the couch, her knees pulled up to her chin and Grosset by her side.

He sank into the chair near her and pushed a hand through his hair with a heavy sigh. "Doing okay with the demon thing?"

She looked at him and wrinkled her face. "Are you crazy? How am I supposed to be okay with the demon thing?"

"Yeah, that was a dumb question. I know this is a lot for you to absorb." He looked at the book. "Read that, okay? It will answer a lot of your questions."

She turned her face away. "I just want to be left alone. I want to go back to my life as it was four days ago, even with the death of my foster mother, the debt, and the dumping. Why did the warlocks want me? Why go to all that trouble for *me*?"

Theo considered her a moment, deciding how best to answer. "The warlocks have been abducting and converting vulnerable witches to their cause since as far back as we know. Lately, though, they've been taking more. Almost like they're building an army."

She shook her head. "I'm not military material."

"Stefan seems to have taken a special interest in you. Or at least, normally he doesn't meet personally with witches they've abducted, let alone go on the initial kidnapping. He doesn't take risks, you know? He's got underlings for that. Hell, ever since Isabelle almost nabbed him, he never even goes anywhere without bodyguards. He took a risk for you and he's given you all kinds of personal attention, but we don't know why you're so special."

"I feel like Alice and I just slipped down the rabbit hole."

"So who does that make me?"

A smile flickered across her mouth. "Not the Cheshire cat, that's for sure. You don't smile enough for that." She frowned. "You don't smile at all."

"Yeah, well, not much to smile about these days."

"God," she breathed, looking down at her lap and toying with a small hole in the knee of the sweatpants. "*My mom.* I always just assumed she was schizophrenic. The human torch thing, well, no one had an explanation for that."

"Now you do."

"I'll say."

"Micah told me that it made all the supernatural unsolved mystery shows."

Suddenly, she looked about ten years older. "Yes." She sighed. She looked down at the book in her lap again. "So, does this mean I can go home now?"

"Isabelle is downstairs in the library. I'll take you to her. She'll give you some clothes to wear that fit, something decent to eat, and take you home."

She looked up at him. "Isabelle sounds really nice, but if it's okay, I'd rather you just took me home now." She glanced down at her clothes. "I mean, as long as you don't mind that I'd be taking your clothes with me. I'll wash them and return them—"

"I don't mind that you're wearing my clothes."

Actually, she looked damn good in them. He let his gaze wander down her torso. His clothes engulfed her slim body, making him wonder what lay beneath all the bulk. Making him want to undress her and find out. It was intimate to think that the material that had lain against his skin now lay against hers.

Theo ripped his gaze back to her face. Clearly, he needed to get laid sometime soon. It had been too long. He hadn't taken a lover since Ingrid had died last year.

There had been no great love between him and Ingrid. They'd been in the relationship for the sex and the companionship, to ease a little of their loneliness. But Ingrid had been a good friend and she'd died in a horrific way. It had hit him hard and he was still grieving her loss.

"Will you just take me home, then? I want to get back to my stuff. Familiarity, you know? I have phone calls to make. Friends of mine will be worried, not to mention my boss."

"Okay. I'm ready whenever you are."

She pushed off the couch. "Then let's go. It's not like I have a lot of luggage."

He walked toward the door, stopped, and turned back to her. "Uh, except . . . I drive a bike."

"A bike? You mean like a motorcycle?"

He twisted his lips. "You think I ride a ten-speed? I drive a Harley."

"That figures. I can't really see you driving a sedan." She only waved her hand absently. "As long as we can get Grosset home on the thing, I'm past caring. I just want my own bathtub and bed tonight."

SIX

Theo brought his Harley to a halt in front of Sarafina's home, which was housed in an older building that had been converted into apartments. He let the bike idle as Sarafina unwrapped her hands from around his waist and got off.

They'd strapped Grosset to her for the short ride to her house and he'd seemed to enjoy the trip. Theo had to admit Sarafina looked cute in the helmet he'd given her. She unstrapped it and handed it to him.

"That was fun!" Her eyes were shining bright with excitement. He liked that look on her face much better than the anger or sorrow he'd been seeing.

He shut the bike down and got off. "I'm coming up to ward your place. Since we don't know why Stefan took such a special interest in you, there's no telling if he'll come after you again." As an earth witch, Theo possessed the ability to ward, and his wards were stronger than most.

She looked alarmed. "You mean the bad guys aren't done with me yet?"

"We don't know if they are or not. After the raid, Stefan went on the run, so I wouldn't worry too much about it. The wards are just a precaution."

He'd leave off the part where he was hoping Stefan did show up. He was using her as bait.

"Ward? What does that mean?"

"It's a magickal barrier that's set up. A perimeter. It wards away certain types of people or magick, whatever you charm it for."

"Uh-huh. And what about the creepy demon?"

"A demon won't go out of his way to track you down when there's easy prey all around him. It's the Duskoff you need to be concerned with."

"Great."

Together they mounted the stairs to her apartment. When they reached the top, Sarafina stilled, staring at the door. Theo followed her gaze, saw that it was ajar.

"Stay back," he ordered her. "And keep the dog quiet." He approached the door carefully, wincing every time the old floorboards beneath his feet squeaked. With his metaphysical grasp, he loosely fisted a couple of defensive charms from his stores of magick and pushed the door open the rest of the way.

Sunlight streamed in from huge windows in the living room and small kitchen, bathing brightly patterned furniture and throw pillows in buttery light and nourishing the five hundred houseplants in her apartment. Nothing seemed out of place in the small, comfortable-looking place. Her apartment was a lot like her: friendly and beautiful.

But someone was in here; Theo could sense their presence.

Behind him, out in the corridor, Grosset yapped.

A brunette stepped out of the kitchen at the sound, took one look at him, and let out a scream so loud Theo swore his eardrums popped.

Sarafina raced past him and threw herself into the woman's arms, who only then ceased her ear-piercing shriek of terror. Grosset danced around the woman's feet.

"Maria, it's okay! I'm okay," Sarafina said.

Maria held her at arm's length, letting out a stream of Spanish before switching to English. "Where the hell have you been? We've been so worried about you." She glanced at Theo, then at Sarafina's clothes. "Don't tell me that you . . . you . . ." She waved her hands.

"Uh, Maria, this is Theo," Sarafina interrupted, blushing. "Theo, Maria. She's a good friend of mine. Theo is . . . he's . . ." Sarafina's blush deepened.

Maria gave him a slow once-over, female appreciation on

her face. He was familiar with it, even though he almost never welcomed it.

Theo shifted and looked out the living room window, clearing his throat.

"So, what's going on, sweetie?" Maria asked. "Everyone expected you home from Kentucky three days ago. When you didn't show up for work, Daniel was really concerned. You need to call him. Even Alex has been beside himself."

"I'm sorry, I—" Sarafina broke off. Clearly, she was looking for a way to explain her absence without revealing the truth and was at an uncharacteristic loss for words.

Theo stepped forward and smiled. Sarafina's mouth snapped shut. "It's my fault. Sarafina and I have been seeing each other for a while, and when I saw how much she was grieving the loss of her foster mother, I insisted she drop everything and come away with me." He paused. "I didn't even let her pack a bag, which is why she's wearing my clothes." He stepped to Sarafina and took her into his arms, pulling her up against his side. "Isn't that right, sweetie?"

Sarafina stiffened. "Uh." He rubbed his hand along the chilly skin of her upper arm. "Uh," she said again.

"Wow, Sarafina. Dating for *a while*? You never told me. What about Alex? You guys just broke up like two weeks ago!" Maria gasped and grinned mischievously. "Were you cheating on him?"

"Did I say a while?" Theo asked. "Actually, we just met. It just feels like I've known her a long time." He pressed a kiss to her temple and Sarafina's eyes widened. "Isn't that right, snookums?"

"Maria . . ." said Sarafina with a shaky smile. She pulled away from Theo and led Maria toward the door. "I'm really tired. Thank you so much for your concern. You are the best of friends. Once I get myself in order, take a shower, and call Daniel, you'll be the first person I contact, and I'll tell you everything."

Maria grabbed her purse off a small bright red and blue painted table by the front door. "Okay, you promise to call me? We can go out for *mojitos* or something."

"Absolutely."

Maria hugged her again. "I'm just so relieved you're all right. Never do that again!"

"I promise. I just . . . just got carried away." She cast a furtive glance over her shoulder at Theo. "We're kind of, uh, into each other right now."

Maria leaned forward and whispered something in Sarafina's ear, glancing at Theo. Sarafina giggled nervously. Then Maria disappeared out the door.

Sarafina turned. "Thanks. I had no idea what to say."

"What did she whisper to you?"

She smiled, her eyes sparkling. "No wonder, he's gorgeous."

Theo cleared his throat and looked away.

Sarafina laughed. "You're bad with people, but especially women, it seems. A pity, since . . . well, it's a pity."

"It's a pity since what?" His voice came out a gravelly, low growl and he narrowed his eyes at her.

"Uh, because most women probably think you're pretty hot. Most women would agree with Maria."

"Most women? That include you?"

She tipped her head to the side. "Are you . . . *flirting* with me, Mr. Winters?"

He grunted and turned away from her. "I'll do the warding now." While he pulled the proper charms from his stores and cemented them around her windows and doors, Sarafina went into her bedroom and changed out of his clothes.

The wards snapped into place just as she emerged from the bedroom with his clothes neatly folded over her arm. Now she wore a pair of tight-fitting, worn blue jeans that did good things for her ass and a long-sleeved blue shirt that did good things for her eyes.

Not that he noticed her ass or her eyes in any way but a perfunctory one.

She handed him her clothes. "Sorry I didn't get a chance to wash them."

"No problem. Your wards are in place. They'll keep out Stefan or any of the Duskoff." He jerked his head at the book she'd placed on her coffee table. "Read that and get back to me."

"Oh, that's my first priority. I'm making a pot of tea, maybe some dinner, and settling in to read." She glanced at a small table near her kitchen. "Right after I listen to the fifty messages I have on my recorder, probably all of them panicked."

Damn, she had fifty-two messages on there. Apparently, Sarafina had lots of people to care about her. That must be nice.

He left the apartment, intending to walk down the stairs and go back home. Instead, he turned in the hallway outside her apartment to look at her. He didn't want to leave her. It bothered him. There was something odd about her, something off, something he wasn't comfortable with—

"Why are you staring at me like that?"

"Was I staring?"

She rolled her eyes. "You know, you really need to work on your people skills. Good night, Theo." She slammed the door in his face.

Something really *irritating* about her.

SARAFINA SLID INTO HER OWN BED, WITH HER OWN sheets and her own pillows, snuggled down, and sighed. It was almost perfect. She was just missing . . . Grosset jumped up and settled at her feet. Ah, *now* it was perfect. She smiled and closed her eyes.

Immediately, an image of Theo popped into her mind. Her smile faded and she shook her head a little, grimacing.

She tried to snuggle back down and immerse herself in the treat that was her own bed and apartment after the hellish few days she'd had, but rest didn't come. Really, it was no surprise. The book Theo had given her lay on her bedside table. She'd spent all afternoon and evening reading it.

It was not material that made for good dreams.

Warlocks—witches gone bad—and demons? Demons? *Really?* And she was part demon? Or at least, created through a demon's magickal tampering. It was all so unbelievable. Yet she'd felt the power inside her. She'd wielded it. She knew it was all for real, no matter how bizarre it was.

Earth, air, water, and fire. She was fire. At the thought, the seat of her magick gave a little pulse.

There are more things in heaven and earth, Horatio, than are dreamt of in your philosophy. That was Shakespeare, she was pretty sure. Had it come from *Hamlet*? She wasn't sure, but wherever it had come from, it was true.

She'd spent most of the evening stunned that she wasn't more surprised by the contents of the book and by what had happened to her. In an odd way, the information she'd been given completed a circle of knowledge within herself. She'd always known there was something more, that *she* was something more, but until now she hadn't known what.

Like a puzzle piece finally fitting into place. Now she had the complete picture.

Her mother had been crazy, there was no doubt about that, but maybe she hadn't been quite as crazy as everyone thought.

Ugh.

She couldn't think about her birth mother without a cold knot settling in the pit of her stomach. As she always did, Sarafina turned her mind from the woman who'd given her life . . . then had tried to kill her. Anything else caused too much pain.

And who knew that witches were men, too? She'd always thought that women were witches and men were . . . wizards or warlocks or something. The term *witch* had always meant something feminine to her.

There was certainly nothing feminine about Theodosius Winters.

Why did she have to keep thinking about him? He was like some kind of virus she couldn't shake.

It was true she did feel better with the wards up around her apartment. If she concentrated, she could sense them: solid, unyielding, better than a moat around a castle. Ironically, Theo would help her sleep tonight.

Forcing Theo and the book from her mind, she closed her eyes. After her foster mother's death, she'd taken all her paid vacation from work and planned to use the time to get her head together. She would just have to ask her landlord to give her an extension on her rent. If she gave blood or something, maybe she could actually afford a few groceries and some dog food.

Double ugh.

First thing on her agenda tomorrow was a trip back to the Coven. That meant she needed to get some rest tonight.

Eventually, she drifted off only to be awoken by a crash in her living room. Grosset jumped up and started barking. Sarafina shushed him so she could hear.

More movement.

Panic sending an icy jolt through her body, she threw the covers off and grabbed the baseball bat she kept by the side of her bed. She still wasn't comfortable enough with her fire magick to use it as a weapon. Thanks to the warding, at least she knew it couldn't be Stefan or any other warlock—well, she hoped like crazy, anyway—but it could be a burglar. The way her luck had been running, she wouldn't doubt it.

She inched to the doorway of her bedroom, holding a hand up to keep Grosset on the bed. He sat down and put his head on his paws with a whimper. Something crashed in the kitchen and Sarafina winced. It sounded like a wild animal was loose in her place.

She peered around the doorjamb at her darkened apartment. Luckily, she was a lover of nightlights, so she could see a little . . . enough to know a hulking dark form blocked her path to the front door. She'd hoped she could grab Grosset and make a break for it. She'd had quite enough of fight or flight during the last few days, thank you very much. This time around she was choosing *flight*.

The large form turned and ambled toward her room. *Oh, no.*

Sarafina turned quickly, her back pressed against the wall of the bedroom and her hands clenched on the baseball bat. Her breath came fast and hard and her nerve endings were electrified with terror. Grosset had his nose buried under his paws, seemingly as nervous as she was. God, she hoped he wouldn't bark.

What was that smell, by the way? It smelled dry and sort of bitter. How odd. There was something about that kind of scent in the book, wasn't there? She searched her memory, knowing she'd read something about a smell like that. Wasn't it caused by . . . Her whole body shook as realization took hold.

Daaeman magick.

Demons.

The intruder reached her doorway and she swung her bat high and hard, aiming for the man's face. The trespasser simply grabbed her bat and swung her instead. She slammed into the doorjamb with a crack of blinding pain. She collapsed on her ass, stunned for a moment.

Grosset went ten different kinds of Pomeranian wild at the man's feet.

"*Vae* Sarafina. It is good to see you."

SEVEN

SHE LOOKED UP AT HIM, RECOGNITION BLOOMING. RED eyes . . . killing rage. That's what the red eyes meant, right? *Right?* She couldn't answer, couldn't move. Terror and pain had frozen her in place.

Her thoughts came in quick succession. Demon. The same demon that had visited her at the farmhouse. There was a demon in the room and she was going to die.

Grosset grabbed the demon's pant cuff and shook it, growling. The demon's massive red-eyed head swung toward the dog and he jerked his leg, sending Grosset flying. The little dog hit something and yelped.

Fury exploded through her. *"You bastard!"*

She lunged across the floor, grabbed the baseball bat, and rolled to her feet. Giving a battle cry that came somewhere from the very depths of her body, she swung the bat with all her strength at the demon's head. This time she connected with a satisfying thump that sent the demon careening sideways into the wall.

"Bai? Is that your name? Don't ever, *ever* touch my dog!" She drew back to hit the demon again, but a hand grabbed it before she could swing. Sarafina looked behind her to see Theo, who grunted at her and stalked toward the demon. Theo's magick rose in the room, making the hair all along her body rise. The scent of freshly turned earth filled the air.

The demon pushed away from the wall with an animalistic bellow and turned his attention to the earth witch. Theo pushed her to the side and stepped toward him. Ordinarily, she might have been miffed, but in this case, if Theo wanted to fight the demon, it was her pleasure to be pushed aside. He could *go for it*.

Sarafina ran to the corner of the room and scooped a cowering Grosset into her arms. He immediately licked her face and she sighed in relief that the little dog was all right.

Magick exploded around her for the second time in two days. The bitter scent of demon magick burned her nose, mingling with the earth power Theo wielded. The demon blasted a hole in her wall in an effort to hit Theo, who'd leapt out of the way. Smoke filled the room and made her cough. Her night table exploded, along with her bookshelf, making it rain paperbacks and the occasional hardcover.

A mound of earth doused the fire that had erupted from the burst of demon magick. In front of her the floor churned to a soil-like consistency and swallowed the demon whole.

Eyes wide and mouth agape, she stared at Theo over the mound.

"Go!" he commanded. "Get to the Coven. Now!"

She went. Holding Grosset close to her, she dodged the odd grave in the center of her bedroom and dashed out the front door of her place just as the mound exploded in the bedroom and the demon roared his disapproval.

Sarafina raced down the stairs, wondering just how long it would be before her neighbors woke up and discovered the battle of titans going on her apartment. Or the floor turned to mush. How was she going to explain *that* to her landlord?

She kept an extra key in a holder hidden in the wheel well of her car. Holding Grosset in one arm, she found it and extracted it with shaking fingers. Across the street flashes of light burst from the windows of her apartment. She'd lose her lease and never get her deposit back at this point. The thought made crazy-sounding, nervous laughter bubble up.

As if losing her lease was her biggest worry.

Once in the car, she put Grosset on the passenger seat, jammed the key in the ignition, and took off with the tires squealing.

As soon as she got to the Coven she'd go to Thomas Monahan and send help to Theo. She only hoped it wouldn't be too late.

* * *

"WHAT THE FUCK IS GOING ON? WHY WOULD AN *Atrika* go after you like that?"

"Oh, goodie, I get to be special again. First I'm special to the head warlock and now a demon wants to cuddle with me in the middle of the night." Sarafina dabbed a Q-tip covered in disinfectant over a nasty scratch on Theo's face. He winced and she blew across it. Poor big baby. "This guy, Bai, asked for me by name."

Theo had come back to the Coven about an hour after she'd hightailed it there and sent some witches to aid him. She'd come into the dark, quiet Coven screaming for help, since she hadn't known where to find anyone of importance. Thomas, Jack, and Claire had helped Theo drive the demon off.

Grosset was uninjured. It seemed he'd hit the mattress of her bed, not the wall. Now he was fed, watered, petted, and amply cuddled and curled up on Theo's couch, fast asleep.

Theo rubbed his chin. "I guess this means what we'd suspected is true. Somehow the Duskoff have found a way to ally with the *Atrika*. I'd bet anything that demon was running an errand for Stefan."

"Uh, from what I read in Micah's book, an *Atrika* wouldn't be anyone's errand boy."

"Something is drawing them together. The law of averages is against both the Duskoff and the *Atrika* taking a special interest in you at the same time."

"I really wish I were less interesting."

He glanced at the clock. "It's only a couple hours until morning. The rest of the Coven might be able to make sense out of some of this."

"Have I said thank you yet?"

"You looked like you were doing a pretty good job before I got there."

She snorted. "That was a lucky shot."

"Took guts."

Lifting a shoulder, she said, "He made me mad."

"Remind me never to do that."

She held a bottle of disinfectant in one hand and a bag of cotton balls in the other. She glanced pointedly at his ripped and bloody shirt. "Take it off."

He gazed past her while he pulled the garment over his head and tossed it on the coffee table, looking far away in Musing Land. Suddenly, Sarafina was all there, though, momentarily struck dumb by the confusing, alluring, beautiful expanse of his body.

The first thing she noticed were the tattoos. They covered his arms, shoulders, chest, and back in swirling and swooping black tribal designs. Underneath those, or meshing with them, really, were scars—thin, white, raised ridges of flesh. Perhaps once they'd been wounds made with a knife? Maybe even a whip. The scars dovetailed with the tattoos, flirted and danced with them. The effect was clearly deliberate and oddly beautiful.

The second thing she noticed were the muscles. The sheer physical strength displayed in his upper body was as breathtaking as the tattoos. She allowed her gaze to travel the sculpted gorgeousness, every dip, curve, mountain, and valley. This was a man who took care of himself, who worked out on a daily basis and had a body fit for any male modeling job, scarring be damned.

His gaze was now centered on her and his face wore an expression of challenge. "Got a problem?"

Sarafina blinked and cleared her throat. "Problem? No, no problem. Your body is just, just—"

"Scarred? Disfigured? Disgusting? Pick an adjective."

"God, no, you're gorgeous!" she blurted and immediately wished to call the words back into her mouth. "I mean, the tattoos are very well done."

"Thanks."

She busied herself squirting some of the antiseptic onto a cotton ball. Not only was his chest decorated with ink, he had a couple of nasty gashes that needed attending. "Did you do them?"

"Yeah. I had help for the places I couldn't reach, but I did a lot of it."

"That's crazy."

"I do them for lots of the earth witches here, and some of the others who just want them for aesthetic reasons." He paused. "Why? You want one?"

She smiled. "Too late. Got one already."

He lifted his brows.

"You'll never see it, buddy." She grinned and swiped a drenched cotton ball over a gash.

He yelped.

"Sorry. Considering you just fought a demon, you're really kind of being a wimp about this."

He only glared at her in response.

"How'd you get past the warding on my apartment, anyway?"

"I created them, Sarafina, that means I can break them."

Of course. Duh. She mentally slapped her forehead. "So you were watching my place? Sitting out there on the street, monitoring me?"

"Yeah."

That was a little creepy. "So, I guess you still think I'm a bad guy."

He didn't answer for a moment. "No. Not after tonight. I was watching you to see if—"

She nodded, anger prickling through her. "You were using me as bait, weren't you? To see if Stefan showed up again."

"Yeah, there was that," he answered with a one-shouldered shrug. "But it was also to make sure you stayed safe. Scout's honor."

Her lips twisted. "Somehow I can't see you as a Boy Scout, Theo."

"Got me there. I never was."

"I don't want to even know what my apartment looks like after that battle. Is my landlord going to sue me for damages to his property?"

Theo shook his head. "It's taken care of. I used earth magick to clean it all up. Almost looks good as new. It's a little messy, but there's nothing your landlord will sue you over. I even put up a sound barrier around the place so you won't get any complaints about the noise."

"Wow. Thank you."

"It's standard operating procedure. The Coven doesn't need non-magickals asking too many questions. We're better off left to myth and Hollywood where they're concerned."

He winced again as she swiped more disinfectant over a gash.

"I'm sorry."

"You know healing is a part of fire magick," he gritted out. "It hurts a fuck of a lot less than antiseptic."

"So I read in the handy-dandy witch handbook. However, I'm not even close to trying that out."

"Why not? You're going to have to learn sometime. Might as well be now."

"Are you qualified to teach me this lesson?"

He grabbed her wrists and she jumped a little, startled. His fingers were warm on her skin and his dark, intense gaze drilled into her. "Just find your seat, be one with it, and it will flow naturally. There's nothing to it once you find acceptance of your power. Doesn't matter you're coming to it late in life." He forced her seat to warmth, made her feel the pulse of power that dwelt within her.

Her lips parted a little and her warm breath trickled over him. There was an energy between them. Something hot and fierce. Something that had nothing to do with the way he was currently manipulating her seat.

Theo felt . . . *dangerous* to her.

She suppressed a nervous laugh. "That's very Zen of you."

He shrugged and released her hands. The little pulse of magick between her breasts died. "Everyone's always training, teaching. It's not necessary. Those skills are already a part of you. Natural. Organic. All you have to do is tap them."

"What if I burn the hell out of you in the meantime?"

His full lips twisted. "You think my body can't take a few more scars?"

"I actually didn't mean that wimp comment. I think you can take anything."

"Enough." He grabbed her hand and placed it over one of the gashes on his chest. She fought the urge to *euuuw* out loud. "Now close your eyes, tap your seat, and concentrate on healing."

"Okay." She did as he asked.

It was the same thing they'd shown her how to do at the farmhouse during those first terrifying twenty-four hours. She took some deep, even breaths and concentrated on the space between her breasts. The area warmed a little and began to tingle once she'd located it. The warmth spread down her arms, jumped between her fingers with little electric shots that she concentrated on keeping from Theo's skin.

He was right. She could do this; it was a part of her. This *was* her, the part of her that had always been missing up until now. Now she was whole and it felt *good*.

The tingling warmth down her arms and jumping between her fingers gradually relaxed into a manageable heat, something that almost felt moldable. Instinctively, she directed it at the gash her palm covered.

Theo flinched and she pulled back a little, allowing him to once again settle against her hand. This time she regulated the heat better, concentrating on making magickal tendrils of a therapeutic nature, instead of a burning one. She allowed curative waves to sink into the injured flesh of his wound, promoting healing and knitting it back together.

Under her fingers the wound shifted and smoothed, the edges of the gashes coming together. The heat coming down her arm eased and she sensed she'd given all she could give.

Only by that time she was long gone, lost in the concentration it took to maintain the heat. Her breathing came deep and steady, keeping time with her heartbeat. She was slipping farther and farther away . . .

Theo took her hand in his, his thumb rubbing the underside of her wrist. Her eyes came open slowly; they'd rolled all the way back in her head like she was in meditation. She focused on his face.

Theo continued to hold her hand and now her gaze, too. He had really beautiful eyes, a rich dark brown like the most sinful chocolate. The slow stroke of his thumb on her sensitive skin made bad things—or good things, depending on one's perspective—happen lower in her body. She couldn't bring herself to pull her hand away or to rip her gaze from his.

He released her hand. "All right?"

She blinked and came out of her trance like she'd been freed from a witch's spell . . . funny thought, that. She only nodded in response.

Theo looked down at his gash. "Incredible. I don't think it will even leave a scar," he murmured. "Weren't we just talking about natural skill? It appears you have a lot in the realm of healing."

Sarafina focused on his wound and gasped. His gash was almost completely healed. She jerked her hand away and stepped backward. "I did that? Fire magick can do *that*?"

Theo studied the pinkish mark. "I'll be honest, that's a little beyond the ordinary scope. How do you feel?"

"Drained."

He grunted. "You expended a lot of power to accomplish this."

"What else can fire magick do?"

"All witches have their specialties. You'll have to find yours."

"Okay, but what else can *fire* do?"

Theo grinned. "Burn things. Explode things. It's a great weapon." He paused. "But I think maybe we just found out why you're special, Sarafina."

HOW TO CONTROL THE *ATRIKA*. NOW, THAT WAS A DIlemma.

Stefan had thought that holding the thing they wanted most over their heads would compel their obedience. And, for the most part, the leverage he possessed had been effective.

For the most part.

Ironically, the *Atrika* couldn't control their emotions very well . . . or their libidos, it seemed. One would think such a killing machine would have no emotions, or their emotions would run icy and remorseless. Yet the heart of an *Atrika* beat wild and fierce, their emotions hot and strong. In a way they were like children, acting always from the id.

It made it damn hard to control them and Stefan had been working too long and come too far to allow Bai's dick to screw it up.

"What should we do with the recalcitrant demon, sir?" asked David, a lanky water warlock. He looked so innocent, David did, so . . . geeky. Yet David would slit your throat for a twenty-dollar bill. Stefan loved that about him.

David had been on his father's staff. He'd been there the day William Crane had been pushed out the forty-story window of Duskoff International in New York City by Mira Hoskins, that little bitch of an air witch. He'd also been there when Isabelle Novak had caught Stefan by the balls—literally—a couple years ago. Both times David had escaped. He had a knack for survival, just like Stefan did.

"What to do with a recalcitrant demon? *Oui*, a question for the ages." Stefan sighed and drummed his fingers on the boardroom table of Duskoff International and stared out the window where his father had fallen to his death. Just being in this room made rage boil the seat of his magick, made it shoot through his limbs like he was about to explode.

It made Stefan feel very motivated.

Thomas Monahan and his organization of weak do-gooders had killed his father. He'd told them he'd make them pay and he would.

"Didn't Boyle give you any tips for how to control an *Atrika*?"

"Boyle told me many things, but how to bring an *Atrika* to heel was not among them. That *daaeman* was loyal to his people."

"Of course, sir, silly of me to think he would reveal such secrets."

"*Oui*. How is the air witch?"

"Weak. She is depressingly fragile."

"We're done with her. If you can't break her to our cause, kill her."

"We cannot bring her to the Duskoff, sir. It seems she's too cemented in her former life and lacks our aspirations." David rolled his eyes. "She's constantly crying for her husband and child. It's annoying."

Stefan waved a hand. "Then do with her as you wish and dump the body when you're done. We don't need her anymore."

"Yes, sir." David turned to leave.

"And send Bai to me. All I can do is try and reason with him. He's already tipped our hand."

"Right away."

It took Bai a long time to answer his summons. Long enough for Stefan to down two glasses of Scotch and become even more agitated. However, even though he had leverage over the demon, Stefan wasn't dumb. You didn't push an *Atrika* and expect to keep your head, leverage or not.

The demon entered and Stefan studied him for a moment over the rim of his glass. All the *daaeman*, regardless of breed, were tall and muscular. Physically intimidating. All of them—all that he'd seen, at least—were also good-looking in human terms. The *Atrika* were especially beautiful. Chiseled features, handsome faces. He'd never seen a female demon, but reportedly they were also attractive.

Stefan supposed their good looks had helped to lure women—and men—way back in ancient times to mate with them. It was a sort of weapon, built into their DNA. Perhaps he should be grateful, since it was those couplings, with a little magickal help, that had produced elemental witches. It was the *daaeman* from which all witches sprang.

Those randy *daaeman*.

"I don't enjoy answering when you call," Bai said, first thing. His voice was thick with the sharp, blunt syllables of the accent common to the demons. "Like a common mongrel." Bai was one of the few who spoke English well. That was why Stefan put up with him and all his demands.

Stefan's hand tightened on his glass and he forced himself to release his grip. "*Et merde. J'en ai assez*," he murmured to himself. "I'm sorry, *my lord demon*, but we need to have a conversation about your rash interaction with the woman, Sarafina Connell."

Bai's face relaxed a degree, his jaw unlocking and his thick lips parting a little. "Sarafina? What of her?"

"The agreement was that you could have her *after* you

finished your task. You have not yet finished your task, therefore you cannot have her yet. Do you not recall the agreement, or is there some reason you cannot comprehend it?"

Bai shifted and his eyes flashed red. Most demon's eyes only went red when they were about to go on a killing rampage. Bai's eyes went red whenever his emotions got the better of him and that seemed most of the time. Bai was an especially dangerous demon. "That was the agreement before you lost her."

"I didn't *lose her.*"

"You miscalculated the factors related to her induction."

"No, I was perfectly correct to assume her history would make her a good candidate for us. Without the meddling of the Coven and with a little more time, I feel sure I could've won her to our cause." His jaw locked as he thought of the raid on the farmhouse. "But I know exactly where she is and when this is all over, she will be yours. Until then, no contact."

"Do not give me orders." Bai's eyes flashed red again and Stefan's breath choked in his throat for a moment.

For a moment he almost took a step back, away from the demon who had been denied his candy, but retreating would make him appear weak. And *that* would be suicide.

Bai bared his teeth, now pointy and sharp, a mouth full of fangs. "You are making an error. I care not for anything but Sarafina. She is mine whenever I decide to take her."

He jumped from the room—in that eerie way they had of bending space to travel between two points—and Stefan was alone.

EIGHT

"SO THAT'S TWICE NOW THE DEMON HAS VISITED you."

Theo watched Sarafina shift uncomfortably under Thomas's gaze. She was flanked by Claire and Isabelle. Mira stood nearby. The three had immediately taken her under their wings.

"Yes," she answered. "The first time was like he was simply watching me. Watching me sleep. The second time he was knocking around in my apartment like he owned the place." She shuddered and her voice hardened. "Then I hit him with the baseball bat."

Thomas averted his gaze and looked out the library window for a moment before speaking. "Since Stefan just brushed off the incident at the farmhouse, we're going to assume that he's found a way to ally with one or more *Atrika*."

"Bai is obviously pretty cozy with Stefan," Sarafina answered. "Had the run of the house, apparently."

"My point exactly."

Micah sat in one of the leather chairs near Thomas's desk. He shook his head and frowned. "But that seems totally impossible. The *Atrika* are unable to open any portals between Eudae and Earth."

"It's my understanding that Rue, the head of the *Ytrayi*, is the only one with enough power to do that," Claire broke in. Her lips twisted in an odd smile. "I remember it well."

Yes, so did Theo.

About a year and a half ago, Claire had been trapped on Earth, after having lived her whole life on Eudae. After the

Cae of the *Ytrayi*, Rue, had imbued her with a weapon called the elium, he'd pushed her through a portal and snapped it shut after her when the *Atrika*—the enemy of the *Ytrayi*—had stormed their palace. Two *Atrika* had managed to dive in after her and there had been a life-and-death chase all over the Midwest to avoid them.

That was how Ingrid and many other witches had been killed. That's how Theo had ended up with a broken leg. He'd walked with a limp for months.

"Right," answered Micah, "and we all know how difficult it is to open a portal from this side because we tried it."

"Without using blood magick, you mean," Theo interrupted. "You don't think Stefan would sacrifice witches to open a portal?"

Micah turned and looked at him. "Of course he would, but that spell is complicated. It took Erasmus Boyle years to execute it from this side of the veil." Micah shook his head. "I just don't see how it's possible that Stefan could have forged an alliance with the *Atrika*."

"Maybe," Mira put in, "we should explain what a portal is. Sarafina looks confused."

Sarafina nodded. "That would be nice. It was explained in the book Theo gave me, but I didn't really understand it."

"Who does?" answered Micah. "But here's what we think. Eudae and Earth are layered on top of each other. The matter of each location vibrates at a different rate, creating a barrier. I call the difference in the vibrational rates *the veil*. There are ways to alter the vibrational rate in small patches of these tiny strings of energy, equalizing them and making a place in the veil where it's possible to step through."

"So close, yet so far away," murmured Sarafina.

"Yes!" Micah's eyes lit with enthusiasm. "Once you step through the area of matter that has been equalized, your body changes in structure, mimicking your surroundings and thus allowing you to stay on that side of the veil. For whatever reason, stepping through seems to affect us more coming from Eudae to Earth. It makes you nauseous. And when—"

"Be careful," Theo drawled. "He'll talk about this all day if you let him."

"I think it's fascinating." Sarafina leaned forward a little. "How do you equalize the patches of matter, Micah?"

"That's the big mystery. We know *how* it can be done, we're just not sure *why* it happens. Blood magick will do it." Micah jerked his head toward Claire. "Once upon a time, we were working nonstop on a way to get Claire back from Eudae. Without murdering a bunch of people, it's nearly impossible."

Sarafina looked at Claire, questions clear on her face.

"It's a long story," Claire answered.

She turned her attention back to Micah. "Performing blood magick means killing people or animals?"

"Witches. Specifically, witches of certain elements and levels of power. They must be killed in certain places and at certain times in order to open a portal."

"Yuck."

"Vast understatement."

"Okay, I have a question," Isabelle broke in. "When Boyle broke Stefan out of Gribben, we all thought Boyle had killed him, right? Then Stefan called me later to taunt me about his continued well-being. When I asked him why Boyle hadn't killed him, he told me *other arrangements had been made*. I know we've speculated at length that Stefan somehow made a deal with Boyle—"

"But any deal would have been rendered non-executable with Boyle's death on Eudae," answered Thomas.

Isabelle stabbed her finger in the air. "*On Eudae*. Those are the key words. Yes, perhaps Boyle's death was unexpected and threw a kink in the original deal Stefan made with Boyle. But let's say, hypothetically, that Boyle had a backup plan and planted something on Eudae that would help . . . I don't know . . . open a doorway or leave some way for the Duskoff to make some kind of a deal with the *Atrika*."

Micah shot out of his chair and began to pace.

"Micah?" Thomas asked. "Could she be on to something?"

Micah stopped in the middle of the room and rubbed his chin. "It's a possibility, but there are lots of questions."

Theo shifted his weight and uncrossed his arms. "The

primary question must be why Boyle would help Stefan and what possible reason the *Atrika* would have to agree to ally with the Duskoff. Their goals are not the same. The *Atrika* want Eudae and the Duskoff want more control on Earth."

"I would go so far as to say," Thomas broke in, "that Stefan wants *all* control of Earth. He's got a hell of a superiority complex. I saw it while he was in Gribben. He thinks that because witches have the power of magick we should rule over the non-magickals."

"Yes, but the *Atrika* don't seem to care about Earth," Micah answered. "So Theo is correct. There's no motive for them to form an alliance when their objectives are literally worlds away."

"Stefan Faucheux is not a stupid man," Thomas said, leaning forward in his chair. "I would never underestimate his ability to manipulate a situation to his advantage. I'm sure he could find something to entice the *Atrika*."

"Like *us*? As in female witches?" Isabelle answered, eyebrows high into her hairline. "I hate to point this out. I mean, I really, really hate to point it out, but Boyle took an unhealthy interest in me and this Bai demon is taking an interest in Sarafina. Maybe female witches hold a fascination for them."

"But none of the demons on Eudae took an interest in Claire," Thomas answered. "None but one, right, Claire?"

"That's right." Claire cast her gaze downward. "It was forbidden for any of the *daaeman*, any of the breeds, to show such interest in an *aeamon* female."

Isabelle gestured impatiently. "Yes, but those weren't *Atrika* demons. Claire lived among the other three breeds. Not the *Atrika*."

"Point taken," answered Thomas.

"It's a possibility." Micah threw his hands up. "Anything's a possibility at this point. Again we find ourselves playing a guessing game with the Duskoff, one step behind their agenda while we try to prevent whatever they're planning from coming to fruition. It's a familiar, exhausting dance."

Mira moved toward the door. "I'm going in with air magick." She meant projecting her consciousness from her body so she could travel incorporeally to another place. Strong air witches could do that. "I'll try and find a crack in the warding around their headquarters in New York like I did when they were holding my aunt. Maybe I can find something out. Maybe they're keeping the air witch Emily there."

Thomas nodded. "Good. Let me know if you find something out." He turned his attention to Sarafina. "Now we need to get you sorted out."

Sarafina's eyebrows rose. "I need sorting out?"

"You need instruction. Fire is a volatile element and you need to learn how to wield it with care. To boot, Theo tells me you have more power than most."

Sarafina glanced at him and smiled a little. "I know you're right. I mean, I saw firsthand what uncontrolled fire magick can do to a person."

Thomas nodded as he shuffled some papers on his desk. "Claire and Adam have agreed to allow you to stay with them. They'll train you. Adam is a fire witch, and Claire has control of all four elements. They're the best equipped to help you."

"*No.*"

Thomas jerked his gaze to Sarafina. Few witches talked to Thomas Monahan that way. There was a reason he headed the Coven; he had a way of compelling people to obey him.

Sarafina shifted, her hair moving over her shoulders. "Look, I'm sorry, I don't mean to be trouble, but I don't want to be with anyone but Theo. He's the only one I trust."

Theo stiffened in surprise. Considering the way things had started out between them, that declaration was unexpected.

Sarafina glanced at Claire. "I mean, oh, God, I just stuck my foot in my mouth, didn't I? You've all been nothing but kind to me, and I'm sure you're all great teachers and wonderful, trustworthy people—"

Claire smiled and touched Sarafina's arm. "It's okay. You didn't offend me. I totally understand and I'm sure Adam does, too."

"Of course," answered Adam from across the room. He grinned. "Go ahead, reject us."

"Adam!" Claire shot him a mock glare. "He's just kidding. Adam is almost always kidding."

Sarafina looked at Theo and spread her hands. "It's just, you know, he fought a demon in my bedroom and won. That's sort of . . . endeared him to me." She colored a little and glanced away.

Adam opened his mouth and Theo shot him a look that promised much pain if the words poised on his tongue made it into the air.

Thomas nodded slowly, deep in thought. "That's fine with me as long as it's okay with Theo. Theo is well versed in all the elements, and he's got a lot of control and knowledge. Still, I think you'll learn more paired with witches of your own element."

She shook her head. "I don't care. I want Theo."

"It's okay with me," Theo answered.

Thomas nodded. "It's settled, then. You two can work out the living arrangements. Even though it would be safer for Sarafina to be close to a more experienced witch at all times, if you decide not to stay at Theo's, Sarafina, we've got apartments free within the Coven."

Theo answered, "She stays with me."

Adam raised his eyebrows across the room and Theo shot him another quelling look.

Sarafina shrugged. "I guess my decision has been made for me."

"I can't protect you when you're in a different apartment."

Thomas nodded. "I agree. We don't know if Bai will come back or not." He paused. "You're in danger, Sarafina."

She gave him a sad smile. "It's okay. I have some practice at that."

Theo was certain she was referring to her mother. What hell had the early years of her life been? They'd probably been a lot like his.

"I HOPE THIS IS OKAY WITH YOU." SARAFINA STUDIED Theo's back while he stood in the kitchen, stirring a charm in a saucepan. "I mean, that I wanted you for a bodyguard or teacher or whatever you are."

No response.

"I mean, it's not that I have designs on your body or anything." Her gaze slipped to his ass. *Much.*

His shoulders tightened a degree. "Now that's a pity."

She grinned and stabbed at a bit of random herb on the table with the pad of her index finger. "Did I detect a note of amusement in your voice? Could it be? Has hell frozen over and have pigs grown wings?"

He grunted and continued to stir his pot.

"Anyway, I'm sorry if I pushed you into doing something you don't want."

Theo replied without turning. "Do you really think I'd do something I didn't want?" More silence.

Well, I guess that was as much of an answer as she was going to get.

"So you don't mind the living arrangements?"

"You must stay with me. Bai might try and come after you again and it would be better if I were close. Wards don't work on demons. Not even the kick-ass ones surrounding the Coven. Not much works on demons."

"So you won't mind the pink panties hanging over the towel rod in the bathroom?"

That made him turn. "There's going to be pink panties hanging over the towel rod in the bathroom?"

She grinned. "Actually, I wear thongs. They take up less space."

Theo's grip tightened a degree on the wooden spoon he held.

"I'm joking, Theo, relax. Grosset won't bother you?"

Theo diverted his gaze from her face to the dog in question, who sat on the floor near his feeding dish, panting. "No, but I guess we need to buy some Alpo. He can't live on SPAM."

"I'll take care of that tomorrow. I have to run back to my place to pack a bag and run by the office to finalize paperwork for my leave of absence."

Her vacation had turned into unpaid leave. It was the

worst time ever for her to go unpaid, considering her financial problems. Luckily the Coven was helping her make rent and pay her bills. She'd gladly taken the money, though pride dictated she pay them back when she could.

"You're not going alone."

"I should be fine."

"No way."

"I don't want to trouble you, Theo."

"You're not troubling me. I'll just be doing my job. That job is you."

The way he said it, so intensely, so protectively, made her heart miss a beat. She gave him a light smile to cover her reaction. "Wow, so you'll be *doing* me. My, what will the neighbors say?"

He ignored her comment. "After we return to the Coven tomorrow, we'll go straight to the training rooms."

"Training rooms?"

Theo nodded. "About a year and a half ago the Coven came into some money via Rue, the leader of the *Ytrayi*. Thomas and the Coven's advisors used it to make repairs to the buildings that were needed after we had a major battle with the *Atrika*. When they made the renovations, they added on training rooms for each of the elements."

She shrugged. "Sounds good to me."

He turned back to his bubbling brew and flipped off the heat. "Who's Alex?"

She stiffened. "How do you know who Alex is?"

"I don't. That's why I'm asking you. Your friend mentioned him at your apartment, said she wondered if you'd cheated on Alex."

She studied the tabletop. "He's my ex. We were together for about two years, but the fire was only a flicker at first and then it went out. We stayed together too long. Mostly out of fear of being alone, I think."

"So you're not nursing a broken heart on top of everything else?"

She swallowed hard, her eyes suddenly pricking with tears. "I am, but my broken heart is for my foster mother, not Alex. I'm still grieving for her."

He set the pot to the side and stared down into it for a long moment. "I'm sorry," he murmured without turning around. "It's hard losing your parents." His mother had taken off when he'd been a teenager, but considering her brutal husband, Theo couldn't really blame her much.

"Thanks. She was a good woman. I believe in an afterlife, though, and that gets me through."

"Even now that you know all this about witches, *daaeman*, and other worlds?"

She smiled. "Especially now. What do you believe in?"

He shrugged. "Most witches take a patron goddess or god, but some of us are broader in our beliefs."

"Let me guess, you're broad."

He looked down into the pot. "Yeah, but I believe in an afterlife."

Theo reached over and pinched some herbs from a pot on the counter, then dropped them into the pot. The air popped with a burst of earth magick, teasing her nose with a whiff of freshly turned soil. Apparently, he'd just absorbed the charm he'd made.

He turned. "Don't worry about the dog or your . . . thongs . . . hanging over the towel bar. Just go ahead and make yourself at home." He paused, studying her with his intense eyes. "But, Sarafina, don't make the mistake of thinking I'm not dangerous to you."

A little thrill of alarm jolted through her veins. "What do you mean?"

He gave her a lingering, smoldering look that nearly singed off the fine hairs around her face and made a hot ribbon of want curl through her lower region. Her answer was in his dark eyes, on his face.

Oh. *That.*

Theo left the room, disappearing down the shadowed hallway.

Yes, she was beginning to realize just how dangerous he might be.

NINE

➤

THEO SKATED HIS HANDS DOWN SARAFINA'S SMOOTH arms and decided immediately this was not a good idea. She needed someone else to help her learn to handle her fire magick. A witch of her own element, one who wasn't attracted to her. God, she should have gone to stay with Adam and Claire.

Sarafina shivered a little and extended her arms the way he'd instructed. He set his palm on the seat of her magick, right between her breasts and tried to ignore just how much he enjoyed his hand there.

They stood in the center of fire's brand-new training room. Thomas had spared no expense. Pads covered most of the floor, for practice in hand-to-hand combat. The walls and floor were all fire-resistant. Numerous tools were supplied for aiding new fire witches in learning the finer points of control . . . and Sarafina really needed to use them.

She had an incredible amount of raw talent in healing . . . but that's where it stopped. Defensive fire magick seemed to be a skill beyond her grasp. It was a good thing she hadn't tried to fight the demon in her apartment with magick; she'd have lost.

About ten feet away from them stood a large metal bowl on a pedestal. "Concentrate on hitting the bowl," he said, using a little earth magick to help her draw her thread of power and keep it steady. "This will teach you control."

Taking her time, she aimed a stream of fire toward the bowl . . . and hit the wall behind it with a radiant flash. The ball of fire burst into white-hot brilliance, then faded to a slow burn. The bowl still stood, completely unmolested.

Theo allowed his hands to drop away.

"Wow, I really suck at this, don't I?" she asked, staring at the black spot on the wall.

Theo pushed a hand through his hair. "I think that's a little harsh."

It had been some variation of the same all day long. Anyone who came to their power so late in life should have trouble adjusting and controlling it, but Sarafina seemed . . . exceptional.

"Don't try to sugarcoat it, Theo. I suck."

He sighed. "Yeah, okay, you suck."

She grimaced. "So no gold stars for me today?"

"You probably just need more practice. Look, your healing ability far surpasses anyone's I've ever seen, and you have a lot of raw power. It's learning to direct and control it. That's your difficulty. You just need to train more."

She raised an eyebrow and cocked her hip. "What about all that stuff you said about witches overtraining, and all we really had to do was tap into our seats and be one with the power?"

He studied her for a moment. "Yeah, well, in your case, you need to train."

"Okay, let's do it then. Let me try the candle thing again. I almost got that one."

He pulled out a new taper and placed it in its holder. Then they stepped back away from it. She could light a candle close-up; that had been the first thing she'd learned to do. The objective here was to light the wick from a distance, something that took considerably more control.

She melted the entire thing, even the holder.

Together, they stared down at the bubbling mess. "That was even worse than the first time, wasn't it?" she asked.

"Last time you only melted half the stick."

She sighed. "I'm not giving up. Let's keep going."

And he wasn't giving up on her, either.

They practiced for the rest of the day with varying

degrees of success. Sarafina was tireless in her efforts to learn what he was trying to teach her, and little by little she improved.

At the end of the day, Theo pulled her back ten feet in front of the bowl once more. "Try it again."

Sarafina closed her eyes and concentrated on drawing power and wielding it. An arc of white-hot fire raced from her and exploded in the bowl in a brilliance of sparks, setting off the sprinkler above it. Perfect shot.

She did a little victory dance and then turned to him with shining eyes. "Good?"

Theo stared at the water hitting the faraway fire and smiled. "Much better. I think you're finally getting it."

The woman had so much untutored power it was mind-boggling. It was a miracle she'd managed to get this far in life without torching herself like her mother had. Sarafina was probably among the stronger fire witches in the Coven. Her only hang-up was control.

She stood with her hands hanging loosely at her sides, dressed in a pair of clingy gray cotton workout pants and a burgundy halter top.

"You're improving, but you still need to work. I think I'll have Jack come in to help you with some of the finer points of wielding fire. But this portion of your training is finished for the day. Your seat must be exhausted."

She grinned, but it quickly faded. "*This* portion of my training? What's the other training I'll have to do?"

"Claire will need to teach you how to use your magick against demons. They have effective shields against elemental magick, but there are techniques to get around them."

She nodded. "Okay, that seems like a good thing to know."

"Isabelle will work on training you to use a copper sword."

She nodded. "I read about the sensitivity of the *daaeman* to copper in Micah's book."

Daaeman, all the breeds, had an allergy of sorts to copper. When the Coven had first learned of it, they'd had weapons made to take advantage of it. The *daaeman* could use a type of magickal inoculation against their reaction to copper called caplium, but it wasn't completely effective. Copper, even though it wasn't a surefire way to defeat a *daaeman* in a battle, was still better than nothing. It was one of their only weapons against them and they all trained diligently with the swords.

"And I'll have to teach you self-defense," Theo added. "The non-magickal kind."

Her eyes widened a bit. "Oh. Like kung fu?"

"Something like that." Theo couldn't help but grin at the look on her face. "It's necessary. Magick doesn't always work."

"Hey, if I had known how to kick Stefan's ass back at the farmhouse, I would've tried my best to do it."

"After I get through with you, you will."

SARAFINA LANDED FLAT ON THE MAT, UNDER THEO'S big body. Her heart rate had ratcheted up, but it had little to do with the exertion she was putting forth and a whole lot to do with the man forcing her to exert it.

Theo's breath teased the fine hair around her face. He stared down at her with such intensity it made her breath catch. "Give me more."

More. She closed her eyes.

For the last week that's all he, Claire, Isabelle, and Jack had demanded of her. Theo worked with her self-defense skills, Jack was helping her fine-tune her raw ability with fire, and Claire was teaching her how to use it effectively against demons. Lastly, Isabelle was helping her learn how to use a sword—something she never thought she'd have to do in her life.

God. *Not ever.*

Every night she collapsed exhausted into her bed and slept like the dead until morning. Every single one of all the muscles she'd never known she'd had ached. She understood the gravity of her situation and she'd been giving her all to each of them. That added up to three hundred percent. She had no more *more* to give.

She tried not to let the look in his eyes cow her. "I'll try."

He grunted and rolled off her. "Don't try, just do it."

She pushed to her feet, wincing at a pain in her back. Being slammed down onto a pad by a muscular man twice her weight wasn't fun. "Who are you, Yoda?" Annoyance made the words snap out.

"Just because Bai hasn't been back doesn't mean he won't be."

She let her head droop. "I know, I know. Believe me, if he or Stefan ever come back I want to be ready." She shivered. "I think Stefan scares me even more than Bai."

"Why?"

Sarafina walked over and took a towel from where she'd draped it over a Nautilus machine. They were training in the Coven's exercise room. "Because he's a witch. I mean, I would expect a demon to do hideous and terrible things. I can understand that. But Stefan is *aeamon*, one of us."

Theo uncapped his bottle of water and took a drink. When he'd finished, he put it down and said, "We're all one, Sarafina. As hard as that may be to understand, the *aeamon* are a part of the *daaeman*. We're born of them. The *daaeman* are a complicated race, like humans. Some of them are good and some of them are bad. There many shades of gray. You can count on an *Atrika* being violent and sociopathic. They're made to be that way. You *should* count on it to save your skin. But there are accounts of even *Atrika* falling in love with humans in ancient times. Even they are capable of compassion, apparently."

"So what are you saying?"

"I'm saying you shouldn't generalize and you shouldn't think in terms of *us* versus *them*. Basically, there is good in all demons, witches, and warlocks, but there's bad, too. You can't live by absolutes and you can't trust anyone, not even those closest to you."

Sarafina studied him for a long moment. "Do you really believe that? You can't trust anyone?"

He shifted. "Yeah, mostly."

"I agree with most of what you said, up until the end." She glanced away. "Wow, I'm sorry."

"Why?" The word dropped like a sharpened blade between them and she fought a wince.

She turned and found his gaze. "I'm sorry that whatever life handed you it was so terrible it taught you that you shouldn't trust anyone."

He tipped his head to the side a little. "Didn't it teach you that?"

She smiled and shook her head. "No. Oh, I had a rough time of it when I was a kid and the day my mom died was no picnic, but no. There are lots of people in my life I can trust, and I thank the stars every day for each and every one of them." Just thinking about how blessed she'd been to have Rosemary, not to mention all of her friends, made warmth tingle through her chest.

But Theo's gaze only grew colder. He looked away from her, at the door. "Let's knock off for the night. I think you've had enough for one day."

She tried not to jump up and down and squeal with excitement. Jumping up and down at this point was out of the question, anyway; she was far too sore. "Sounds good to me. I'd love a long, hot bath and an evening of relaxation."

"If we're lucky, Bai and Stefan will give it to us."

They gathered their things and headed back to Theo's apartment. Grosset was lying on the couch when they arrived, looking like a little furry emperor awaiting his evening meal. She collapsed onto the couch next to his happy, squirming body and sighed deeply.

"Speaking of your friends," said Theo from the kitchen doorway. He was probably going to make more charms. It seemed like all he did was make charms or work out when he wasn't training her. The man had no capacity for enjoyment, it seemed. "Do you need to contact them? Aren't they wondering where you are?"

She smiled as much as she could under the weight of her fatigue. "I've been fielding text messages for the last week. You provided me with the perfect cover. Maria has sung your praises to our entire circle of friends and acquaintances. They all think you've taken me away again to help me get over my grief."

If only she really could disappear for a while and nurse the heavy, sad undercurrent of emotion that seemed ever-present since Rosemary's death. That luxury was denied her.

He nodded. "So in their eyes I'm your boyfriend." He could've used the same tone to say, *I've been sentenced to be hanged at dawn.*

"That's your fault, dude, not mine." She let her head fall back against the cushions out of pure fatigue and closed her eyes. She couldn't even gather enough energy to be offended.

Grosset hopped off the couch and ran into the kitchen, where Theo was clanging pots and pans. She knew he'd feed the little dog and could hear him talking to Grosset in his low, rumbling voice. Eventually, as her exhaustion got the better of her, she heard nothing at all.

She awoke inside a dream. Or at least in the brief interlude between sleep and wakefulness, Sarafina thought she had.

Theo leaned down over her, fresh from the shower, wearing nothing but a towel around his narrow waist. His skin smelled of soap and the slightest bit of aftershave. His long dark hair lay damp and tangled over his broad shoulders. Her gaze seized on his chest, which was rarely bare despite the amount of training they did every day. The breathtaking expanse of muscular yumminess tapered to a narrow waist just barely covered by the white towel. For a moment she hoped it would slip. And, God, she was dying to ask him about all those scars.

"You fell asleep," he rumbled, helping her up from the couch. "You'll wake up sore if you sleep that way on the couch, and we have more training to do in the morning."

She groaned and allowed him to pull her to her feet. "I can't get any more sore than I already am," she grumbled and staggered toward the bedroom. Heavy drowsiness confused the signals transmitted from her head to her feet and she stumbled. Theo caught her and steadied her, but not before she fell against all that lickableness. That woke her up a bit.

"Take a shower and get into whatever you sleep in and I'll give you a massage."

She stumbled again. "A massage?"

"I'm good at them."

She started to ask who he practiced on. He didn't seem to have a lot of friends, let alone girlfriends. His life was all about magick, training, and gaining revenge against the Duskoff and demons. But pointing out he had no life was not a good way to treat someone who'd been generous enough to open his home to her, not to mention put himself in front of a demon for her.

Anyway, the thought of having his hands on her made her knees go weak.

"Okay, I won't turn the offer down. A good massage would make me sleep much better."

They stopped outside the guest room doorway. "Make sure you wear something"—he paused and made a slow sweep of her body with his gaze—"appropriate."

Sarafina scowled at his back as he walked down the hallway to his bedroom. Wear something *appropriate*? What did he think, that she intended to try and seduce him? Did he think she was planning to light a few candles and slip into a black lace teddy or something?

She curled her lip and watched him disappear into his room. She might think he was hot and more than a little mysterious, but she had no intention of trying to jump his bones. Good thing, since he'd just made it clear there would be none of that, anyway. He'd rejected her before she'd made a move . . . and she hadn't even been planning to make a move!

Teeth gritted, she went in and took a hot shower. Finding a pair of boxer shorts and a tank top, she declared them "appropriate." She assumed he wanted her body as covered as possible, but she didn't own any grannie nightgowns that covered her from throat to ankle. He'd simply have to settle for her normal nighttime attire.

Wincing, she made it over to the bed and collapsed facedown. Her eyelids immediately drooped. The hot water of the shower had made her muscles feel a little better and it had made her extra sleepy. Grosset bustled into the room, followed by Theo.

Wordlessly, Theo started on her right foot, massaging it

competently with strong hands. Sarafina groaned, feeling all the tension and soreness leak from her body the farther he moved up her leg.

And the farther he moved up her leg the more poignantly aware she became of his touch. He worked silently and in a very businesslike manner. This was not a man who'd suggested the massage as a way to try and get into her pants. Clearly, he meant only to work out the knots in her muscles so she could sleep better and they could get back to work the next day.

Considering what he'd told her about her clothing being appropriate, she should be offended. She certainly should not be enjoying the slide of his calloused palms over her skin and the deep, strong pressure of his fingers massaging her calves and thighs. It relaxed her body and also made her feel tingly in places he most certainly was not touching.

His touch also made her feel oddly comforted and protected. When she gave in to the fact that she liked his hands on her—really she didn't have any energy left to fight it, anyway—her body tipped so far into drowsiness that it was impossible to recover.

When Theo reached her shoulders and turned the muscles there into melted butter, the comforting darkness of sleep closed over her head like a wave crashing onto the beach.

Theo noted Sarafina's breathing deepen to slumber as he finished working the tension from her back. Once he was satisfied that he'd helped her recover from the stress and strain of the grueling week she'd put in, he withdrew and took a moment to watch her sleep, totally unable to resist the urge.

She turned onto her back and lay half covered by the sheet that was twisted around her legs. As she shifted, the boxers she wore rode higher up, better exposing the silky, pale shape of her thighs. He'd just had his hands on them and he knew how soft and velvety her skin was.

She threw an arm over her head and the action caused her breast to press against the material of the tank top she wore.

If he looked hard he could see the outline of her nipple. He was a man; he looked. He even imagined what it would feel like under his fingertips, what it would taste like against his tongue.

His gaze traveled upward again. Her eyelashes were swept down over creamy pale skin and her full lips were slightly parted in sleep.

Yeah, she was attractive. Maybe even a little more than merely attractive. Most men would probably call her cute, but Theo found her beautiful.

Grosset lay on her other side, snoring. The dog snuffled against her back and almost woke her up, so Theo turned and walked out of the room. The last thing he needed to be caught doing was staring at her while she was sleeping. All the trust she thought she had in him would disappear.

And he liked that she trusted him.

TEN

❧

SARAFINA TURNED DURING YET ANOTHER TIRING training session and regarded Claire. "Where is his family?"

Claire dropped to the padded floor the three balls she held in the air with air magick. She'd been juggling them while Sarafina had been practicing throwing fire the special way Claire had instructed her. Together the two of them were probably better than Ringling Bros.

She blinked. "Who?" A knowing look enveloped her expression. "Oh, you mean Theo."

Sarafina nodded.

"He doesn't talk much, our Theo. I'm sure you've noticed."

Claire spoke with an odd, very subtle accent, something that people might presume was Dutch. It had come from growing up on Eudae, Sarafina understood. It was hard to believe that Claire actually spoke fluent Aemni, the demon language.

"He especially doesn't talk much about his past or his family," Claire continued. "I do know that he's estranged from his parents and has been since he was a teenager. I don't think he had a good life with them. His father abused his mother and I believe she left when Theo was a teenager." She lifted a shoulder. "I don't think he has any siblings, but I'm just not sure. Theo is reserved. He doesn't share much about himself and he's hard to get close to."

Sarafina shifted and glanced away. "Yes, sometimes people who have their spirits broken when they're young close themselves off from the rest of the world, to protect the unbroken part of themselves. It's hard for them to risk because they understand just how much there is to lose."

"You sound like you're speaking from experience." Claire's voice had gone quiet and gentle.

Sarafina laughed. "I suppose having my mother try to kill me in my neighbor friend's sandbox qualifies as a spirit-breaking childhood event. I closed down, too, but my foster mom helped me see what I was doing early on and correct it." She paused and swallowed hard; a rush of grief for Rosemary rose up to swamp her for a moment. "I had help. Not everyone gets that."

Claire gave her a small, secret smile. "I had help, too."

Sarafina figured she was referring to Adam. The two of them were always together, obviously committed, and deeply in love. There were several couples in the Coven that way—in the kind of relationships that made people around them get lumps in their throats.

One day Sarafina wanted something like what Claire and Adam had. Something like what she saw when Jack met Mira's eyes from across the room, or when Thomas brushed the back of his hand against Isabelle's cheek when he thought no one was looking. A relationship like that wasn't in the cards for her, at least not anytime soon.

Sarafina returned her smile, happy—if not just a little jealous—for the other woman's good fortune. It was natural. Everyone wanted to be loved, didn't they? Even Theo needed to be loved somewhere down deep under all the gruff.

"Can you tell me what happened to his chest to create all those scars?" Sarafina asked. She couldn't resist asking the question, she just couldn't.

"The Duskoff, who else? I'll let him tell you the details, though."

Sarafina raised an eyebrow. "Think he will?"

"I think he's bonded with you better than I've ever seen him bond with anyone. Even Ingrid."

"Ingrid?"

"A fire witch who died in a blood magick spell performed by an *Atrika daaeman* about a year and a half ago. Theo was sleeping with her, but no one really knows if it was more than that." She glanced away. "I feel responsible for her death in a way because the demon's spell was worked to find me. Her death really affected Theo deeply."

"That's horrible."

"It was a . . . bad time."

"I'm not sleeping with him, you know."

Claire looked up in surprise. "Huh? I never thought you were."

"Well, but you said Theo was bonding better with me than he had with Ingrid, a woman he was sleeping with. I'm not with Theo like that."

"Oh, sorry. I didn't mean to imply I thought you were."

"I just want to make that clear." Sarafina waved a hand at her. "I'm staying in the guest room and we have different bathrooms. I've never even seen him naked, well, except for the waist up, and—"

Claire laughed. "Okay, I got it. I think someone is protesting a little too much."

Sarafina felt her cheeks heat. "I just don't want tongues to be wagging, mostly for Theo's sake."

"Okay, gotcha." Claire winked. She turned and headed for the door. "I'll see you tomorrow, Sarafina."

"Okay, see you tomorrow!" Sarafina waved and then smacked her forehead with her open palm once Claire had disappeared. She hadn't completely clued her in that she was crushing a little bit on Theo, had she? Nah, not at all . . . Sarafina cringed.

She headed out of the room as well, more than ready to knock off for the night. All the way up to Theo's apartment she kicked herself for running on at the mouth about sleeping with Theo. As much as she tried to deny it, the more time she spent with the man, the more she imagined what it would be like.

Theo was so *intense*. Would he be that way in bed, too? How would all the focused, passionate emotion that teemed under his constant brooding translate between the sheets? Just the thought made her shiver.

She'd read that certain elements were attracted to each other. Air and fire fed each other. Earth and water nourished each other. When two people who were already attracted had elements that complemented, that attraction was intensified. Earth and fire had nothing special—no pumped-up attraction.

On her end, it mattered not a whit.

Sometimes before she went to sleep at night she imagined what it would be like to kiss him. He had such a sensual mouth, such full lips. How would they feel slipping and sliding against hers? How would his toughened, powerful hands feel moving against her most intimate places? She knew firsthand from the massage he'd given her that he could be gentle and strong at the same time.

Would he be uber-dominant in bed, or would he allow her to take the lead?

Oh, God.

She stopped in front of his door, trying to calm the furious flush that had entered her cheeks. It was the curse of the fair-skinned. She had to get control of her fantasies. Theo had given her absolutely no indication that he was at all interested in her that way. He'd made that one remark in the kitchen, but, hell, she could have misunderstood. Then there'd been that comment about appropriate clothing.

No, he wasn't attracted to her.

She walked into an empty living room. Grosset was in his usual place on the couch. She set her bag down on the floor by the coffee table and noted that his apartment had been much tidier since she'd been staying with him. Probably a combination of her picking things up and Theo becoming more conscious of not simply stripping as soon as he got through the door and dropping his clothes willy-nilly.

Not that she'd mind if he stripped as soon as he got through the door.

Theo walked down the hallway. "Did you have a good session with Claire?"

She sought Grosset's leash and nodded. "She taught me how to ricochet my magick to get around *daaeman* shields and how to deflect their blasts."

Theo watched her walk toward Grosset with the leash in hand. "I already took him out."

"Oh, great. Thanks." She put the leash back.

"Mira has been hearing some disturbing whispers. It appears that the air witch the Duskoff captured has been killed."

Sarafina jerked. "Really? That's horrible."

"That's the Duskoff. If they can't bend you, medicate you, or if you're of no further use to them, they kill you."

"But wait." She turned to him. "Why wouldn't they keep her alive? I mean, they need witches of all four elements to cast a demon circle, don't they? Why wouldn't they use her in one of those?" She chewed her lip, thinking. "They didn't use her to bring Bai through, or she would have been dead long before now, since the witches in the circle are sacrificed to pull a *daaeman* to Earth. But they could have used her to pull a second *daaeman* through, right?"

Theo bared his teeth in something Sarafina assumed was supposed to be a smile. "Very perceptive. Thomas thinks it's one of two reasons. Either the witch didn't have enough strength to bring an adequately powerful *daaeman* through, or they don't need to cast a demon circle. Considering Bai is here and no one knows how he arrived, Thomas is leaning toward the second thing."

"You mean, the Duskoff didn't keep her alive to toss her into a demon circle because they already have their demon."

"Yeah."

"We just don't know how he got over here."

"Yeah."

"Sounds ominous."

"It's never anything less." He moved the coffee table to the side of the room as if it weighed nothing. "Because of recent developments, I want you to show me what you know."

"What? Is this a pop quiz?"

He stood in the center of the room and faced her. "Yeah. I'm going to attack you and I want you to throw me off. I want you to prove to me you can do it."

She glanced around at the furniture. "Shouldn't we do this down on the mats?"

"Do you really think your attacker will wait until you're somewhere convenient?"

"Good point."

"What are you waiting for?"

"You haven't attacked me yet."

He rushed her. Having a man twice her weight careening across the room at her was just about enough to stop her heart for a moment. Then instincts took over, driven by his training over the last two weeks. She didn't really think, she just reacted.

Moving to the side, he rushed past her. Her tactic didn't work. He grabbed her around the waist and lifted her, spinning her around. Her breath crushed out of her and her magick flared, running over her body, just far enough away to keep from burning her . . . but not him.

Theo yelped and pushed her away, the fabric of his shirt smoking. In a moment, he was on her again, the scent of earth magick flaring in the air. Grosset started barking. Just as a bolt of power spiked toward her, she ducked, hitting the floor, and rolling back up onto her feet.

He grabbed her from behind and they struggled. She brought her elbow back into his solar plexus, making him grunt. Then she pivoted on the balls of her feet and brought her palm up against his nose, pulling back only at the last minute so she didn't break it. He *oofed* and whirled to the side, tripped and fell against the corner of the wall.

That saying about the big guys falling harder was true.

"Oh, my God! I'm sorry!" Sarafina rushed to Theo's side, placing her hand on his back and hoping like hell she hadn't injured him too badly.

"I guess you pass the test," Theo said, holding a hand to his head.

"Come on, let me see." She pulled his hand away from his face and saw that he'd beaned himself in the forehead. Those kinds of head wounds bled a lot, and this one was no exception. She gasped and bit her lower lip. "I'm really sorry, Theo. I didn't mean to hurt you."

She led him over to sit down on the couch. Grosset eyed

them both warily. Sarafina pushed his hair away and examined his forehead, wincing.

"I asked you to hurt me. Don't be sorry. You proved that my training has actually done some good."

She frowned. "You seem to get hurt a lot."

The ghost of a grin passed over his lips. "I let you win." He caught and held her gaze. "Anyway, this gives you a chance to practice your healing on me again."

Sarafina stilled, captivated. This was the longest he'd ever looked directly into her eyes. His pupils dilated a little, the color turning a deeper, darker brown. Her lips parted and her breath caught at the intimacy of the moment. The silence between them seemed pregnant with possibility . . .

Her next sentence came out in a near breathless puff of air as she stared deeply into his beautiful eyes. "Take off your pants."

That pregnant, intimate moment popped like a bubble.

He blinked. "What did you say?"

Mentally, she smacked her forehead. *Brilliant, Sarafina, brilliant!*

"I meant your shirt, not your pants. I'll try to get the blood out of it." She gave a nervous laugh. "Why would I ask you to take off your pants?"

He gave her just the briefest hint of a smile. Because of its genuineness, it was the most stunning thing Sarafina had seen in a while. In one smooth move, torso rippling with power, he removed his shirt and gave it to her.

Flustered, she rose and scrubbed the hell out of the bloodstains before dumping the shirt into the washing machine. She returned with bandages and disinfectant. "Let me clean the wound before I do the healing. I don't like the possibility of accidentally sealing an infection in there."

Theo nodded and she sat beside him. Sarafina was becoming accustomed to patching up his wounds by now. It didn't take her long to clean up the blood and disinfect the gash. Then she used fire magick to close it up. In the end, she didn't even need the bandages.

She sat back and admired her handiwork for a moment. All that remained was a rapidly healing ridge of flesh. Damn, she was getting good at this. "So, the air witch being killed was bad news, especially for the air witch, but Bai hasn't tried to rip us to shreds in a whole two weeks. I count that as good."

"I don't think he'll try and rip *you* to shreds, Sarafina." He paused. "At least not right away."

The implication of what he'd just said made her shiver. She swallowed hard.

"I don't want to lie about what I think Bai wants from you."

She raised an eyebrow. "Well, there's this saying about ignorance and bliss . . ."

"Ignorance only gets you killed in this world."

"Still, I think I liked it better when you weren't talking much."

"I only speak when there's something worthwhile to say."

She nodded. "No idle conversation for you."

"I don't enjoy shallow conversation." He shifted. "But if you would feel more at ease, I can try."

"I don't enjoy *shallow* conversation, either, big guy." She ran her gaze down his chest. "So, in the spirit of avoiding such topics, do you want to tell me how you got these?"

He glanced down at his chest. "The Duskoff put them there. They captured me when I was a teenager and tried to break me physically. They wanted me to tie myself to them, become one of them."

"How would physical torture help their cause?"

"They try seduction first. Torture is a last resort. It works like all abuse works. They break you down completely and build you back up in their image. By the time they're done with you, you'll give them anything." Long pause.

"Did they whip you?"

"A little, but mostly these were made by a knife tip. There was a man there who got off on giving pain that way. It excited him." Theo's jaw locked. "He had a whole set of knives that he kept so sharp they didn't even hurt when they sliced your skin." He paused. "Not at first, anyway. He liked to draw patterns on people, considered himself a true artist."

Queasiness roiled her stomach. "God, I'm so sorry."

"It's over and done. I don't look back at the past."

Hmmm, maybe, but she could hear it in his voice—it still clung to him, anyway. They shared that burden—having a heavy past. Wanting to let it go, yet not being allowed to release it, not completely. In this one thing, she understood him. In this one thing, they shared a common bond.

The difference between them was that she'd not allowed herself to become emotionally scarred by her past and Theo had. That was clear enough.

She reached out and traced a long, thin white scar running from his shoulder down over his pecs. His flesh shivered under her touch and his breath caught almost too softly to hear. She flattened her palm against his warm skin and savored the steady, strong beat of his heart thrumming under her hand.

"What you've done with these scars—you've made them magnificent. You've transformed them into something your own, art of *your own*. Taken your wounds and made something beautiful out of them."

He caught her hand in his so fast it made her gasp. Theo stared down at her. "Don't push me." He stood and walked toward the hallway.

"Push you? What are you talking about?" She rose from the couch.

Theo turned and stalked toward her. "You know what I mean. I'm attracted to you, and you know it. Don't push me. This isn't a game."

"What?" She shook her head, confused. Honestly, when she traced the scar on his chest the last thing she'd been thinking about was sex. She'd simply been moved by his experience and the marks he'd always wear to remind him. "Theo, I wasn't trying to push you. Maybe I never should have touched you. I overstepped our boundaries. I'm sorry."

"I can't be around you without wanting you." He turned away from her, once again walking toward the hallway. Probably, he meant to escape into his bedroom. Run away.

Sarafina followed him. "Theo, wait. We need to talk this through."

Theo whirled and pushed her against the wall.

ELEVEN

HER BREATH LEFT HER IN A RUSH OF SURPRISE AND a spike of fear. She had to quickly remind herself that she trusted Theo and he meant her no harm.

His arms pinned her on either side of her body and his head dipped, his warm breath teasing the fine hair at the edges of her face. Goose bumps erupted all over her body. "The last thing I want to do with you is *talk*, Sarafina." Theo moved his hand from her waist slowly down to her lower stomach, splaying it there.

Her stomach muscles tightened and her breath caught. "I didn't know you were attracted to me," she whispered. "You gave me no reason to think so."

"I'm giving you reason now." His voice was low and melodic in a raw, masculine way. He spoke right next to her ear, sending shivers through her body.

Her breathing hitched. Yes, yes, he was giving her a reason now, *ample* reason. So much it was making her head spin.

His hand dropped an inch, toyed with the button of her jeans. "And if I can't make myself walk away right now, I'll give you even more reason." His voice came out a low, velvet purr.

Sarafina closed her eyes and fought not to reach up and touch him. Her sex responded to his words as surely as if they were foreplay, growing damp and tingling in anticipation of his touch. Her nipples grew tight and the slightest brush of the material of her shirt against them sent ripples of pleasure through her. She shuddered just a little, wanting more from him.

Theo did all this to her with only his voice.

She had wanted, yearned for, many men in her life, but she wasn't sure she'd ever desired one as much as she desired Theo right now. By his own admission, he was restraining himself, but what would this man be like when all his self-control was unleashed?

His warm breath eased along the skin near her collar-bone, his lips barely brushing the curve where her shoulder met her neck, making her shiver.

"Sometimes when I watch you," he murmured, "I wonder just how you'd like to be touched. I wonder where you're the most sensitive and which parts of your body make you sigh and moan when they're stroked and kissed."

Images of his big hands running down her bare body assaulted her mind. She imagined his bare chest rubbing her breasts, his knee parting her thighs . . .

Sarafina tried to reach up and touch him, but he grabbed her wrists and pinned them to the wall on either side of her head, his body pressing against her and keeping her still.

Theo's voice lowered. "Then I wonder what it would be like to fuck you. If you like it fast and hard or slow and easy. I wonder what you sound like when you come."

Guh.

Sarafina made fists and pulled against his unyielding grip, unable to find an adequate reply. Theo had gone from frigid to scorching in a half second flat, and she wasn't processing it all that fast.

He released her wrists and she raised her head, meeting his gaze. Confusion and desire warred for supremacy within her and she had no idea how to react to this turn of events.

Theo's jaw locked. All he did was look down at her mouth, staring at her lips. After a long moment, he lowered his head and tasted them. It was so gentle, so at odds with the way Theo had acted up until now. Sarafina closed her eyes and melted a little, her knees going weak. Her fingers found the front of his shirt and twined in the material, holding on for dear life as his lips skated over hers, savoring her.

Sarafina parted her lips a little, urging him to take the

bait. He did, parting her lips farther, slanting his mouth firmly over hers and sliding his tongue within her mouth. The brush of his tongue against hers was like fire and set her pulse racing.

His hands slipped to the small of her back and he pushed, drawing her flush up against his chest as he slanted his mouth across hers and deepened the kiss. Sarafina's mind shut down for a moment as she was immersed in Theo—the feel, smell, and heat of him.

The softness of the initial kiss was gone, replaced by hot, brutal need. Now his lips were almost harsh against hers, his tongue seeking as much contact with her tongue as he could get. Like he wanted to consume her. Like all he wanted in the world was to kiss her and this would be his only chance.

Sarafina whimpered deep in her throat. In all her life she'd never been kissed this way. Hell, the way Theo did it made her feel like she'd never once been kissed at all. Her mind spun and she could do nothing but grip his shoulders, fingers finding anxious purchase in the material of his shirt. His muscles bunched and flexed as he moved, accentuating how large and imposing a man he was. Sarafina didn't want the kiss to end.

But then he was gone.

Tottering unsteadily on her feet, she opened her eyes and saw him disappear down the hallway. Her lips were swollen and her body tingled with awareness of him. Unable to move, she just stared at his retreating form, feeling like she'd been a hit-and-run.

"Theo." His name came out in a croak.

He didn't stop.

She pushed off the wall and forced herself to go after him. She realized it was a bit like chasing a wild wolf. Theo was dangerous and unpredictable; he'd just proved that. Still, she couldn't stop herself. "Wait a minute. You can't just *do* that, *say* that . . . *kiss me* and then run away."

He halted in the threshold of his bedroom doorway, back to her.

She stopped behind him. "Theo," she repeated.

"I told you not to push me," he said, his back to her.

"I just want to know what's going on here. I'm confused. Turn around and talk to me."

He stood there for a long moment, then simply stepped into his bedroom and closed the door in her face.

TWELVE

BAI LOOMED OVER HER, EYES RED. HIS BREATH *smelled of old bones and hot blood.*

Sarafina screamed and sat bolt upright in bed. Grosset cowered nearby.

Theo skidded to a stop in her doorway, his hair a tangle, wearing only a pair of boxers. He held a copper sword in his grip. "Where?"

Her breathing came harsh in the cool night air. Sarafina held out a hand, watching it tremble. "It was only a nightmare." Her voice shook, too. "About Bai."

"Fuck, Sarafina." The words came out of Theo on a relieved sigh. He lowered his weapon.

She pushed a shaking hand through her pillow-mussed hair, then threw the blankets off of her and swung her feet to the floor. "I need a drink and I don't mean Kool-Aid."

"Don't."

She stopped in mid-motion. *"Don't?* You're not in a position to tell me what to do, Theo." Now her voice trembled more from anger than fear. She hadn't forgotten about his reaction to her earlier. She was also more than a tad riled from her nightmare. Being terrified and out of control pissed her off.

"Alcohol can impair your judgment and slow your reaction time. It can also make your mind more open to Bai's influence."

She sat back down on the bed, the thought making ice water course through her veins. "What?"

"You have to consider that the nightmare wasn't just a nightmare."

Great. Now she wouldn't sleep for the rest of the night, maybe not for the rest of her life. "What? Like Freddy Krueger? They can do that?"

He nodded. "He can't actually hurt you, Sarafina, but he can mind-fuck you."

She ran a hand over her face. God, she was so tired. Grosset came to curl up next to her. "Unbelievable."

Theo fidgeted in the doorway. "Are you all right?"

"Fantastic."

"Do you think you can sleep anymore tonight?"

She snorted. "That would be a *no.*"

He leaned his forearm against the door frame and rested his head there. His voice was muffled when he spoke. "When I can't sleep, I take a drive."

"On your motorcycle?"

He raised his head. "Yeah, the night air is good for you, you know?"

"So, was that like an offer or something?"

"Yeah."

"Your generosity and verbosity overwhelm me."

He sighed. "You want to go or not?"

Anything to break the spell of the nightmare. "Yes."

Minutes later they were dressed and on Theo's cycle, barreling down an empty early morning highway fast enough to blow the memory of her nightmare straight out of her brain. The cool air infused her lungs and spread a smile over her face.

It was like they were flying—like they were *free.*

Now Sarafina could see the appeal of motorcycles, whereas before she thought they were only the domain of the crazy, the stupid, or men having midlife crises. On the back of a bike, hurtling through the black, you could find freedom—if only temporarily—from everything behind you.

All the weight on her was gone, eradicated by the force of the road underneath the cycle's tires. All the pressure of her past—for right now, anyway—had vanished, forced away by the vibration of the vehicle beneath her.

No wonder Theo loved his bike.

Eventually, they came to a park and Theo pulled over,

bringing the cycle to a rumbling halt. It had to be around two or three in the morning. Sarafina released her hold around his midsection, pulled off her helmet, and dismounted. The trees stood tall and silent under a night sky strewn with stars. They were pretty far from the light pollution of the city, judging by the beauty of the sky.

"How long have we been riding?" she asked as Theo got off the bike.

"We're about an hour out of Chicago. I come here sometimes to get away from the city lights. You can actually see some stars out here."

She looked up at the sky, the slight breeze cooling her head, which had been warmed by the helmet, and rustling the fine hair that framed her face. Sarafina closed her eyes and sank into the moment, letting it fill her up like water pouring into a pitcher.

When she opened her eyes, Theo was leaning against the bike and staring at her. "Do you feel better?"

She smiled and nodded. The rage that had tightened her muscles earlier was absent now. "Thank you."

He stared at her for a moment, their gazes locking, then he pushed away from the bike and walked into the nearby copse of trees. Somewhere in the distance, a night bird called, breaking the near-perfect silence. "I like it out here at this time of night."

"You like it because there are no people?" It was an educated guess.

"Yeah, definitely."

She walked over to stand near him. "Right now, I completely get that."

They stood in companionable silence for several moments. Finally, Theo spoke. "I love this park. If I ever have kids, I'll take them camping here on the weekends."

The words had slipped from him as though he hadn't meant them to, like a stray thought had been trapped in a bit of breath and set free by accident.

Somehow the image of Theo having children, let alone *camping* with them, didn't jive. Roasting marshmallows over a fire? Backpacking in the woods? It seemed odd, yet in some ways Theo would make a great father. He'd be protective, that was for sure. If he ever had a daughter, her boyfriends would have to tread very carefully.

She gave him a sidelong glance. "Do you want kids?"

He glanced at her and shifted a little. "Yeah, maybe. One day."

"I just thought that—"

He turned toward her. "What? That a person with an upbringing as fucked up as mine wouldn't want to risk parenthood?"

"No!" She held out a hand as if to ward off his belligerent tone of voice. "I wasn't thinking that at all. It just seems like your life is all about your work. You seem so hell-bent on taking the Duskoff down and not really all that interested in dating, let alone building a family."

He rubbed a hand over his mouth. "Yeah, well, maybe one day we *will* take the Duskoff down and I can concentrate on other things." He paused. "More important things, like marriage and a family."

"I hope so."

"Maybe," he said again. "If I can ever find a woman crazy enough to stay with me."

She laughed. "You have your charms, Theo, even if they're a little buried under a crust."

He grunted, turned, and walked toward the cycle. "You ready to head back?" His tone really didn't invite disagreement. Apparently, it was time to go.

She turned toward him. "I would like to be your friend, Theo."

He halted with his back to her. His shoulders tightened. "That's nice. Do you want to hold my hand, too?"

Sarafina blew out a frustrated breath and walked to the bike. "I'm trying to extend an olive branch here."

"I didn't know we were fighting."

"It's just that, things seem tense between us after what happened, you know, in the hallway . . ."

"You mean when I kissed you, Sarafina?" He turned toward her and she stilled like a deer in a hunter's line of sight.

His voice had gone a shade lower, a bit more velvety. Almost . . . seductive.

She couldn't take another kiss-and-run.

"Yes, you kissed me, then pushed me away."

Theo turned back toward the bike. "That was a mistake."

"What was a mistake, the kiss or pushing me away?"

He fiddled with the helmets lying on the cycle's seat. "The kiss, Sarafina."

"Not from where I was standing."

"Your perspective might change if you knew that every woman I become involved with ends up dead somehow."

"What?" She put her hand on her hip. "That sounds really ominous, Theo. What exactly are you saying?"

He turned toward her. "*I* didn't kill them, Sarafina. I'm just saying they have a habit of turning up dead."

She opened her mouth, then closed it. "I have no idea what to say to that."

"Don't say anything. I don't want to talk about it."

"Okay."

"Come on, I'll let you drive for a while."

"Huh?"

"I'll teach you how to drive a motorcycle."

"Oh." She eyed the huge heavy . . . *hog*. Isn't that what they called them? "Um."

"It's not hard. Come on." He extended one of the helmets toward her.

She took it, knowing this was his olive branch.

ADAM'S BLADE MET THEO'S AND REVERBERATED down the length of his arm. Theo pushed back with a grunt and sent Adam backward. Adam swung around, slashing upward with his sword and forcing Theo back into the defensive.

Theo whirled, his tail of hair lashing him in the face, and blocked Adam's powerful swing. Adam was one of the best swordsmen in the Coven and Theo loved to engage him. It was a challenge. Today he craved the burn in his muscles and the state of mindlessness that combat gave him. It provided a much-needed escape.

Sweat poured down Theo's chest as he took the offensive again, pushing Adam back in a flurry of flashing copper blades and ringing metal. Channeling all his current frustration and rage into the battle, Theo pressed Adam farther and farther back. His muscles straining and his arms and legs screaming, he gave a loud bellow and forced Adam to stumble backward onto the mat.

Adam threw his sword to the floor and swore at the top of his lungs. He shook his sweat-soaked hair and yelled, "All right, enough! I give in! *Gods damn!*"

Theo let his sword dangle at his side. He tipped his head back and closed his eyes for a moment, savoring both his rare victory against Adam and also the satisfying physical strain in his body from the exertion it had taken to gain it. Then he reached down and offered Adam his hand. Adam took it and Theo hefted the other man to his feet.

"Good fight," said Theo.

Adam eyed him warily. "You're only saying that because you won."

Theo grinned. "Maybe. Want another go?"

Adam rotated his shoulder. "Hell, no. You're out for blood today. I want to keep my head on my shoulders. I have a woman at home to think about."

Yeah, Theo had a woman at home right now, too. That was a turn of events he'd never counted on. At first he'd figured it wouldn't be a big deal. She was his job. Sure, she was pretty, but there were lots of pretty witches in the Coven and he'd been able to resist almost all of them. Theo wasn't like how Adam had been pre-Claire, chasing after every woman he came into contact with.

But after just a week of living with Sarafina, his resistance had been worn to a nubbin.

Her constant presence—the subtle, sweet scent of her invading his nose at every turn, the sight of the nape of her neck when she twisted her hair up onto the top of her head, or the curve of her calf and her small bare foot when she sat in the recliner and rocked herself while she read a book. All of those tiny little things had added up. Now her presence in his apartment was all a tease to him—foreplay. It excited him. Like waving a steak in front of a starving tiger.

He'd had nothing but contempt for Jack McAllister when he'd begun sleeping with his charge, Mira Hoskins, way back when. And when Adam and Claire had fallen into bed while Adam had been helping to keep Claire safe from the *Atrika* a year and a half ago, Theo hadn't been surprised, but he had been a little disgusted. He'd sworn both times that if he were Adam or Jack, he'd never follow the whim of his dick and nail the body he was supposed to be guarding.

Now here he was trying hard to think with his big head and ignore the little one.

"So what the hell is with all the extra energy?" queried Adam, rubbing a towel across the back of his neck. "You always fight hard, but that was exceptional." He raised an eyebrow. "Sexual repression, maybe?"

"Shut up, Adam."

"Yeah, well, if it is sexual repression, keep it away from me, all right? I don't swing that way."

Theo readjusted his grip on the blade. "I just wanted a good fight today, that's all. Knew I'd get one from you."

"Everything going okay with Sarafina? She seems like a really cool chick. Claire likes her a lot. Shouldn't she be training with the copper blades by now?"

"She is training with the swords, but she's doing it with Isabelle." He paused. "Everyone likes Sarafina."

He glanced at him. "You including yourself in there? I know you two got off to a rocky start. You know, what with you dragging her through the cornfield and all."

Theo lifted the blade and examined the edge. "Yeah, things were rocky back when I thought she was a warlock. There was something suspicious about her."

"Suspicious?" Adam shook his head and snorted out a laugh. "Yeah, well, she's never looked like much of a warlock to me. An angel, maybe, not a warlock."

"Sometimes people who look sweet and innocent really aren't."

"Yeah, true. Okay, got me there." Adam glanced at him. "She's kind of hot, too. Don't you think so?"

Theo rested his sword against the wall and pulled a bottle of water from the small fridge nearby. "You think every woman is hot," he said with a snort before uncapping it and taking a long swallow.

"I don't," he protested, turning toward him with sword in hand. "I'm committed to Claire now, but that doesn't mean I don't notice an attractive woman when I see one. I just don't think any of them hold a candle to my wife."

Theo just grunted. It was true that Adam was a different man now that he'd met Claire.

"You never answered my question." Adam danced toward him playfully, sword in hand. "Admit you think she's cute."

Theo took a step backward and was forced to set his water down. "Adam, I'm not in the mood for games."

He danced closer, blade at the ready. "Fuck, Theo, when are you ever? Come on, admit you think she's cute. It's not a hard thing to do." Adam feinted, making Theo duck and back away.

Theo was forced to take his sword back up and block Adam's jab. "Gods damn it, you're a fucking pain in the ass."

"Like that's news." He slashed upward toward Theo's chest and Theo blocked his swing. Metal clanging on metal filled the air anew. The hit reverberated down his arm. "Admit it already."

"Don't make me hurt you, Adam." Theo growled.

Adam took a swing that Theo blocked at the last second. "Just admit it."

"Yeah, okay, fuck! She's cute!"

Adam raised an eyebrow and turned on his heel, bringing his blade down fast and hard toward him. "Now we're getting somewhere."

Theo had only a moment to wonder why Adam cared what he thought about Sarafina before he was on the offensive and back in the battle again.

* * *

THE IMPRINT OF THEO'S KISS STILL WEIGHED ON Sarafina's lips. The time that had passed since he'd pressed her up against the wall hadn't diminished it. In fact, every time Theo looked at her—which was never directly these days—the memory became even heavier.

She shifted on the small couch she sat on and tried to focus on Thomas's update and not on Theo, who leaned against a nearby wall with his arms crossed over his chest.

They'd gathered in one of the Coven's general meeting/receiving rooms. All of them were lushly furnished with overstuffed couches and chairs and had fresh flowers on the tables.

Somehow, some way, she'd been admitted into the Coven's inner circle. She'd gone from non-magickal office worker, to being a suspected warlock, to being a confirmed fire witch who was intimately involved in the most powerful witchy organization of the realm.

She couldn't think about it too much without seriously doubting her sanity, so she didn't. Going with the flow seemed the best way to proceed at this point.

Sarafina assumed she'd been included in the inner circle because of her as of yet unknown *special* status. That she was of interest to Stefan Faucheux and his pet *daaeman*, Bai, was not in question. But for whatever reason they'd decided to include her, she'd been summoned along with about fifteen other witches to listen to periodic updates made by Thomas and Micah.

Even Isabelle's perfectly groomed and highly fashionable mother, Catalina, was here for this discussion. Catalina, so Sarafina had been told, was doing her best to mend her relationship with her daughter. Apparently, when Isabelle had been growing up, Catalina hadn't parented her well. However, now she was trying her best to make it up to her daughter, and so spent a lot of time at the Coven.

Today there were representatives from the East and West Coast Covens, too, an occurrence she'd gathered was rare. The Chicago Coven was not only the witchy headquarters for all the Midwest and the South, it was also the largest coven in the United States. However, there were smaller covens in

Boston and San Francisco as well. Today Eleanor Pickens, an earth witch, had come in from the San Francisco Coven, and Darren Westcott, a water witch, had come from the Boston Coven.

The news they'd borne had not been comforting.

"There have been two killings that seem *daaeman*-like to us," said Eleanor. She nodded at Darren, who sat on a chair not far from Sarafina. "Darren says they've had one in their area, too. Now, it could be a sick serial killer, but seeing as how the murders are scattered all over the country, it seems unlikely. The victims weren't witches, but they were dismembered and disemboweled like an *Atrika* would do it. Not killed for blood magick, but likely for sport."

"So you're suggesting *Atrika* are loose all over the country?" Micah interjected.

Eleanor shrugged. "You tell me. I'm just stating the facts. We've already established that the warlocks are getting rowdy everywhere, kidnapping more often, and taking bigger risks to build up their ranks. We've already established that there's at least one *Atrika* Earthside." Eleanor jerked her chin at Sarafina. "The one that's so interested in her."

What a depressing thing to be known for.

Eleanor continued, "We don't know how that one came through, so it's not really a big leap to assume that others came through, too."

Silence.

Sarafina shivered, imagining more than one Bai loose in the world.

Micah cleared his throat and sat forward in his seat. "I think we should dangle a few juicy prospects in front of the Duskoff, hope they take the bait, and get some of our people in there to see what's going on. There are a few Coven witches who look younger than they are, and who have backgrounds that would make them seem like good recruitment material. We should talk to them and see if they're willing."

Thomas shifted and drew everyone's eye. He walked from where he'd been standing by a wall into the center of the room. "We talked about this before and I have misgivings. First, there's no telling if we managed to get witches undercover into the Duskoff whether they'd be privy to any of the warlock's sensitive information. They'd be considered merely soldiers, nothing special. Second, it's too big a risk. If the witches who go in are discovered, they're dead. Simple as that."

"You talk about risk, Thomas," Eleanor interjected. "What about the risk to all of us if the Duskoff have somehow allied with the *Atrika*? Imagine a world overrun with the most violent *daaeman* breed, led by the warlocks? Try to imagine the carnage to both witch and humankind."

Sarafina hadn't been around when Erasmus Boyle had terrorized the Coven, or when the other two *daaeman* had come through hunting Claire. Yet she knew all too well what a creature like Bai was capable of. She thought about Maria, Robin, Nick, and the rest of her friends. What if *Atrika* ran amok on Earth? What if a *daaeman* got their claws into one of them?

The thought was terrifying.

"You're right, Eleanor. I know what you're saying," Thomas answered. "But it's too much to ask—"

"I'll do it," she announced. The abrupt words made even Sarafina jump in surprise. Theo's head swung toward her, his eyes going dark. "I'll go. I'll do it."

THIRTEEN

❦

HER VOICE WAS SHAKING A LITTLE. "THE DUSKOFF will let me in. Stefan was all buddy-buddy with me, remember? I can go back to him, say I've thought things over and I want to join them. I can get Stefan to tell me what's up and I can find out why I'm so special to them all in one go."

"No way in hell," Theo interjected from where he stood near the wall. He unfolded his arms from across his chest and took a step forward into the room. He seemed to fill it suddenly, and every inch of him was menacing. "You've got an *Atrika* after you, Sarafina. Have you forgotten?"

"No, I most definitely haven't forgotten," she countered, staring up at him. Anger laced her words and made them sound hard. "That's one of the reasons I'm volunteering. I need to find out what the hell is going on. I don't want to just hide in the Coven and wait for him to come back for me."

Theo fisted a hand at his side and a muscle twitched in his jaw. "You're barely a witch, Sarafina. Your training isn't even finished yet and you'd be putting yourself right into their nest without any backup."

"That's bull, Theo, and you know it. I'm strong. *Exceptionally* strong, isn't that what you told me?"

"In *healing* you're exceptionally strong, Sarafina. You're stronger than most with fire, but you lack the skill to wield it properly. You're not ready for something like this."

She continued on as if he hadn't spoken. "And the fact that I'm inexperienced works in my favor. I'll tell Stefan I spent some time here at the Coven, but you-all were too goody-goody for me. I'll tell him I want to be with the ones who can

help me maximize my skills and turn a profit from them."
She paused. "I was in theater in high school. I can do this."

Theo glared down at her. "No. Gods damn it, getting the
lead in *My Fair Lady* can't prepare you for something like
this."

She bristled. "You're not my—"

"Enough!" Thomas roared.

The room was plunged into silence once more.

"I agree with Theo," Thomas said. "It's too dangerous."

Sarafina gestured with one hand. "It's perfect. I have the
best way in of anyone here. Stefan was already willing to
talk to me personally. All I have to do is convince him I
want to go warlock and I'm sure he will let me in again."

Thomas raised an eyebrow. "And Bai? Aren't you forgetting about him? Maybe all Stefan wants to do is feed you to
his pet *Atrika*."

Sarafina shook her head. "No, he told me that he would
keep Bai under control and away from me."

Theo snorted. "Do you really think that Stefan has any
control over Bai?"

She turned and speared him with her gaze for a long moment before answering, "You don't, either, Theo. No one
does. I either sit here and wait for Bai to come for me, or I go
back to Stefan and wait there. It's the same damn thing. But
if I go back to Stefan, I might actually glean some information that could help the Coven and maybe all of mankind to
boot. Is that such a bad thing?"

"Here you have me to protect you, Sarafina," Theo ground
out in response. He glanced around at the roomful of
witches, all of whom had their eyes on her. "Here you have
everyone to protect you."

A part of her wanted to deny that she needed protection
because admitting that she couldn't fight all her own battles
made her feel weak and fragile. But all Sarafina had to remember was the look in Bai's eyes, and it made her snap her
mouth shut and swallow her denial.

Claire, sitting beside her, touched her knee. "*Everyone*
needs protection against the *Atrika*, Sarafina, even the great
and glorious Theodosius Winters." Sarcasm bit into the last

few words. Perhaps Theo was getting on Claire's nerves, too.

"So maybe Theo can go with her." That came from Micah. Everyone turned to stare at him. Micah spread his hands. "Theo has had little direct contact with the Duskoff since he was a teenager. Mostly, he hunts down wayward warlocks and lawbreaking witches away from the organized structure of the cabal. He did have that skirmish with Stefan a couple weeks ago, but there are earth charm glamours that can be used to change his appearance enough for him to avoid recognition. He might be able to go in with her."

Thomas pursed his lips together and examined Theo. "I don't know."

"I don't want Sarafina in there." Theo growled.

"We've established that at length," Thomas responded drily, rubbing his hand over his chin. "Let's consider our options."

"There's nothing to consider." Theo snarled.

Thomas shot him a dangerous look. "Last time I checked, you weren't the one in charge of Sarafina."

"You made it my job to guard her. Putting her in the middle of a nest of warlocks and within reach of a *daaeman* who has an unhealthy fascination with her is not guarding her."

"We need to do what's best for the Coven," Sarafina answered evenly. "I will do whatever I can to help defeat those who might mean innocent people harm." She turned to look at Thomas. "You said Mira can't break through the Duskoff's warding?"

Mira spoke from across the room. "It's smooth as glass and ten thousand times stronger. I can't find a way through and none of the earth witches can find a way to break it. I've been all over it, every inch, and I can't find a flaw. It's almost as if it's not made by witches, like it could be . . . well, I hate to say it, *I really do*, but it could be *daaeman* warding." She shook her head. "I can't hear a thing unless it's said outside Duskoff walls and they're being very careful never to slip."

Sarafina turned her attention back to Thomas. "So how else can we gather the information we need? Someone has to go in."

Thomas said nothing in response. He only stared at her stormily. She was right and everyone in the room knew it, no matter how much they might not like it.

Theo swore under his breath.

"Look, let's leave off on this issue for now," Thomas said. "We'll consider it. I'm not saying it's a good idea yet, just saying it bears more scrutiny."

"You can't win a war without taking risks," Sarafina added softly. "And this is shaping up to be a war, right?"

Theo jerked his head to stare at her, dark eyes narrowing.

The witches filed out of the room. Sarafina watched them go, noting that Theo hung around by the door, waiting for her, undoubtedly.

Oh, goody, a scolding.

"That was pretty gutsy," Darren drawled in his Boston accent from where he sat in an armchair near her. He had glossy black hair and a Vandyke that made him look just a little wicked.

"Is gutsy a synonym for stupid?" Her hands were shaking.

God, what had she just volunteered for? Was she totally insane? She was a paper-pusher, a cube farm animal, a freaking data entry professional! She was not James Bond.

Darren laughed. "No, I didn't mean it that way. I meant I think you're brave."

"Well, thanks. Maybe you'll say something nice at my funeral. Hey, by the way, I'm sorry for your loss."

His smile faded. "You mean the air witch, Emily. She was a member of our Coven. She lived mostly with the non-magickals, though. Her skills were so low-grade she really considered herself nothing more than a human with a few spooky abilities. I didn't know her all that well."

"Any idea why they would have been interested in her, seeing as how she wasn't very powerful?"

Darren shook his head. "No. Really, we have no idea." He frowned. "I guess she was vulnerable enough that she could be taken easily, so they did."

Sarafina nodded.

Theo shifted near the doorway and continued to look

pissed off. Of course, he always looked pissed off. Did he want her to hurry up so he could berate her?

Yeah, whatever.

She turned her attention back to Darren.

"It's just weird," Darren said. "She wasn't even powerful enough to use in a demon circle. Why they snatched her and then turned around and killed her . . ." He gestured into the air, trailing off. "We don't know."

"None of this makes sense."

That's why she wanted to see what she could get out of Stefan. For Emily. And for the non-magickals who'd been killed across the country, perhaps by *daaeman* for sport.

Darren smiled. "Thanks for thinking of her."

"Of course."

"Maybe, if you have some free time later today, we could get a cup of—"

"Sarafina," Theo interrupted, coming toward her. "Let's go."

Sarafina jerked her gaze from Darren and focused on Theo. "Do we have an appointment or something, Theo? I don't remember making one."

"Training." Theo pushed the words out from a nearly locked jaw. "If you're going to offer yourself up on a platter to Bai, we'd better make sure you're well garnished."

Darren stood. "I need to go, anyway. It was nice to meet you, Sarafina." He turned and nodded at Theo. "Theo." Masculine challenge stood clearly on both their faces.

She and Theo watched Darren leave. Theo shut the door behind him, then braced his hand on the back of the door and spoke. "Making new friends, I see."

"Are you jealous?"

"Of course not." His voice was harsh. "Flirt with whomever you want. That's not why I'm pissed."

Sarafina stood. "Look, Theo, I'm not a child. I understand that I just put myself in grave danger."

Theo stared at the closed door for a moment before turning toward her. "No, Sarafina, you just promised yourself death." He paused. "Is that what you want? I've met lots of people in my life who do, either consciously or subconsciously. I would not put you in that category. You are . . . life. You are harmony, laughter, and magick."

She blinked and jerked a little at the awe in his voice. It was almost reverence. Okay, she hadn't been expecting words like that. Her jaw loosened a little, dropping a degree.

"Don't do this." He swore low. "Take your offer back. Stay away from the Duskoff."

"No."

"Sarafina—"

She pushed past him, toward the door. No way would she stand here and let him chastise her like he was her father. He grabbed her shoulders as she went past and held her fast.

"Let someone else go," he said in a low voice.

But someone else didn't have the access that she had.

"I can't, Theo." Her whole body shivered at his proximity, remembering his kiss. It was an event indelibly marked on her mouth.

"I won't let you get hurt."

"Then come with me and make sure I don't."

THEO'S GAZE SLIPPED DOWN THE CURVE OF HER throat. His fingers itched to stroke the fine blond hairs on the vulnerable back of her neck.

She wasn't looking at him; she was looking at the door. An unconscious tell. Sarafina wanted away from him. Her jaw was tight and her eyes a little narrower. She was pissed off and he'd done it.

She was right about being the best person to approach the Duskoff, but Theo didn't care. The thought of putting her deliberately in harm's way made every protective instinct he had go on red alert.

Somewhere along the way he'd decided Sarafina was his to keep safe, his responsibility.

"Yes, of course I'll go if you go." He paused. "But they won't allow me near Stefan."

She looked up at him. "But you'll be near *me*. That's all that counts."

"Stefan undoubtedly thinks you're beautiful. That won't

hurt your cause at all. Even if they let me in to the Duskoff, I won't be able to protect you all the time because he'll try and keep you close and me away. He'll want you to himself."

"Beautiful?" She blinked. "What an odd thing to say. Why do you think Stefan would consider me beautiful?"

He said nothing and made sure to school his expression. Fuck. Had the woman never looked in a mirror? She was light to his night—fair of skin, hair, and eye. Her body was fragile, delicate-looking, but he knew just what a wallop she packed, not only magickally but physically. He loved that dichotomy in her.

And she was small. So small and light that he could pick her up with no problem. The sexual possibilities of their difference in sizes had not gone unexplored by him. He bet anything he could lift her, press her against a wall, and fuck her with no difficulty at all. It was also likely that he could easily flip her while they were having sex, bringing her to her knees so he could take her from behind with hardly any effort.

Fuck if he didn't want to try that sometime.

Sarafina arched a fine blond brow. "Have we gone silent once again?" She made a mock moue. "And you were doing so well."

He shook off the fantasy playing out in his mind. With Sarafina it was hard for him to keep his thoughts on business. He wanted her. That want was growing worse every damn day and it was becoming distracting.

She rolled her eyes and tried to push past him again. He tightened his grip, staring down at her. Words about how pretty he thought she was wouldn't come. He wasn't good at saying things like that.

Anyway, he shouldn't say them.

Their relationship didn't have room for bullshit like that. Still, he had trouble letting her go. They stayed locked that way for several long moments.

Finally, Sarafina ripped herself away from his grasp. "God, Theo, what's your deal? Let me go."

He watched her stalk from the room and fisted a hand at his side when the door closed behind her.

* * *

"I DON'T KNOW WHAT TO MAKE OF HIM," SARAFINA said to Mira. "He's so odd." She sipped her iced tea. "How can a man so gorgeous be so odd? It's like a crime against nature or something."

She, Claire, and Isabelle were in the Conservatory, sitting at one of the tables in the communal area after dinner. It was late and darkness had closed like a fist around the Coven.

"He's a powerful earth witch," answered Mira with a shrug of a slim shoulder. "From an entire line of powerful earth witches, from what I've heard. His parents were a nightmare, and his childhood was pretty violent. Then there was that whole deal with the Duskoff when he was a teenager. He's bit different because of all that darkness."

Claire took a sip of her drink and then said, "Adam and I were surprised you chose to stay with Theo, actually. He's a wonderful man and one of the best people to have your back in a fight, but he's so sullen all of the time. He's so hard to communicate with."

Mira shook her head. "I adore Theo, but I don't understand him."

Isabelle dragged her finger through some of the condensation left on the glass-top table and played with the water droplets, letting them whirl out into the air and dissipate. *Show-off.* "With certain people you have to keep your expectations low. Take what they're offering and try not to demand too much more from them. Men had to keep their expectations low where I was concerned for a long time." She looked at Sarafina and smiled. "Then I met the right man."

Sarafina returned her smile. "It's not like I want marriage and children from Theo, but I do have to live with him for now. He's a good man and all, I just . . . I don't know. He intrigues me, I guess."

There was no way she was going to tell them about the kiss she'd shared with Theo. That had just been a one-off, anyway. He showed no interest in ever kissing her again, only interest in dictating her behavior and decisions. *That* didn't fly with her.

Claire laughed. "You and half the other women in the Coven."

"Oh, really?" Sarafina answered. "I didn't know." She shrugged and laughed. "I shouldn't be surprised, though, he's hot."

"And selective," Claire answered. "According to Adam, Theo could pretty much have his pick of women, but he's only taken one lover ever as far as Adam knows."

And Sarafina knew who it was. "Ingrid."

Mira nodded. "She was abrasive, but a good person in her heart. It was a blow to the Coven when she was killed."

"She was one of Thomas's seconds, along with Jack," Isabelle added. "It was a real loss."

Sarafina nodded. "Once he told me that all the women he was ever involved with turned up dead somehow."

Mira frowned. "That's interesting. I only know about Ingrid, but Theo gives *reserved* a new meaning. He's not exactly an easy guy to get to know."

"Yeah, that's for sure."

"So what was Alex like?" Isabelle asked.

"Alex? He was . . . nice."

"Oh. *Nice*." Isabelle grinned. "I'm sorry."

Sarafina laughed. "He was really personable and friendly, very motivated in his career path. He was a man my foster mother would have called *a provider*. He treated me well, and we almost never fought. It's just that there wasn't that . . . that . . ." She trailed off, searching for the right word. "That spark." She snapped her fingers, making fire flare. "You know?"

All three of the women laughed. "Yes, I think we get it," answered Mira. "That spark you're talking about is pretty important to a fire witch."

"Alex was a great guy, but we shouldn't have been together. It just wasn't right. He wasn't—"

"Tall, dark, and mysterious?" Isabelle supplied, grinning. "Brooding and reticent? Complicated and just a little bit dangerous?"

"Hmmm, sounds like someone we all know," added Claire in a teasing tone of voice.

Sarafina glanced down at the table, letting a small smile cross her lips. "Can we add aggravating, controlling, uncommunicative, stubborn, and indecipherable?"

Claire nodded. "We can."

"I know what you're getting at, though." Sarafina shrugged a shoulder. "Maybe. Or maybe it was because Alex wasn't a witch. We lacked that thing in common. I didn't know I was a witch when I was with him, but somewhere deep within I always knew I was different."

"Honestly, Sarafina," said Mira. "I can relate because I was in relationships with non-magickals before I found out I was an air witch. It's just not the same with someone who doesn't share in magick. I'm not saying that relationships with non-magickals can't work. There are some in the Coven that do just fine in them, but I think it helps to have that shared base."

"Well, I guess I'll find out sooner or later since I'm sort of starting a new life here at the Coven, turning a new page, or whatever. Maybe eventually I'll be in a relationship with a witch and I'll have a basis for comparison."

Isabelle leaned forward and grinned mischievously. "Maybe you'll be in a relationship with Theo."

Sarafina relaxed back in her chair with a laugh. "I don't think Theo's looking for that. I'm certainly not."

"I did notice Darren looking you over quite a bit today." Claire raised an eyebrow over the rim of her glass.

Sarafina felt a blush tinge her cheeks, though it had little to do with Darren's attention and a lot to do with Theo's fit of jealousy over it. Was she a bad person if she admitted she'd gotten some pleasure from that?

"Yes, well, he'll be going back to Boston soon. Anyway, we've got more pressing matters to think about right now. Perhaps soon I'll be headed back to the Duskoff." Sarafina pushed away from the table and stood. "So, I better get to sleep. Theo's all about training early in the morning."

The women said their good nights and Sarafina strolled back through the Conservatory smiling to herself, the light along the gravel path she walked glowing intermittently.

Apparently, *Atrika* had destroyed most of the Conservatory

about a year and a half ago, as well as a good part of the rest of the Coven. They'd used a gift of diamonds from the *Ytrayi* to make repairs. Now the Conservatory was a beautiful place once more, and Sarafina was glad it had been salvaged.

She was grateful for many things at the moment. Grateful that she now knew her true nature and had an explanation for her mother's insanity. It didn't make the weight of those memories any easier to carry, but at least they were less perplexing. She was also grateful that she'd made friends within the Coven. Claire, Isabelle, and Mira were wonderful women and easy to talk to about her new life.

Could she count Theo as a friend? Sarafina frowned. No, he remained only an enigma. Still, she was grateful for him, and *to* him as well.

The Coven was dark now, settling in for the night. The corridors were empty and she knew she'd catch hell from Theo for staying out later than she should. She hurried up the stairs and turned the corner of the corridor leading to Theo's apartment, her mind awash with a million things.

Sarafina looked up and stopped short.

Bai stood there.

Her mouth gaped and her mind stuttered to a halt. Over three weeks had passed and *nothing*. There'd been no sign of him. Now here he stood, between Coven walls.

And judging from the expression on his face, he wasn't taking no for an answer this time.

FOURTEEN

"THEO!" SHE YELLED AT THE TOP OF HER LUNGS.

Sure, she'd trained in defensive measures, but this was *a demon* standing in front of her. All six and a half enraged feet of him. She wasn't dumb enough not to want backup.

Her power rose in response to the acrid scent of the *daaeman* in front of her. She parsed out a thread and threw it at him, twisting it just right in order to get it past Bai's natural elemental shields. It popped in his face like a firecracker and she took the opportunity to run like hell.

Bai made a low, animal-like sound of anguish and followed her. The tromp of his massive feet on the floor of the Coven echoed behind her. She careened around the corner and nearly collided with a couch. Sarafina knew she had to prevent him from touching her. If he touched her, he could jump her anywhere on the planet.

She so, *so* didn't want that.

Feeling like she was playing a game of life-or-death tag, she pounded down some stairs with Bai close behind and raced down an unknown corridor. Good God, this place was huge and she had no idea where she was running. At any moment she could be trapping herself in a corner. Doorways on either side of her led to parts unknown. Every single one was a question mark and a potential pathway to death.

Sarafina came to a set of double doors that appeared to open into a large room. She rolled the dice, hoping there was an exit on the other side or at least a good place to hide.

She careened into the room and skidded to a stop, closing the door behind her. In the half light shining through the windows, it appeared she'd entered some kind of ballroom. Of course, owing to her recent trend of bad luck, it was completely naked of furniture.

And there was no exit.

Behind her, a roar shook the floor beneath her feet.

Sarafina did the only thing she could do; she turned and made a stand. Raising as much power as she could, she waited, balancing on the balls of her feet for the *daaeman* to come through the doors. She screamed when he jumped in behind her instead.

She moved from pure instinct, bringing her elbow back hard into his solar plexus. He grunted in pain, releasing her, and she scrambled away from him. As she went, she ripped power from the center of her chest and held it loosely, ready to wield.

"What the hell do you want from me?" she snarled.

"I want nothing *from* you, Sarafina. I simply want *you*. You will be mine soon. It's been arranged."

The double doors crashed open and Theo walked in, the scent of earth magick filling the air. "You can't have her, *daaeman*. She's already mine."

Bai's lips peeled back from his pointed teeth. "Do you think you're a match for me, *aeamon*? I will come for her when this is over, and you won't be able to stop me."

"Screw you both," Sarafina yelled. She wasn't about to be claimed as anyone's property.

She unleashed the huge amount of magick she'd pulled from her seat at Bai. White-hot fire exploded around him in a magnificent flash that nearly blinded her. The hard and fast use of her power drove her to her knees, gasping. She gripped her chest, every breath an agony.

Theo let loose with a string of swear words. The air filled with the scent of freshly turned earth, vanquishing the hot scent of fire. What had been searing hot now went cool and dark as the deepest part of the Earth.

Sarafina forced her head up and saw that Bai had disappeared. Where he'd stood was now a scorched circle and a pile of dirt.

Theo's hands gripped under her arms and he pulled her

up and against him. "Damn it, Sarafina, what did you do?"

She gasped, pressing her hand to the center of her chest as if she could chase away the pain. "I pulled . . . as much . . . as I could."

Theo scooped her into his arms. The action surprised the hell out of her, but she had no energy left to protest. All she could do was hold on as he bore her out of the ballroom and up to his apartment. Once inside, he laid her on the couch. Grosset hopped into her lap and wildly licked her face, perhaps sensing she was in great pain.

Theo stood back and gazed down at her. "You have to take care of your seat, Sarafina. You can't rip out massive amounts of magick the way you did."

She glared up at him. "There was a *daaeman* standing in front of me." The words sounded choked.

"Do not speak!"

Anger, even more acute than her pain, made her straighten her spine and try to shout at him, even though it came out more a harsh murmur, "Don't tell me what to do!" She collapsed back against the cushions and closed her eyes, drawing a ragged breath and fighting unconsciousness.

He gestured inarticulately for a moment before seeming to gather his thoughts. He took a deep breath before speaking. "Look, Sarafina, you can't just yank out huge chunks of power from your seat. If Bai were to show up again right now, you'd be completely defenseless."

"You're right." She nodded. "I know . . . you're right."

"Don't speak." This time he said it in a gentler tone. Theo held up a hand to stop her from continuing. "You'll injure yourself further. I understand what happened. You were faced with all that *daaeman* in front of you, and you panicked. You yanked out a big chunk of power to throw at him, as much as you could."

She nodded. God, her throat and chest hurt.

"It's a rookie mistake, right? Can you see that? We've talked about this."

Sarafina closed her eyes for a moment and nodded again. Yes, she saw that. She'd screwed up.

He knelt on the floor by the side of the couch. "I understand why you did it, but that has to be the last time. Pulling that shit in the middle of a battle can get you killed. You dole out power little by little, using it to best advantage. Don't gamble it all away in one go."

"I see what you're saying," she whispered.

"Good. Now what can I do to help you feel better? You won't have enough power to heal yourself for a while."

Sarafina blinked. The man was actually having a normal-type conversation with her, with eye contact and everything. It was jarring.

"Hot tea with lemon." Her voice came out in a low rasp. He rose to go into the kitchen, but she laid a hand on his arm. "Let me."

"No way. Sit here and rest."

Sarafina leaned her head on the armrest of the couch and closed her eyes. Suddenly, she was really glad that he'd insisted on getting the drink for her. Her head was pounding.

Soon she felt the press of a warm ceramic mug into her hand. She opened her eyes and saw Theo sinking into a nearby chair. "That's lemon verbena tea. Mira is always dropping it off for me even though I never drink it."

She took a sip and let the warmth fill the aching empty place in the center of her.

It was funny how before she'd known she possessed magick, that place between her breasts had seemed like any other part of her body. She'd never given it much thought. But now that she knew she was a witch, when the seat of her power was damaged, it was the only part of her body that mattered.

"There are two pieces of good news. First is that you've learned your lesson and won't ever do this again."

Sarafina rolled her eyes at his high-handed comment and the tone he'd delivered it in. God, she couldn't wait until she could speak freely again; she had a lot to say. Did he even know how infuriating he could be? He seemed completely oblivious.

"Second is that you're a strong witch and should recover quickly."

Well, now, that *was good news.*

Once her tea was mostly gone, she let her eyelids drift closed once more. Theo groaned in the chair next to her, an oddly sexual sound that made her come out of her half sleep with a spike of awareness. One day she'd love to make him groan that way using her hands, tongue, and teeth. The thought made her shiver.

It was incredible how one minute the man was pissing her off and the next she wanted to jump his bones.

There was something about him that flipped her switches, that was for sure. Maybe it was simply the challenge of bringing a man that big and that bad to his knees sexually. Maybe if she ever scratched that particular itch, she wouldn't be so attracted to him anymore.

Nah, he'd be like crack. One taste and she'd be addicted.

There was also something nice about having a man as big and as bad as Theo watching over her while she drowsed, vulnerable and injured, on the couch. The knowledge that Theo would protect her if Bai decided to return warmed her inside as surely as the tea.

In his presence, she felt safe. Despite everything, she trusted Theo completely, no matter how annoying he could be sometimes.

He slipped the cup from her grasp, dropped a blanket over her, and soon she drifted to sleep with Grosset at her side.

WHEN SARAFINA WOKE IN THE MORNING, THEO WAS still in the chair near her. He looked uncomfortable— slumped down with one arm thrown over the armrest. His head had lolled back and his dark hair trailed over the side of the chair. He still managed to look luscious, though. The hem of his black T-shirt had ridden up, exposing his washboard stomach and the enticing button fly of his jeans.

She swallowed experimentally and when pain didn't shoot through her body, she sat up a little. The seat of her power was flushed and full once more, like a battery recharged. She closed her eyes, dragging in air through her nose and letting it out slowly. Ah, much better.

"Okay?" That was Theo's gravelly morning voice. It sent goose bumps all over her body.

She looked over at him and smiled. "Worlds better." Her stomach growled. "I feel so good I could eat a stack of pancakes, but since we don't have those, I'll go make coffee."

He moved a little and winced, instantly making her feel guilty. He'd slept in the chair because of her. "I'm going to shower," he mumbled, pushing a hand through his hair.

Later, while she sipped coffee at the kitchen table, Theo walked in . . . with just a white towel around his waist. Again.

Sarafina almost dropped her mug.

Apparently, he had no idea how good he looked like that. If he knew the thoughts that went through her mind every time he traipsed around the apartment that way, he'd put on some clothes.

Theo walked to the coffeemaker and poured himself a cup. She watched his rippling back muscles where she could see them through his damp dark hair. The man was a menace to any woman within a thirty-foot range, and he had absolutely no clue.

She directed her gaze down to her coffee cup. "Shouldn't we be notifying Thomas about what happened last night?"

He turned, cup in hand. "Already done. I called him as soon as I knew you'd be okay last night, once you'd fallen asleep."

She nodded. "What did he say?"

"Nothing I didn't know already. He said stay on you. We're mated, you and I. Inseparable from here on out."

Great. She had catnip just out of her reach 24/7 now.

"Mated, huh. Wow, and here I never really wanted to get married." She set the coffee cup down. "Can I pee by myself?"

"Please do."

"How about shower?"

"Yeah. We're not getting ridiculous about it."

She set her empty cup down and pushed up from the table. "My turn." Her knees went weak, and he was there in a second, steadying her.

"Are you sure you're okay?"

She nodded. "I'm fine. Just got up too fast." She shook her head, walking to the bathroom. "I hope Bai stays away today, though."

"I hope Bai stays away forever."

She looked up at him, a weak smile passing over her lips. "Not much chance of that."

I simply want you. That's what Bai had said. The words hung heavily between herself and Theo, unspoken.

So when did an *Atrika* ever not get what he wanted?

SHE CAME OUT OF THE BATHROOM RIGHT WHEN Theo was walking down the hall to his bedroom. "Oh, sorry."

He crowded her a little against the wall and Sarafina didn't have time to wonder if it was on purpose before all the saliva in her mouth dried up. His breath eased over her shoulder and his chest rubbed against hers. Under her shirt, her nipples hardened.

He stayed that way. Right. Up. Against. Her.

"Uh, listen, Theo. I know you said we had to stay close, but does it have to be this close?" Her gaze flicked down to his towel.

"Does my state of dress bother you?" His voice rumbled out of him and reverberated deep within her.

She tried really hard not to stare at his chest. "I think you mean your state of *un*dress, and let's just say that you walking around like that might give me a heart attack. If you wanted, you could save Bai all the work."

"That would be a pity, but I'm happy to know I affect you that way."

She snorted. "You'd affect any woman that way. The charming thing about you, Theo, is you don't know it."

He reached out and took a strand of her hair between his fingers. She had no nerve endings in her hair, but that didn't matter. Sarafina felt that touch straight down to her toes. "You scared me last night. *Bad.* You take risks that I don't like, Sarafina."

"Why do you care what risks I take? You barely know me."

"Maybe I know you better than you think." A muscle twitched in his jaw. "Maybe I'm starting to like you, too."

Her heart rate kicked up a bit. "I didn't think you liked anyone."

"You thought wrong." His gaze was intense, like every part of Theodosius Winters. He said nothing more, but his eyes had gone dark and *that* said everything. His pupils were dilated, which meant he was turned on.

She glanced down and hooked her freshly dried hair behind her ear. "Listen—"

He pulled her up against his chest and kissed her. His mouth slanted over hers and consumed her gasp of surprise. There was no sweet tasting like there had been last time, this was all taking. Her hand pressed against his chest as he parted her lips and slid his tongue in to brush against hers. Sarafina's knees went a little weak at the hot taste of him.

Theo broke the kiss after a moment, but kept her there, pressed against him.

"We have to stop doing this." Her voice came out a little breathless.

"Yeah, but I don't think we can."

How right he was. A laugh bubbled up from somewhere inside her, but what he did next stopped her from voicing it. He pulled her into his bedroom.

Straight to his bed.

She landed on his mattress, and he came down on top of her. His mouth came back down on hers for round two.

The man didn't do anything halfway and that included kissing.

She wiggled beneath him and made a sound deep in her throat. Theo lifted his head and stared down at her. "I can't think of a reason to stop right now, but I've been trying not to do this," he murmured.

"I like *this*."

"You're willing to take your chances, then?" He nipped at her lower lip, sucking it into the hot recesses of his mouth and then dragging it through his teeth.

Oh. That wasn't what she'd expected him to say. It was hard to form words, but she had to try. This was important. "Just one woman isn't women, Theo." She was thinking of Ingrid. "And it wasn't your fault."

"Ingrid wasn't the first. Neither of them were my fault, but they both turned up dead, anyway." He nibbled the tender place where her shoulder met her throat, then dragged the flat of his tongue over the tiny bite mark he'd left.

She gasped, then moaned. "Coincidence. Superstition." His kiss left her sex feeling warm and wet. She wanted more, would do anything to get it. "Please, don't stop, Theo."

He ran his hand from her collarbone down over her breast and cupped it. Her nipple went hard and tight against his palm, stabbing up through the material of her shirt. Staring into her eyes, he stroked it, teasing along every ridge and valley until she bucked beneath him and sank her teeth into her lower lip.

"How do you like to be touched, Sarafina?" he murmured. "Do you like it when a man strokes your breasts and sucks on your nipples?"

"Ah," she breathed. "All of the above."

Theo grinned wickedly. "Okay, then."

He pushed the hem of her shirt upward and pulled it over her head. Her bra was gone in an instant, leaving her bare from the waist up, exposed to Theo's hungry, roving gaze.

"You're so fucking beautiful, Sarafina," he murmured.

Then his mouth descended on her breasts and he showed her just how much he believed what he'd just said.

FIFTEEN

LUST CRUISED THROUGH HER BODY AS HIS LIPS closed around the peak of her nipple. She squirmed a little beneath him and he grabbed her wrists in one of his broad hands before pressing them to the mattress above her head. Then he forced her body to bow toward him, lowering his mouth once again to her breast.

His tongue followed every ridge and valley, every pucker and peak until she was barely able to keep quiet. She'd never come from just a man's tongue on her nipple, but Theo was close to making her.

Then he did the same thing to her other breast.

She moved her hips on the bed. The sight of his dark head working over her and the feel of his long silky hair brushing along her skin was almost enough to make her crazy.

"Theo," she murmured. "You're killing me. This is . . . this is—"

"Me, making you come."

He moved his hand between her thighs, finding her clit through the material of her clothing. With perfect, expert motions, he circled it, using the seam of her jeans to rub against the swollen, sensitive area. Pleasure arced through her body, bowing her spine. Theo rode her through it, making it go on and on.

The climax came to a gentle, rolling halt, leaving Sarafina feeling boneless. "Theo," she whispered. He'd released her wrists, so she guided his face to hers. God, she wanted to return the favor. She couldn't wait to get her hands on him.

But his facial expression was tight where she was sure

hers was languorous and anticipatory. It was odd how clearly she could read his emotions right now. His mask was completely gone—burned away—replaced by a roiling sea of intense desire and *anger*.

Sarafina lifted her head, suddenly very aware of her nakedness, where a moment ago she hadn't been at all. "Theo, what's wrong?"

"I didn't want to push this far with you."

Well, hell, she wanted to push further.

Sarafina braced herself up on her elbows. "You started this, not me." She sounded like a seven-year-old, but she didn't care. He'd given her a taste of him and now she wanted more. That was his fault.

"I know I did. Apparently, no matter how hard I try, I can't resist you." He got up and pulled on a pair of sweats, then sat down on the edge of the bed and pushed a hand through his hair. "Then last night you scared me so bad, made me crazy. I had to touch you today."

"So let me touch you back."

"That wouldn't be a good idea."

Sarafina sat up, pulling the blanket over her. "Look, Theo . . ."

In the living room, Theo's cell phone rang. He retrieved it and gave a snarling, "Yeah," into the receiver.

She collapsed back onto the mattress as Theo spoke to whoever was on the other end in low, forceful tones. Then silence.

She raised her head and saw Theo standing in the doorway.

"Thomas wants to talk to us."

THEO STOOD BY THE WINDOW AT THE FAR END OF THE Coven library trying really hard not to hurl something through the floor-to-ceiling glass. He'd known this was coming. As soon as Sarafina had mentioned it to Thomas, Theo had known Thomas would take her up on her offer.

Thomas Monahan was a good man, but the Coven always came first. He'd put Sarafina at risk to gain information.

In a heartbeat.

"So even though Bai attacked her here at the Coven, you're still willing to send her back to the Duskoff." Theo spoke without turning around to face Thomas and Sarafina. His voice was hard. Right now all he could do was stare straight ahead and use all his willpower to resist destroying something.

"Not long term. I just want her to go in for a day or so and I want you to go with her," said Thomas.

"I want to find out what Bai wants me for." Sarafina countered Theo in a combative tone.

Theo snorted. "And you think Stefan is just going to tell you?"

"He might if I offer something in return. He knows the Coven got to me. I can offer to give him information."

"You're not prepared for this. Last night proved it."

Sarafina sighed. "Theo, Bai is coming for me one way or another. There's no place to hide, no place to run. I feel better meeting this head on."

Theo turned to face her. Last night had made him realize just how much he was coming to care for her. This drove him insane—watching her march herself right into a nest of black mamba. "Do you even know where Stefan and the Duskoff are right now?"

"New York," answered Thomas. "Stefan hightailed it back to headquarters after the raid on the farmhouse. You'll have to go there."

"How do you know?"

"Mira. She can't hear anything within the warding, but she notices it when Stefan moves somewhere and comes out from behind Duskoff walls. She's tuned to him and he knows it. He's not making any slips, unfortunately, though Mira will be there if he does."

"I'm going in with her. I'll cut my hair and—"

"You will not!" That came from Sarafina. "I won't allow you to cut your hair, Theo."

"I'm not sure I can work up a charm powerful enough to disguise it."

Sarafina shook her head. "No way. I know that's where you store a lot of your spells and charms. I'm not letting you diminish your power base for me."

"I'd rather help keep you alive than have my power base at full flush." He reconsidered. "I'll work on a charm today and see if I can come up with something. If I can't, it's coming off."

"Do that," said Thomas. He fingered his own hair, tied at his nape. His hair, also a part of his power storage, had been shorn on Eudae by the *Ytrayi*. "It takes a damn long time for it to grow back in. Either way, I want you both on a plane tomorrow morning."

THE NEXT DAY SARAFINA WALKED WITH THEO UP the steps of a tall granite building in Manhattan. The large sign in the square in front of the skyscraper read DUSKOFF INTERNATIONAL.

It gave Sarafina chills to see firsthand just how entrenched and established the warlocks were in the human world. Duskoff International was a powerhouse of a company, privately owned by the Crane family until just recently when it had been taken public—owing to Stefan Faucheux's greed, undoubtedly. The stock price was sky high. Sarafina knew next to nothing about the business world and even *she* knew all that.

Who would be able to believe that warlocks sat in the boardroom? Three weeks ago she never would've.

They'd left for New York yesterday and settled into the swank that was the Hotel Indigo in Soho. Thomas Monahan had a place here in New York, but staying there was out of the question. They weren't sure if the Duskoff had the place under surveillance, but they probably did. Grosset was back in Chicago, staying with Claire and Adam.

Theo had been able to design a convincing glamour for himself. Just an hour earlier in their hotel room Sarafina had watched him drink the foul-smelling concoction and stared in awe as it worked.

Apparently, glamour charms weren't easy to make. Only earth witches as powerful as Theo, Thomas, and Micah, three of the strongest in the Coven, could concoct them.

On the downside, the charms were fragile and only lasted about twenty-four hours. By this time tomorrow the magick would erode and the carriage would turn back into a pumpkin . . . not that Theo's body could be compared to a pumpkin. And there was no re-creating the charm and altering your appearance exactly the same way again. These were onetime deals, suitable more for novelty than espionage.

The upside was, wow, the changes wrought were impressive.

Theo hadn't been able to create the illusion that his hair was shorter, but it was a different color now—a blond nearly as light as her own. His skin was lighter, too, less swarthy Italian and more winter-loving Nordic.

The charm had made him seem shorter and a bit less bulky—less aggressive, all around. It had softened the brutal, grim lines of his face, curving the granite-hewn edge of his jaw and making his lips thinner and his mouth less expressive. It had smoothed his forehead and relaxed the severe set of his eyebrows. His pupils were blue now, transformed with a pair of ordinary colored contacts, but his eyes still revealed every breeze disturbing the ocean of his emotions.

It was eerie just how much Theo did not resemble himself. Yet his severity and seriousness somehow seemed to radiate out from the charmed suit he wore, ruining the illusion of harmlessness he'd been striving for.

"They'll make sure I'm separated from you first thing," he said in a low voice when they reached the frosted double glass doors. "You'll be on your own, but I won't be far away."

"So what do I do if they try to kill me?"

"Retaliate. You have fire." He paused. "Oh, and scream real loud."

"Great," she muttered as they pulled the doors open. Why the hell had she volunteered for this again? Oh, yeah, she was the Coven's best chance for information.

Hell, she wanted some of her own, too.

The lobby was sleek and polished and filled with people in business suits. It looked like any other office building on a Tuesday morning, bustling with commerce and with the scent of greed heavy in the air. Apparently, not all their employees were warlocks. Many of the lower-tier people were non-magickals with no clue about the sort of otherworldly dealings this conglomerate dealt in. Amazing.

They approached the receptionist's desk. She was most certainly a warlock. Sarafina could almost feel heat coming off her—fire. The two security guards standing near the desk were warlocks, too. She was a young redhead—fitting for the element she commanded. The guards eyed them with mocking expressions on their faces, probably recognizing them as kindred magickals, yet not their kind.

The receptionist raised her gaze to them as they approached, a pair of stylish square glasses perched on her pert little nose. The nameplate on her desk read BELINDA. "Can I help you?"

"We'd like to see Stefan Faucheux," answered Sarafina. She'd dressed up for the occasion, a Ralph Lauren black wool sheath dress and a matching pair of Prada peep-toe pumps, all provided by Thomas Monahan. She'd done her hair up high on her head and had taken a lot of time with her makeup. She knew she looked like she belonged here. If only her friends back in Bowling Green could see her now.

Belinda blinked. "Do you have an appointment?"

"No, he's not expecting us."

The receptionist snorted delicately. "Do you think he sees just anyone?" A delicate sneer seemed to be a natural part of her voice. She gave Theo a sloe-eyed once-over, a woman's assessment of a man. From the speculative look on her face, she found him to her liking. A flare of totally misplaced possessiveness rose up in Sarafina.

Sarafina smiled saccharine sweet and leaned in a little. "He'll see *me*. Tell him Sarafina is here."

Belinda gave her a dirty look. "Do you have a last name?"

Sarafina tilted her head to the side and batted her eyelashes a couple times. "Do you really think with a name like Sarafina I need to give it? Stefan will know who I am."

The receptionist's lip curled, but she reached for the phone. "There's some *Southern* woman here named Sarafina who says Mr. Faucheux will see her *without delay*." The last words dripped with sarcasm. "She's got a Mr.—" She covered the phone with her hand and looked at Theo. Suddenly, she wore a dazzling smile. "What's *your* name?"

"James Anwar." He waited a beat. "We're from the Chicago Coven."

The woman jerked a little and paled, her smile gone. "You're Coven witches?"

"At the moment. That's what we've come to discuss with Mr. Faucheux," Theo answered.

The person on the other end said something and Belinda glanced at Sarafina, then turned away and spoke low into the mouthpiece. She set the receiver back into its cradle and looked up at them. "Tell the elevator operator you want the thirteenth floor."

They thanked her and walked across the busy foyer to the bank of elevators on the other side.

The thirteenth floor wasn't even on the menu of options, Sarafina noted when they entered one of the elevator cars. Theo undoubtedly knew that already since he'd fought in the big battle waged in this building several years ago, the one in which Mira Hoskins had sent William Crane careening out one of the top-story windows with a blast of air.

She glanced at Theo, standing beside her in the elevator with his hands clasped in front of him. His malevolent gaze was fastened completely on the back of the head of the elevator operator—a warlock. Theo had been here before . . . and killed here before. At the moment, despite his disguise, he looked like he wanted to kill again.

As if it were some bizarre inside joke, Marilyn Manson's "I Put a Spell on You" played in the background—the elevator music version. *Cute, really cute.*

They rode up a few floors past thirteen, let out the two nonmagickals in the elevator, then rode back to their requested floor.

The doors opened into a lobby. Another curved receptionist's desk lay directly in front of them with another pretty warlock receptionist. Potted green plants sat in the corners of the room, flanked by rows of chairs where visitors could wait for the person they had an appointment with, she guessed. On either side of the receptionist's desk stood a glass wall with frosted doors, revealing a corridor of offices.

She was in warlock central.

It was so different from the Coven. This place was all business, no nonsense. Gleaming, polished marble, designer suits. *Money.*

The Coven was comfortable and easygoing. Sarafina realized in that moment just how much she'd come to think of the Coven as her home in such a short amount of time. The Coven and the people in it had become family.

Well, okay, maybe she didn't quite want to think of Theo as *family.* That would be weird.

Powerful wards pulsed to either side of the frosted glass doors. They'd passed through another set of doors at the entrance to the building and one more when they'd crossed the threshold of the thirteenth floor. It had felt like walking through a cobweb. This ward was much stronger and Sarafina could feel it even from ten feet away. No one could get past it unless they were a warlock or invited in by a warlock.

The black-haired receptionist motioned them over with a crooked finger. She spoke to Sarafina. "Mr. Anwar will wait here for you." The receptionist pointed at the door to her right. "Tenth office on the right."

Theo nodded at her once—it was nothing he hadn't predicted, nothing they both hadn't expected—and went to sit in one of the chairs. Cold fear suddenly rushed through her veins. She stared at the door for a moment, feet frozen to the floor.

"Sarafina." Theo's voice was low and warm. It thawed her. "Give my regards to Mr. Faucheux."

She jerked her gaze from the door to Theo, drew a deep breath, and then walked in to her appointment with the devil.

SIXTEEN

WHEREAS THE WARDING DOWNSTAIRS HAD BEEN LIKE a cobweb, this warding was like walking through a bead curtain. Not bad, all in all, but much more potent. Warding away what, Sarafina wasn't sure. Mira's power, for certain. If Sarafina hadn't had the go-ahead from Stefan, she was certain it would've felt more like a brick wall.

Low, hard music emanated from Stefan's office. When Sarafina entered, his back was to her—sheathed in an expensive gray suit and framed by a huge window overlooking Manhattan. He slid the heel of his Italian loafer along the floor and spun to the beat of the music.

"Mr. Faucheux?" she queried loudly.

He pointed the small remote he held at the stereo system and the music faded away. Then he turned and regarded her. Bastard was handsome. Sarafina could see why all the world adored him, what they knew of him, anyway. "Ah, the angel seraphim."

"My name is Sarafina." Her voice had an edge she'd best get rid of fast. She smiled. "Mr. Faucheux."

He inclined his head and motioned to a deep leather chair in front of a large mahogany desk. "Sit."

As she found her seat, Stefan took a fat cigar from a case on his desk and lit it with a snap of his fingers. Sarafina tried not to cough on the smoke and veered away from making a Freudian allusion aloud.

A view of the New York cityscape spread out behind him. It was a large office, complete with a sitting area, a putting green, and a sizable bar. Nice. Not to mention the stereo and large-screen TV. The place was twice the size of her apartment and furnished much better.

Of Stefan Faucheux could she expect anything less?

Behind her the door snicked closed and she jumped a little, turning around to verify the event.

"*Merde*. I will not harm you, Sarafina. Please."

Sarafina drew on some place of inner strength she'd been cultivating since childhood. She could do this. She could put on an act and make it believable.

She turned back around, shooting him a look of skepticism. "You did kidnap me, Mr. Faucheux. Remember? I think I have a right to be a bit jumpy."

"Stefan." He sat down in his chair and propped his expensively clad feet onto the shiny surface of his desk.

"Stefan. So you can see why trust may not be on the menu."

He spread his hands, cigar smoking from between the fingers of one hand. "And yet you are here, my petal. You have come all the way from Chicago, in fact, to seek an audience with me." His expression darkened. "After having spent three weeks with Thomas Monahan and his *Coven*." He sneered the word *Coven*.

"I did spend three weeks at the Coven, you're right. I spent three weeks there and decided they aren't for me."

Stefan smiled and took a puff. "Cigar?"

"No, thank you."

"Tell me more, my petal. Tell me about the man you have arrived here with."

"James Anwar. He's an earth witch I met at the Coven. We came to the same conclusions about the place at around the same time." She leaned forward. "I don't want to talk about James, I want to talk about the *daaeman* who is—"

"Is he your lover?"

She bristled. "James? Why should that matter?"

Stefan wore a small, secret smile that she didn't like at all. He leaned forward and rested the cigar on the edge of an ashtray, letting it smoke. "It matters to the demon who hunts you."

The saliva on her tongue dried instantly and her body

went stiff. *Demon* and *hunts you* didn't go well in the same sentence.

"He would not take kindly to you sleeping with any *aeamon*."

"Why?" Her voice came out pinched. "What are you talking about?"

Stefan reclined in his chair, placing his hands behind his head, looking fat and happy as a cat who'd just consumed a juicy mouse. "Come back to us and I can provide you a measure of protection against him, my petal. Having you roam free is . . . upsetting him."

Sarafina took a couple deep, measured breaths and willed her imminent panic attack away. "How did he even get Earthside?"

"Let's just say I have my ways."

"Are there more? More *daaeman* than Bai?"

Stefan spread his hands. "Isn't Bai enough? Really, Sarafina, I'm not the man most likely to spill Duskoff secrets into the lap of someone who has been contaminated by the heroic leader of the Coven and all his do-gooder minions."

"I want no part of them." She studied her hands clasped in her lap and channeled Meryl Streep. "You kidnapped me, but *so did they*. They assumed I was a warlock because you were meeting with me personally. They yanked me from that house with the use of an earth witch so brutal he dragged me through a cornfield."

"Mmmm, yes, Theodosius Winters. He's quite the cold bastard, that *sorcière*. Like they all are. He has a particularly large grudge against the Duskoff, however. Some of the warlocks saw him dragging you from the house that day."

Oh, good. *That was very good, indeed.*

She nodded. "He locked me in Gribben and abused me until it was verified I was an abductee and not a member of the Duskoff."

Stefan nodded sympathically. "I know too well how vicious they can be. I have experienced Gribben firsthand. It's the only thing in this world I have encountered that has the power to break me." He leaned forward. "To lose your magick that way, it's hellish, is it not? So painful. I would rather die than go through that again."

"Even only having recently discovered my magick, it was . . . awful." She was bluffing big-time here, since she'd never once stepped foot in Gribben. Apparently, the place had had quite an effect on Stefan, however.

Stefan's cleanly shaven jaw locked and a muscle twitched near his eye. "I would like to give them a taste of the torture they put those prisoners through, wouldn't you?"

She looked up, holding his gaze steadily. "I've fantasized about it."

His gaze warmed. "A woman after my own heart."

"When they finally let me go, Theodosius Winters stalked me, waited outside my apartment to see what I would do, if I would run back to the Duskoff or not. He was there when Bai showed up and for that I'm glad, but afterward, after I returned to the Coven to seek refuge, that's when the pressure to join them began. They wouldn't let me leave. I was a captive once again."

"So you finally broke out and traveled here to see me."

"With James's help, yes."

"And now you want back into the Duskoff."

She tried her best to look conflicted for a moment, then rose and paced the room. "I'm not sure yet. I'm so confused. Both organizations have done me wrong."

"I can understand why you might see it that way, but truly, we had no choice but to do as we did. Anything less would have sent you running for the hills."

She whirled and stared at him. "You *kidnapped* me."

He inclined his head. "We did, and I'm sorry for that."

Frowning at him, she shook her head and continued pacing. "It took me a while to see it, but I think I get the difference between the Coven and the Duskoff now."

"Tell me, my petal."

She stopped in the middle of the room and looked at him. "The Coven is all about *harm ye none* and *live and let live.* They believe in responsibility and restraint." She allowed a hint of shine into her eyes. "But witches are special! We have power like no human has! The Coven ignores that superiority. They refuse to use it to their advantage. The Duskoff can and do. So it's the Duskoff, not the Coven, that can help me make the most of myself."

Stefan studied her for a long moment and then smiled. "I'm glad you've seen the light. The Coven is for the weak. The Duskoff is for the strong." He paused, his smile fading. "But have you forgiven the way I indoctrinated you? Have you decided to join us?"

"The *daaeman*, Bai. You need to tell me more. Why is he so interested in me?"

"Bai saw you long before I ever did, my petal. He's the one who brought you to my attention, in fact. I have been trying my best to keep him from you. I am the only one who can do that. If you were closer to me, it would be easier."

"What does he want me for?"

"I fear I cannot answer that."

"Why not?"

"Because I choose not to. At least not yet. Prove to me you have rinsed off the taint that is Thomas Monahan, prove to me you truly have rejected the Coven, and I will give you more information."

"How do you propose I do that?"

"Stay in New York. I will find you an apartment. Come to work here at Duskoff International. I will give you an excellent salary, more money than your Bowling Green–born self could possibly imagine. You will have the best of everything if you join us."

If only you agree to bleed for me. The words went unspoken, but she knew that's what he meant.

"Why do you want me so badly?"

"You are very strong, my petal, stronger than you imagine. I am like any other executive of any other company; I search out the best and brightest for my staff."

"And Bai? What of him?"

"If you stay close to me, I can control him. Together we will work on that problem."

She bit her lower lip. "I haven't decided what I'll do yet."

Stefan said nothing for a long moment. "And Mr. Anwar? What will he do?"

"He is also exploring his options."

He picked up his cigar once again and leaned back in his chair. "I'm disinclined to take him. I know nothing about him, and he requires a thorough background check."

"Of course."

"Are you fucking him?" Stefan took a puff and smoke curled around his face.

Sarafina didn't answer.

"If you are, stop. You don't want to rile the *Atrika* any more than you already have."

"I will live my life as I choose."

"Do you have a self-destructive streak?"

Her jaw locked for a moment before answering. "I am no one's slave. Not yours. Not Bai's."

He laughed. "Yes, you are a fire witch. There is no doubt." Stefan leaned forward. "My petal, it is necessary that you choose a side and choose it soon. We are in a war and all those who stand in the middle risk obliteration."

"DON'T MAKE ME LOSE MY TEMPER, SARAFINA. TRUST me, you won't like it." Theo paced across the hotel room, fear making every single nerve in his body sing to life.

Fear for Sarafina.

The trip to Duskoff International had gone well as far as things went. No *daaeman* had popped up to kill them. Stefan seemed unaware of the ruse, thanks to Sarafina's plausible excuse for having come.

They had gotten a bit of information they hadn't known before—Bai was personally interested in Sarafina, and it didn't sound like he just wanted to kill her out of hand. They also knew without a shadow of a doubt that the Duskoff were in league with Bai. However, there were a lot of whys and hows still hanging in the air.

Why did Bai want Sarafina?

Why had the Duskoff allied with Bai?

How had they pulled him through and were there others?

And here they were sitting on a great opportunity to find out. All they had to do was risk Sarafina's life.

"Dissolve that charm, Theo. It's unnerving not to see the real you."

There was no reason to keep it. The Duskoff viewed him as too great a risk. He'd anticipated getting no farther than the door. Sarafina could go much farther than that if she played along, but she'd have to do it on her own.

Which was why Theo was so pissed.

Drawing a bit of power that made his scalp and tats tingle, he dissolved the glamour. Then he whirled and stalked toward her. "You're not doing it."

"You can't tell me what to do, Theo. I'm getting really sick of you trying."

She was pissed, too. He glimpsed fire dancing between her fingers, running up and down her arms in tiny fiery rivers of rage.

He turned away from her and walked to the other end of the posh hotel room. "If I have to lock you in the room, I'll keep you from going back there tomorrow morning."

"You know you can't do that. I'll just burn my way out."

Theo turned to face her. "This was not the plan. We're not prepared for this and we don't have backup."

"What about Darren and his witches? They're not far. They're, what? Four hours away by car."

His jaw clenched. "You'd still be going in alone."

"But there'd be backup if I ran into trouble."

He stared down at her, running out of excuses to stop her. The protectiveness he felt toward Sarafina was like nothing he'd experienced before—or at least like nothing he'd experienced since he'd been seventeen. That memory was what fueled his intense desire to keep Sarafina safe. The last thing he could bear was for history to repeat itself.

And here they fucking were, right on the cusp.

Why he'd developed such intense emotion for this particular woman, he couldn't say. Maybe it was because he'd taken her from the Duskoff's clutches, even if at the time he'd thought of her as the enemy.

For whatever reason, the truth of the matter was that for the first time in his adult life, he'd decided that a woman meant something to him. He'd put an invisible, indelible mark on her—a claim. No other person could harm her without risking his wrath. She could not endanger herself without making him seriously insane.

But she was a woman used to taking care of herself, making her own decisions. As much as he wanted to, he couldn't prevent her from doing this if she chose.

And he disliked the name *Darren* coming from between her lovely lips. He disliked even more the interest that had been in Darren's eyes when he'd looked at her back at the Coven.

Was he jealous?

The thought jarred him. Jealousy would mean he'd claimed Sarafina as his in more than just a protective way. It would mean that he'd claimed her in an emotional way. That couldn't be. He couldn't do it.

Gods, having this woman placed under his guard was making him crazy. Just like it had made Jack McAllister and Adam Tyrell crazy. Damn it!

He turned away from her. "You're right, I can't stop you from going back to Stefan. If you choose to do that, I'll call Darren and make arrangements for him to come down with a small guard of witches."

Sarafina let out a long breath. "Thank you. Thanks for not making me fight you."

"Doesn't mean I like this. Doesn't mean I think it's smart."

"It's our best hope at the moment."

"Yeah, well, I'd rather have Thomas's opinion on that score." He fished his cell phone from the back of his jeans.

It rang in his hand.

Theo answered with a hostile, "Yeah," knowing already who it would be. They had no warding around them right now, and Mira would've heard their conversation had she been tuned to it. She would've relayed it to Thomas.

The conversation was short and tense. Theo snapped the

phone closed and paced away from Sarafina, toward his section of their two-bedroom suite. He fought not to snarl the words as he threw the cell to the couch, "You have Thomas's blessing."

SEVENTEEN

Her mother slammed open her bedroom door so hard the knob stuck in the wall, making a hole.

Sarafina jumped in surprise and gripped her doll close to her, as if it could protect her from the insane glint in her mother's eyes. Her mom's frizzy blond hair stood up all around her head as though she'd been electrified, and her body gave off a constant heat that Sarafina could feel even across the room. Her body always gave off that heat, like she was ready to boil.

Today it was even more palpable. Perspiration beaded her mother's forehead even though it wasn't warm in the room, and her face was flushed as if she had a fever. Her flowered sundress clung to her damp skin.

But heat wasn't the only thing emanating from her mother today.

Today the off-balance quality that her mother always displayed seemed more severe. Today Sarafina suspected something had sent her mother over the edge of the precipice she always balanced on.

Today was a dangerous day.

Sarafina's body tensed. On the dangerous days she went to bed with bruises on her arms and legs, sometimes even odd burn marks from where her mother gripped her skin. Dangerous days were the ones when Sarafina knew to get out of the house fast and stay out.

Her mother took another step toward her, eyeing her narrowly. "You have a wickedness inside you. You have fire in your soul. We have to purge you of the evil, my child, so you can go to God pure."

Purging at her mother's hands meant pain.

Sarafina noted her mother was moving closer to the bed, leaving the door open. Her gaze darted toward escape as she gripped her doll tight.

"Just like me, Sarafina. Just like your grandmother. Like your father, too. We are all cursed with the hellfire of the devil."

Her mother lunged for her, but Sarafina dove off the side of the bed, leaving her beloved doll behind, and darted past her, feeling displaced air at the nape of her neck where her mother almost grabbed hold of her.

"Sarafina!" her mother raged as Sarafina ran full bore through the living room and out the front door. "Come back here!"

Sarafina ran across the front lawn and down the street, feeling the heat of her mother as she drew closer. Glancing back, she saw the glint of something long and sharp in the morning sunlight. Her mother had a weapon.

Neighbors, out in their yards on such a fine day, stared. Too stunned, too complacent. Whatever the reason, no one did anything to help Sarafina as she ran screaming down the street.

She darted between houses and ran through backyards, her short eight-year-old legs pumping as fast as she could make them.

It wasn't fast enough.

She was no match for the long, adult legs chasing her and every step she took felt like a step backward. The farther she ran, the closer her mother got—her heat and the flash of that pointy thing she held bearing down on Sarafina.

Sarafina's sandal caught the edge of a sandbox in her friend's backyard and she went sprawling face-first into it. She scrambled forward, sending sand flying, and turned over just in time to see her mother looming over her.

Sarafina threw her hands up, as if her tiny arms would be enough to ward off the weapon coming toward her and the wild glint in her mother's eye.

"I'm trying to save you, child," her mother yelled. "Don't you see?"

"Momma, no!"

Light erupted in a brilliant display. Her mother cried out.

Sarafina scrambled back away from flame, stared for a moment at the sight before her.

Then she screamed.

"Shhh . . . it's all right. Sarafina, wake up. Wake up."

Sarafina roused with a gasp to a warm, hard body against hers. "Alex?" But it couldn't be Alex, she thought groggily. Alex was out of her life now.

"No," came a low, rumbling voice. "It's not Alex. You were screaming in your sleep, Sarafina."

"Theo." She blinked back tears, a remnant of her nightmare. She had that one so often. Over and over. Like her subconscious just didn't want her to forget that day. Her conscious mind did, though. Oh, she wanted so much to banish that day into the blackness of nevermore.

Why couldn't she just let it go, *all* of it? That memory didn't serve her and she wanted it gone. Anytime her mind brushed past that event when she was awake, she veered from it, refusing to remember.

But when she was asleep, in her dreams, her subconscious played it over and over on a loop.

"Oh, God, make it stop," she whispered, melting against Theo's chest. She couldn't get enough air. Her throat was closing up. "Why can't I make it stop?"

He rubbed her back and held her close. "It's okay, Sarafina. It's over now. You're awake. All over. Sometimes when a new witch starts training, stuff gets dredged up. The encounter with Bai probably didn't help, either."

She shook her head. "The dreams have always been there." She could barely get the words past her constricted throat. "Nothing I do makes them go away." Her voice held a thread note of hysteria.

"Relax, Sarafina. Take a deep breath."

She gulped in air and let it out slowly.

"There you go. Good. Now, do it again."

Sarafina fought for another lungful and let it out slowly, again and again until the tenseness in her body eased. A sob escaped her, but she didn't cry. Sarafina was done crying for the woman who'd borne her. She hadn't truly been her mother, Rosemary had.

Rosemary had been the one to help her cope in the days after this incident. She'd been the one to see Sarafina through her adolescent and teenage years. Rosemary had been the one to help Sarafina banish the cripplingly low self-esteem she'd had as a child from it.

Her foster mother had been the one who'd patiently taught her about life, the one who had loved her. Rosemary had been the one who'd helped her pick out her prom dress and who had held Sarafina while she'd cried from her first heartbreak.

The woman who'd borne her wasn't worth a thought, a memory, let alone a traumatic reoccurring dream.

If only Sarafina could convince her subconscious of that.

"Are you all right?" Theo murmured, stroking her hair.

She drew a trembling breath and took a moment to respond. "I'm better. I'm glad you're here." Her voice shook a little.

His arms tightened around her a degree, but he said nothing in response.

Sarafina clung to him in the dark. After the recent couple of awkward days they'd shared since their encounter in his bedroom, she supposed she should've felt ill at ease holding on to him so tightly right now. She clung to him like he could save her from the scary monsters in her brain—and maybe the ones who weren't in her brain, too. The feel of Theo against her only comforted her. He was hard and warm and real, strong enough to dispel residual shadows clinging to her psyche.

"Thank you for waking me up." Her whisper sounded loud in the dark.

Again, he said nothing in response, but she'd grown used to his less-than-loquacious nature. His silence was more of a comfort than anything else. Anyway, it was just him. Just Theo.

They lay twined together for close to an hour, just breathing. The intimacy warmed her chest, made something inside flutter and dance. His presence chased away the dark memories of her childhood, if only momentarily.

As relaxed fatigue settled heavily over her limbs, Theo rolled her to the side, beneath his big body. "Let me touch you." The words came heavy and silken in the dark.

Whoa.

She stiffened a little, not because she didn't want him to touch her but because she hadn't been expecting him to ask.

"Yes." The word came out in a soft rush. God, she was pathetic. But to feel something right now, something *else*, would be a gift.

His voice shook a little. "Let me taste you."

She shivered, fine ripples of pleasure running through her body. Maybe she was dreaming this. If so, she didn't want to wake up. "Theo, I'm yours."

She spared a thought for Bai and what Stefan had told her. Where was that mysterious *daaeman* now and why, exactly, did he care whom she slept with? The various reasons why an *Atrika* would lay such a claim on her chilled her blood.

But then Theo slid his hands along her body and her blood warmed, her muscles made the slow slide to soft butter. All thoughts of Bai, all thoughts of anything but Theo's hands on her, dissolved like so much sugar into water.

He worked her boxer shorts down and off. Then his big hands were planing her inner thighs and spreading her legs. His chest brushed hers as he worked his way down her body, her nipples tightening just from the memory of his tongue on them. Finally, his breath warmed the skin near her sensitive sex, making her hot and achy before he ever even touched her.

"Why are you doing this, Theo? You confuse me. You leave me alone and then show up in the middle of the night like this."

"Stop talking and let me touch you. I just need a taste—"

"But why?" She moaned as his breath warmed her intimate flesh. "If I'm here and I'm willing, I don't understand—"

"I don't know." The words came out agonized. "Sarafina, I don't know why I can't let myself."

"Let me touch you, too." She reached out to place her hand on his shoulder.

"No." The word was uttered forcefully enough to make her draw her hand back. "If you do that, I'll lose control. I just need to touch you a little."

She groaned and let her head fall back. "What if I want you to touch me a lot?"

"Let me do this. *Give me.*"

Of course, he wasn't really asking for permission. Theodosius Winters didn't do that. So before she could respond, he just took what he wanted. In the half light of the room, she watched his head descend to her sex.

Her back arched as his tongue swept over her folds, his hands bracing her thighs wide apart. He held her down like he was afraid she'd try to escape. His tongue found her clit and she relaxed into the pillows as his lips played along it, teasing it to the point of orgasm. Sensation spread out in slow waves, enveloping her body and swamping her mind until she couldn't think straight.

Soon she was helpless against him, moaning beneath him and trying not to beg for more. Theo made low sounds of pleasure that dovetailed with hers, like he loved the taste of her and couldn't get enough.

His tongue slipped deep inside her sex, filling her up, then went back to the slow, teasing slide against her aroused clit. Again and again, he pushed her to the point of climax, drew back, then built her up again. He pressed his fingers inside her, finding a sensitive place deep within and stroking it over and over in a semblance of what his cock would do—driving her crazy with need.

Over and over he did this, playing her body like it was an instrument. The pleasure zinged through her veins and built to a fever pitch before exploding over her. She shuddered and cried out his name, trembling from the force of her climax. After it was over, she collapsed, sated.

He swiped his tongue over the small tattoo high on her

hip, a sun and moon intertwined like a yin-yang symbol. "You said I'd never see it."

"I was wrong," she murmured.

Theo came up to lie beside her.

Sarafina turned to him. "Please don't run away this time. Give me that, at least."

Silence.

She reached out and touched his chest, but her hand on him only made him stiffen. "I want to touch you."

"No. This has already gone too far."

She withdrew her hand, even though her fingers itched to explore his chest, to trace the scars and tattoos. Her fingers curled a little at the thought of delving past the button fly of his jeans to discover the treasures below it.

"I don't understand you," she said finally. The words fell into the stillness of the room like rocks.

"No one does." Pause. "Not even I do."

"But I want to get to know you."

He said nothing. The moonlight shone in from the curtainless window, painting his face and throat in pale silver and bleaching the color from his hair. His eyes were open and his face troubled.

"Will you let me try?" she whispered.

"Let's just get through tonight. Tomorrow will take care of itself."

That was not an answer at all.

"Don't leave tonight, Theo. Stay here with me."

He didn't reply, but he did close his eyes. Sarafina took that as acquiescence. Closing her eyes, her mind was a jumble of Theo. What was going on in his head? What drove him to behave this way, waking her up in the middle of the night to touch her like she was his fix? To tell her in a roundabout way that he needed her and at the same time hold her away from him with one hand?

Theo *did* need her. Sarafina could see that. She needed him, too. With every passing moment he became more intriguing to her, more a person she simply had to get to know.

She just wasn't sure how to break down his barriers enough to make that happen.

THEO STAYED WITH HER ALL NIGHT. HE WRAPPED himself around her body and saw her through until the morning.

But when she woke, Theo was gone.

She could hear low voices in the living room of the suite, so she rolled off the side of the bed and discovered she was naked.

Oh, yeah. Right. Now she remembered.

The eroticism of her encounter with Theo in the early morning hours came rushing back to meet her. Her knees went weak as her body recalled the broad, hard press of his hand against her inner thigh and the slow stroke of his tongue along her sex.

She sat down on the side of the bed and drew a deep breath before recovering enough to make it into the bathroom for a shower.

When she emerged, she dressed from head to toe in Ralph Lauren—a filmy eggshell blouse, a gorgeous lavender skirt, and designer heels that brought the two colors together. The clothes had again been gifts from the Coven. It was important that Stefan thought she desired the "good" things in life.

As she curled her hair becomingly around her face, she decided that her mind was a little clearer from the hot pound of the water. She touched up her makeup and exited the bedroom.

Theo sat on the edge of the couch, wearing only a pair of faded blue jeans. His hair was still mussed from the night before, and he held an empty coffee cup in one hand.

His gaze rose to meet hers, his pupils dilating. The memory of what they'd done together the night before seemed to dwell in his dark gaze. It made her cheeks heat and her sex along with it. Sarafina had to look away quickly.

Darren sat in an armchair, wearing a pair of expensive-looking gray trousers and a light white sweater. Two unfamiliar women and a man sat nearby.

She nodded. "Darren."

He gave her a head-to-toe sweep. The kind men gave women when they thought they were attractive. Sarafina's face warmed again. "Sarafina."

"I see you're eager to get back to the Duskoff." That was from Theo, and it came out friendly enough to the uneducated ear. Sarafina heard the aggressive undercurrent, however.

She managed to meet his gaze levelly. "I'm eager to do what needs to be done."

Theo motioned with the empty coffee cup toward a cart in the corner of the room, near the small bar. "I had break-fast sent up."

She nodded, unwilling to look at him.

"I'd like you to meet Gina, Lily, and Carl," said Darren. He motioned to the Boston Coven witches, who all nodded and said their hellos. "I brought ten total. The rest are staying in various places around Manhattan. We're here just in case."

Yes. Just in case.

"Thanks for coming."

Darren shrugged. "Give us a crack at Stefan Faucheux, even the possibility of one, and we'll take it." His voice and expression had gone hard.

"So what's the plan?" asked Gina, a dark-haired earth witch with a heavy build.

Sarafina walked over to the spread, picked up a croissant, and nibbled on the end. "The plan is," she said in between bites, "I go back to Stefan this morning and tell him I want in. I find out as much as I can about what they're doing. Simple enough." She turned around to seek a cup of coffee and realized her hands were trembling. Damn it. Her stom-ach had a cold, empty, fluttery feeling, too: stage fright.

"What about the *daaeman* who is so enamored of you?" asked Darren.

"The *daaeman* is Stefan's pet." She sipped a bit of the hot black blend, closed her eyes, and relaxed for a moment. *Ahhh, that was better.* "I do think he intends to feed me to the monster at some point, but he wants something from me first. Until Stefan gets that from me, he'll control Bai as much as he's able."

"But you're not safe from him."

She turned to face Darren. "I'm not safe from Bai anywhere."

Darren gave her another slow sweep of his gaze, respect now lighting his eyes. He was a water witch and typically water and fire repelled each other. All the same, Darren seemed quite attracted to her. But Sarafina was all filled up with Theo. She didn't share Darren's feelings; hers were already reserved.

Too bad she'd picked a lost cause.

Theo stood. "Come here. I have a charm to give you."

She set her mug and croissant down and walked over to him. He took a small silver necklace from his back pocket and dangled it in front of her. It winked prettily in the morning light.

"Do you understand the significance of the pentagram?" he asked her.

She reached out and fingered it. The metal was still warm from his body heat. "I know the Wiccan hold it dear, but I don't know what it symbolizes. My birth mother raised me Baptist, so it's a little, well . . ." She trailed off, not wanting to offend anyone.

Rosemary had been agnostic and Sarafina's churchgoing had ended with her. Still, as a throwback to her childhood, the thought of Wicca made her sweat a little. The upright pentagram, as a symbol of that pagan religion, made her a bit nervous, she was ashamed to say. Early childhood experiences cut deep, it appeared, clung hard to the psyche. Her recurring nightmares were evidence enough of that.

She looked up at Theo who studied her solemnly. Theo probably was Wiccan. Figured. What he'd said earlier about the afterlife had made her think that. Everything else about him made her sweat, so why not his religion, too?

"It's not a symbol of Satan," said Theo. "That's a myth fundamentalists believe, partially based on stuff cooked up by fifteenth-century Christian propagandists to vilify pagans. Wiccans don't even believe in Satan."

She nodded and licked her lips. "I know. I mean, I've read that."

"Good." His hand closed around hers. He placed his index finger to each point as he spoke. "Air, water, fire, earth. This last one is for spirit."

She frowned, feeling the pendant. "It's thick."

Theo nodded. "It's got water in it, water I charmed this morning so that Darren can use it to track you. Wherever you go, we'll follow."

She turned and gathered her hair on top of her head so Theo could put it on her. Was it her imagination or did his fingers linger at the nape of her neck longer than they should have? Did they brush the tiny hairs there a little? His touch gave her goose bumps, made her tremble.

Theo stepped away from her; she noticed the loss of his body heat. "It's also calibrated to gauge your emotion. If you have a surge of fear or panic, we'll know something is wrong and come in after you."

"Okay, then." Shivering a little, she let her hair drop into place and turned. "Let's go."

EIGHTEEN

BACK TO BELINDA.

Sarafina approached the desk in the lobby of Duskoff International, feeling the charm that Theo had given her resting in the hollow of her throat like a talisman against evil.

"You're back," Belinda greeted her, dropping her nail file to the desk with a curl of her upper lip. She sounded absolutely thrilled.

"I need to see Stefan."

Belinda shrugged a shoulder, clad in a beautiful gray silk blouse. "You can't. He's not here."

She placed a hand on the top of the desk and leaned forward. "What do you mean? Where did he go?"

She sneered. "Mr. Faucheux is a busy man. He's supposed to wait around here for you?"

Damn it.

"It's really important that I talk to him."

"Don't get your Hanes Her Way in a bunch. He's traveling this morning. Mr. Faucheux left word with me to send David to you. He'll get you where you need to be." She plucked a pink Post-it from her desk with manicured fingertips. "The note Mr. Faucheux left for you says, 'If you're serious about what you said yesterday, meet me at the airport.'" Belinda glanced at her watch. "But you'd better hurry, he's taking off soon."

"Where is he flying to?"

Belinda made a face. "How the hell would I know? I'm just the receptionist." She picked up the phone and pressed a button. "David will be right down."

* * *

SARAFINA FIDGETED IN THE BACK OF THE SLEEK black limo as they turned onto the street that would take them to the airport.

Finally.

Across from her sat David, a water warlock, who was apparently something like Stefan's personal assistant. He wore an expensive tailored suit and a mocking expression a lot like Belinda's on his narrow, horselike face. He was suave, cultured, a bit androgynous, and superficially at least, seemed to fit right into New York City like a puzzle piece.

Sarafina had the impression he'd murder her in a heartbeat if he thought he'd get something out of it.

David, she was pretty sure, had served William Crane, too. She'd heard Thomas and company talk of him before. Every time the Coven and the Duskoff had a magickal smack-down or conducted a raid, somehow this guy escaped.

They'd scurried across town in midday traffic to an airport that dealt mostly with private jets. The entire trip David had either been on his Blackberry or his laptop and had spared little more than a glance at her. Really, the only time he'd opened his mouth was to take little jabs at Thomas and the Coven. Sarafina had handled her anger like an Oscar-winning actress, but she *so* wanted to punch this little weasel.

Sarafina sat ramrod stiff, staring out the window of the limo, her mind turning her situation over. She was currently careening through Manhattan traffic as fast as the limo driver could push his way through, in a mad dash to meet Stefan's private jet, which would whisk her away immediately to parts unknown.

There would be no way for Theo and Darren to follow her, nifty charmed necklace or not. Was Stefan doing this on purpose? To ensure she wasn't being watched by the Coven? If so, did he only suspect she still had ties to Thomas Monahan . . . or did he *know*?

The limo came to a stop next to a sleek midsized white jet with multicolored lines running down the fuselage and two huge engines mounted near the tail. Six windows lined either side. This was Stefan's private plane, so of course it was top-of-the-line.

The limo driver opened the door for her, letting in the morning sun. She looked at the plane and then turned to David. "I don't have anything with me, not even my toothbrush."

David twisted his lips into a sardonic smile and let his Blackberry drop into his lap. "If you want to join the Duskoff, you'll be expected to bleed for us." He tipped his head to the side and gave her a withering look. "If you can't even manage a day trip without your toothbrush, then you're certainly not ready for the rest."

Point taken.

The driver helped her out and guided her to the stairs. At the top waited Stefan. "Sarafina, I'm so happy you decided to join me." He motioned to her and she climbed the stairs to the top. "Step into my parlor."

He placed a hand to the small of her back and led her into the passenger cabin of the plane. It was narrow, but packed with luxury. She took a moment to scan the fine leather furniture, thick carpeting, a wide-screen television and a stereo system, and fully stocked bar.

Stefan motioned to the two heavily muscled men sitting at the front of the cabin, near the cockpit. "My bodyguards. They only speak when spoken to, so they won't be disturbing us."

Someone moved in the corner of the cabin. The pilot? The man turned and guided icy blue eyes to her face.

Bai.

The airplane door slammed shut behind her.

NINETEEN

FIRE ROSE AS FAST AS HER FEAR. SHE WOULD FIGHT to the end because no way was she going down easy. Power rippled from her center, winging down her arms to her hands, where fire danced and sparked between her fingers. Through Theo's training, she was on the balls of her feet and ready to move fast.

"Peace, my petal," said Stefan. "He won't hurt you."

"Except every time he sees me, he tries," she answered through gritted teeth.

"Misconstrued intent. You always attack him first, yes? Out of fear?"

Sarafina kept her gaze locked on the *Atrika*. "That's because *he's scary*. He breaks into my house, hovers over my bed at night, surprises me in darkened corridors."

"Well," Stefan spread his hands, "The *Atrika* aren't very well versed in the ways of our culture. Bai is one of the few who even speak English."

She gave him a dirty sidelong glance. "If he never truly meant me harm, why did you tell me you could protect me from him?"

Stefan grinned. "Ah, that. Well, I actually didn't lie, my petal. There's no telling what Bai might want to do to you in the future." Bile rose up into her throat at those words. "I meant it when I said you are safer closer to me, where he can see you easily from time to time, and where I can remind him of his commitments to me. But as of *this* moment, Bai is no threat to you."

If the charmed pendant Theo had given her was working,

he was probably going nuts right about now. Talk about emotional spikes.

"What is he doing here?" she asked in a low, shaky voice.

"I thought you wanted answers. The best person to give them to you is Bai himself. I am trying to earn your trust, as you are trying to earn mine. This is my gift to you, Sarafina. He has much to tell you. Right now I believe he wants only to watch you, be in the same room with you. Perhaps later he'll be moved to speak."

Watch her? This was off the creepy meter.

Sarafina remained frozen, staring at the *Atrika daaeman*, while Stefan wandered over to the bar and poured amber liquid into a short, chunky crystal glass. "Drink, anyone?"

Sarafina could sure use one right about now even though it was before noon, but she was pretty sure she'd just throw it back up from nerves. She shook her head.

"Sit, my petal. Relax. You're in no danger at all and we're about to take off." Stefan picked up a remote control and aimed it at the stereo. A slow, dark, hard alt-rock song about suffering rolled out softly from the speakers. How fitting.

Bai's alien eyes bored into her face. She couldn't move her gaze from his. If she did, what would he do? God, she'd managed to trap herself on an airplane with Satan and his demonic minion.

Go, Sarafina.

Stefan strolled over to a seat like nothing was wrong and sat down. "You look as though you're about draw pistols on each other. This isn't . . . what's the name? The O.K. Corral. Sit, both of you."

Bai shifted his gaze first. He moved to stand near a chair, but didn't sit.

Sarafina sank down into the chair farthest from them both just as the plane lurched forward and began to move toward a runway.

"Where are we going?" she asked.

"It's a surprise," Stefan answered.

Oh, goody.

Theo had undoubtedly worked himself into a serious

lather by now. He wanted so much to protect her, even when she was capable of protecting herself. The fact he couldn't get to her now would be bothering him much more than it was bothering her.

Right now her heart ached for him, something deep and painful inside her. She wanted him—the feel of his solid body and the scent of his skin. The desire was so strong it brought tears to her eyes.

"So how is Isabelle?" Stefan took a sip of his drink.

She blinked in surprise at the question, then quickly remembered the history he had with her. Isabelle had been the one responsible for his imprisonment in Gribben. She'd considered Stefan responsible for the death of her sister at the hands of a demon and had trapped him in his limo one night, allowing the Coven to rush in and scoop him up. If it hadn't been for Erasmus Boyle breaking him out of Gribben—initially with the intention of killing him—Stefan would still be there.

"I only met her a few times," she answered evasively. "She married Thomas Monahan."

Stefan tipped his drink at her. "Yes, I know. I sent them a toaster as a wedding present. Such a wonderful couple." Sarcasm dripped from every word. "And Mira Hoskins—oh, her last name is McAllister now, isn't it? She's a lovely woman, too. Killed my father, you know."

Sarafina nodded. "I heard that. I'm sorry for your loss."

"Most of the Duskoff thought I would welcome his death, since leadership of the Duskoff and all its wealth then fell to me. They were wrong. I loved my father. He took me in when no one else would. He taught me everything I know today."

Sarafina was familiar with the story. Stefan Faucheux had been born in Paris and still sported the heavy accent that marked him as a Frenchman. When he'd been a boy, he'd run away from the country's protective services and lived on the streets. On a trip to Paris, William Crane had come across the child and recognized him as a very powerful fire witch. Crane adopted him and brought him back to the States to raise.

Many assumed that Crane had been replacing his biological son—also a fire witch—who had run away at a young age. William Crane's biological son was Jack McAllister, Thomas's heir apparent for Coven leader. At any rate, Stefan had proved malleable in William's hands. He'd turned into a fine warlock, vicious enough to follow in his father's footsteps.

"Everything I do is for love." Emotion threaded Stefan's voice. He raised his gaze to hers. His eyes were a pretty, clear blue—the same eyes she'd seen gazing out from magazine covers all her life as she stood in line at the grocery store. "Everything I do is for my father, to make him proud of me. He might be gone, but I still believe he watches over me." Stefan paused and looked distant. "He would want me to avenge him."

Bai was staring hard at her. It was making her hands clammy.

Moistening her lips and placing a look of concern on her face, Sarafina leaned toward Stefan. "I'm sure that William Crane could not be any more proud of you."

He took another sip of his drink. "I miss him."

"I'm sure you do." She glanced up at Bai, who stood still as a Greek statue by Stefan's chair. "I can understand your loss, since I recently lost my foster mother."

He nodded. "Then you understand that even though I told Mira that I forgave her for killing my father, I may still have to make her pay."

The cold threat in his words made her body stiffen and her breath catch in her throat. She wasn't sure what to say in response.

"*En fait*, my father killed Mira's parents in a demon circle, so I could see why she would want to retaliate."

"Yes." She scowled at him. "Wasn't your father trying to kill Mira in another demon circle when she shot him out the window? It was self-defense, wasn't it?"

Stefan gestured with his glass. "Yes, there was that, too. At any rate, I forgave Mira for killing my father. I forgave Isabelle for her sins against me as well."

The plane took off, tipping her backward. She grabbed

the armrests, having disdained the seat belts. Bai still stood, not moving a muscle. Nothing seemed able to budge him.

She'd like to try a flamethrower.

Stefan ran a finger around the rim of his glass. "But I may have to go back on my word."

That last sentence was murmured in a quiet voice that reminded her of a serial killer. His words were spoken in a way that made brutal, disgusting images of slain animals slick through her mind.

Stefan wanted Isabelle and Mira dead—and in a gruesome way.

Again, she found herself at a loss for a response. What could she say to that?

Sarafina swallowed hard during the intervening silence, knowing he expected her to say something. This could even be some kind of a test to see how she reacted.

She chose her words carefully when she could finally speak again. "They're both powerful witches and both protected by Thomas Monahan. Mira is his cousin and Isabelle is his wife. How do you propose to get to them?"

Bai shifted beside Stefan. It was the first time he'd moved.

She leaned back in her chair. "Oh. You intend to use Bai."

He gave her a brutal little smile and inclined his head. "After a fashion."

"Speaking of Bai." She shifted her gaze to the *Atrika* and narrowed her eyes. "Let's talk about you a little, shall we? So? What do you want with me?"

Sarafina stared up at Bai and refused to look away, no matter how badly she might be trembling with fear. She clenched her fists in her lap to hide it. Having Bai detect her terror would be akin to a shark scenting chum in the water.

Or maybe it was more the equivalent of a striptease?

"I told you at the Coven before you threw your fire at me," said Bai. His voice was low and flat, expressionless. She'd been told the *Atrika* were all about emotion, but there was none in his voice. "I want nothing *with* you; I simply want you."

"Well, Bai." She leaned forward and raised a brow. "You can't have me. Option B?"

His face clouded with anger. Ah, so there was the emotion. It simmered under the surface of icy stoicism. How oddly familiar. "You have no choice in this matter."

"I am a free being, Bai, and I won't be pushed into doing something I don't choose. Be more specific about what you want me for."

Oh, God, she wasn't sure she wanted the answer now that she'd asked.

"I wish you to bear my children."

THEO SLAMMED HIS FIST DOWN ON THE DASHBOARD of Darren's sedan as they squealed through the gates of the airport just in time to see Stefan's plane taking off.

If he'd had his cycle, he would have been able to dodge the traffic and would've made it here sooner. Although arriving any earlier probably wouldn't have mattered unless he'd planned to stow away in the luggage compartment.

Theo watched the plane lift off and sail into the blue sky while the bottom dropped out of his stomach.

"So much good the charmed pendant is doing us." Darren brought the car to a halt. "We need an alternate plan and fast."

"We get the log and find out where they're going." He paused, watching the plane disappear into the horizon. "Then we follow them."

Darren watched the jet disappear on the horizon. "And we call Thomas."

"DID YOU REALLY THINK I WOULD BRING YOU WITH me all the way to my final destination?" Stefan said, as they pulled up in front of an understated, yet clearly posh hotel in downtown Louisville, Kentucky. The tires came to a stop on a narrow cobblestone street, office buildings rising on either side of the car, and sandwiching the hotel between them. "I have sensitive things to do here. Things I don't trust you enough with yet."

"I can understand that."

Stefan planned to leave her at this hotel while he conducted his business. It was a very nice place with a historical flourish.

Sarafina was still shaking from her conversation with Bai on the jet. The things he'd told her had caused her brain function to seize and she was only now regaining it.

Bai had told her all kinds of things she'd never wanted to know, and had especially never, *ever* wanted to pertain to her. Things that had made her wish—no, *long*—for her days lived in ignorance, when she'd had no idea she'd been a witch, when she'd been a pod potato, living out her days in a small cubicle, typing her way to oblivion.

Instead, an *Atrika* had decided she'd make a good broodmare. She didn't even have wide hips.

An insane giggle rose of out her. Yes, when a *daaeman* claimed you as his mate, a bit of brief insanity did ensue. That was another one of those things she'd never wanted to know firsthand. Sarafina figured the craziness was normal . . . if there was a normal for situations like these. If Bai had his way and took her as his mate, maybe she'd get lucky and succumb to insanity completely. It certainly would make things more bearable.

"Are you all right?"

She fixed her gaze on Stefan. "I am most assuredly *not* all right."

Stefan clucked his tongue. "If you join us, I will do everything in my power to keep you safe from Bai."

"Yes, so you keep saying." She laughed again, but this time it was totally sane. "Do you expect me to believe that?"

The two bodyguards were in the limo, too, but they were pointedly ignoring their conversation.

Stefan spread his hands. "You heard Bai tell the story. He was the one who saw you first, a gem of an undiscovered fire witch. Powerful and ignorant of her abilities, just waiting to be molded like so much putty in the hands of the Duskoff. It was Bai who brought you to our attention and laid claim to you first. It is I who will try to extract you from his amorous claws. We want you for our own."

Sarafina speared him with her gaze and narrowed her

eyes. "So now I know what Bai wants from me, but what do you want from me, Stefan?"

Stefan leaned forward. "I want from you what I want from all members of the Duskoff—your blood, your sweat, and maybe even your life. In return for your loyalty and your commitment, you will receive riches and luxuries like you've never imagined." He paused a beat. "And for you, Sarafina, *power*. You are one of the most powerful fire witches I've encountered. I would want you close to me. You would be high up in the organizational structure." He raised an eyebrow. "The fact I want you so much is extra incentive that I will keep you safe from Bai. You should feel comforted."

Sarafina swallowed a burst of laughter. Yes, having Stefan Faucheux covet her for his organization of warlocks was *very* comforting.

The limo driver opened her door. She glanced at the doors of the hotel, then turned back to Stefan. "Take me with you."

Stefan gave his head a shake. "No, my petal. It's too soon. You were living with the enemy for weeks. You've been contaminated. As much as I would like to trust you, I cannot let you too close to my plans now; they mean too much to me. There is a room reserved for you. Check in, wander down to the hotel shops, and buy some clothes. The clothing selection is surprisingly superb here." He produced a wad of cash and handed it to her. "Consider it my treat. We'll talk more when I return."

She allowed the driver to help her out of the limo and watched as it pulled away from the curb.

"Damn it," she said aloud as one of the doormen approached her. "Damn it, damn it, damn it!"

"Can I help you, miss?" the doorman inquired.

Just then a motorcycle pulled up outside the hotel. It wasn't a Harley like Theo's. It was a red crotch rocket. The kind of bike that would make Theo sneer. But it looked fast. Fast was good.

How different could a crotch rocket be from a Harley? Okay, probably a lot different. Anyway, she'd only driven

Theo's Harley for a short time. That hardly made her an expert at maneuvering a motorcycle.

But this was an emergency.

"No," she answered the doorman, her eyes all for the bike, "but *he* might be able to." She walked with purpose to the cycle's owner, who'd just dismounted. He took her in with one appraising, appreciative sweep of his eyes. It was these times in her life she was glad men seemed to find her attractive.

The man was in his midthirties, probably monied. Good-looking in an ordinary way. Sandy blond hair and brown eyes.

"I have a huge dilemma and need to rent your bike." She shoved the wad of bills at him, with the sinking feeling that this was never going to work. "Can I use your bike for a few hours?" She shoved her purse at him, too. "Here's my identification, my credit cards, everything. You can hold on to it until I return."

He flipped through the bills, his eyes widening. "There must be close to ten thousand dollars here."

She nodded, surprised herself at the amount Stefan had given her. "Just for a few hours, I swear."

"You even know how to drive one of these things?"

Well, kinda. She nodded and looked up him, infusing her smile with all the sweet, angelic innocence her blond hair, blue eyes, and peaches-and-cream skin conveyed. She'd gotten away with so much in her life because of the way she looked . . . let this just be one more thing.

He waggled the wad of bills in her face and grinned. "That's a lot of money, honey, but the bike is worth a whole lot more. How do I know you'll bring it back?"

She gazed down the street and twisted her face in anguish as the limo's brake lights illuminated and the vehicle turned a corner. *Gah.* Every moment she stood here was another moment Stefan got farther away. It might even be too late to catch him now.

Sarafina dragged her gaze back to the motorcycle owner. "You don't. Please, sir, it's an emergency."

He considered her for a moment. "Keep your money." The man handed her the wad. "Name's Eric and I'll tell you what, honey, climb aboard and I'll trail that car you're following so closely with your eyes. I could use a bit of excitement in my life."

God, anything! She needed to find out where Stefan was going, even if that meant dragging a non-magickal along for the ride.

She nodded. "Yes, okay, let's go." She was practically dancing on the sidewalk in her anxiousness to get going. "Follow the limo that just left here. Not too close, though. You can't let him know we're behind him."

"Hey, I've seen movies. I know how to do it. Climb on." Eric threw his leg over the cycle and she got on behind him. He handed her his helmet. *What a gentleman.* "Put this on."

Once she was secure, Eric took off with a jolt that made her scream with surprise and grab on tight.

He let out a holler and took off down the street at a speed that made Sarafina cling to his back for dear life.

TWENTY

STEFAN TOOK THEM QUICKLY OUT OF THE DOWNTOWN area and straight south for about an hour and a half. Several times Sarafina figured Eric would tire of the novelty of this experience and want to return to his comfortable hotel, but he never seemed to lose his enthusiasm for the hunt.

Apparently, luck had been with Sarafina when she'd approached this man. The only tricky part was that Eric was a non-magickal—a civilian. Sarafina only hoped she could keep him from being exposed to anything that would make his reality shift and his head explode.

Once they got off the highway, following the limo had become much more difficult. Eric handled it with the aplomb of a CIA agent, staying just far enough behind to keep an occasional eye on the rear bumper. It was peculiar to see such a symbol of power and prestige backdropped by rusty trailers and prefab houses.

Deep in the heart of the country, the limo pulled onto a narrow, overgrown lane, an entrance to what appeared to be a large piece of land. It seemed they'd reached their destination. She tapped Eric's shoulder and asked him to halt the bike at the entrance. He brought it to a stop and dismounted.

"Now what?" Eric turned to her, his blue eyes lit with eagerness.

"I need to take this next part solo."

He motioned at the small driveway. "You mean go in there all by yourself? That can't be safe."

She smiled. "I can take care of myself, but thanks for

your concern. And thank you so much for the lift." She offered her hand to shake. "I can take it from here."

He took her hand, shook it, but then held on to it. "What's your name?"

Oh, shit. She understood the look in this guy's eyes and that the slow drop of his gaze meant he was wondering what she'd look like naked.

She hesitated, but he'd driven her all the way out here. This was no time to be rude. "My name's Sarafina."

"Would you agree to have coffee with me sometime, Sarafina? Maybe you can tell me all about your mysterious self."

"That's so sweet, Eric, and I think you're a fabulous guy—"

"But?"

"I'm not in the market to have coffee with anyone right now."

"I don't see a ring, but there's a man, right?" He finally released her hand.

She shrugged. "Maybe." Sarafina glanced at the driveway. "I have to go, Eric. Thanks again."

He rolled the bike over to the bushes and hid it in the depths of the greenery. "Oh, no, honey, I'm not leaving you. You go on in there and do what you need to do." He settled down under an oak tree. "I'll be here when you get back."

Relief swelled a bit since she actually had no idea how she was going to make it back to Louisville. Finding out what Stefan was up to out here in the middle of the Kentucky countryside had trumped that concern.

Thank God for Southern men.

"Eric, you're a good guy."

He winked. "Maybe so good I can get you to forget this man who is preventing you from having coffee with me." He settled back with a sigh and closed his eyes.

She laughed and shook her head, disappearing down the overgrown lane.

It was a long lane.

Panting, she finally made it to the end where it opened up into a clearing. She was also now highly unhappy with her choice of skirt and heels. Of course, she'd imagined herself basking in the air-conditioning of Duskoff International all day, not slapping mosquitoes in a field near the meandering Ohio River.

Sunlight glinted off the top of a vehicle in the distance. Keeping to the tree line, she mounted the slope of the hill hiding the bottom half of the car and found a building.

A gleaming, shiny building right in the middle of the clearing.

It wasn't a house; it was more industrial than that. Yet there was nothing to tell her exactly what the structure was meant for. The building was bland, nondescript, and very out of place here in the tranquil surroundings.

It was high afternoon, inching toward twilight. High afternoon was the hottest part of the day and Sarafina's hair was limp and lay plastered to her head. She slipped off her shoes and let them dangle from her index fingers as she padded through the cool grass toward the building. The few windows there were had coverings over them, but there was a door at the back of the structure.

Of course it was locked. Stefan wasn't going to hide a building way out here and not lock the doors.

Stymied, Sarafina turned in a circle, wondering what she could do. She was so close to finding out what Stefan was up to. She was *right here*, if only she could take a couple steps closer.

Trees surrounded the building. In the distance, down the bluff, was the river. She couldn't get into the building, but that didn't mean there wasn't more to find *around* the building. Perhaps a search of the land would turn something up.

SEVERAL HOURS LATER SARAFINA HAD SEARCHED every last inch of the property and had nothing to show for it but bug bites. Stefan's limo was still parked outside and no one had come in or gone out.

Twilight had long since faded into night, taking the warmth from the air and leaving only chill. It was time to go back to the mouth of the lane and hope Eric hadn't left. She'd return to the hotel and try something else.

Sarafina pushed a branch away and turned to head to the lane, her heart heavy with defeat. Just then she glimpsed something she'd missed before. It was an opening under a hill and an outcropping of rocks. Some branches had been placed in front of it that seemed unnatural, as though deliberately laid there to hide something.

She pushed them away and uncovered the small mouth of a cave. Standing in a spill of moonlight that bleached the color from the overhanging rocks, she considered it. Someone had hidden it on purpose and judging from the way her spine was tingling madly, it was something very important.

There was only one way to find out.

Going spelunking hadn't been on her list of things to do today. Yet this might be her only chance to explore it. She slipped her shoes back on. Then, crouching down, she made her way through the entrance, praying there were no spiders or snakes.

On the other side it was high enough for her to stand. It was cool inside, quiet, and completely dark. Extending her hand, she lit a small fireball in her palm. Her magick was nice that way; she didn't even have to pack a flashlight.

Graffiti decorated the craggy rock walls, and a few empty beer bottles littered the sandy floor. The air smelled faintly of pot. Perhaps that was why the branches had been covering the entrance; maybe the former landowner had been trying to discourage teenager interlopers.

Another small opening led off into yet another room. Shining her bit of fire within, she saw there was a warren of rooms going back farther and farther. Somewhere deep inside one of the caverns, water dripped.

It seemed like an ordinary cave. There were lots and lots in this region. Kentucky, in particular, was known for them. And yet . . . there was something *else* here. Something more. She could feel it, sense it, *breathing* here somewhere deep in the dark.

She shivered, her heartbeat quickening. A presence entered the small room with her, alien body heat emanating out and warming her. Though she could see no one, hear no one, she knew it.

Oh, God, she wasn't alone.

Sarafina turned to leave and ran into something hard. Her fire extinguished. She screamed, but a hand clamped over her mouth before she could fully voice it.

"It's me."

Theo removed his hand from her mouth and she hyperventilated for a moment before she could speak again. "Theo, what are you doing? Can't you make a little noise when you're sneaking up on someone in a dark cave? You scared at least five years off my life!"

"Making noise would defeat the purpose of sneaking, wouldn't it? I wasn't totally sure it was you until you ran into me. It could have been someone else with your pendant. Anyway, consider it payback. You scared some years off my life, too, chasing you all over the country."

She touched the pendant he'd given her. "It works, I guess."

"Yeah." His breath eased across the skin of her cheek and he pulled her against him. "Fancy meeting you in a cave in central Kentucky." He nuzzled her hair for a moment before stepping back a little.

"You saw the limo, right? You must know why I'm here."

"Yeah, we met *Eric* down by the road. Everything he had to say was very illuminating. Of course, most of it was about how hot you are." There was something in his voice that shouldn't be there. It was dry, brittle, a bit sarcastic.

"Ha! He waited for me. What a guy."

Silence. Theo didn't respond, but his body stiffened. This time his silence spoke louder than words.

"You're jealous!" The realization washed over her like cold water, waking her up and making her gasp. "You were jealous when you thought Darren was interested in me and now Eric—"

"I'm not jealous."

She laughed. "Yes, you are, Theo. I know jealousy when I hear it. Listen, buddy, you have to let me know you're interested in me before you have any right to be jealous of other men."

He pulled her up flush against him and lowered his mouth

to hers. "And those couple nights in bed? They didn't prove my interest in you?"

"Sexually, maybe." Her breath hitched in her throat. "They showed me you want to fuck me, and you're conflicted about it, nothing more."

"Yeah, I want to fuck you." He let his lips brush hers. "I want to keep you in bed with me all night long, make you come so many times you can't see straight."

Oh . . .

Sarafina swallowed hard and steadied herself in his grasp. "So what's stopping you?" Her voice came out breathless.

"I forget."

He nipped at her lower lip, sending a wave of gooseflesh over her body, then crushed his mouth to hers, hot and hungry. Theo parted her lips and slid his tongue inside, making a low sound in his throat as though she tasted good. It made her shiver.

When they broke the kiss, Sarafina was breathing heavily and a little shaky on her feet. "Uh, when we get to a hotel or somewhere with a bed—actually a couch will do, even a futon—remind me to remind you that you forget."

He laughed, a low rolling sound. It was the first time she'd heard him do it, and it filled her with a deep joy. "I won't need reminding."

Outside the cave she heard movement. Footsteps. She stiffened.

"It's okay. It's probably Darren or Thomas."

"Thomas came down?"

"We pulled into the airfield right as your plane was lifting off. Once we figured out where Stefan was taking you, we all hopped the first plane to Louisville. From there we followed the pendant. We were only a few hours behind you."

Theo followed her through the passageway and back into the night air.

A hand grabbed hers and helped her to stand. She came face-to-face with Darren. Thomas stood near him. Once Theo was through, he put a hand on her waist and drew her away from the water witch.

"Anything in there?" Thomas asked.

Sarafina shook her head. "I thought there was something, but maybe it was my imagination. I think I just creeped myself out."

"That's Stefan in the building, right?" asked Darren.

"Yep."

"Anybody else in there with him?"

"His driver and the two bodyguards in the limo were the only other people in the car. He didn't stop to pick anyone up. Bai was in the airplane with us—"

"What?" Theo and Thomas said it both together.

She nodded. "And boy do I have a lot to say about *that*. Anyway, Bai popped off before we landed. Bottom line? I don't know, but there's three more warlocks in there besides Stefan for sure. Bai may or may not be in there with them."

"I think we should go find out," said Darren.

"I think we should go haul Stefan's ass back to Gribben," Theo added.

Thomas rubbed his chin. "The thought had occurred to me, too. No time like the present. We can take three bodyguards and a limo driver."

"And Bai?" asked Sarafina. "What if Bai jumped back to his supposed master's side and is in there right now? How many witches did you bring with you?"

Thomas grinned at her. "Scared, Sarafina?"

"Hell, yes! And if you-all had any sense at all, you would be, too."

Darren began to walk back toward the clearing. "Let's do it." The other men followed.

"Just like that?" Sarafina hurried after them. "Right here, right now?"

"Thanks to you, we have an excellent opportunity," said Thomas, pulling his cell from his pocket. "We have the element of surprise. I'm not about to waste it. Let's take him down." He talked low to someone on his cell and then snapped it shut. "They're sending the motorcycle guy home and will meet us at the building in two minutes."

Oh, goodie, a magickal smack-down. Sarafina trudged ahead, looking forward to this quite a bit less than the boys.

* * *

THERE WERE NO WARDS ON THE BUILDING, SO THEY just strolled right in. The steel door broke against Theo's foot easily, after being softened a bit with a charm. In the back, Thomas did the same thing. The plan was to meet in the center, trap everyone in the building between them. The witches they could handle.

The only wild card was Bai, whether or not he'd pop back in.

The interior of the building was dark and oddly bare, yet the dry, bitter scent of myriad herbs hung in the air.

"They're spell-casting," Theo muttered to himself. "This is earth magick, but there's another note in the air."

Darren inhaled deeply. "Demon magick."

Theo took a step forward, his hand securely in Sarafina's. Damn, he did *not* like her in here. "What the hell—"

Something exploded at the back of the building, down a set of stairs leading into the darkness. Jack and Adam, both fire witches, stepped in front of him, blue flame licking eerily along their arms and torsos to light the way.

Theo had a charm of his own to use. He lit a small white orb that floated in front of him to illuminate the darkness. Then he gestured to Sarafina, who held fire in her hand to light her way, and they progressed down the stairs.

He didn't want Sarafina to be a part of this confrontation. It would be her first as a Coven witch and she was still so new to her power. It was true that after a few hard bumps in the road of her training, she'd finally gotten the hang of defensive magick, but she lacked experience. Tension sat in his shoulders and back at the thought of her in a battle.

Yet in a battle with Stefan Faucheux, as much as the protector in him might want to shelter her, he couldn't hold her back. He couldn't stifle her and make decisions for her. Anyway, Sarafina had proved time and again that she was more than capable of taking care of herself.

None of that was going to stop him from watching her back like a hawk in here, though.

The stairs let out into a long corridor that fed into a circular area with many more hallways. The smell of the herbs was growing more pronounced the farther they went into the structure. It seemed like they were headed in a downward direction, too, down into the earth. Theo could feel the resonance of it, thrumming through his blood and making his tats tingle.

"Shit," said Adam, turning around. "This place is like the haunted house at the state fair."

"What is Stefan doing in here?" Jack muttered.

"It's dark, in the ground, and smells of earth magick with a twist. Smells like *daaeman* magick." Theo paused. "He's spell-casting with Bai in this place."

The sound of something slamming to the floor and shouting came from their right. The scent of combined elemental magick rose, drowning out everything else. Apparently, the group Thomas led had found pay dirt.

Theo and the others ran toward the commotion. Light glimmered at the end of the corridor they'd turned down. Another flight of stairs.

Farther down into the earth.

The stairwell emptied into a large room with concrete floors and stainless steel tables. A battle was already under way. Furniture had been smashed, tables overturned, herb crushed underfoot. The air witches—Claire and Mira—had been busy.

The scent of all the elements hung heavy in the air along with . . . along with . . .

"No," Sarafina breathed beside him. "It can't be."

But it was.

The room was not filled with warlocks spell-casting demon magick with Bai as they'd presumed. The room was filled with *Atrika*.

TWENTY-ONE

❦

IT WAS THEIR WORST NIGHTMARE COME TO LIFE. The monsters weren't a world away anymore, they were here. Sarafina, like the other Coven witches, was momentarily speechless at the sight.

It didn't matter that it should have been impossible that so many *Atrika daaeman* were Earthside; somehow they were.

Stefan turned from the fray and centered his gaze on her. "You!" he bellowed. "*You little bitch.* You led them right to my door."

Just then a huge—hell, they were *all* huge—*Atrika* with long blond hair noticed the newcomers and lobbed a massive dose of demon magick at them.

"Sarafina!" Theo bellowed right before they were forced to part. The Coven witches scattered. Sarafina threw up a shield and rolled to the right, finding a table and hiding behind it as the demon magick slid past her in a bitter wave, scorching the concrete floor of the room.

Across from her, Theo rolled back up to his feet and retaliated, pushing the *Atrika* back. A bowl of some kind of herb went flying past her and smashed into the wall, followed by a demon.

Well. You didn't see that every day.

The dark-skinned *Atrika* sprawled on the floor for a few moments, stunned, then spotted her and snarled. Sarafina scrambled to her feet and raised power. Clearly, she couldn't hide behind the table forever, darn it.

She hit the *Atrika* with a blast of white-hot fire before he could completely recover, making sure she remembered not to tap all her power in one panic-fueled rush this time. The *Atrika* howled, hit dead-on, and Sarafina backed away, ducking flying debris.

Turning in a slow circle on the balls of her feet, she surveyed the room. Chaos ruled the day.

The room was awash in battle. To her left, Theo was tag-teaming an *Atrika* with Adam. Across the room, several *daaeman* were ganging up on Claire. She was a strong witch, but she was clearly in distress. Remembering Claire's history with the *daaeman*, Sarafina strode across the room, raising power to aid her as she went.

Before she made it there, Stefan grabbed her by the shirt and whirled her around to face him. "How did you do it? How did you find me out here? How?"

Sarafina plunged her hands straight into his chest and funneled fire magick from her seat straight into his. Stefan blocked with his own power at the last moment, but the force of the hit sent him careening backward all the same. He hit a table, flipped over backward, and lay still.

Just when she'd dodged that bullet, a seven-foot-tall *daaeman* with jet-black hair grabbed her upper arm almost hard enough to snap the bone. She cried out in pain as he whirled her around and slammed her into a table. Pain erupted through her stomach and she fought the urge to collapse on the floor and curl up in a fetal position, retching. No way could she raise power. She'd been rendered helpless.

Then Theo was there, drawing the monster away from her. She heard him calling to her, but she couldn't respond. Sarafina held her hand to her stomach and drew deep breaths, recovering. Out of the corner of her eye, she saw Theo attacking the black-haired *daaeman* with everything he had.

The second she could, Sarafina drew power and threw it at the back of the *Atrika*. Fire exploded and he went down with a mighty roar, smoking. Theo met her eyes for only a moment before another *Atrika* engaged him. Theo could take care of one *Atrika*. She was worried about Claire and her *three*.

Adam was also busy with an attacking *daaeman*, but he kept throwing worried looks over at Claire. She followed Adam's glance and watched Claire pivot, obviously weary and tapped of energy. The three *Atrika* circled her, stared her down, scenting her weakness as if the wind carried the clue.

As a whole, the *Atrika* obviously had it in for Claire. If they had their way, the former handmaiden of the *Ytrayi Cae* wasn't leaving this place alive. That was clear enough. They were teaming up on her more than they were Mira, who was the other most powerful witch in the room.

No, the *daaeman* knew who Claire was. Knew she was the one who'd carried the elium for a time and who had caused the death of two of their best warriors.

And they were holding a hell of a grudge.

Sarafina dove forward, putting herself in front of a red-headed *daaeman* that clearly intended to extensively torture Claire before he blasted her to Eudae and back. At the same time, she raised a wall of white-hot fire between herself and Claire. She practically collided with Adam, who had extricated himself from the battle. He wrapped his arms around Claire and leapt to the side, rolling her away from the *Atrika*.

The sheet of fire separated her from the attacking *daaeman*, but Sarafina knew it wasn't going to last. She scrambled backward, crab-walking away as she gathered more energy. What she'd done was the equivalent of teasing a grizzly with a platter of salmon.

Guess who was the salmon?

"Sarafina!" Theo was battling an *Atrika* to her right, casting glances over his shoulder at her. "Sarafina!"

"I'm okay!" she called back.

The wall of fire collapsed, leaving the huge, angry red-headed *Atrika* standing before her. His eyes matched his hair—killing rage. The air around him crackled with power.

Then again, maybe she wasn't okay.

"Sarafina!"

The *daaeman* Theo was fighting sent a massive bolt into Theo's side, sending him careening backward. He cracked his head on the floor and lay still. Sarafina screamed, momentarily forgetting the enraged *daaeman* advancing on her.

But she couldn't forget for long.

Power rose like a massive wave, prickling over her skin. She was the tiny sailboat in the water; her defenses were not enough to stop the wave from crashing down over the top of her. Like she had in the ballroom, she gripped a fistful of magick from her chest, knowing it would incapacitate her. She just needed to get through this encounter; she'd worry about the next one when it came.

The *daaeman* in front of her roared. She jerked in the face of the sound, terror coursing clear and icy through her veins. Her hold on the bundle of magick she'd pulled from her seat never wavered.

And then Bai stepped between them. The *daaeman* glanced at her, baring his teeth briefly, then turned and roared back at the redheaded *Atrika*. They engaged, teeth ripping, throats snarling, claws tearing.

Sarafina blinked. Then she rolled to the side to avoid the spray of demon blood and the acid burns that would come with it. From a safe distance, her hands gripping an over-turned chair, she watched.

It was like a scene from *King Kong*. She was the favorite of a monster, and he meant to keep her safe from all the other monsters.

Surreal. Sarafina wasn't sure if she should feel relieved right now, or really, *really* alarmed.

The two *Atrika* rolled on the floor, sounds of animalistic bloodlust sending chills through her body.

Theo came from her left and she practically leapt into his arms. "You're all right," she cried. His head was gushing blood.

He half carried her away from the fight, over to the side of the room toward the door.

"Desist!" Stefan bellowed in the middle of the room. Nothing happened.

The head warlock muttered a stream of French and then, "Stop! I hold your leashes, and I'm yanking them. This is over!"

In amazement, Sarafina and Theo watched as one by one the *Atrika* stopped fighting. Stefan was indeed commanding the *Atrika*.

Every one of the *daaeman* in the room stopped their battles except Bai and the redhead. Soon their snarling was the only sound.

All around them Coven witches and the handful of warlocks left pulled themselves up from the floor and limped to a safe place to see what would happen next.

"Bai!" Stefan bellowed.

The battle between the two *Atrika* finally came to a close. Bai's great head swung around and fixed on Theo, who had his arm around Sarafina's waist.

Bai snarled and stalked toward them. Theo stiffened and drew power, just as she did.

"Peace, Bai, let her have her fun." Stefan smiled slowly, holding a hand to his head where he'd hit it against the table she'd catapulted him into. He fixed his gaze on her and smiled a cold little smile. "Soon she'll be all yours. I can't think of a more fitting punishment."

Stefan snapped his fingers. "*Allez!* Somebody get me out of here."

An *Atrika daaeman* reached out, touched his shoulder, and they all winked out, even Bai, leaving only Stefan's hapless warlock bodyguards and the limo driver behind.

The room went silent, but for the occasional whimper or groan of pain.

Sarafina surveyed the wreckage, thinking it looked a lot like a battlefield after a war.

Theo turned her to face him. "What does Bai want you for?"

Fear welled up inside her, then settled like a cold, hard rock in the center of her stomach. "He wants me to bear his children."

Theo said nothing in response, but his grip on her shoulders grew a little stronger.

Adam approached them, helping Claire who'd twisted her knee in the fight. "What did you say?"

Sarafina shook her head and pulled gently away from

Theo's grip. "Apparently, there's a shortage of *Atrika* females, and they're having trouble kidnapping *daaeman* females, of the other breeds. *Aeamon* women are considered the next best alternative. Bai saw me in Chicago and took a liking to me." She snorted. "Says he can tell I'm fertile and that I'm strong enough to bear good stock." Her voice sounded thin and bitter.

Thomas had come to stand near them, accompanied by Isabelle. Isabelle was pressing a wet cloth to a gash on Thomas's head. Her expression was one of horror.

She was welcome to join the club.

"I am telling you right now that will never happen." Theo growled. "Not while I'm drawing breath."

She shivered and hugged herself. The thought of Bai killing Theo over her was too much for her emotions to hold.

"Someone give me a body count!" Thomas yelled abruptly, startling her.

"The limo driver's dead," Jack called back, then paused a beat. "Two dead Coven witches. A bunch of minor injuries. A few more serious. Lots of acid burns. Marcus probably broke his leg. James and Kelly are out cold."

Thomas swore, pulled out his cell phone, and turned away from them. Probably calling for aid. He snapped the phone closed after a few moments of talking in a low voice to someone on the other end. "Search the building. Get Micah down here to take a look at these herbs and try to figure out what they might have been doing." He glanced at one of the warlocks sitting on the floor trying to stop a bloody nose. "Drug up the surviving Duskoff and get them back to the Coven. Throw them in Gribben, and we'll question them."

Theo pulled her to the side. "Are you injured? How are your stomach and your ribs?"

"I'm okay. I don't think anything's broken." She touched her sore belly. "Just scrapes and bruises." Bad bruises.

Thomas's shoe crunched some broken glass on the floor behind them, making them turn. He swung around and pointed a finger at Theo and Sarafina. "Theo, you don't let her out of your sight from now on. I don't want her so much as *peeing* without you in the room."

Sarafina frowned. "Uh."

"I mean it." Thomas pointed at her again, like a father reprimanding a child. "Don't make me handcuff you together. Go back to Louisville and find a good hotel. I don't want you far from us. Sarafina, on the way there, call Micah and tell him everything you just told us."

Thomas started to turn away, then stopped and turned back. "And Sarafina, you did an awesome job here. Thank you for rushing in to defend Claire the way you did. If you want a job with the Coven, it's yours."

THEO FUMED THE ENTIRE WAY BACK TO LOUISVILLE, his hands tight on the steering wheel of their rented SUV. He couldn't bring himself to speak or do much beyond concentrate on the road in front of him. The rage he felt at Bai and Stefan boiled through his veins, and he didn't trust himself not to explode, so he just kept silent.

Beside him Sarafina sat staring out the window, deep in thought. He couldn't blame her. Being earmarked for broodmare status by a *daaeman* would bring much contemplation along with it.

They reached the hotel where Stefan had originally intended to lodge and left the vehicle for the valet. Stefan's limo was still parked back on the land and the Gods only knew where he was by now.

Eric's flashy red bike was parked outside. Theo couldn't help but sneer as he passed it on the cobblestone street.

They were both a mess. They needed to get up to the hotel room before anyone started asking why they were dirty and blood-streaked.

When they entered the lobby there was the man himself, sprawled in the lobby on a sofa near one of the gift shops. Eric had probably been waiting for her. His face lit up when he saw Sarafina and he rose to greet her, but Theo extinguished the man's enthusiasm with one cold, hard stare.

"Thanks again, Eric!" Sarafina called over her shoulder with a smile as Theo pulled her past, toward the reception area. "I appreciate all your help!"

Theo checked them into a one-bedroom suite and then asked that the concierge send up supplies, like a change of clothes, a first aid kit, pajamas, and toiletries. Then he took her upstairs, away from Eric, away from everyone.

He needed her to himself right now.

As soon as they cleared the threshold and the door was shut, he pulled her against him and crushed his mouth to hers. Her body compressed against his, soft against hard, and her breath hissed from between her lips as they broke the kiss.

"You were right about not needing to be reminded," she said breathlessly. He loved that he could make her sound that way. Her smile was a little lopsided. "Maybe there can be something good about today, after all."

"I want you, Sarafina. I'm sick of denying myself."

He also wanted to put his mark on her, make sure the world knew in some way that he cared about this woman, that she was his. Not Stefan's pawn.

And not Bai's broodmare.

He needed to get her naked and make sure she truly was all right—that she was alive and well, warm and wanting him. They were both hurting, injured, but that wasn't going to stop them.

He raised his head, sour realization blooming through him. "Fuck, *condom*." He growled. "I don't have one. *Damn it*."

"It's okay. I'm nowhere near the time of the month when I could get pregnant."

"Are you sure?"

"I know my body, Theo. I'm totally sure."

"Thank the Gods."

Theo lifted his head long enough to ascertain where the bedroom was and then moved her toward it, his hands pulling at her clothes as they went.

Once in the bedroom, he slammed the door so hard with his foot that the walls shook, closing it just in case the concierge arrived with their packages while they were busy.

He yanked her skirt down her hips and slid her grass-stained blouse the rest of the way off her shoulders, letting both drop to the thick carpeting beside the bed. She wore a red silk bra and matching panties that made Theo's mouth go dry.

The only thing better would be to get those little pieces of nothing off her.

TWENTY-TWO

❧

"YOU'RE NOT GOING TO RUN AWAY AGAIN ARE YOU?"
Sarafina ran her lips over the warm skin along his collar-
bone, making him groan. The scent of him intoxicated her,
man and magick.

"I'm not going anywhere," he murmured, finding her lips
and nipping at them.

"Good." She smiled. "I don't think I could take another
hit-and-run."

He bit the curve of her neck, sending a shock wave of
want through her, followed by goose bumps.

They were both dirty from the day, bloody and battle-
bruised. Her stomach and arm ached, and Theo had cracked
his head really good, but none of that mattered now. All that
mattered now was their skin, sliding hot and silky against
each other's. All that mattered now was the bed behind them
and the different ways they wanted to show how much they
cared about each other.

He dropped to his knees and pulled her against him, gently brushing his lips over the bruise that was blooming over
her abdomen. "Are you all right?"

"I'll be fine." She let her fingers brush through his hair.
"Touching you makes all my pain go away."

Theo stood, slid his hands around her, and unhooked her
bra, but she sidled back away from him with a mischievous
smile before he could free it. She finally had a chance to
undress him and see every inch of his gloriousness; no way
was she allowing him to get distracted by her breasts.

She sank down on her knees and pushed the hem of his tight black T-shirt upward, revealing the tanned, tattooed expanse of his washboard stomach. Pure delight warmed her as she scattered kisses over it, feeling the brush of the line of dark hair that ran down past the waistband of his jeans against her lips. Sarafina closed her eyes, breathing in the scent of his skin and savoring the smooth hardness of his abdomen before she rose and pushed his T-shirt up and over his head, leaving him lusciously bare from the waist up.

Oh, yeah. Candy. And she still had the entire lower half. This was better than Christmas.

Sarafina took her time exploring, her fingers tracing his muscles and the hills and valleys of that mouthwatering geography. She brushed his nipples with the flat of her fingers and he shuddered, closing his eyes and tipping his head back on a groan that sounded caught somewhere between pleasure and torture.

He slipped off his shoes and socks at her urging, and she held his gaze while she dropped her hands to the button fly of his jeans and slipped it through the loop. She pushed his boxers and jeans to the floor.

For the first time, *he* was naked and *she* was clothed . . . at least a little.

Savoring the moment, she held his gaze while she drew her hand up and circled his cock. Dark lust flared through his eyes the moment she touched him. He was long and wide, gorgeous—just like the rest of him. Stroking him from base to tip, she allowed her tongue to travel along some of the ridged tattoos on his chest, loving the slow shudder of his body and his heavy, even exhalation.

Unable to resist, she sank down on her knees and took him between her lips. Theo swore out loud and tangled his hands in her hair as she pushed his cock back deep into the recesses of her mouth and let her tongue play along his shaft.

"Sarafina, for the love of all the Gods, you are going to drive me insane," he gritted out from a half-locked jaw.

She ignored him, nibbling her way up and down his

length and allowing her tongue to play with the extra-sensitive place just under the crown.

After a few more moments of oral torture, Theo jerked her upward and pushed her back onto the bed. She fell against the soft comforter and Theo stared down at her like she was a five-course meal and he'd not eaten for weeks. She was more than willing to offer herself up on a platter.

"Take your bra off for me." His voice was low and a little harsh. "Then take off your panties. Do it slow."

Her breath caught a little, but she did as he asked, the silk sliding along her skin as she removed her final bits of clothing.

His gaze roved her nude body restlessly. "Part your thighs."

She spread her legs, revealing her warm, damp sex to his eyes. Doing this made her feel so vulnerable. She knew how she looked to him. Her nipples were hard little peaks and her clit was excited and pulling from its hood. Sarafina wanted him to touch her so badly.

Theo raised his gaze to her face. "Do you know how beautiful you are?"

She moistened her lips with a tongue that had gone mostly dry from the look in his eyes. "I feel beautiful whenever you're looking at me, Theo." She paused. "I feel even better when you're touching me."

"Your clit is excited. It's swollen and just begging to be petted. Stroke it. Show me how you want me to touch you."

This was a game she'd never played before. She hesitated at the request, but then held his gaze as she allowed her hand to drift downward between her thighs. As she circled her clit with two fingers, Theo stroked his cock from base to tip, his eyes on the motion of her hand. She watched the muscles of his arm flex as he touched himself, making lust flare through her body as if it was he who touched her.

Slow, melting pleasure blossomed from her sex and spread throughout her body as she caressed the aroused bundle of nerves until she balanced on the precipice of an orgasm. She tipped her head back into the pillows, her breathing coming faster.

Then Theo was there beside her, his tongue playing over
one erect nipple while he toyed with the other. "Is that good,
Sarafina?" he murmured. "Is that how you like to be touched?"
He placed his hand over hers as she worked her clit, driving
herself closer and closer to climax.

"Yes," she whispered.

"And this?" he asked, sliding first one finger deep inside
her, and then adding another, stretching the muscles of her
sex. "Does that feel good, too?"

Sarafina moaned and dug her heels into the mattress as
he drove in and out of her.

"Are you going to come?"

She nodded and whimpered, unable to reply.

Theo maneuvered downward and moved her hand away.
While still stroking his fingers deeply in and out of her, he
sucked her clit into his mouth. His tongue skated up and
down against it, pushing her straight into a climax.

Ecstasy poured over and through her, making her cry out.
Theo held her down, his tongue and mouth sucking her clit
until it hurt, then felt good again, and then made her sputter-
ing orgasm fire back into life. Once again, she was moaning
under him.

Theo flipped her before she could catch her breath and
dragged her beneath him. She spread her thighs and lifted
her buttocks as he pulled her hips up, fitting them together,
her bottom to his pelvis.

His cock found the hot, slick, already well-pleasured entrance to her sex and pushed inside. Sarafina clawed at the
blankets and pillows as he stretched her muscles more and
more with every inch he gave her.

Theo's legs braced her thighs apart and his huge hands
held her motionless as he slid in to the root. She gasped at the
sensation and the massive way he filled her. Her sex plumped
with need once more, eager for his touch.

Theo stroked her aching clit with one hand, bracing the
other on the mattress beside her, and began to thrust. His
cock slid out to the crown and then back in, over and over,
faster and faster. Sarafina's climax crashed over her body,
her sex pulsing around his thrusting length.

"Ah, Sarafina," he groaned as he came.

They collapsed together onto the mattress, a tangle of sweaty limbs and heaving chests.

Sarafina laughed, just for the joy of it. There'd been a couple times when she'd had multiple orgasms with a man, but it had never been like that. It had never been so deliciously intense.

Theo drew her close and kissed her lips, her eyelids, her cheeks. "I hope that means it was good."

She nuzzled his throat. "Mfph," she murmured, then fell silent. Apparently, her verbal capabilities were spent for the time being.

After a few moments of cuddling her, he reached down and pulled his jeans up from the floor. While he dug in his pockets, she flopped bonelessly back onto the pillows and stretched like a cat. For the first time since they'd entered the room, she noticed something other than Theo. They were on a king-size four-poster bed. Antique furniture scattered the room and a fireplace lined one wall. Nice place.

Theo rolled over with a groan and handed Eric's business card to her between two fingers. She took it and turned it over. His cell and home phone numbers were listed there.

"Eric gave that to me to give to you," said Theo, settling back against the pillows with a deep sigh of pleasure.

"Uh-huh." She chuckled and shook her head. "You have to give it to the guy, he's relentless."

"Yeah, well, he's about to relentlessly smash his face against my fist," Theo muttered with his eyes closed.

Sarafina chuckled. "Temper, temper, Theo. Anyway, you have no cause for concern." She ripped the card in half and tossed it to the floor.

Theo popped an eye open, then reached out, snagged her, and pulled her against him. One tug and she was beneath him on the bed with his big body covering hers. "I know. Don't you think I have more confidence than that?" he asked right before he kissed her.

Sarafina went speechless as his lips traveled down her jawline, her throat, and then latched onto her nipple. He worked it with his tongue and gently nipped at it until her sex warmed and tingled yet again.

She squirmed beneath him. "Ah, Theo, I think you're going to make me come again." Her voice was a mere whisper. "I've never been so incredibly multiorgasmic in my life."

"Mmmm." He reached down amid the blankets and found her clit and stroked it, making her gasp. "Maybe you've discovered a new talent. I'll help you practice, okay?"

He brought her slowly to climax this time and when she finally came under his fingers and tongue, he latched his mouth to hers and consumed every last gasp of pleasure she made.

While she lay sprawled noodlelike across the bed, he rolled off, pulled on his boxers, and exited the room, leaving the door open. Sarafina lay staring up at the ceiling trying to will herself into motion and failing miserably.

A few moments later he returned laden with shopping bags. "The concierge delivered the stuff we asked for. I figured you were hungry, so I ordered a couple cheeseburgers for us off room service. The food will be here in about twenty minutes. Just enough time for us to take a shower. That okay with you?"

Her stomach growled. "Did you order fries?"

He nodded, rummaging through the bags.

She pushed off the bed. "Then it's great with me." She walked over to Theo, who was taking all the purchased items from the bags. She distracted him by tilting his face toward hers and kissing him.

Theo dropped everything in his hands and pulled her against him, slanting his mouth across hers and kissing her deeply until she was dizzy. He picked her up and walked her toward the bathroom. She wrapped her legs around his waist and held on for the ride, chuckling against his mouth.

One-handed, he worked the faucet in the shower. The spray of hot water hit them both as he stepped inside, Sarafina still in his arms, laughing and kissing him.

Theo was actually laughing, too. The sound of it warmed Sarafina more than the water ever could.

He set her to her feet and they soaped up their hands and washed each other, stopping occasionally to lick the water droplets off particular locations of each other's bodies.

Theo pressed her against the wall of the shower, his hands on her hips, his lips brushing hers. "Bai's not taking you away from me." He growled. "You're mine, Sarafina Elizabeth Connell. You're all mine."

She smiled against his mouth. "Say it again."

"You're mine." He crushed his lips to hers.

THEO WATCHED SARAFINA'S FULL LIPS WRAP AROUND a French fry and restrained himself from leaning over and nibbling the opposite end like the pasta scene from *Lady and the Tramp*. Although his intentions were a lot less innocent.

He'd had a taste of Sarafina in bed and he wanted more. Theo had figured she'd be responsive and uninhibited in bed, though she had been a little shy about touching herself in front of him at first. His mind was awash with the ways he could push her further. She'd go anywhere he wanted her to go; he had no doubt on that score. Sarafina had a body and mind ripe for erotic exploration.

And Theo so wanted to help her with that.

She sat on an armchair in front of the cart that room service had sent up. She wore a short, silky gray bathrobe and had her long, pale legs crossed. The expression she wore on her face was faraway and dreamy. He'd helped chase away the bogeymen for a while, which had been his ultimate goal for the night. The entire ride back to Louisville, she'd been stiff with tension and worry.

The worry was now held at bay for him, too. His mind, his body, even his heart—all of it was filled up with Sarafina right now.

"Tell me about Ingrid," she asked, nibbling another fry.

Theo leaned back in his chair. "Ingrid? Why?" He pushed a hand through his damp hair. "What do you want to know?"

"You said something once that interested me. You said she was the second woman you'd been with who had died."

Oh, that. Maybe he hadn't helped push current events to the back of her mind as much as he'd presumed.

"Why do you want to know all that, Sarafina? Are you thinking about death tonight?"

She smiled and studied her fry. "Kind of hard not to after a day like we had, finding about a bajillion *Atrika* Earthside. They're like death on legs." She paused. "But no, I'm not. I'm thinking about you, wondering a little, I guess about your past. I know that Ingrid was a fire witch, like me, and that the *Atrika* killed her to perform a blood magick spell to locate Claire. It's your personal relationship with Ingrid that I'm wondering about right now."

He'd been less than forthcoming about his past with her up until now, just as he was less than forthcoming with everyone. However, Sarafina wasn't everyone, not anymore. He owed her a little piece of his past, no matter how much it might hurt him to give it up.

Theo took a careful sip of his drink before replying. "Ingrid was hard and strong, unyielding, but there was another side to her, one that only her lovers saw."

"And you were one of her lovers."

"Yes, though don't put too much weight on the word *lover.* Ingrid never wanted to be tied to one man. Instead, she flitted around the Coven, taking men to her bed as she chose. I was one of them. I think, like many of us, there were reasons she found commitment difficult, but she never shared hers with me. There wasn't much romantic about what we shared, but she was a friend. A very good friend."

"Jack McAllister was one of her men, too, I heard."

"Before Mira, yes." Theo nodded. "Anyway, we were in a relationship when the *Atrika* killed her. You remember the roadside killer? The one that dismembered his victims and left them on the side of the road? He made all the papers about a year and a half ago."

She nodded.

"That was really the *Atrika* who were chasing Claire. Ingrid was one of the victims."

She threw her half-eaten fry back onto her plate. "I remember seeing her face all over the news. There was a man killed, too?"

Theo nodded. He remembered the day they'd found out about the murders like it was yesterday. Sitting in that coffee shop in Missouri with Claire and Adam, the waitress coming over . . . "The non-magickals thought it was a disturbed individual. They could have no idea it was a demon. The police still think he's out there somewhere."

"So, what about the other woman you said was killed while you were dating her?"

Theo stood and walked to the other end of the room. He didn't want to think about Colleen, let alone talk about her.

TWENTY-THREE

SARAFINA'S HAND CLOSED OVER HIS SHOULDER. "I'M sorry, Theo. You don't have to talk about it."

He turned to her. "No, it's okay. It's just that while I don't feel responsible for Ingrid's death, I do feel responsible for Colleen's."

"Sometimes talking helps."

He snorted. "I like pretending it never happened. That helps me."

"Yes, but it never makes it go away."

"Nothing makes it go away, Sarafina. You just have to learn to live with it."

He studied her eyes for a moment. They were such a clear, pretty shade of blue. He reached out and smoothed his thumb against her cheek and she turned her face to his calloused palm and laid a kiss there.

When she did that, look up at him with all that emotion in her eyes, Theo could deny her nothing. He would do anything for her.

"Colleen was my girlfriend when I was a teenager."

Understanding swept over her features. "She was your high school sweetheart and when you—"

He shook his head. "Not high school. My life at home was unstable. I never made it through high school."

"Okay, I didn't know. But she was involved when the Duskoff kidnapped you somehow, wasn't she?"

"Colleen was my first love, my only love." He didn't elaborate on the fact that he thought he might be falling in love with Sarafina. It was too soon for that and the circumstances didn't need to be any heavier than they were. "She kept me sane when my father was beating my mother up." Anger arced through him as memory flooded his mind. His voice was hard when he spoke next. "Eventually, I beat him up."

"I'm sorry, Theo."

"It's over now. My mom took off, and I haven't heard from her since. My father's gone, too. Colleen was the one solid person I had to hang on to. Strangely enough, she was also a fire witch. Anyway, she was with me when they kidnapped me, so she was caught up in it."

Theo closed his mouth and went silent, fighting the unwelcome recollection. Images of Colleen under the brutal hands of the Duskoff, tied up and given to Reece, the bastard who'd cut him.

Reece had done much, much worse to Colleen.

Theo shut his eyes as if he could make the memories disappear. "You don't want to know what they did to her. I've spent close to twenty years trying to forget. She didn't deserve any of it and I was the one who caused it all." He shook his head. "She tried to fight them."

Sarafina didn't say anything for a long moment. "She sounds like a hell of a girl."

He pressed the heel of his palm into his eye socket, but that didn't make the mental pictures go away. "She was."

"But you weren't responsible for her abduction or her death, Theo. Tell me you know that."

He looked down at the floor. "I do know that. Ultimately, she was caught up in the situation because of me, but it was the Duskoff who were responsible. *Reece.* I've been making them pay for it every chance I get, too." He gritted his teeth. "I made Reece pay long ago. *Slowly.* Then I threw his ass in Gribben. He's there right now, suffering every single day."

"And now here I am, a fire witch and involved with you. Does that slate me for death?"

He smiled at her, but he knew it had a bitter edge. "Can you see why I resisted? I'm bad luck."

She laughed. "Yeah, but I'm not superstitious, Theo. I believe we make our own luck."

Gods, he needed to change the subject. "So, I told you all about my exes, sad stories all. Tell me about Alex."

She snorted. "I don't even miss him."

He caught her chin and tilted her face to his. "Good. That's what I like to hear."

Someone pounded on the door. Theo answered it, using the peephole first.

Thomas stood on the other side along with Micah. "The front desk told me what room you were in." Thomas had two sword sheaths in hand, which he handed to Theo. "I brought these for you and Sarafina."

Theo backed away, allowing the two men to enter. They said their hellos to Sarafina and then settled onto the couch.

"So did you find anything interesting in the building?" asked Sarafina, settling back into one of the armchairs and crossing her legs.

Thomas and Micah exchanged The Look. Theo knew what the The Look meant and it wasn't anything good. He set the sword sheaths down next to a chair and crossed his arms over his chest.

"We found evidence of *daaeman* magick," said Thomas. "No big surprise there since we could all smell it once we entered the building."

Micah spotted the room service cart and got up to peruse it for leftovers. "Either Stefan is brewing a really big pot of herbal tea, or he's planning a very strong spell against all of witchdom. I'm going with the second thing." He turned and wagged a French fry at them. "You guys going to eat this? I'm starving."

"Go ahead," answered Sarafina. "How do you know it's targeted at all of witchdom?"

Micah picked up the plate of lukewarm fries and replied with his mouth full. "I strongly *suspect*. The combination of herbs that were found there suggest it. Not all of the herbs were from Earth, by the way."

"Any idea what kind of spell?" Sarafina asked.

"If I knew that my life would be all kittens and sunshine." Micah threw the remains of a fry back onto the plate, his voice turning sour. "Instead it's all *daaeman* blood and warlock guts. I'm sifting through it all now." He speared Thomas with a look of disdain. "It would have been nicer to have a tidier site to investigate. Acidic blood melted a lot of the evidence."

Thomas coolly looked away from Micah to Theo. "We'll be staying here in Louisville for a while until we can get a handle on what's going on. We've got Claire and Micah analyzing the building and have sent for more witches from Chicago to guard the place if Stefan returns. I want you to go with Mira and Jack back up to Chicago. We have reason to believe that Stefan might be there. Jack and Mira are your backup if Bai shows up prematurely." Thomas paused and seemed to choose his next words carefully. "But it seems clear that Bai won't come for Sarafina until Stefan's plan, whatever that is, plays out."

"And when that happens, we'll be ready for him." Theo growled out.

"When the *Ytrayi Cae* came here to collect Claire, he offered us an alliance," Micah ventured, his gaze on Thomas.

"Yes, and I refused him, said there was no reason for one and there never would be." Thomas passed a hand over his face. "Rue told me he hoped I never regretted those words. With so many *Atrika* Earthside . . ."

"You regret your words now," Micah finished.

Thomas sighed. "The *Cae* of the *Ytrayi* obviously doesn't know what's going on since he hasn't contacted us. There's no way he wouldn't show if he believed Claire might come to harm."

"And there's no way to contact him," Theo added.

"You know as well as I do that it's impossible to open a portal from this side." Thomas shook his head. "Somehow the Duskoff managed it, but short of killing seven witches in an intricate blood magick spell, it's unfeasible. And it's not like we have an interdimensional telephone."

"So we find a way to defend ourselves against the impending threat," said Micah.

"Or we take the offensive," Theo asserted. "And attack them first."

Thomas met Theo's gaze and smiled. "Or we take the offensive. You reading my mind now, Theo?"

"Yeah, well, first we need to find Stefan," Micah said. "I'll bet anyone in the room five hundred bucks he's gone underground again."

Thomas smiled bitterly. "Bet you five hundred bucks Mira has heard him whispering."

TWENTY-FOUR

~

THE BLACK CAULDRON WAS A POSH LITTLE NIGHTCLUB in a bad part of town. Frequented by witches, it fairly teemed with pulsing elemental power. Sarafina stopped a half block away, feeling the thrum of the music shaking the building on its foundation.

Mira stopped, too, swaying against the brick wall of a storefront in a way that Sarafina now recognized meant she'd caught something on the air. A whisper, a murmur, something leading her to Stefan. It had been happening a lot lately.

Jack caught her by an elbow and kept her from falling over. "Did you hear something?"

Mira nodded. "Stefan's in there, all right, but there are two *Atrika* with him." She glanced at Sarafina. "Not Bai, but that doesn't mean he might not show up."

Sarafina swallowed down a cold surge of fear at the possibility. "I know. It's okay."

"I don't like this," said Jack. "It's too fucking easy. Why isn't Stefan taking more care not to let you hear him?"

Theo shifted beside her. "Because it's a setup."

Mira shook her head. "I don't think so. I think Stefan's confident, cocky. I don't think he feels like he needs to shield his conversation from air magick anymore."

"He's cocky because he has an army of *Atrika* to call on." Theo growled. "Since Kentucky, we all know that. There's no reason for him to be coy or careful anymore. He has no secrets left to guard now."

"He might have an army of *Atrika*, but we have an army

of witches," Mira answered. "Maybe Stefan will become overconfident and we can take advantage of that."

Theo just grunted in response.

It was pretty clear to everyone that Stefan had the upper hand. It was nice that Mira could be so optimistic, though. They needed that.

Annie, an earth witch, was standing by the entrance. "The others are all ready."

Jack was in charge here in Chicago while Thomas was still in Kentucky. He had ordered a group of Coven witches to enter the building earlier. Now they were mingling with the magickal and non-magickal patrons of the club.

"Good." Jack nodded. "If our suspicions turn out to be true, one of us will send a text message. That will be your cue."

They weren't going in there without all their bases covered. There was a plan in place.

Annie, a diminutive brunette, smiled. "We'll be ready. I hope we get to kick some warlock ass tonight." She turned and reentered the club.

"Shall we?" Sarafina asked, moving toward the building.

They entered the building and were immediately enveloped in darkness. The beat of the trance music pounded in their ears and the club seethed and pulsed with dancing bodies and roving colored spotlights.

Theo pulled Sarafina close to him, up against his body to make sure she didn't become separated from him in the crush. Sarafina remembered the story about Isabelle and Erasmus Boyle in this very club. Thomas had lost sight of her for only a second and Boyle had snagged her and dragged her out to the alley at the back of the building. Clearly, Theo didn't want the equivalent to happen to her with Bai.

Sarafina wanted to tell him that she could take care of herself, but that would be a lie. Everyone needed help when dealing with the *Atrika*. Everyone, even the most powerful witch, needed someone watching their back. She was glad she had Theo to do that for her, and she would watch over him as well.

Anyway, she enjoyed the press of his body against hers.

Mira moved toward the back of the club and the four of them moved with her, since she had the best idea where to find the warlock. The best-case scenario would be to somehow draw the *Atrika* bodyguards away and take Stefan back to Gribben if they could.

Sarafina let her hand stray to her back pocket, where she had a syringe full of Ketamine, a drug to render Stefan witless, alongside two syringes of hard-to-make and very rare liquid copper for the *Atrika*.

She had two syringes of the liquid copper since Bai was after her; but because the ingredients for the magickal spell that kept the copper in an injectable form were hard to come by, she was the only witch who carried the weapon.

If they were lucky, the Ketamine would make Stefan docile enough to bring back to Gribben. The trick, of course, would be getting it into him before he torched the place.

Theo and Jack wore copper swords sheathed to their back under long black coats that were a bit out of place in the warm club. They were weapons of last resort, since pulling copper blades on demons in the middle of a club where there were non-magickals was not the best scenario.

The team from the Coven walked to the back of the club and saw Stefan at a table in the back with a redheaded bimbo crawling all over him. Two *Atrika* stood nearby.

So, it was true, Stefan was living it up without a care. He felt that confident in his plans. Well, maybe it was time they broke up the party.

Sarafina and Jack approached Stefan first. Sarafina fisted a thread of power loosely in her hand, ready to throw if she needed it.

"Hey, Stefan," Sarafina said, one hand on her hip. She was wearing a pair of tight leather pants that had made Theo slobber earlier that evening.

Stefan grinned at her. "Hello, Sarafina. Are you looking for Bai? I can call him for you, if you like." He didn't seem surprised at all to see them.

Theo stepped up close behind her and she placed a staying hand on his chest. Behind Stefan, the two *daaeman* also moved a bit closer to protect their charge.

"Enjoying a night on the town?" Sarafina answered.

He motioned to the two hulking *Atrika* behind him. "Why not? It's not like you can do anything to me here in a public place. Not while I have such muscle to defend me. I have an image to uphold, after all." He pulled the redhead close to him. She smiled and simpered up at Sarafina. "There are paparazzi everywhere. You can do nothing."

He wasn't lying. The photographers lounged along the bar, one eye always on Stefan. Anywhere Stefan went, so did the photo hunters. To the non-magickal world, Stefan was a God among men. He sneezed, and his snot made first-page news.

Sarafina raised an eyebrow. "Think what you will. I'm glad you're having fun, Stefan. That's good. You should take advantage of the time you have left."

Stefan rolled his eyes. "Did you come here to talk trash? Shall we unzip our pants and compare our cocks? I guarantee mine is bigger."

The redhead giggled. Mindless twit.

"I think Isabelle would disagree," Jack answered with a grin. Isabelle was the only one of them who had firsthand—literally—experience with the size of Stefan's equipment.

Stefan's face shuttered, and he took a long drink of his cocktail. "Do you have a reason for tracking me down? Didn't you get enough of me in Kentucky?"

Sarafina stalked over to Stefan, yanked his chair out, and leaned in close. Her anger had flared at the insolent look in his eyes and the practiced boredom in his voice. His bodyguards moved in, but Stefan waved them away with a cocky smile on his face.

"Let's stop playing games, shall we?" Sarafina said. "Tell us what spell you're trying to cast."

Stefan laughed. "How delusional. Do you think I'd actually tell you? Do you think you intimidate me?"

Sarafina moved around Stefan's chair so that the warlock faced her, then she slammed her foot between his legs. Leaning down close to his ear, she announced, "I haven't even tried yet."

"Oh, ho! Sarafina!" Stefan purred with a saucy smile. "I did not realize you were so attracted to me. If I had known we could have had a quickie in the limo."

"Shut up."

An explosion sent a wave of all four elements through the club, making the patrons scream and scatter. Things were going according to plan.

Mira had eased away once they'd found Stefan and joined Annie and a few Coven witches of the three other elements in another part of the club. Together, the witches were creating a diversion. All four elements used at once made a magickal signature a lot like Claire's. Knowing how much the *Atrika* hated Claire, they figured it would draw off Stefan's muscle. They'd been right. Stefan's *daaeman* guards jumped in less than a fraction of a second to investigate, leaving Stefan alone and unguarded.

Not quite vulnerable, though. They had to act fast, before Stefan realized what was going on.

The second the magickal explosion occurred and the *Atrika* lit out, Sarafina had yanked the Ketamine syringe from her pocket and slammed it into Stefan's chest. A moment after she'd shot the drug into him, she pulled fire from her seat and shot it through her foot, dangerously close to Stefan's family jewels. He yelped and backed away, succeeding only in tipping his chair backward and landing on his ass.

Jack and Theo were on him in a moment, yanking him up and slamming him against the tabletop while the club went frantic around them.

Theo had cast a spell on the paparazzi's cameras when the initial magickal explosion had gone off, preventing them from taking pictures. They'd all been too busy fleeing or dodging elemental magick to try, anyway.

"Oh, I'm sorry, Stefan," said Sarafina, "I didn't mean to make you relive bad times."

"You're a fucking—" Stefan's eyelids dropped. "A fucking—*merde*, you'll never get away with this."

Jack leaned down into Stefan's face with a feral grin. "Looks like we just did, warlock."

* * *

"SLEEPING LIKE A BABY," SAID MIRA WITH A HARD little smile, staring down at Stefan who remained passed out and sprawled on one of the uncomfortable prison beds in Gribben.

Theo curled his lip, looking down at the warlock.

Because of the ambush and diversion they'd created, magickal firefights had broken out all over the Black Cauldron. In the explosion of chaos, non-magickals and witches alike had run for cover.

Since the *Atrika* had been occupied searching for a non-existent Claire, Theo had just picked Stefan up, slung him over his shoulder, and walked him out of the club. In the commotion, it had been easy as pie.

No one was sure how all the magick was going to be explained away, but desperate times called for desperate measures. In any case, humans had a tendency to find answers for even the most bizarre of occurrences. They'd done it to explain Sarafina's mother's death, and they'd do it for this, too.

"He'll be out for the night," said Jack. "Mira and I will be here when he wakes to question him. We'll have to hurry, since we don't know how long it will take for his horde of *Atrika* to figure out what happened."

"We'll wait with you," Sarafina replied.

Jack shook his head. "There's no sense in all of us being miserable. Come back in the morning and we'll question him together."

"What if the *Atrika* show up before then and find you all alone?"

Jack shook his head. "We won't be. Thomas, Isabelle, Claire, and Adam are all due back momentarily. This will be the first place they come, don't worry. Go get some rest. I know you've been on guard and not sleeping well. Claire and I know how that is. Get the hell out of Gribben for a while, and we'll call you if we need you."

"Do we look that poorly rested?" Sarafina asked.

"Yes," said Mira with a gentle smile. "Go sleep a little."

Theo didn't have a problem with the idea of getting away

from Gribben. The place was awful. With powerful spells etched into the very mortar, it was the one place on Earth that was completely magickless. No witch or warlock once having passed its threshold could access their power. It was akin to being stripped and raped. Theo lost his breath every time he came through the doors. Here he felt bare and raw, heavy and oddly plain. Melba toast. That's how Thomas described it. Dry, flavorless, easily breakable.

Gribben was the Coven's prison, where they kept all warlocks and offending witches before they were tried and sentenced. Some were inmates for life. For any witch of great power, it was a potent punishment. The stronger the witch, the worse Gribben felt.

The last time Stefan had been housed here, he'd become suicidal. But an *Atrika* had broken him out, and if the *Atrika* could figure out where the Coven had taken him, Theo had no doubt they'd break him out again. Their gamble right now was getting as much information from Stefan as they could before that happened.

He took Sarafina's hand and led her out of the cell. "If you guys insist, I'm not arguing," he said as they left.

Theo only started to feel alive again by the time they reached his apartment. Once through the door, Sarafina kicked off her shoes with a heavy sigh. Neither of them had been sleeping well.

He scooped her into his arms before she could draw another breath. Ignoring her yelp of surprise, he carried her into the bedroom and laid her on the bed.

She rose up on her elbows and crooked a knee. Giving him a come-hither look, she murmured, "Does capturing warlocks excite you, Theo?"

He let his gaze wander down over her tight leather pants and the creamy exposed skin at her midriff where her filmy red shirt had ridden up. Where Sarafina was concerned, he was always excited.

"Sleep," he said gruffly, turning away. "You're exhausted. I'll stay up and keep a lookout."

"Oh, Theo . . ." Sarafina purred. The sound of a zipper being undone and leather brushing over satiny smooth skin met his ears. He knew the feel of that skin against his lips, tongue, and hands.

Drawing a deep breath for strength, he turned. She lay in only the low-cut club top and a pair of skimpy blue silk panties.

He wanted to take them off with his teeth.

She tipped her head to the side a little. "Don't you think we need to unwind a little before we sleep? We deserve to celebrate after what we just did. Annie gave me a birth control charm when we got back to Chicago, by the way. We're totally safe now."

He traced the curve of her thigh with his gaze. "Don't tease me, Sarafina. You need to sleep so you're ready for a fight later. There will be one; it's just a question of when."

She pulled her shirt off and dropped it to the floor along with her bra. Her small pert breasts were topped with luscious hard red nipples—like little suckable berries. "Are you absolutely sure?"

Theo lingered for a moment, staring at her, then stalked across the floor to loom over her. She relaxed back into the pillows, the look of a vixen on her face. Sarafina was a woman who knew she was beautiful and she knew exactly how to use her beauty to greatest effect. It was part of what made her so dangerous.

He leaned down, bracketing her with his arms on either side of her body. Her facial muscles relaxed a little as she realized she'd won the battle and now would reap the spoils.

Theo leaned in and captured her full red lips against his, sliding over them torturously slowly, just the way he knew drove her crazy. He flicked his tongue into her mouth and allowed it to brush her tongue while he moved one hand between her perfect thighs to press against the warm, damp silk covering her sex. He found her clit and stroked it beneath the material until it grew engorged and ultrasensitive.

Sarafina shifted and moaned under him, her arms seeking to twine around him and draw him down onto the mattress with her. He caught her lower lip and dragged it slowly between his teeth. She shivered and moved her hips, seeking more contact.

Instead, he drew away and kissed her forehead. "Two can play that diabolical game, baby," he murmured a moment before he backed away far enough that she couldn't draw him to her. "Sleep now."

She protested, but he ignored her. He only sank down into a chair in the corner of the room and watched her glare at him.

Sarafina grabbed her boxer shorts and T-shirt from a nearby chair and slipped them on. "You're evil."

He smiled. "Maybe a little. Sleep now and I'll be even more evil later."

SARAFINA WOKE THE SAME WAY SHE'D GONE TO sleep—aching for Theo. She craved the feel of his body against hers, his tongue on her skin, his hands on her body. Being with him, having him inside her, was the only time she truly felt safe anymore.

Her eyelids fluttered open and she moaned, stretching under the sheet that covered her. Theo was no longer in the chair. Actually, he was no longer in the room. That was strange since he rarely let her out of his sight.

She rose, not bothering to cover herself. "Theo?"

No answer.

She navigated the room in the predawn, headed to the hallway, and hit her shin on the bed frame. "Ow!" She hopped on one foot toward the living room, hand to her shin. "Theo?"

"I'm here." A warm body pressed against hers, crowding her back against the wall.

"Theo," she murmured, smiling. The dawn light just barely kissed the edges of his hair and bleached the color from his normally well-tanned skin. Shadows played over his face, obscuring his eyes. She reached up and let his long hair curl through her fingers. "I was worried you'd left me."

"Of course not."

But he would. Eventually, he would leave her. He'd push her away because he didn't feel worthy of her. The pain that Theo had had to endure all his life—goodness, it had started at birth—had shaped him that way. Too damaged for love. His life had molded him in such a way that he felt unworthy of anyone's kindness, anyone's total commitment.

And, damn it, she'd fallen in love with him. Didn't bode well for her, did it?

"I—" She snapped her mouth closed and swallowed hard. The darkness closed around them like a smaller room within the room. "I want you, Theo," she whispered against his lips. "I need to have you inside me. I want to feel close to you, as close as I can get."

He turned her toward the wall and pushed her hair to the side, his fingers running over the skin of her shoulder in a sensual sweep. His hands slipped over her bare breasts, caressing her nipples as his lips and teeth caught her earlobe and nipped.

A shiver ran through her and goose bumps erupted over her skin. Her sex plumped, excited, eager.

"Dally with the *aeamon* now for I'll be coming for you soon."

Bai's voice.

She stiffened and opened her eyes, all her excitement was gone in a rush of cold fear. She turned. Bai stood there, not Theo. His eyes glowed red and when he parted his lips, his teeth were pointed and sharp as knives.

Sarafina screamed.

TWENTY-FIVE

"SARAFINA!"

She lunged forward in bed, the sheets a tangle around her legs. Bright daylight streamed in through the bedroom window. Theo caught her in his arms and she fought him for a moment, not certain who he really was.

"Shhh, it's okay now, you're safe." He pressed her head to his shoulder and wrapped his arms around her to keep her from thrashing.

Sarafina closed her eyes and whispered, "God, it was so real." She shuddered, shaking and cold from the memory of Bai's breath on her skin.

Theo pressed a kiss to the top of her head. "It was just a dream."

She pushed away from him a little so she could see his face. Theo, yes, it was Theo. "No. No, that was no dream. I could feel everything. Oh, God, I thought he was you. He touched me." The words came out a horrified whisper. "I thought it was you, but it was Bai."

"It wasn't real. It was a mind-fuck, Sarafina."

She shook her head and flipped the sheets away to expose her shin. "I hit my leg on the bed. I can still feel the pain." There was no bruise there, at least not yet.

Theo pulled her close. As his embrace tightened she closed her eyes, letting out a breath of tension. She was safe now, safe.

After a moment, he pulled her away from him so he could look into her eyes. "He's playing with you. The *Atrika* like to stalk and they like their prey scared. It excites them.

He entered your subconscious as you dreamed and he woke your sense of self. It was like a lucid dream, understand? He can't hurt you physically there, he can only scare you. If you allow him to scare you, he wins."

"But I hit my shin!" She shuddered. "And I felt his hands on me . . . his breath."

"He can make it seem real, as real as waking reality." Theo let out a slow breath. "Making you afraid, it's like fore-play to him."

Bitterness rose to sting the back of her throat at the thought. She swallowed it down. "Yes, I get it. I understand. Don't let him see how terrified he makes me and I win. Oth-erwise it . . . excites him."

"Exactly. Come here." He pulled her still trembling body closer against his and stroked her hair.

"I'm okay. It was just thinking he was you and then . . . having it not be." She frowned at the daylight and pushed away from him. "How long have I been sleeping?"

"Stefan's awake and Thomas is back. They're question-ing him. No sign of any *Atrika* yet. I let you sleep as long as you wanted since you needed it."

She raised an eyebrow. "And you? You don't need sleep?"

"I'm fine."

"Bullshit. Lie down and take a nap, big guy. It's my turn to watch over you." She pushed him backward onto the bed, but he grabbed her by the arms and pulled her down on top of him.

Sarafina gave a yelp of surprise and found herself rolled beneath his body in one second flat, his mouth on hers.

Just as Sarafina was starting to relax a little and shake off the horror of her most recent encounter with Bai, Theo's cell phone rang. He fumbled for it, took one look at the interface, and said, "We have to get to Gribben."

GRIBBEN LOOKED LIKE A WAR ZONE. NOT UNLIKE THE one they'd left behind in Kentucky. Theo was getting sick of the carnage.

Theo lost his breath and Sarafina her step as soon as they

crossed the threshold of the prison, but it didn't slow them down for more than a heartbeat. The guards were away from their posts and the series of gates leading into the heart of the prison were flung open to allow Coven reinforcements to enter. All the prisoners were in lockdown and as they passed, they could see faces peeking from behind the small square windows in their heavy metal doors.

The prisoners were all smiling, laughing, pounding on their walls. They knew exactly what was happening—their Coven captors were getting their asses handed to them by *daaeman*.

So what else was new?

They made their way down into the bowels of the prison, where they'd put Stefan. The *Atrika* had either finally deduced where the Coven witches had taken their fearless leader, or they'd performed some kind of locator spell to find him. Either way, they were here now and locked in a battle with Thomas and the others.

The problem was both simple and profound: the Coven witches had no power here and the *Atrika* did.

It made for bad odds, all in all.

The sounds of the battle grew louder the closer they got. An *Atrika* blocked the open steel door they needed to get past in order to get to where Thomas and the others were, filling the frame like a freight train jamming the mouth of a tunnel.

They came to a skidding halt. Theo reached back for his sword and held it between himself and the monster who stood snarling in front of them. Sarafina held her sword in hand, too. Without magick to wield, Theo felt vulnerable as a newborn babe and he was certain Sarafina felt the same. A copper blade just wasn't the same as magick.

The *Atrika* raised power. It crackled through the air like a spark finding dry tinder. Just as the creature threw it, he and Sarafina parted, each leaping to the side. The bolt of magick went straight past them, exploding against one of the prisoner's doors where it made a big black smoking crater. That was one warlock who probably wasn't celebrating anymore.

Before the creature could raise more power or focus on Sarafina, Theo lunged forward and sliced deeply into the thigh of the *daaeman*. The creature roared and lunged toward Theo, who only narrowly dodged his grip and rolled away to avoid being hit with any blood. The blood splashed, smoking, on the wall, and the demon's wound popped and snapped from the copper.

Sarafina came up from behind and hefted her sword, driving it into the side of the *Atrika*. More *daaeman* blood gushed and they both danced to avoid it.

The *Atrika* let out a battle cry that seemed more animal than anything resembling human and turned toward Sarafina, who had backed away, holding her sword up. The creature raised another bolt, making Theo's ear pop from the pressure.

"Sarafina, watch out!" he yelled.

She barely had time to duck the flare of magick that probably would have taken her head clean off. She rolled on the floor, sword tight in her hand, just like he'd taught her.

Theo swung toward the *daaeman* and caught him in the shoulder. Again the creature roared and lashed out magickally. This time Theo took a sideswipe bolt to his sword arm. Pain flared vibrantly through his body, making him drop his blade. The flesh of his upper arm was open and glistening— badly burned.

The *daaeman* charged him, but Sarafina was on his back in a moment, slashing at him as hard as she could to draw him away. She cried out as droplets of blood from the *Atrika* spattered her and ate right through her clothes.

Theo picked up his sword and forced himself to grip it. The *Atrika* was staggering a little, listing to the side as he chased Sarafina around the corridor, trying to corner her. It might have been a reaction to the copper blades slashing deeply into him, or perhaps it was from simple blood loss. Whatever was causing it, it was good.

Sarafina darted to avoid a blast of power and the *daaeman* feinted, managing to grab her by the arm and throw her up against the wall so hard she dropped her sword. He gathered power in a hard rush, clearly intending to drive it straight in the center of her while he pinned her there.

Anger and fear bubbled out of Theo, hot and bitter. He swung his sword with all his might, ignoring the searing agony of the movement. He aimed for the neck of the *Atrika* and caught him dead-on. The demon's head separated from his shoulders and the body fell lifeless against the wall. Sarafina dove to the floor, just narrowly avoiding the spray of blood.

Theo grabbed her arm and helped her past the toxic gore. The floor and walls still smoked from the splattering of blood. She'd gone from sheet white to nauseated green, and he didn't blame her. It was a gruesome sight.

Once they were far enough away, Theo went down on one knee, his wounded arm in shock at all the movement he'd made. It felt like someone had taken a blowtorch to his injured limb.

"Let me see." Sarafina's fingers were gentle as she angled his arm to take a look and whistled low. "It's bad."

"I figured that," he gritted out. "Better my arm than the center of my chest, though."

The crash and a bellow of *Atrikan* ire echoed through the open door. Theo lurched to his feet, gripped his sword, and charged through it with Sarafina right behind him.

Two more *Atrika* lay headless on the floor of the corridor where they'd stashed Stefan. A couple of witches lay on the floor, too, dead for sure. Another few lay wounded, their backs against the wall, breathing shallowly.

Stefan's voice echoed from inside one of the cells and he and Sarafina ran toward it. Inside were Thomas, Isabelle, Claire, and Adam. Stefan stood surrounded by three *Atrika*. The head warlock's skin was ashen and his shoulders were slumped. Gribben had taken its toll.

Sarafina had told Theo that Faucheux had said being imprisoned in Gribben—or at least, losing his magick—was the only thing that had ever come close to breaking him. Seeing Faucheux now, Theo believed it.

The head warlock fixed his gaze on Sarafina, hatred

making his eyes bright and his face pinched, before he reached out, touched the *Atrika* nearest him, and they all jumped.

Gone.

The witches stood in silence for a moment. Theo could hear nothing but the moaning from the corridor.

Adam swore loudly. "And for the second fucking time Stefan escapes Gribben. The only person ever able to do that."

Isabelle threw her sword to the concrete floor with a clatter. "He didn't escape. He was *poofed*. Don't give him more credit than he deserves, which is none."

Thomas turned toward the door, throwing his sword down, too. "It's done. Let's tend the wounded." He sounded as frustrated as Theo had ever heard him.

SARAFINA AND THE OTHERS FOLLOWED THOMAS OUT of the room, already finding Jack, Mira, Micah, and the other unharmed Coven witches helping the wounded and ensuring any injured *daaeman* were well and surely dead.

She was still shaking from their encounter in the hallway with the *Atrika*. Seeing Theo hit by *daaeman* power had nearly stopped her heart. He'd come close to being killed.

She couldn't imagine a world without him in it.

As he walked toward her, she studied his open wound. "Let's get out of Gribben so I can heal you up, Theo. You're no good here until your arm is treated. After that's done, we'll come back and lend a hand with the injured."

He nodded and they made their way out of the prison. Stepping past the front gate and having the flush of her magick return to her was almost better than sex. They leaned against a stone wall outside and dragged in lungfuls of fresh air.

"Okay, come on," she said almost immediately. They didn't have time to burn.

He turned toward her, offering his arm for her inspection. She'd never tried to heal anything this extensive before and wasn't sure she could do it.

"It's all right if you can't heal the whole thing, Sarafina." He must have read the look on her face. "You're the only fire witch I know who could even come close, who could even attempt it."

She let a faint smile flicker over her mouth. "My defensive skills might suck, but healing is something I can do."

"Your defensive skills looked pretty damn good to me just now. Ow!"

"Sorry."

As she worked, the others helped the wounded from the prison and brought out the dead. Once she was done, the wound looked as though he'd had a massive amount of stitches and a couple weeks of healing. It had taken a chunk out of her seat to do it, though.

He looked at the reddened, healing wound. "Amazing."

"Feel better?"

He cupped her chin and tilted her face toward his. "*Amazing.*" They held each other's gaze for a moment, then parted. It was time to go back in.

Ugh. She really didn't want to enter Gribben again.

Together they descended into the depths of the prison, and then dove in, helping the others.

Theo started to turn away, to go down the opposite direction of the corridor, then stopped. "Thanks for the help in the hallway. We tag-teamed him pretty good." A rare grin flashed across his mouth.

She smiled. "I keep telling you we work well together."

His grin faded and he turned away. "Be careful."

"Oh, stop nagging," she muttered and turned to find someone she could aid. There were plenty to choose from.

She walked down the hallway toward where Adam and Claire were aiding the medics.

"I hope all this was worth it. Did Stefan tell you anything before the *Atrika* came for him?" Sarafina asked Claire, kneeling to check the pulse on a dark-haired male water witch. He had a nasty burn wound in his side, the material of his shirt seared onto the poor man's skin.

Doing something like this—checking for someone's pulse and half expecting not to find one—would have seemed inconceivable to her a month before. Hell, she probably would've tossed her cookies on viewing a wound like this one or having the scent of charred skin in her nose.

After all, that particular scent brought back some pretty bad memories.

But now not so much. She was finding out there were plenty of ways being a witch benefited her life. Still, this was not one of them. Luckily, the wounded witch still lived. He was only unconscious. Good thing for him, judging from the severity of his wound.

They needed to get these people beyond the prison walls so the fire witches could do their work.

Someone handed her a wet rag and she went on to the next victim, a small redheaded female earth witch, and wiped away some blood from a gash on her forehead.

"Yeah," Adam answered for Claire, "get Stefan into Gribben and the sheer force of this place breaks him. That's why we did it. We found out something really interesting."

Sarafina paused in her work to glance at him. "So, are you going to tell me?"

Claire did it instead. Her voice was tight and her expression even tighter. Her voice was little more than a whisper. "Somehow, some way, Stefan got hold of the elium. That's how he's commanding the *Atrika*. He's got it stashed somewhere, protected and hidden. The *Atrika* would do anything to get the elium, so they're acting as Stefan's personal army to gain it."

Sarafina noticed now that Claire's face was pale. She didn't think it had much to do with treating the dead and wounded, either.

The elium was a ball of *daaeman* magick that worked as a neutralizing agent against power. It was the nuclear bomb of magickal weapons. Whichever *daaeman* breed controlled the elium controlled Eudae. Last the witches had known, the *Ytrayi* had possessed the elium.

Sarafina frowned and went back to her work. The earth witch she treated was sliding in and out of consciousness, babbling incoherently. "The *Cae* of the *Ytrayi* holds the elium, though, right? It's inside him, isn't it?"

Claire's face twisted for a moment in anguish. "Yes, Rue holds the elium. Or he did, anyway."

Sarafina knew that Claire had served as Rue's handmaiden from childhood up until the time the palace on Eudae had been attacked by *Atrika* and Rue had imbued her with the weapon to protect it. He'd sent her to Earth and slammed the doorway between the dimensions closed behind her, but not before two *Atrika* had dived in behind her. Claire managed to retain her freedom after much fighting, and Rue had been able to get the elium back.

Even though Claire had been, for all intents and purposes, Rue's slave, she had tumultuous, conflicted feelings where he was concerned. Rue thought of her as his daughter. Most likely Claire was worried about him.

A medic came and scooped the unconscious earth witch into his arms. Sarafina rocked back on her heels and cast a worried gaze at Claire. "Do you know what happened to Rue?" she asked gently.

Claire shook her head and turned away, tending to another fallen witch.

THEO AWOKE TO LIPS SKIMMING HIS ABDOMEN. Immediately, his cock took notice of the light head hovering over his stomach and the hands pushing their way down his boxers. His shaft hardened to steel as Sarafina's fingers touched it and he groaned.

"Mmmm, you're awake." She purred. "You've slept ten hours and you told me to wake you after eight."

"Why didn't you wake me at eight?" He groaned and dropped his head back against the pillows as she stroked him.

"Two can play the overprotection game, Theo." She nipped his stomach lightly.

He rolled her over and had her cotton shorts shimmied down her legs in about two seconds flat. He pulled her leg to the side, exposing the vulnerable part of her upper thigh and nipped her there, savoring the tender flesh between his teeth and against his tongue.

"Let's see what other games we can find to play." He lowered his mouth to her sex and latched onto her clit.

"Theo," she murmured, her fingers curling in his hair. "I'm not objecting."

He slid a finger deep into her sex. Her silken muscles clasped it eagerly, so he added a second and worked them in and out until she moaned his name again. "I thought you wouldn't. Take your shirt and bra off."

She wiggled her T-shirt up and got her bra off, all the while he held her legs down and parted so she couldn't move them, gliding his fingers in and out of her. Under his tongue, her clit had grown full and needy. If he took his index finger and caressed her there with steady pressure, she'd come for him so quickly and sweetly. But he had other plans.

"So, you like to play games?" He purred against her inner thigh. "Let's play, then."

TWENTY-SIX

❧

HE REACHED DOWN AND PULLED A BOTTLE FROM HIS bottom nightstand drawer. Grosset was sleeping soundly in his doggie bed in the kitchen. That was good. He had some significant plans for Grosset's mistress and he didn't want any canine interruptions.

"What are you going to do with that?" Sarafina asked lazily.

He didn't answer, he only squirted some of the lubricant onto her lovely, aroused sex and let it drip down to the area of his immediate fascination.

"What? Theo, I've never—"

"Hush. Lie back and put your hands above your head, Sarafina. Place your wrists together. Consider yourself tied and unable to move. My words are your rope. Break it and I'll tie you up for real. Got it?"

She studied him for a moment, her lower lip caught between her teeth and insubordination on her face. He reached out and slid his finger through the lubricant, massaging it into her clit. Her eyelids dropped and her head fell back on a moan. She lifted her hands above her head the way he'd asked.

Ah, that was better.

Theo liked to be in control in the bedroom. He suspected Sarafina liked him to have it, too. He slicked the lubricant down to her rear and played there a bit, waking up all the nerves.

"Theo," she said, her voice breathless. "I've never done this. I've never had a man touch me there before."

"Virgin territory? Lucky me. Do you trust me, Sarafina?"

She nodded.

"I'm excited by this, Sarafina. I'm excited by the fact that when I touch you here, I can see your sweet sex becoming even more eager for my cock." He used a finger of his opposite hand and speared deep inside her sex. She shivered. "You may not have ever had a man touch you here, but you're curious, aren't you?"

"A little," she admitted.

"Do you want me to stop?"

She bit her lower lip and shook her head.

Suppressing a smile, he slid the tip of his finger inside her rear and she gasped, then moaned. "Can you feel all your muscles stretching?"

"Yes, oh, God, yes."

He pushed in deeper, making sure there was a lot of lubricant to ease the way. Her legs widened even farther in an unconscious gesture of surrender.

"Ah, there you go. It's good, isn't it?"

She nodded and moved on the bed, arching her back and stabbing her breasts into the air. He added a second finger to the first and maneuvered so he could rub her clit with his thumb at the same time, knowing she needed that stimulation to add some sweet pleasure to the unfamiliar play at her rear.

"Gods, you're so pretty like this." His voice was shaking and his cock was hard as a rock, watching how excited this made her, watching his fingers slide simultaneously in and out of her. He loved that this was new to her and that he was the one to introduce it to her.

"I'm going to come, Theo," she whispered. "Oh . . ."

She came, her body rocking and spasming under his hands. Before the last of her climax had run out, he lifted up, pushing his boxers down to his knees impatiently and slid root-deep inside her.

Her silken inner muscles were still pulsing. They gripped his shaft warm and tight, milking him as he began to thrust in and out. He rode her fast and hard, his hands on either side of her head and his gaze holding hers as he moved deep within her.

Her eyes were a little glazed and her facial muscles slack from the aftermath of her climax. She hooked her legs around his hips and met him thrust for thrust, driving him as far into the center of her as he could go.

Gods, how happy he was to be able to touch her so deeply. As deeply into her body as she'd touched his heart. It was frightening how much he'd come to care for her, but he couldn't deny it.

"Sarafina," he murmured roughly. He wanted to say so much more. But it wouldn't be fair to either of them.

She kissed him, reaching out and pulling his head close to hers. Their lips touched softly at first, then needier and needier, like they couldn't get enough of each other's taste. Their tongues meshed, hot and soft as their bodies fused, becoming one for such a short period of time.

He wanted it to be forever.

The thought was pure and deep, singing through his blood like a promise of something he wanted with every inch of his heart and soul, yet could never have because he knew he would destroy it, crush it.

Obliterate it.

He pushed the thoughts away as pleasure rose up from his balls, crashing over him like a tidal wave he couldn't stop.

"Sarafina." He whispered her name as she came for the second time, "Theo" spilling from her lips simultaneously.

Together, limbs intertwined, they dissolved into ecstasy.

Once it had passed, he rolled to the side and pulled her close, inhaling the scent of her hair. When he was with Sarafina, he felt content. At peace. It was the only time he ever did.

There was a part of Theo that wanted to welcome Sarafina into his life and keep her with him always. But to do that, he would have to be certain that he was making her as happy as she made him. Anything less wouldn't be fair to her.

And Theo had never been the one to make anyone happy.

"Theo," Sarafina murmured sleepily, "that was incredible. I never imagined it would be like that. It was so . . ."

"Intimate?"

"Yes."

For being a beautiful woman with a bevy of men at her beck and call, she was surprisingly innocent. There were so many things he wanted to show her. No, so many things he wanted to *share* with her.

She cuddled closer to him. "Theo, I—" She broke off the sentence and then started again. "I love you." It came out barely a whisper.

Theo stiffened. "Don't do that." He pulled away from her and rolled off the bed.

"Don't do what? Don't love you?" She scooted to the edge of the mattress, holding the sheet to her bare body. "I can't just stop, Theo. I don't have control over it." She paused and her voice went softer, less certain. "I just thought you should know."

Theo sat for a moment, digesting all the emotion roiling through him until it shut him down, just like it always did. Shut him down, shut him up. Numb. Cold. Under the surface his heart breathed fire, but he'd learned to keep it well sectioned off.

He stood and walked to the bathroom. "I'm taking a shower."

"Theo?" Her voice had a note of brokenness to it—defeat.

Theo hesitated, but kept walking. It was for the best.

SARAFINA WATCHED HIS RETREATING FORM WITH anger simmering in her gut. How dare he discard her words and her feelings like that and just *walk away*. She understood the baggage that Theo carried was heavy and she'd known the rules of the game when she'd started playing.

But she loved him, damn it, and she wasn't letting him push her aside.

Sarafina rose from the bed and stalked into the bathroom after him. He was in the shower already and steam billowed through the room. She opened the door and slammed it hard behind her, her ire fully piqued. His back was to her, his tribal tats glistening with water.

"Theo, you're not getting away with that. I won't accept that bullshit from you. Are you a coward? Are you scared of me? Are you—"

"You talk way too much." He turned and drew her close, his mouth coming down on hers. He kissed her until she was warm all over and it had nothing at all to do with the temperature of the water.

Her knees swayed when he released her. "And you know nothing about me." He growled. "*Nothing*. So don't start."

She frowned. "That's just more bullshit, Theo. After living hip to hip with you for these many weeks, I do know you. I probably know you better than anyone in the Coven, maybe the world."

Sarafina yelped when he pushed her up against the wall of the shower. The tile was slick and smooth on her bare back.

"You know this about me, Sarafina." He kissed her again, his tongue snaking between her lips. He broke the kiss, breathing hard. "And this." He went to his knees and ran his hands over her rear, pulling her toward him. His tongue snaked between her thighs and laved over her clit with a masterfulness that made her eyes roll back into her head.

She tried to stay on task, but his hands and his tongue on her sex made all the thought that had been in her head suddenly blow away as if it had never existed. She rested her head back against the wall and moaned out his name.

She struggled against the distraction, but damned if he wasn't doing a really good job. "We fit well, you and I, Theo. Come on, you can't deny it." Her sex was becoming excited again, her clit plumping and growing more sensitive. Only he'd ever been able to do that to her—push her from one climax straight into another.

Theo rose to his feet and lifted her, settling her thighs over his hips and sliding his cock deep within her.

She gasped in surprise at the quick movement and the strength it took to do it, then she moaned at the sensation of having him filling her once more. The world only felt completely right when he was inside her, a part of her.

"Yes, we do fit well together, he murmured, pinning her against the wall and thrusting deep inside her.

"Don't make this into something sexual." She slurred her words as if drunk. "I didn't mean sexually, even though . . . *oh!*" He jabbed up inside her, increasing the pace and length of his thrusts. "Even though the sex between us is really, really, *oh*, good."

"Stop talking." He nuzzled her throat and bit the tender part where her shoulder met her neck.

"No," she whispered. She closed her eyes for a moment. The head of his cock was brushing her G-spot in this position. "I won't stop because—"

He backed away from the wall and deposited her on the slick tile floor of the large shower and flipped her onto her stomach. He slid a hand under her abdomen and lifted her, fitting them pelvis to rear before thrusting his cock roughly back inside her sex.

Theo liked to take her this way. Maybe because missionary was too intimate? After all, in this position he didn't have to look into her eyes. Now it was all about the joining of their bodies—not of their hearts.

But, unfortunately, where Theo and sex was concerned, she seemed to be powerless and soon all her rational cognition was gone in a tidal wave of primal need.

He took her fast and hard, animal-like, there on the floor. He spread her thighs as far apart as they'd go and slammed in and out of her, rubbing her clit from the front until she couldn't help but climax. It was almost forced out of her.

Sarafina orgasmed around his pistoning length, long and powerfully. Theo came again, too, groaning as his cock jumped within her.

After a moment, he pulled away from her and walked to the door of the shower. Before he left he turned toward her. "*That's* all you and I share, Sarafina. Get it through your head."

TWENTY-SEVEN

❦

SARAFINA SLAMMED THE PLASTIC BOTTLE OF WIN-
dow cleaner down on Theo's kitchen counter and tossed the
rag she'd been using after it. She stared at the stove for a moment, almost blinded by its polish.

Theo's apartment was cleaner than it had probably ever
been. She'd spent the whole day scrubbing, wiping, polish-
ing, and spraying everything in sight. She'd even cleaned the
upholstery on the couches. Grosset had wisely parked himself on the freshly vacuumed sofa and was staying out of her
way.

Theo was still in the apartment, of course, because he
was guarding her body. Doing other things to it, too, while
he repeatedly slammed her heart against the floor. He was
especially good at that last part.

So he remained in close proximity, but not too close,
lest she decided to take her broom to his head. Whenever
she entered a room, he left it. It had made for an interesting
day, her cleaning his apartment to hell and back and chasing him from room to room.

Now she was exhausted, but she felt better. Sarafina wasn't
totally sure why she felt compelled to clean when she was
upset, but it always did the trick. Perhaps cleaning the house
made her feel like she was in control. With her two hands
and a little effort, she could change her environment to suit
her.

She sure as hell couldn't control or change Theo, that was
for sure.

Sensing the man in question was standing behind her, she

stiffened. He was silent as a cat, but she still knew he was there. Sarafina could feel the touch of his gaze on her as though he brushed her with his hand.

She turned toward him. "You know, Theo, you're all big and bad and ride a Harley and wield a sword"—she gestured widely with her arms—"and maybe all the demons quake in their demon boots when you approach, but you're still the biggest coward I ever met." She pushed past him into the living room, where she meant to stop, but instead she kept on going, right out the door.

If Bai wanted to come for her, so be it.

"Sarafina," said Theo from the doorway. "You can't be alone. You can't just walk away from me."

"Ha!" she threw over her shoulder. "Watch me."

She took a page from his book and kept walking away without another word. With every single fiber of her being, she needed to be away from him right now. Sarafina would even risk Bai to get peace.

The sound of Grosset's jangling collar met her ears and soon he was trotting at her heels. At least she still had the love of her dog.

She found her way to the Conservatory. At this time of the evening, the place was dark but for burning torches and accent lights decorating the pathways. There were only a few people enjoying the tranquil surroundings.

That's what she needed. Tranquility. Just for a few minutes. Then she would go back to the apartment and Theo's brutal stoicism.

Sarafina found a bench tucked between a tree and a huge flowering bush. She collapsed onto it with a heavy sigh. Grosset jumped up beside her and laid his head in her lap.

"Sarafina?"

She looked up to see a petite woman with a pixie cut looking at her from a nearby pathway. She had a book tucked against her body. "Hi, Annie."

"Are you all right?"

She smiled. "I'm okay. Just looking for a little solitude this evening."

"Me, too." Annie glanced down at her book. "This is a

good place to read. How's the birth control working out for you?"

"Good." Not that she'd be needing it anymore. "Thanks again for your help."

Annie nodded. "Hope you find a little tranquility." She walked away.

Yeah, so did Sarafina.

She'd been in many relationships in her life. Since she'd been sixteen she'd gone only short times in between steady boyfriends. She was not inexperienced when it came to the opposite sex. Yet Theo stymied her. By the way he looked at her, the way he touched her, she knew, *knew* he had feelings for her.

And she had feelings for him like she'd never had in her life. What she felt for Theo blew all her other relationships out of the water.

So this was love.

All the country-western singers wrote songs about how much it hurt.

Boy, they were right.

THEO STOOD A SMALL DISTANCE AWAY FROM WHERE Sarafina sat in the Conservatory, concealed by trees and bushes. He understood she needed to be away from him, but he couldn't let her out of his sight . . . for more reasons than one.

She had her eyes closed, her head resting on the trunk of the tree growing behind the bench she sat on. Her hands were sunk deep into Grosset's fur, and her facial muscles appeared tight. He allowed his gaze to trace the lines of her chin and travel down the slope of her neck.

He loved her so much.

His hands fisted at his sides. Never in his life had he wanted a woman like he wanted her. The problem was that he wasn't built for love. His life had twisted him in a way that made it impossible for him to hold on to anything beautiful or precious.

In a way, he was like the *Atrika*, built for battle, for conflict, for revenge and killing. He was a monster, not fit to hold an angel like Sarafina in his hands. She was too precious to this world. He would only crush her.

Why couldn't she see that?

Once he'd dreamed of finding a woman like her, of settling down and having children, giving those children the kind of life he'd never had—full of love and stability. Now that he'd met Sarafina he realized how impossible something like that would be for a man like him.

Theo had always worried his father's brutal heart beat within his chest. It did to some extent, although it was the warlocks who suffered his wrath, not a wife. One thing Theo knew was that he would never raise a hand to anyone he loved. That was one part of his father he'd been lucky enough not to inherit.

Yet Theo had never managed to successfully maintain a relationship in his life. His mother had fled, and Colleen and Ingrid had been killed. Theo knew he wasn't responsible for any of that—not really—but it still made for a hell of a bad track record.

Sarafina was too precious to gamble with. Theo couldn't bear the thought of investing all of his heart in her and then losing her.

Gods, it would kill him.

And *of course* he would lose her. He simply wasn't equipped to do anything but fumble a relationship with a woman like her.

She deserved someone like Darren or even Eric. Someone who had lived a normal life, who hadn't had the love and compassion tortured and beaten out of him. His scars went deeper than his flesh and they weren't easily healed. Sarafina had to realize that.

He was just trying to keep her from being hurt.

He might love her and she might love him—there was little question of that—but sometimes love just wasn't enough.

Theo indulged himself a moment longer, gazing at her silhouette through the foliage, then melted back into the shadows to keep watch over her until she decided to return to the apartment.

When she finally stepped though the door, he was moments behind her.

She rounded on him in the living room as Grosset trotted into the kitchen to look for food. "Did you follow me?"

Theo shut the door behind him. "Of course I did."

"Why? Why do you even care, Theo?"

"Sarafina." He walked to stand directly in front of her. "Of course I care."

"I thought I was just sex to you."

"Fuck," he murmured under his breath. "We're not right together, you and I. I'm not the best man for you. You need someone who can make you laugh, who can—"

She made a hand gesture to cut off his words. "Stop right there. I can't listen to these lies you're telling yourself a moment longer. I'm going to bed."

Theo watched her stalk to her room.

She turned in the doorway. "I need you, Theo. I want . . . *need* the intensity of your love and your protectiveness. It's true we're different enough that most people wouldn't think we'd fit together, but sometimes jagged edges fit just right, puzzle pieces falling into place. That's how I feel about us."

He shook his head. "You don't understand, Sarafina."

"I understand more than you think I do. In fact, I understand even more than you do." She paused, looking sad. "And you need me, too, Theo. More than you realize."

SARAFINA WASN'T GOING TO THINK ABOUT THEO. She'd decided that right after their conversation the previous night. He didn't want her, so she shouldn't want him.

If only it were that easy.

Instead, after uneasily falling into a fitful sleep, she'd awoken to find Theo in the armchair in the corner of her bedroom, slumped over in an uncomfortable drowse. He'd watched over her all night long. Grosset was snoring in his lap, the traitor.

Her gut reaction had been to go to Theo and help him into bed, so he could get at least a couple hours of worthwhile rest, but she'd stopped herself. The stubborn man. She wasn't going to show him how much she cared for him.

Not when he was being such a slave to his fears.

Anyway, she'd opened her heart to him once and he'd made it bleed. She certainly wasn't going for a twofer.

Now it was midmorning and she wasn't going to worry about him and how tired he looked, standing up against one of the library walls, away from the group as usual, while Thomas conducted a meeting.

She wasn't going to think about Theo at all, let alone care about him.

Yeah, right.

It seemed that Theo wasn't the only one good at lying to himself.

Sarafina pulled herself back from the quagmire of her own mind and emotions and tried to concentrate on what Thomas and the others were saying.

"We're organizing another raid, this time on Duskoff International."

Whoa, now Thomas had her full attention.

"We'll leave in the morning. Darren is already there, preparing. Once the workday is done, the warlocks remain. That's when we'll enter."

"What about the wards on the thirteenth floor?" asked Sarafina. They were of *daaeman* make, according to Mira. They couldn't break them.

"That's still a problem."

"Are you sure all the non-magickals will be out of the building?" asked Mira.

Thomas hesitated, then shrugged. "No."

"What are we going—"

"*Je suis arrive!*" The voice came from beyond the open door of the library, from roughly the area of the Coven's foyer.

Sarafina froze in her chair. It was one of the voices that haunted her dreams and stole all the sweetness away. She knew that voice well.

"What the—" Adam bounded to his feet across from Sarafina.

"Maybe we don't have to raid Duskoff International, after all," said Theo. He'd taken about three steps toward her from his place across the room. "Maybe the raid has come to us."

Thomas bolted from behind his desk toward the door. "How did he get through the wards? The *daaeman* would be able to get through, but Stefan should be barred."

"The *Atrika* probably just broke the wards so he could get in," answered Claire. "That would be nothing but child's play to them."

Sarafina stood, a cold, hard knot of tension in the middle of her stomach. If Stefan was here, that meant *Atrika* were here. If *Atrika* were here, that meant Bai was probably here, too.

Theo caught her hand. She wanted to pull away from him, even as she pulled him closer. Right now Sarafina was so hurt by him that even the touch of his skin on hers made her want to cry. At the same time, there was no one else in the world she wanted at her side right now, no one she felt safer with. How ironic.

"You don't leave my side, got it?" he said. It wasn't really a question.

Together they followed the rest of the witches who'd been gathered in the library for the briefing out into the foyer. The other inhabitants of the Coven had begun to filter here as well. Word of Stefan's arrival had spread through the building quickly.

Stefan stood in the middle of the large area, his feet planted comfortably and firmly on the marble floor of their home. He was surrounded by a contingent of *Atrika*, who guarded him like his own personal force of bodyguards. Warlocks also surrounded him, all looking cocky and pleased with themselves.

Rage at the sight bubbled inside her. She couldn't imagine what Thomas Monahan must be feeling.

"What are you doing here?" asked Thomas. He sounded controlled and calm, but Sarafina could see his fists were clenched at his sides and rage clearly sat in the stiffness of his shoulders.

"What the hell did you do to Rue?" Claire yelled, lunging toward the ring of *Atrika*. Adam caught her and held her back, trying to quiet her down.

Stefan laughed. "I let that slip in Gribben, didn't I? Of course I could hardly hold it back under the circumstances." He glanced at Thomas. "Thomas holds the *Cae* of the *Ytrayi* to task for torturing him on Eudae, yet Thomas tortures as well. That makes Thomas a hypocrite."

"I do what I need to do in order to protect my people."

"As Rue might say, too, yes?" Stefan raised a pale eyebrow. "So I also do what I must to protect my people. I do what I need to do to protect the Duskoff way of life and to improve upon it. Any action I take against the Coven is a step toward that goal, since the Coven seems set against preventing us from living the way we see fit."

"*Harm ye none.*" Thomas ground the words out. "The Duskoff crushes that principle under its boot heel."

"*Harm ye none.*" Stefan made a raspberry. "How about to each their own?"

"You really care that much about the well-being of your people, Stefan?" Mira shook her head. "I don't buy it."

"Ah, Mira, just the witch I wanted to see today. I cared about my father, but you ended that for me, didn't you?"

Mira's mouth snapped closed. Everyone knew that William Crane had been seconds away from sucking all the magick and life from her when she'd retaliated and killed him. Stefan made it sound like she'd done it in cold blood.

Stefan pulled something from his pocket. Sarafina couldn't see what it was, but it fit in the palm of his hand. "I came to finish the job my father started, although with a slightly different ending." He motioned to the *daaeman* surrounding him and gave a careless one-shouldered shrug. "I've already pulled through all the demons I could possibly ever have a use for. I have different priorities that are a bit more personal."

Theo's grip tightened around Sarafina's hand. The tension in the room ratcheted upward. They'd ambushed Stefan twice, and now he'd ambushed them. No one had their swords. No one but Sarafina even had any syringes. She only had one because of Bai's interest in her, kept in a special leather sheath on her hip at all times.

All they had on hand to fight the *Atrika* and whatever Stefan had just pulled from his pocket was their elemental magick and their determination.

Coven witches from all over the building had now converged in the foyer. They stood behind the core group of nine—Mira, Jack, Thomas, Isabelle, Claire, Adam, Sarafina, Theo, and Micah—lining the massive curving staircase that led to the second floor and crowding the corridors leading off from the foyer.

Sarafina had the gut reaction to turn and tell them to go—to run—even though she knew they'd come to fight. They stood there like a bunch of moths drawn to a flame. Whatever Stefan held in his hand had to be deadly.

"Do you remember what it was my father tried to do to you, Mira?" Stefan said with a hard smile. His blue eyes glittered in the light. "Right before you pushed him out the window?"

"It's kind of hard to forget," Mira responded, her voice edgy and thin sounding.

"He set you in a demon circle and almost squeezed the power from your seat. But my father failed. He underestimated you and underdrugged you. He didn't take into account the love you shared with Jack McAllister and the fact that nothing could prevent him from coming to your aid." Stefan paused. "Here's how I succeed where my father failed." Stefan's hand moved.

"Everyone hit the floor," Thomas yelled.

Theo pulled Sarafina down and covered her body with his. From beneath the protection of his chest, she could see Stefan standing triumphantly in the middle of his bitterest enemy's lair. A smile had spread across his face—the beaming smile of a man who finally had victory within his grasp.

Stefan threw the small glimmering object up into the air and murmured a few words like an earth witch would.

But this was not elemental magick. This was *daaeman* magick.

The small ball of alien power crackled and pulsed for a

moment, hanging suspended in the air above Stefan's head, glowing like a tiny blue star. Acridness filled the air, burning their noses, tinged with the scent of both familiar and strange plant life. The very molecules around them seemed to pulse and expand, like the object drew the essence from everything around it, growing pregnant and swollen with power.

And then it exploded.

THE ONLY THING THEO COULD THINK ABOUT WAS keeping Sarafina safe from whatever that blue egg of death had hatched in the air.

A bolt of sizzling light blue magick whizzed past his head and exploded on the floor near him. It did nothing, only evaporated on the marble in a shower of sparks.

Near him one of the bolts hit a brown-haired earth witch Theo thought was named Brian. Brian gasped and hit the floor, grasping fistfuls of his shirt near the center of his chest and curling into the fetal position.

Dragging gulps of air into his throat and his eyes bulging, Brian reached out to Theo with one hand. "My magick, it's gone. It's completely gone."

TWENTY-EIGHT

❦

"COME ON, BABY, WE GOTTA GO." HE PULLED SARA-fina to her feet, shielding her body from the scattershot and made his way toward one of the corridors. The rest of the Coven had also figured out the score and were doing the same thing, trying to dodge the magickal shrapnel.

They found no refuge in the corridor. The bolts from the *daaeman* magick found them there, too, ricocheting off the walls and sparking on the floor and ceiling. Theo and Sara-fina were too busy dodging the bolts to even think about raising power.

And the *Atrika* were coming.

To his left, Miranda, a fire witch, took a stand, raising power to fight the *Atrika* who were charging her like a freight train. A shot of the blue *daaeman* shit hit her straight in the chest and the flare of power she'd *poofed* into exis-tence fizzled like a candle doused by a tidal wave.

Miranda gasped in shock and fell against the wall, grasp-ing her seat with both hands, a look of utter despair trans-forming her features to shocked ashen gray. The *Atrika* who'd been gunning for her before simply passed her by. She wasn't a threat anymore.

"Theo!" Miranda yelled, her eyes wide. "Get out of here. Get out!"

What an awesome idea.

"Come on," said Sarafina, seeing an opening in the throng. They were all edged into the corridor like cows ready for slaughter.

"Watch out!" Miranda yelled.

A bolt of *daaeman* magick sailed toward them. He and Sarafina leapt apart, each going in different directions to avoid the projectile. This was like some fucked-up, deadly dodgeball game.

When Theo rolled back to his feet, Sarafina had been swallowed up in the crowd and was nowhere to be found.

SARAFINA STRUGGLED BACK TO HER FEET AND IM-mediately had to duck to avoid another bolt of blue. The damn bullets of despair didn't always explode harmlessly on the wall or floor; sometimes they bounced and changed direction, aiming for another witch.

All around her people were being hit. The sounds of grieving met her ears and tightened her chest and stomach in empathy. She couldn't imagine what it would be like to lose her power, not after she'd just found it.

It wasn't going to happen to her, goddamn it.

She looked up from her place on the floor and couldn't see Theo anywhere. Their only chance was to get out of the Coven, away from the spell that Stefan had unleashed. She glanced past the throng in the foyer and saw that the *Atrika* and warlocks were guarding the exit. Of course. They'd probably been ordered by Stefan to hem everyone in, the better to hit them with the alien magick.

Near her Annie was hit in the shoulder by a bolt of blue. The diminutive brunette spun from the impact and then sank to the floor, hands covering her face and keening in grief.

"Annie!" Sarafina cried out, crawling toward her.

Annie either didn't hear her, or was too in shock to answer. She remained on her knees, face hidden in her hands. Sarafina couldn't get to her in the throng and could only catch a glimpse of her from around the panicking witches.

Moments later, in absolute horror, Sarafina watched Annie calmly stand up and put herself in the way of an *Atrika* barreling toward her. It looked like a pure act of suicide.

"Annie, no!" Sarafina lunged toward her from her kneeling position on the floor, but to no avail. The *Atrika* just ripped out Annie's throat as he went past and her lifeless body collapsed.

Just like that.

Numb at the sight of the once vibrant witch on the floor, eyes sightless and her blood pooling on the marble, Sarafina rested against the wall behind her for a moment and closed her eyes in anguish. Somewhere in the distance she heard things crashing above the din of terrified witches on the verge of losing all they held dear.

Things crashing. *Yes.* Somewhere out there Claire and Mira were kicking some demon ass with air magick.

Again she scanned the throng for Theo but couldn't find him. In the foyer, her gaze seized on Thomas, Isabelle, and Micah. The three were trying to get to Stefan, who still controlled the magick blue ball of death.

Stefan.

Sarafina scrambled to a crouching position and made her way toward him. Their best hope was to take Stefan out and stop the alien magick filling the Coven. Then they'd have to deal with the *Atrika*, which was another issue.

Just as she reached Thomas, Isabelle, and Micah, a shot of blue came streaming right toward Thomas. Sarafina paused in mid-crouch, her breath catching in her throat.

Oh, God . . . no. Not the head of the Coven.

"Thomas!" Micah lunged toward his cousin, knocking him to the side and out of the way of the bolt. It hit Micah in the side.

Micah rolled on the marble floor of the foyer, holding the center of his chest, his face contorted in agony.

"Micah!" Thomas grabbed Micah by the shirt and yanked his cousin toward him on the floor, Isabelle coming down on the other side of him.

Sarafina reached them just in time to see Micah staring up with wide, glazed eyes. *"Oh, my Gods, it's gone. I'm empty inside."*

Sarafina looked up at Stefan who stood with the spinning, spitting ball of light above his head, looking down at the scene with a smile on his face.

Her jaw clenched in a surge of rage, she stood and threw a huge volley of white-hot fire at him, only to have her blast blocked by an *Atrika*. One bat of the huge *daaeman* paw and it evaporated into the air as if it had never been.

Stefan fixed his gaze on her, his lip curling in disdain. Without Stefan even lifting a finger, a shot of blue came right at her forehead. Sarafina ducked as the bolt whizzed past her, hit the floor, and ricocheted into a nearby witch. She closed her eyes for a brief moment as a sob clenched her gut, listening to the witch's cry of anguish.

Isabelle stood near Micah's side and pulled a lot of magick fast and hard. Water coursed from the pipes, down the hallway, everywhere and anywhere she could call it from.

The other water witches in the foyer caught on fast and called water, too. Soon Sarafina lay in an inch of it, then another inch. Rising fast, the water all made for Stefan, forming a conical wave around him and his *Atrika* bodyguards, who had difficulty staving it off.

Even better, the contingent of *daaeman* guards were now distracted and busy.

Seeing an opening, Claire, Mira, Thomas, and Sarafina all mounted an attack. They tossed all they could at the now struggling and preoccupied *Atrika*. Sarafina caught one in the side of the head with a burst of fire that sent him reeling back, howling.

The water coursed in, soaking Stefan's shoes, and began to rise fast. It was already up to Sarafina's calves. Most likely the water witches had tapped the water pipes, the streams in the Conservatory, and the Coven's pool. She could smell a note of chlorine underneath the heavy scent of elemental and *daaeman* magick.

Thomas lobbed an earth charm at Stefan, which made Sarafina's ears ring from the power. The charm made it past the *Atrika* and hit Stefan full in the chest, sending the warlock careening backward to slide on his back in the water.

Now out of Stefan's control, the ball floated up into the center of the foyer, near the chandelier. It continued to emit *daaeman* magick, but judging from the swear words coming from Stefan's mouth the warlock had lost complete power over it. Now it hung like a deadly *daaeman* disco ball near the ceiling. It was sure making the witches dance all right.

Something growled to the left of her and Sarafina turned her head to see Bai pushing witches out of his way to get to her.

Okay, time to go.

She pushed into the throng and tried her best to disappear. The last thing she needed was for Bai to jump right next to her in the crowd and take her away. He could do it so easily. Her only chance was to stay as far from him as she could and not allow him to touch her.

Weaving in and out and back and forth, all the while dodging blue bolts, she forced her way to the back of the crowd, where more *Atrika* and warlocks stood trying to guard the exits and keep all the witches in the vicinity of the *daaeman* magick. Water sloshed around her calves here, too. She could feel a current and she was working against it. The water witches were still calling it toward Stefan.

Sarafina ducked into a room off the corridor. Water streamed in after her and it was a struggle to get the door closed again. She found herself in a storage room filled with cleaning supplies.

Channeling fire, she shot a burst of it at the wall separating this room from the next. It created a ragged, smoking hole she could climb through. With some luck, she could just go around the guards.

Drastic times called for drastic measures.

THEO CALLED FOR SARAFINA AGAIN. WHERE THE fuck had the woman gone? He dodged a bolt and it smashed into the water at his feet, apparently dissipating on contact.

Stefan had lost control of the *daaeman* magick, but that only meant the ball was shooting off randomly. It was almost as bad as having Stefan direct the thing. The only positive was that now the warlocks were being hit, too.

Fighting the crowd that was working its way to the back of the foyer and the corridors leading away from it, Theo pushed his way forward toward Stefan. If he knew Sarafina, she would have gone for the source of the problem rather than running from it.

Theo came upon Isabelle kneeling in the water with Micah half in her lap, her wet hair sticking to her face. Theo went down on his knees beside Micah. "Are you hit?"

"His magick is gone," said Isabelle. "Completely gone."

"Oh, fuck."

Soaked, Micah looked up at him with haunted, blank eyes. "Find me a sword," he ground out. Rage transformed his face, made his expression tight. "Theo, find me a sword!" he repeated, louder his time.

There was a brutal cast to the scholar's face that Theo had never seen on him before. It was an expression he was more used to seeing reflected in the mirror.

Right now, Theo could deny Micah nothing. He'd find the man a sword.

Theo glanced toward the corridor leading off to the opposite side of the stairway. An *Atrika* blocked the end of the hallway, but he could get into the room. There might, with luck, be some weapons in there.

"I'll be right back," Theo said and rose, sloshing through the water and picking his way past fallen witches to make it there, keeping an eye out for stray bolts of the blue demon magick.

After breaking the locked door down, he found only three swords within and managed to get them back through the crowd without the *Atrika* noticing. He gave one to Isabelle and one to Micah. Micah caressed the hilt with a finger, looking nothing like the happy-go-lucky geek Theo knew. Micah wanted to spill blood and Theo hoped he'd get his chance.

"You see Sarafina anywhere?" he asked Isabelle. Everyone had to shout over the din of battle, grieving, screaming, and rushing water.

"She was here, Theo, but then she took off like the devil was chasing her." She pointed toward the back of the foyer, at the other corridor.

Maybe not the devil, but Theo was guessing it was somebody just as bad.

Theo melted back into the crowd in the direction Isabelle had pointed in. He had to find her.

SARAFINA EDGED HER WAY DOWN THE CORRIDOR. This part of the Coven was dry, at least. All the water was being directed to the front part of the building.

Some of the Coven witches had also managed to make their way past and were convening, trying to devise a way to mount an effective attack against Stefan and the invading *Atrika* from the opposite direction.

She was just trying to get away from Bai.

Her best bet was to get out of the Coven completely and keep moving. Having lost Theo in the foyer, she knew she was alone now. Against Bai that made her chances slim to none.

On the lower floor of the Coven, she turned a corner and headed toward the Conservatory, past the doors of the ballroom. There was an exit leading out onto the sprawling lawn from the back of the Conservatory if her memory served her. After her narrow escape from Bai down this very corridor, she'd memorized every part of the building so she'd never get trapped again.

Stefan's hand clamped over her mouth and he dragged her kicking back into the recessed doorway of the ballroom. God, she hated this room! She bit his hand, tasted blood, and he released her.

How the hell had the bastard traveled from the foyer to this part of the Coven so fast? Her blood went cold as she realized there was only one way.

There was an *Atrika* here, too.

Sarafina spun, raising power, but a big, black-haired, dark-skinned *Atrika* simply snuffed out the fire before it could reach him.

"Are you always going to need someone to fight your battles for you, Stefan?" She clucked her tongue. "So sad."

He gave a loose shrug of one shoulder. Such a French gesture. "They're useful. I don't disregard the tools at my disposal."

Sarafina shifted her gaze to the dark-skinned *Atrika*. "So you're a tool, huh?" The lips of the *daaeman* curled back in a thin growl. "I thought the *Atrika* breed had more pride."

The *Atrika* turned his attention to Stefan, his eyes flashing red.

Stefan gave an unsure sidelong glance at his demon-on-a-leash, looking like he wondered if the *Atrika* might break his chain.

Sarafina raised a brow. "Worried, Stefan? You should be. I wonder what the *Atrika* will do to you once you give them whatever leverage it is you're using. It's the elium, right?"

Stefan turned his attention back to her. "Don't make me shut you up." Every word was a lash of a whip.

Oh, looked like she'd hit a nerve.

Stefan glanced at the *Atrika*. "Go back to the foyer. I don't need you here. I can handle a witch like her with one hand tied behind my back."

The *Atrika* jumped away, leaving them alone.

Stefan stepped out into the corridor. "So many women of the Coven have offended me, Sarafina. Mira killed my father. Isabelle tried to kill *me*. Yet out of all of them, I think I'm most affronted by you. You're the only one who never had a good reason for wronging me. Mira and Isabelle both had personal debts to settle, but you . . . you're just a flat-out bitch."

He took another step toward her. Sarafina's stomach clenched, but she stood her ground. "You kidnapped me, Stefan. That's pretty personal."

Sarafina pulled a thread of fire and held a small line of white-hot flame in her hand. It was useless, but it made her feel better.

Stefan glanced at the fire. "You've learned so much in such a short time. You're wasted here."

She channeled fire into the palms of her hands and stood on the balls of her feet, ready to move. He circled her, an odd expression of pleasure on his face.

Sarafina tilted her head to the side and smiled a little, batting her lashes. "So does that mean you'll take me back?"

"No, my petal, you're not mine to claim anymore."

The world went perfectly silent and the hair on the back of her neck stood on end. Sarafina's skin prickled at the sudden flush of *presence* in the corridor. She knew the press of that particular existence in the air around her, on her soul. Pressing, taking . . .

It was Bai.

"You will come with me now." Bai's voice was deep and even. He sounded satisfied, happy. Sarafina supposed he had no reason to feel otherwise. Apparently, the bad guys were winning and Bai had what he wanted. That would be *her*.

Slowly, she turned toward him. All six and a half feet of her future children's father filled up the corridor behind her. The fire in her palms died.

Behind Bai, Sarafina saw Theo turn the corner and freeze. Their eyes met and held past the *daaeman* blocking the pathway between them.

"Sarafina." Theo growled her name and then shouted it again as he began to run toward her. Power gathered in an arc from here to there.

The *Atrika* was about ten feet away. He disappeared and Sarafina ran toward Theo, her feet pounding madly on the carpet of the corridor. She knew what was coming next. It gathered like the doom of Armageddon at the back of her throat and behind her teeth—bitter fear of the inevitable.

Bai jumped in right in front of her. She screamed in terror. He reached out and touched her and she was gone, obliterated in every way that mattered.

GONE. SARAFINA WAS GONE.

Theo stood in the center of the corridor, seeing his worst nightmare come true. Bai had disappeared, reappeared, and then disappeared with Sarafina. Theo had been too far away to stop it.

He stood for a moment in cold, painful shock, then raised his gaze from the place where Sarafina had disappeared to the smirking warlock not far away. Sarafina had slipped through his fingers, but there was someone here to take all his aggression out on.

Gathering power, he ran toward him, intending to make him into a warlock mash. Stefan sent up a wall of white-hot fire. Theo countered, pulling earth right through the floor of the Coven to put out the flames. The walls shook and the floor moved in a wave that didn't trip Theo up for a moment. He leapt over the smoldering ridge of earth and kept going.

On the other side, Stefan was just disappearing around the corner at the opposite end of the hallway. Theo pounded after him, his sword heavy in his hand. Rage and grief twisted inside him, but he couldn't let it get the better of him. Instead, he used it, transforming it into speed and a deadly will to make Stefan pay.

Theo caught him on a staircase somewhere near the Conservatory. Pulling a charm, Theo used it to trip Stefan, who went sprawling on the steps. The warlock flipped and shot a wave of white-hot flame at Theo that he only narrowly managed to dodge.

"She's gone." Stefan snarled. "Bai's taken her to Eudae. You'll never get her back now."

"Then I've got nothing to lose, warlock." Theo advanced on him. "You'd better start praying."

TWENTY-NINE

SARAFINA PRESSED HER PALMS AGAINST THE FLOOR and retched. Her whole world was focused only on that for a moment. When she finished, she closed her eyes as another wave of intense nausea swept through her.

The scent of the place wasn't helping. It smelled of old blood—tangy and metallic—and a twist of unfamiliar, decaying plants. The spot where she'd landed seemed to exude death and violence. When she moved her hands, cold dirt and grit bit into her palms.

The *Atrikan* part of Eudae. It had to be.

The look on Theo's face . . . He'd been shattered, terrified. What could he be feeling now? Sarafina couldn't venture a guess. He'd be feeling like this was his fault, like he'd failed her. Theo thought he failed everyone. This would destroy him.

Her heart grieved that more than anything, even more than the fact that when she lifted her head she would find herself in a brutal alien world with no hope of rescue or escape.

Oh, God, she missed Grosset so much. It hurt like a physical pain in her chest and gut. She knew Theo would take him in as soon as the smoke cleared. As gruff as Theo acted toward her pet, she knew he had a soft spot for Grosset. The little dog would be okay. But she'd never be able to bury her face in his warm fur again.

And Theo.

She squeezed her eyes shut and tears splashed to the concrete floor. Sarafina couldn't even think about that loss right now. It hurt too much.

Anyway, she'd lost him before Bai had ever grabbed her.

The wave of nausea faded and she rocked back on her heels, taking stock of her situation through her tangled hair. She blinked, not believing the scene that met her eyes. "What?"

They were back in the building in Kentucky, in the room where they'd had the knock-down, drag-out fight with Stefan and the *Atrika*.

Bai hadn't moved her to Eudae.

She wondered why for a fleeting moment before a surge of incredible joy made her entire body sing. If she wasn't on Eudae, there was a slender thread of hope to hold on to. Her euphoria tamped out like a candle in a tornado as soon as she saw the shadow in the corner.

Using one of the tipped-over chairs to help herself up, she stood and grabbed an old towel from one of the tables to wipe her mouth clean. The fabric smelled of herbs.

"What are we doing here?" Her voice echoed eerily in the large, empty space and raised goose bumps along her arms. Dropping the towel, she hugged herself.

Silence.

She sighed. "Look, if you expect me to play broodmare, expect me to bear and raise all your brats, you'd better answer me when I ask you a question, buddy."

He moved his gaze from where he'd been staring off into the distance at some unknowable thing and settled it on her. All her bravado evaporated. "Eudae is not like Earth for *Atrikan* females. You cannot expect . . . respect."

"I'm not an *Atrikan* female."

"You're not a full blood, but you carry our spark in your DNA. You are descended from the *Atrikan* line, I can smell it on you. Why is it do you think I am so attracted to you?"

There was so much wrong with that last sentence she couldn't even begin to fully digest it. She had *Atrika* in her DNA? Oh, wow, that was so *not* a compliment.

Bai took a step toward her and she took a step back involuntarily. "You have just the barest trace, as do several others in the Coven." He tapped his nose. "It's a special talent of mine."

Another step. And another. For every one he took toward her, she moved back. She knew she might be backing herself into a corner, but she couldn't stop herself. She didn't want Bai within ten feet of her, even though Bai wanted to get much closer than that.

Much closer.

The backs of Sarafina's thighs hit an overturned table and she almost went sprawling. The feet of the table scraped against the concrete floor—loud in the otherwise quiet space.

Sarafina spied an abandoned sword on the floor and scooped it up, holding it between her and Bai. Uneasily, she inched around the table to put more distance between them.

Bai held out a huge hand. "This doesn't have to be unpleasant, *vae* Sarafina."

She raised her sword and gave a grim laugh. "Oh, I intend to make it pretty damn unpleasant, Bai."

"You could learn to accept your circumstances, accept me. It's my hope that one day you will."

"You mean actually learn to like having sex with a monster, carrying and raising little *daaeman* bratlings? Serving up raw meat for dinner every night? I think not."

"You have seen only *Atrikan* battle behavior, not our everyday life."

"I've imagined it, and it makes me shudder with revulsion. How do *Atrikan* children play, anyway? By dismembering small animals?"

His eyes glowed red and his lips pulled back a little, revealing sharpened teeth. Man, she really needed to learn to keep her thoughts to herself.

He turned his face to the side and closed his eyes. When he turned back his eyes were no longer red. Apparently, he'd mastered his sudden flash of temper. That was good news for her.

He held out a hand. "Come with me, *vae* Sarafina. You are so beautiful, like the human image of an angel. Your mother named you well."

She clenched her hands around the sword handle. "Why haven't you taken me back to Eudae yet?"

"I cannot until Stefan gives us what he has promised."

"The elium."

Bai nodded. "He is not stupid, this warlock. He has managed to manipulate us well, but we will have the better of him in the end."

Sarafina had no doubts on that score. Stefan was stupid—or desperate—to have tried to control this *daaeman* breed. He deserved anything he got, in the end.

"Stefan somehow gained control of the one thing the entire *Atrikan* breed never could. How did he do it?" she asked.

Bai smiled. It was a terrifying sight. "Love."

"What?"

He motioned at the sword. "Put the sword down and I'll tell you how he managed it."

She hesitated, staring at him.

"I will not hurt you, *vae* Sarafina. I want you to mother my children, after all. At the Coven when Stefan released the magick, I was afraid for you. I searched until I located you with the intention of protecting you."

That made sense in a horrifying, stomach-lurching, bile-in-the-back-of-her-throat kind of way. Sarafina set the sword down on the floor at her feet, then rose and waited expectantly.

"When your head mage, Thomas Monahan, and his woman were pushed into Eudae, preceding them went an *Atrika* named Ashe. The humans and the *aeamon* knew him as Erasmus Boyle."

Sarafina nodded. "He was some kind of military leader, wasn't he?"

"Long before he was pulled through the *daaeman* circle by the Duskoff, he had been high in our military, yes. However, he was in our version of prison for crimes against our people at the time he was yanked to Earth."

Sarafina tried not to imagine how horrible the crimes must have been to land an *Atrika* in prison.

"He was murdering women and children for pleasure," Bai answered, perhaps correctly reading her expression.

She screwed her face up. "I didn't need to know that. So, Ashe was pulled through the demon circle and then what?"

Bai recounted the story, explaining that the demon circles that the Duskoff performed were dark magick, blood magick. The warlocks would gather powerful witches from each of the elements and put them in a charmed circle that pulled their magick and life force from their bodies. That helped create a doorway between Earth and Eudae. Through it, they called a *daaeman* who would be tied to them for a time to do their bidding.

The *daaeman* called through always matched the emotional energies of the summoning warlocks. That meant the Duskoff always called *Atrika* through, not *Ytrayi*, *Mandari*, or *Syari*. In addition, the *daaeman* who was called through always matched the power of the witches sacrificed in the circle. The more powerful the witches, the more powerful the *daaeman*.

Erasmus Boyle had been called to Earth from the circle that had killed Mira Hoskins's mother. Boyle was megapowerful. "He lived here until he devised a way to open a doorway to return home," Bai explained.

Sarafina nodded. "He killed six witches to do it." She knew the story.

Bai nodded. "In the course of his quest to return to Eudae, he developed a fascination with Isabelle Novak, whom he decided to use as the last witch to secure the doorway. In order to win her regard, Ashe kidnapped Stefan Faucheux from Gribben and intended to kill him. However, Stefan convinced him to spare his life. Instead, Ashe and Stefan struck a bargain."

She lifted a brow. "A bargain?"

"The warlock formed an alliance with Ashe. Ashe intended to return to Eudae, you see, to urge us to form an interdimensional partnership with the Duskoff, using the portal he had opened. Ashe believed bringing us this partnership would convince us to spare his life."

Sarafina shook her head. She didn't understand. "But that never happened. Thomas and Isabelle wounded Ashe before he limped over to the other side and was beheaded by the *Ytrayi*. Thomas and Isabelle were sucked in after him because the doorway was so unstable and they were there when Ashe was killed. They saw it. Ashe never hooked up with the *Atrika*, so no alliance could ever have been formed between the *Atrika* and the Duskoff."

Bai smiled.

Sarafina fought the urge to tell him to stop. The smile of a *daaeman* was nothing happy. All those teeth didn't warm her heart.

"You are correct," Bai answered. "Before he died, Ashe planted a small bit of *daaeman* magick on Eudae for Stefan, which allowed communication to be sent back and forth through the use of an air witch. Ashe loved his people above all else. He must've deemed the alliance with the warlocks as something of benefit to the *Atrika*." Bai paused. "Indeed, it has been an advantage and will be even more so if Stefan produces the elium."

Sarafina frowned, trying to wrap her mind around it all. Then she remembered the kidnapped air witch from Boston. The one who'd only had enough power to send and receive messages. The woman they'd kept awhile and then simply killed without trying to use in a demon circle.

Had she acted as their telephone?

Sarafina blinked at the implication. "But how did Stefan get the elium?" She shook her head. "For that matter, how did you-all open a doorway between Earth and Eudae and get over here in the first place?"

"Ah, that brings us to *love*. Stefan manipulated Rue, the *Cae* of the *Ytrayi* and the holder of the elium, into believing that he and the Duskoff had kidnapped Claire and intended to kill her. Thus, Stefan led him into opening a doorway in a specific location. Once they did, the Duskoff was ready for him. It was a trap, you see."

"So they extracted the elium and killed Rue?"

Bai shook his head. "No. It is my understanding that the Duskoff are keeping the *Cae* alive for the time being and the elium intact within him. I don't know how they have done this or where they are keeping him, but we have been promised his body and the elium once we have accomplished what Stefan requires of us."

"The destruction of the Coven."

Bai nodded sharply. "Yes."

"What do you intend to do with Stefan and the Duskoff once you have what you want?"

Bai blinked. "We are not without honor."

"That's not an answer."

"The *Atrika* do not take well to being placed on a leash and told to heel." His voice had taken on a sharp quality and his eyes flashed red. "Stefan Faucheux has destroyed himself in his quest for revenge. He wanted it badly enough to risk his life and, thus, he will likely lose it."

"You'll kill Stefan, then take the elium from the *Cae*, return to Eudae, and overthrow the *Ytrayi*."

Bai nodded once. "You will see it all because you will return with us . . . with me."

He stepped toward her and she glanced down at the sword. "And what if I say no?"

He bared his very sharp teeth. "You cannot. Your magick is strong and you're perfect in every way to carry my children. You'll return to Eudae and do that."

"How many other wives do you have?"

He looked surprised. "You will be my only one."

"How will I carry your children? Your blood is acidic." The thought of carrying an acidic *daaeman* child in her belly made her shudder, not to mention the mental picture of how it might get in there.

"There are ways," he replied calmly. "Our ancestors bred children on humans in ancient times through the use of—"

"Yes, yes, I know. It's how elemental witches came into existence."

"The concept is much the same."

"What if I'm in love with someone else?"

He roared and Sarafina almost wet herself. "Don't speak to me of love. *Love* is for children. Love only gets people in trouble, like it got the *Cae* of the *Ytrayi* in trouble."

She couldn't argue with that last part.

He closed his eyes for a moment and drew a deep, steadying breath, once again trying to master his emotions. Bai reached out to her. "Now come. Let's get to know each other a little while we wait."

Oh, hell *no.*

Sarafina scooped the sword from the floor and ran for the door. She'd spent an entire day exploring this piece of land; surely she could find a place to hide.

Behind her Bai roared again. His boots clomped on the concrete as he chased her.

Only she'd better hurry.

Good God, this was worse than nightmares she had as a child. The monster in her closet was real and it wanted to do a whole lot more than just kill her.

THIRTY

❦

THE SENSATION OF STEFAN'S THROAT SQUEEZING between Theo's hands was pleasing. Especially since the action stopped such phrases like, "Bai has taken Sarafina to Eudae." Those were words he never wanted to hear and could not believe were true.

Stefan's eyes bulged and he scrabbled at Theo's forearms, under far too much duress to even consider calling fire. Theo was armed with plenty of earth charms that countered fire, anyway. In the paper-rock-scissors game of elemental magick, strong earth magick usually won out over flame.

They were somewhere near the Conservatory. In the foyer, the *Atrika* and the Duskoff were still in battle with the Coven witches. The blue ball was still shooting off sparks of power-stealing magick. Even this far into the building Theo had to dodge them from time to time.

His primary concern was making sure Stefan didn't live through the day.

"Too bad you sent away your pet demon, isn't it, Stefan?" Theo growled. "Looks like you need someone to protect you from me."

Two huge hands landed on his shoulders and pulled him backward. Theo landed on his side, hard, while Stefan coughed and choked. Looking up, Theo had a half a second to see an *Atrika* standing over him before he had to roll to the side to avoid a blast of demon magick.

Guess he'd spoken too soon.

"Kill . . . him," Stefan gasped, holding his throat and staring at Theo with razor-slit eyes.

Theo bolted, grabbing his sword from the floor and whirling to face his demonic adversary, a hulking blond *Atrika* who looked like he enjoyed bone crunching as one of his hobbies.

The *Atrika* rushed him, gathering power, and Theo moved to the right, dodging a blast and cutting upward with his blade. He hit his objective, the demon's thigh. The wound popped and snapped. Acidic blood dripped while the creature roared in pain. Apparently, this one hadn't taken the caplium that would partially protect him from copper. That was cocky of the *daaeman* and very good news for Theo.

The *daaeman* recovered fast, though, and lunged at him, catching Theo around the waist with a roar and whirling him around to crash into the wall. A hard wave of pain slammed through Theo's body. The demon's acidic blood dripped onto Theo's thigh and made him bellow. Burning agony sank deep into his skin.

Gripping the sword's handle tightly, he brought it up and slammed it into the side of the demon's head. The *Atrika* released him and turned away, staggering. Theo slumped to the floor for a moment, then forced himself back up to fight again.

Magick rose fast and hard and Theo moved to the side, avoiding the bolt that followed. It burned a hole in the wall right where he'd been standing a moment before.

Theo turned and slashed with his blade, only narrowly missing the head of the *daaeman*. Before Theo could even take another breath, the *daaeman* hefted him up with two hands and held him over his head like he weighed nothing.

Stefan sprawled on the steps with a grin on his face as the *Atrika* tried to snap Theo in two like a dry branch. Theo's spine cracked and he bellowed from the sharp wave of pain.

Gods, Sarafina. He should have told her how he felt about her when he had the chance.

Then the thought was gone, replaced by a red haze of pain as the *Atrika* broke him in half.

* * *

BAI CAUGHT HER IN THE WOODS. HE FELL ON TOP OF her, rolling her into the leaves underneath a tall pine tree. The needles stuck into her skin, but it was only a breath of annoyance compared to the enraged, red-eyed *Atrika* pinning her down.

How could she possibly hope to defeat a being that had the capacity to bend space and time? She didn't have a prayer.

Pushing that negative thought from her mind with a healthy dose of rage, she fought him like she imagined any bar brawler would do—throwing punches, kicking, screaming. She figured she was pretty safe. After all, he wasn't going to damage his future children's mother, right?

His hands clamped down on her upper arms and his huge body weighted hers into stillness. "Stop." He growled. "Don't force me to do something I will regret."

"You couldn't do anything worse than taking me from my world and forcing yourself on me, Bai. That's worse than death for me!"

"I could kill the one you claim to love. I could do it while you watched." He bared his teeth. "It would give me pleasure."

She went absolutely motionless. "You leave him alone." The words came out thin and shuddering with terror. They sounded as weak as she felt.

"If that's what it takes to break you, I will do it." He growled again, leaning in close to her face. She wanted to gag from the stench of his breath—rotted meat—but bit it back with effort. "Because I do intend to break you."

She struggled against him to no avail. The man outweighed her by an entire person. "Bastard." It was pathetic, but it was all she could do. Her stomach had turned to a wad of frozen dough.

Contorting enough to unsheathe her syringe, she brought it up, slammed the needle deep into his side, and pushed the plunger down. Then she held her breath.

Please, let it work.

Bai laughed. "*Vae* Sarafina, do you think me stupid? I learned from my predecessor's mistakes. I have taken enough caplium to protect me against even a direct injection of charmed copper."

Well, that was just great.

"I think it's time we cement our relationship." His face dipped toward hers.

In her mind that translated into . . . well, a very bad thing. She couldn't even think the word when it pertained to this being.

And it *wasn't* happening.

She did what Theo had told her to never do. She yanked a huge hunk of power from her seat and exploded it between herself and Bai, using the technique Claire had taught her to get past a demon's natural shields, while also protecting herself from the magickal backlash.

Fire arced, pushing Bai backward. The scent of burning *daaeman* flesh made her gag and this time she couldn't suppress it. Groping for her sword, she pushed to her feet to run while she had a chance. She staggered, fell, caught herself one-handed in some dead leaves, and pushed back up. Her chest felt on fire.

Bai was rolling on his back, groaning as if in severe pain.

Pain arced through her, too. Staggering and falling to the ground for a second time, she gasped in agony, clutching her chest and crawling in the deadfall for a few moments before forcing herself to her feet. She'd just tossed everything she had on the table and it probably wouldn't be enough.

Sarafina forced herself to run, even as her head swam. All she wanted in the world was to pass out, but passing out now would ensure her defeat. Gripping the sword, she ran into the woods, headed toward the road. It was late afternoon, still light outside. Maybe she could reach the road and flag down a car. Once she was in the company of a human, she might be safe.

Maybe.

Her shoes crunching on twigs and leaves as she raced toward her destination, she tried not to think about what might be happening back at the Coven. She tried not to think about what might be happening to Theo.

A sob escaped her. All she could do now was concentrate on escaping Bai. She had to take this moment by moment.

Just as she reached the small lane that led from the main part of the land to the road, she heard a *whoosh*, *pop*, behind her. Suddenly, Bai was there. He'd jumped from his last destination to here, probably figuring where she'd be headed. His face and arms were badly burned, the fabric of his shirt curled and melted. Yet she could see he was already healing.

The bastard.

He reached for her, but she swung her sword first. The tip of the blade sliced his throat. Acidic blood gushed, but it wasn't a deep enough cut to send him down. All it did was piss him off.

Bai stood for a moment, stunned, his hand to his throat, blood seeping between his fingers. Then he fixed his gaze on her and growled low.

Sarafina stepped back and tripped on a fallen branch. Using the tip of the sword on the ground to maintain her balance, she continued backward. Bai advanced on her, power gathering around him like dark clouds.

Daaeman magick sizzled and sparked in the space around his body. Sarafina was certain it was enough to kill her where she stood. Perhaps he'd decided she was more trouble than she was worth.

The power exploded and Sarafina dove to the side, literally leaping into the air as though she thought she could fly. She came down hard on her side and rolled away from the *daaeman*, coming to her feet still gripping the sword. Thank God for all the training Theo had given her.

Every square centimeter of her body ached.

She'd missed the killing blast, but Bai still leapt on her. His blood dripped onto her chest and she screamed, fighting against him. It was like trying to beat up a brick wall. She gouged his eye, which fortunately was not a brick wall—it was soft, squishy, and vulnerable. Digging deep, she took advantage.

Bai yowled and pushed away from her. She sprang to her feet and swung the sword, cutting deeply into his side. The *daaeman* roared and backhanded her. Sarafina went sprawling to the ground again, pain exploding through her face.

The *Atrika* followed her, looking as though he intended to simply rip her apart and bypass magick completely.

Seeing an opportunity to end this right now, Sarafina angled her sword upward. Bai fell heavily against the tip, his momentum driving the hilt deeper into his body than Sarafina could have ever hoped to achieve on her own.

She let go of the handle as Bai rolled away from her, the sword still deeply embedded in him. He came to a rest on his side in the deadfall. His body twitched and shuddered, low moans coming from between his thin, white lips. Blood coursed from his wounds, making a dark and smoky puddle in the dirt.

Sarafina also lay on the ground, her breathing coming fast and shallow. Pain had blossomed in her seat and was enhanced by the injuries from the fight—the acid burn, the bruises and cuts she'd sustained. There wasn't a square inch on her that didn't hurt, and blood—her own—had dripped onto her shirt and pants.

Her magick was tapped, gone. Her capacity to do physical battle was also gone. If Bai wasn't dead, if he pulled a horror movie monster move and got up now, she was done for.

When Bai no longer made a move or any sound, she forced herself up onto her feet. Dragging herself to Bai, she saw that the copper blade was still stabbed through his gut. Blood caked the wound on his throat. His eyes were open, but unseeing.

Sarafina knew from Micah's book that the *Atrika* would go into a coma if they were badly injured. It was how they healed severe wounds and regenerated. Was Bai in one of those healing comas now?

The only way to be totally sure he was dead was to cut off his head, but the sword was *in* the *Atrika*. She supposed she could go get one from the building. There were more in the basement.

God, she didn't want to cut off his head. All she really wanted to do was pass out.

Her body protesting every moment, she walked back toward the building. She didn't want to, but she had to. It was the only way to make sure he never came after her again. It was the only way to ensure she ever enjoyed another night's sleep.

As she approached the building, she remembered the cave. When she'd been in it, she'd felt like something— someone—had been in there with her. At the time she'd thought it had been her imagination, and then Theo had shown up and she'd been distracted.

She went into the building and found another sword. On impulse, she grabbed a flashlight, too. She couldn't produce so much as a flicker of fire right now.

On the way out, she turned toward the cave and stood, considering her options. Something about that place nagged at her.

The cave was not far from the building and she didn't have enough energy to walk back to the *daaeman*, behead him, and then walk back.

What to do? Behead a demon or explore a cave? Decisions, decisions.

Knowing from Micah's book that she had some time before Bai woke from his coma, if that's what it was, she turned and walked toward the cave. It was probably nothing, but she needed to check it out—no matter how much she really didn't want to go spelunking today.

She entered the cave and made her way into the recesses, taking a few turns here and there. There was only one way through as the passageways were just big enough for one adult witch.

The only good part about being in the nasty, damp cave was that if Bai came out of his coma thing prematurely, he wouldn't be able to find her. The bad thing was that she half expected to stumble across a bear or some other wild animal in here, or worse—a pile of dead bodies or something. It was on Duskoff land, after all.

Finally, she reached a largish cavern-type room. Having freaked herself out by that time and finding nothing but rock inside, she turned around to leave. That's when her light caught something up against one of the walls.

She stopped and turned, shining her flashlight on the object once more. It looked like . . . a casket. Somebody's coffin.

Oh, hell no.

Sarafina wavered on her feet for a moment. Her head was telling her to go have a closer look, but the rest of her body screamed at her to run away fast.

Her head won and she forced her body to obey.

She hadn't come this far to not investigate the thing that had piqued her senses. Apparently, this is what she'd come in here for.

She inched closer and closer to the shiny black casket, hoping like hell the top wouldn't open and a vampire or something wouldn't pop out. Really, she'd expire where she stood.

As she grew closer, a humming sound reached her ears. Walking around to one side, she shined the flashlight at the back of the casket and saw electrical cords hooking the thing up and running straight into the stone wall.

Well, that was odd.

Frowning, she reached out and touched the brass handle on the side. Maybe it wasn't a casket, after all. It was pretty big to be one, unless the person inside was a giant. Or . . .

A *daaeman.*

An *Ytrayi?*

Rue.

The thought spurred her to push the top open. It wouldn't budge. Then she saw the latches on the side. She undid the latches and cold steam poured from the edges of the top— like dry ice. Gathering her courage, after all, she'd killed an *Atrika* single-handedly—well, maybe—she pushed the lid the rest of the way open.

Inside lay a man. Easily seven feet tall, broad-shouldered,

blond, with a chiseled, handsome face. It was a *daaeman*, all right. Sarafina would bet money she'd found Rue, the *Ytrayi* breed's missing *Cae*.

With him, she'd found the elium.

The only problem was that both the *daaeman* and the elium were frozen solid.

THIRTY-ONE

SARAFINA STARTED, COMING AWAKE WHERE SHE'D fallen asleep propped up against the cave wall. Or maybe she'd passed out, she wasn't sure.

She'd opened the casket all the way and yanked all the electrical cords out in the back, probably destroying thousands of dollars worth of equipment. Eventually, the dry ice had evaporated.

Of course, she had no idea what she was doing. She'd paced back and forth in front of the frozen *Ytrayi*, wondering about alien metabolisms and trying to recall every science fiction movie or book she'd ever seen or read.

But what was she supposed to do? She was stuck in a cave in the middle of Kentucky trying to thaw out a demon with a weapon inside him. Things didn't get much stranger or less comprehensible than that. She could only do what she thought was right and hope for the best.

She especially hoped that Rue didn't kill her if he woke up. Boy, that would really suck. She was so close to getting her life back.

After that, she'd sat down to rest only for a moment, intending to get up and go take care of her grisly task before Bai woke up. Instead, her body had decided she needed to sleep—or she'd passed out. Probably the latter.

She wasn't sure how long she'd been out, but it couldn't have been long. Her flashlight wasn't any dimmer and flashlight batteries went dim fast.

Something scraped in the coffin and moaned. Every hair on her body stood up. She scrambled to her feet and cautiously approached it. The *daaeman* was still lying motionless, his eyes closed. Slowly, he opened them and winced at the light. She directed the flashlight away from his face.

"I'm Sarafina. I-I'm on your side." She wanted to establish that right off the bat. "I'm a Coven witch and I know Claire."

He blinked at the name and tried to sit up. "Claire? Is she all right?"

Sarafina's breath hitched. "Honestly, I don't know, sir. The Coven's been attacked by warlocks and the *Atrika*. She's there now, in Chicago. I'm here in Kentucky where they've been keeping you." She paused. "Are you all right?"

She needed for him to be all right *soon*.

"The *Atrika*? How did the *Atrika* get Earthside?" He swore low in some strange language. "All I remember is finding out the Duskoff kidnapped Claire. I jumped through a portal to find her and was hit by an overwhelming amount of magick as soon as I was Earthside. *Impossible*." He shook his head. "What's going on?"

Sarafina told him everything. *Fast.* Luckily, Rue figured out the gravity of the situation and pulled himself out of the coffin. He was shaky on his feet, looked a little green, and was soaked with clammy water. But given the strength of the *Ytrayi*, she had no doubt he'd recover fast.

Rue took her hands in his. "You're wounded."

"A little." She hesitated. "Okay, a lot. I just fought an *Atrika*."

"I can't restore your magick, but I can make you feel better and heal a few of your wounds."

"I would appreciate that."

Warmth emanated from the hands of the *Cae* into her body, spreading out and soothing the sore and injured parts of her. Her seat still felt barren and cold when he was done, but the acid burns and the massive bruise on her face where she'd been backhanded felt nearly healed.

Right before they jumped to the Coven, they made a stop at Bai's body. This time Sarafina only wanted to vomit a little. Apparently, jumping through a fold in the space/time continuum, or however they did it, got easier with practice.

Of course, the sight of Bai's body made her want to vomit a lot.

"Did I kill him?" she asked, staring down at his mangled form with her hand pressed to her mouth. She could hardly believe she'd done all that violence.

Rue flicked his wrist and Bai flamed and then turned to ash. "I don't know, but now he's dead for sure."

They jumped again, this time to Chicago.

THEO'S SPINE CRACKED.

Unbelievable agony shot through his body. He knew this was the end. Having nothing else to lose, he twisted hard in a final, desperate bid for life, using his weight to pitch forward.

It broke the hold of the *daaeman*.

Off balance, the beast threw him forward. Theo landed hard, his breath knocked out of him. His sword went clattering and sliding across the marble floor.

Theo pushed to his feet, but not before the *Atrika* was on him again. Together they rolled, fighting until they hit the wall of the corridor behind them.

Forgoing magick altogether, Theo gave him a hard uppercut to the chin, stunning the creature. He extricated himself and faced the *Atrika*, ready to fight once again. Raising power, he tossed it at the *daaeman*, who only partially blocked it. The beast staggered backward, at the same time gathering a bolt of *daaeman* magick to launch at him.

Like all the Coven witches, Theo was growing weary and his magickal stores were badly depleted. Soon he'd have little power left to shield himself. Soon the *Atrika* would simply wear them all into defeat, and one by one the magick ball of death would pick them off. The warlocks could just sweep them up after that, like empty, bland refuse strewn on the floor.

He blocked the blast and rolled to the side, coming back to his feet to see something at the end of the corridor that he shouldn't be seeing.

Rue, the *Cae* of the *Ytrayi*, stood there . . . and Sarafina was beside him.

"Theo!" Sarafina cried, glimpsing him.

He blinked.

Something hard hit him from behind. He went sprawling forward, catching himself on the floor with his palms and rolling quickly to one side to avoid another blow.

"Theo!" Sarafina screamed again.

He didn't have time to answer. He raised power—the little of it he had left—and readied it to throw at the *Atrika* coming at him.

Distantly, in the foyer, the intensity of the ruckus increased. Sarafina was still at the end of the corridor, but Rue was gone. It was only something Theo noticed out of the periphery of his awareness since he was pretty busy dodging a bolt of demon magick. Perhaps Rue had jumped to the foyer. That would definitely cause a stir.

Theo grabbed his sword from the floor and swung around, hitting the demon in the chest. The *Atrika* moved back, stunned by the surprise attack, and Theo charged forward before the demon could regain his ability to put up an offensive. He caught the demon right in the neck.

Theo whirled, avoiding the acidic spray of blood. Gods, he was getting better at this. The body fell thickly to the marble floor.

Theo rested by the beheaded body, bent over with his palms on his knees, his sword held loosely in one hand. He needed a nap.

"Theo!"

He raised his head to see Sarafina running toward him. He dropped the blade and caught her, swinging her up into his arms. Her clothes were ripped, bloodstained, and dirty. Bloody scrapes marked her arms, legs, and face. A yellow-green bruise bloomed on her cheekbone.

All Theo wanted in the world was to kiss every single inch of her precious body. He wanted to spend the rest of the week, the month, the decade . . . his life just with Sarafina.

Perfect bliss and contentment filled him at the sensation of her in his arms. He nuzzled her hair and inhaled the scent of her that overrode the smell of blood, death, *daaeman* magick, and battle.

"What happened?" he murmured near her ear.

All around them rose the sound of renewed battle, but at the moment they were together, enjoying a sense of peace he wanted to expand into forever.

Casting his gaze toward the stairs, he saw that Stefan had disappeared.

She pushed away enough to see his face. "Bai took me to Kentucky. After I managed to get away from him, I found Rue in the cave. Do you remember the cave?"

He nodded.

"Stefan had rigged it so he could keep Rue frozen in there. It was the only way to keep him subdued, I guess."

"Is Bai dead?"

"As a doornail." She winced. "A really crispy one."

Relief filled his chest with a sudden burst of lightness.

Something rocketed past them and crashed into the wall behind them. They could only drag their eyes away from each other for the barest moment to see that it had been a chair.

Blue light flashed out of the corner of his eye. Theo pushed Sarafina to the floor. The blast exploded on the remains of the chair.

"We can talk about this later," said Theo.

"Uh-huh," answered Sarafina with wide eyes.

They got to their feet and made their way out to the foyer. There, right where Stefan had been standing with his blue ball of doom, was an interdimensional doorway.

Theo had seen one only once before. It was not something you forgot. Light flickered and pulsed around the portion of matter that had been twisted and altered to form a bridge between Earth and Eudae.

Through it came the *Ytrayi* in a blessedly heavy stream. The *Atrika* didn't look very happy to see them, either.

The blue ball pulsed in Rue's hands, no longer emitting the magick-killing shots that stole elemental power. Theo and Sarafina watched as he crushed it like a ball of tinfoil into nonexistence.

"Where's Stefan?" Sarafina said beside him.

What a good question.

"The bastard's not getting away again." Theo growled. He'd slipped away after his father, William Crane, had been killed at Duskoff International. He'd escaped from Gribben *twice*. No way was he running away from his punishment this time.

Theo knew that Sarafina's magick had been tapped out, probably from fighting Bai. He could feel that raw, empty spot in her. Why she wasn't flat on her back was a mystery. Looking around at the carnage in the room, Theo realized that many of the Coven witches didn't have any stores of magick left, either as a result of the blue ball or from the battle.

Power exploded near them as the *Ytrayi* and the *Atrika* locked horns. It was nice to have some reinforcements.

"Come on," said Theo, dragging Sarafina by the hand down a corridor. "I want you somewhere safe."

The library was empty but for Micah and Isabelle. Micah sat in one of the chairs near Thomas's desk. Theo didn't have to guess what the problem was.

Micah raised his head momentarily to look at him, then dropped it again.

"Can you get it back?" Sarafina asked, going to his side and laying a hand on his upper arm.

Isabelle looked at her and shook her head.

Shit.

"Stay here, okay?" Theo said to Sarafina. She'd be safe in here. If something did happen, Isabelle was ready to defend. "I'm going to find Stefan."

Theo made his way out of the room and back into the fray beyond the sanctuary. The *Ytrayi* were making quick work of the *Atrika*. They were destroying the Coven, but at least they'd probably win in the end.

Now . . . if he was a slimy, cowardly warlock, where would he be?

Theo was betting Stefan was hiding somewhere, if he hadn't already fled the Coven once Rue and the *Ytrayi* had shown up to rub his nose in shit.

Hmmm. There were lots of places to hide in the Conservatory.

He made his way there, dodging demon battle as he went. The warlocks all seemed to have fled or were defeated. The Coven witches were trying to help the wounded and were rounding up the warlocks they could to throw into Gribben.

The Conservatory, other than having its water all drawn out by the water witches, was largely untouched. It was a change from the last battle that had occurred in here, which had destroyed about fifty percent of the place.

Sounds came from the back of the Coven—sounds of a fight. Theo ran in that direction, sword still clenched in his hand.

At the back of the Conservatory, Theo found Jack and Stefan in an old-fashioned knock-down, drag-out fight. Kind of fitting, since in an odd way, they were brothers. Their magick had been tapped out and Stefan's *Atrika* bodyguards were long gone.

Theo pulled a spell from his badly sapped reserves, making his tats tingle, and threw it at the warlock. It hit Stefan dead-on and the warlock flew backward to land in a bush, where he lay motionless. "That's for Sarafina, you fucking bastard."

Jack collapsed to the ground and drew a ragged breath, bowing his head. "Theo, man, I'm so happy to see you."

Theo offered him his hand and Jack pulled himself to his feet. Together they looked at Stefan, out cold in the bushes.

"What the hell do you want to do with him?" asked Jack.

Theo stalked to him, sword in hand, but killing someone wasn't his first desire, and never when they were lying defenseless. His hand clenched on the sword handle as Theo tried to control his temper.

Then it hit him.

Theo turned toward Jack. "I know the very best possible punishment for this slime."

THIRTY-TWO

 ❧

Sarafina wiped away a tear, watching Isabelle stroke Micah's hair. She couldn't imagine what it would be like to lose her power the way Micah had. Now so many of the Coven witches were dealing with it.

"Isabelle."

Isabelle looked up from Micah's side. "Mother?"

Catalina stood in the doorway, propped up by Thomas. Her normally tanned face was pale, and she looked her age for once.

"She was hit," said Thomas tightly.

"Oh, no." Isabelle rose and went to her mother, allowing her to lean against her as she led her to the couch against one wall. "Damn it," she whispered.

Thomas stepped into the room. His clothes were ripped and blood marked him. He had some nasty acid burns along one arm, but he was alive and he still had his magick.

"It's over," Thomas said. "The *Cae* and the *Ytrayi* have defeated the *Atrika* and are now taking them back to Eudae." He smiled faintly. "We won."

But it had cost them all greatly. That was written all over his weary face. He didn't need to say it.

"Where's Theo?" Sarafina asked.

Thomas jerked his head toward the foyer. "You should all come."

Isabelle helped Catalina from the room with Thomas.

Sarafina went to Micah. "Would you rather stay here?" she asked softly. "I'll stay with you, if you like."

Micah shook his head and rose. "I'm okay."

That was a lie.

Yet he glanced at her and a smile flickered over his mouth. For a moment he almost looked like the Micah she'd come to know. "I lost my magick, but I still have my life. I still have my freedom. That's enough."

They walked side by side out to the foyer where the *Atrika* were being pushed and thrown unceremoniously through the doorway by very pissed-off *Ytrayi*. Thomas, Isabelle, and Catalina stood near them, watching. Some of the *daaeman* were unconscious, others dead. The rest wore collars around their necks. Sarafina guessed it was the same idea as handcuffs, since the *Atrika* who wore them looked utterly defeated.

It was a good look on them.

Theo stood near the doorway with Jack and Adam, a heap of something at his feet. It took her a moment to realize it was Stefan.

The last of the *Atrika* were sent through the doorway and the *Ytrayi*—some of them badly injured and others carrying unconscious or dead comrades—began to also step through.

Rue was across the room with Claire. Sarafina watched them hug, then come to stand near Thomas.

"Once I told you the day might come when we would need to form an alliance," said the *Cae*.

Thomas nodded curtly. "You were right. That day did come."

"It's time we truly open up the pathways of communication, don't you agree?"

A muscle worked in Thomas's jaw. "Yes."

"I propose Claire to act as our liaison. I have devised a way to more easily open a doorway and can give Claire this ability as well. She will act as—"

"Ambassador," Claire volunteered.

Rue inclined his head. "And maybe she can just come for a visit now and then, too."

Sarafina met Claire's eyes briefly and suppressed a smile.

"If she chooses," answered Thomas.

Rue glanced around at the ruins of the Coven. "Do you require more diamonds to repair the damage?"

Thomas shook his head and grinned very slightly. "What you gifted us with before has been well invested. We have enough to repair the Coven and run it for the next hundred years. Thank you for your offer."

Theo had thrown Stefan over his shoulder. He walked over with Adam and Jack. "I was tempted to kill Stefan, but I thought up something better than death, if Rue agrees."

"Tell me," said Rue.

"Take the warlock back to Eudae with you. Lock him up, make him a slave, do whatever you want with him." Theo paused, his expression growing dark. "Just make sure he's miserable every damn second of his life and can never get back here."

"Do you want a pet warlock, Rue?" Thomas asked, with a brow raised and a smile playing around his lips.

Rue rubbed his chin. "I'm sure we can find something useful for him to do on Eudae."

Thomas put his hand on Micah's shoulder. "Ultimately, it's Micah's call. What do you think we should do with him?"

Micah's face took on a brutal expression. He stared hard at Stefan before answering. His hand was white on the handle of his sword. "Lock him in Gribben, send him to Eudae, put him out with the trash—I don't care." He paused, a muscle working in his jaw. "Just make sure he's got no magick before you do it. He should suffer the fate he's inflicted on us."

Rue opened his hand and a blue orb popped to life above his palm. All of them took a step back. Fear clenched Sarafina's stomach at the mere sight of it, and she was sure she wasn't the only one.

Stefan roused on Theo's shoulder, as if somehow knowing the fate that glowed so deceptively and innocently in Rue's hand.

Theo tossed him to the floor.

Stefan exploded in a flurry of French cusswords. At least Sarafina was pretty sure they were French cusswords.

Theo stepped forward and pinned him to the floor with one booted foot on Stefan's chest. "Watch your language."

"Fermes ta gueule et laisses moi me lever!" He shook his

head in agitation and switched to English, since French wasn't getting him very far. "Shut the fuck up and let me go."

Clearly, he had no fire left or he would have used it already.

"No." Theo pressed down and smiled grimly. "And don't make me charm you again."

Thomas stepped forward and looked down at the warlock. "You're defeated, Stefan. This time you're defeated forever. The *Atrika* have been sent back to Eudae by the *Ytrayi*, and the warlocks you brought are either dead or in Gribben. The rest of the Duskoff . . ." Thomas paused and a secret smile passed over his lips. "Well, the Duskoff are soon to be no more."

"What—" Stefan started.

"Shut up."

Even Sarafina wondered about that last comment and the secret smile that had accompanied it.

"Your punishment for kidnapping Rue, allying with the *Atrika*, and attacking the Coven, for using *daaeman* magick against us is—"

"Let me guess," Stefan sneered. "*Death.*"

"No, actually. Your punishment is to be divested of your magick and to live out the rest of your life on Eudae." Thomas smiled again and this time it wasn't so secret. "As a slave to the *Ytrayi*. Somehow I don't think they'll treat you as well as they did Claire."

"You're being neutered," Jack interjected.

"And banished," added Isabelle.

"You can't." Stefan began to fight against Theo. "Just kill me. You can't take away my power. You can't!"

"And yet you were ready to take away the power of others?" asked Thomas calmly.

Stefan's countenance darkened. "You killed my father."

"*I* killed your father," said Mira.

"You're making it hard for the Duskoff to exist," Stefan said. "You're always in our way."

"I'm growing bored," said Rue. The ball flamed in his palm and Stefan's eyes widened.

"No!"

WITCH FURY ◆ 273

The ball left Rue's hand and shot straight into Stefan's chest. The warlock's spine arched and his face twisted in agony. A keening sound erupted from Stefan's throat. It was one she'd heard often during the last few hours, signaling the loss of something precious and beautiful. Something Stefan had misused, something he'd taken from others.

The world would be a safer place with Stefan magickless. The world would be a safer place without him in it at all.

All the people who looked down at Stefan did so with solemn expressions. This was no celebration.

Wordlessly, Rue scooped the warlock up and turned toward the doorway. Stefan fought and bellowed in outrage, but he had no hope of escaping an *Ytrayi*. The *Cae* just gripped him in strong hands, turned around once to meet Claire's eyes, then stepped through.

The sound of Stefan calling, "*No!*" still rang through the silent foyer even after the doorway winked out of existence.

No one moved or said anything for several moments. Then the murmuring began, shuffling, talking. Stefan was gone and the Duskoff defeated—maybe permanently.

She raised her head and her gaze met Theo's. He looked worse than she did. Burns from demon blood marked his clothes and, in places, his skin. His shirt and jeans were ripped. He had scratches, scrapes, and bruises all over his face and body. His lip was split.

Something in her chest clenched. What would happen between them now? The look on his face was cold, distant. It was the same look he'd worn when they first met.

Maybe it was the end of them, too.

She forced herself to hold his gaze and not look away, even though her heart was breaking and that's all she wanted to do.

Well, at least Bai was dead. She could go home now, go back to her apartment to try to pick up the tatters of her life. She had some colorful pieces to weave in, too. Her magick. The Coven. Her new friends. Overall, her life was richer than it had been before.

Of course, it could be even richer.

Suppressing a wave of sadness for what she suspected she

was about to lose, she reached out her hand to Theo. "Come on, let's get you fixed up."

"STOP IT," SARAFINA SCOLDED HIM AS SHE APPLIED salve to a cut on his abdomen.

Pain burst through Theo anew. "It stings." He growled, flinching away.

"Don't be a baby. I want these wounds clean before the fire witches do a healing."

Sarafina still didn't have any juice left and wouldn't for a while, so she'd have Doctor Oliver's nurses treat him. They were pretty busy at the moment, and he could wait. There were others with injuries a lot worse than his.

Sarafina, he'd learned, had been healed by Rue. Now she was showered and had changed her clothes. Aside from having her seat tapped, her wounds were minor.

She finished and threw the cotton swab onto the bathroom counter. He was leaning up against the sink. Sarafina halted for a moment and sighed. "Okay, I'll pack my stuff and be out of your hair. No need to stay now that Bai is gone."

Theo studied her ferociously, a tangle of emotions twisting in his gut. He couldn't get any words out.

She turned and walked to the doorway, then suddenly turned. Tears shone in her eyes. *Fuck.* Sarafina pointed a finger at him. "And no booty calls. I couldn't stand to sleep with you again, knowing you—" She swallowed and shook her head. "Never mind."

Theo stared at the empty doorway for several moments, not really feeling the pain of his injuries anymore. He pushed away from the counter and caught his reflection in the mirror over the sink.

He couldn't do this. He couldn't let her leave like this.

He turned and stalked out of the room, finding her in the hallway, headed toward the door.

"I can't stay here another moment. I'll come back for my stuff," she said, not looking at him. She finally raised her gaze and there was anger there, a challenge. "Don't think you're chasing me away from the Coven completely. I'll be here a lot, so you'd better get used to it."

And every time he saw her, it would be torture.

She pushed past him and made a beeline for the door. "Come on, Grosset. Let's go." Grosset jumped down from the couch and went to her side.

"Sarafina."

She held a hand up. "I don't want to hear it." She turned, her eyes snapping with fire. "And if you ask me if we can be friends, the answer is no." She swore. It was one of the few times he'd ever heard her use a cussword. "I can't be friends with you when I . . . I . . ." She made a disgusted sound and opened the door.

"Sarafina, I have things to say. Sometimes love isn't enough. You wouldn't be happy with me. Eventually, I would ruin our relationship and make you miserable—"

She whirled. "Oh, bullshit! Theo, that's such a load of crap." She stalked toward him, door ajar. "First off, don't you think I know life with you wouldn't be all cream and sugar? You're stubborn and you've got a temper. You're dark and uncommunicative and moody as hell. You're not exactly puppies and sunshine."

"That's why—"

She held up a hand. "Oh, you'd better stop right there and let me speak my piece." Her slight Southern accent had grown thicker with her emotion. "You need to give me some credit for knowing my own mind and emotions. I'm much more familiar with them than you are, and it pisses me off that you presume to know what's best for me."

"Sarafina." He stopped, not knowing what else to say. She just didn't understand.

A tear slipped down her cheek. "Anyway, all that is just more bull. The real reason you don't want to stay with me is because you're scared. Every time you've let yourself get close enough to trust someone, they've either let you down or they've died. Your parents, Colleen, Ingrid. You won't even let the Coven witches in, right, Theo? You can't even risk their friendship because it's too much of an emotional investment. It's just fear, that's all it is." She extended her hands. "I'm here and I love you. I would do anything for you, but you're just going to let it all go, let me go, because you're frightened."

Sarafina stood there for a moment as if willing him to deny it all, to say something—anything. But all the words were stuck in his throat. Finally, she turned and walked out the door, Grosset at her heels.

THIRTY-THREE

❧

"COME ON, SARAFINA, YOU LOVE A GOOD *MOJITO*." Maria singsonged her entreaty and waggled the short glass filled with her favorite cocktail in front of her. "And you know I make them the best."

Sarafina eyed the drink. What she really wanted to do was get blindingly drunk so she could forget Theo, if just for a little while. Otherwise she was going to eat the entire pint of Cherry Garcia in her freezer.

In the last twenty-four hours she'd finally cried. All those tears she couldn't seem to shed for Rosemary after she'd died had arrived with interest. The grief had finally come in an unstoppable flood of deep cleansing, cathartic emotion— the kind that comes all the way from the depths of your stomach. Despite the headache she'd had when it was over, it had felt good to finally vent.

Some of the tears had been for the Coven's fallen—the ones who'd perished and the ones who'd lost their magick in the battle.

Some of those tears had been for Theo, too. Maybe even more than a few.

She shook her head. "No, thanks, Maria. Go on and enjoy."

"Oh, honey, I know it's bad when you turn down a *mojito*." Maria stared at her for a moment, then whirled and walked to the kitchen, putting the drink on the breakfast bar. "*Dios*, if I ever see that guy who played you during such a vulnerable time in your life, I swear I'll beat him up." She turned, a hand on her hip. "You still haven't told me what happened."

Sarafina uncurled her leg from beneath her and pulled her sleeve down to hide one of the small puckered scars she had from being touched by demon blood. Grosset was in the kitchen crunching kibble. It was nice to be home, back in the cocoon of her world, pre-abduction. Even though everything seemed a bit odd—a bit surreal.

"He's not a bad guy, Maria. You don't have to beat him up."

"I'd beat up any man that hurt you, honey." Maria wagged a finger in Sarafina's face, then flounced down on the couch beside her.

"Did you beat up Alex?"

Maria waved a hand dismissively. "Alex didn't hurt you. You two were like a carton of milk a week past the expiration date. That relationship needed to be thrown out. Hell, you hooked up with that Theo guy not even a week afterward, right?" She paused and gave her a meaningful look. "But this guy . . . well, I can tell you love him, and he broke your heart."

Sarafina ripped her gaze from her friend's face. "Maybe a little."

Maria made a scoffing sound. "Maybe a lot. Anyway, let's stop talking about him. You'll tell me what happened when you're ready, though, won't you?"

Sarafina nodded. A highly edited version, anyway.

"'Cause that was not like you at all," Maria continued. "You can be impulsive sometimes, but . . ." She whistled. "I want to know the scoop on this guy for sure."

"He's something else, all right." Sarafina pursed her lips and swallowed hard. She just wasn't ready to talk about him yet.

After a moment, Maria said, "So are you going to take your full leave of absence, or are you coming back to the office soon?"

Sarafina chewed the edge of her thumb, trying to figure out how to best answer that. Thomas had offered her a job at the Coven and she wanted to take it, but the thought of having to see Theo so often was making her consider it at length.

The thought of going back to her cubicle now, though, after all that had happened, made her flat-out cringe. Back to all the non-magickals. Back to everyone who had no idea of the secret side of reality. Sarafina wasn't sure she could do it. Yet Maria worked there and Sarafina would miss seeing her every day.

Of course, so did Alex and she wouldn't miss seeing him.

"I don't know yet, Maria. I'm thinking of a career change, actually. I might take the rest of my leave to look around a little and do some thinking."

"I thought you were tight for money."

Thomas had given her some money, saying it was for her help in vanquishing Stefan and the *Atrika*. At first she'd turned it down, but he'd been aggressive about it. Sarafina had enough to float for a while as a result. "Uh, I came into some unexpected cash."

"Did Rosemary leave you some?"

Sarafina didn't answer. She didn't want to lie to her friend. That's what made keeping the Coven's secrets so hard. Sarafina valued Maria's friendship very much and she hated having to hide this part of her life from her.

Just then the doorbell rang, saving her from having to explain.

"I'll get it," said Maria, rising and going to the door.

Theo was on the other side. He looked over Maria's head at Sarafina, and she touched her hair self-consciously, kicking herself for even caring that she hadn't done anything to it today besides wash it. She was wearing her old, washed-many-times jersey pajama pants, a soft sweatshirt, and the barest minimum of makeup. At least she'd taken a shower that morning.

Maria cocked a hip and pointed a finger at Theo. "Listen, Mr. Muscle, if you think you can—"

"Maria, it's okay," Sarafina interrupted.

She turned. "Should I let him in?"

Sarafina smiled and nodded. "Thanks."

Maria shrugged and walked away from the door. "Okay, it's your heart, not mine."

Theo entered the apartment and stood awkwardly near one of the bookshelves near the door, looking at Sarafina. Grosset barked happily and went to him, tail wagging. Theo bent and scratched his head.

"That's my cue to leave," said Maria, gathering her purse. She leaned down and kissed Sarafina's cheek. "If you want to go to Casey's one night, like old times, give me a call. We can drink a *mojito* and scope the men." She said that last bit with a look of scorn at Theo.

"I will."

Maria breezed out the door without another glance at Theo.

He raised an eyebrow. "Mr. Muscle?"

Sarafina suppressed a smile. "She's a good friend, very protective of me." She paused and pulled her sleeve down again. This time it was a defensive gesture, not to hide her scars but to hide herself. She hated feeling so vulnerable in front of him.

"Why are you here, Theo?"

He hesitated, then walked over to her. Lowering his huge body to kneel at her feet, he took her hand in his. "I'm here because I love you, Sarafina. Because I was wrong and you were right." He paused. "You scare the absolute shit out of me, and you have ever since the first day I met you. At first I wanted to simultaneously push you away and bring you nearer. Later on, I just wanted you, body and heart—but I knew it was a mistake. I knew I wasn't the right one for you."

"Stop."

He shook his head. "But it's not that I'm wrong for you, it's that I'm afraid. Afraid I'll push you away or lose you like I've lost everyone else. I don't think I could stand losing you."

"I know." Sarafina licked her lips, emotion rising in her throat. "The question is, can you get beyond it, Theo? Can you take a chance?"

He took a moment to answer. "Here's what I know, Sarafina. I know I love you and that I can't live without you. The last twenty-four hours have been hell. I know I'm willing to do everything I can to hold on to you. I'll be the best partner I can be."

Sarafina gave a little laugh, her eyes filling up with tears. "Does that mean you'll go to the ballet with me?"

He grimaced a little. "I swear to go to the ballet with you."

She laughed again, trying to picture Theo, with all his muscles and tattoos stuffed into a suit, watching men in tights prance across the stage. "You love me that much?"

He moved between her spread thighs and leaned in to brush his lips across hers. "I would do so much more than endure a night at the ballet for you."

"Oh, I have season tickets," she answered brightly, but then her smile faded. She knew he would endure a night at a ballet for her . . . and so much more. After all, he'd risked his life for her. Put himself in the way of a demon for her. He'd wielded a sword to defend her. Sarafina was pretty sure she could live her whole life and never find another man who'd do any of that for her.

She touched her lips to his. "You're not going to disappoint me, Theo. You'd never be able to do that."

Shadows haunted his eyes. He didn't reply.

Her fingers found the hem of his shirt and pushed upward, feeling the hard, warm muscle beneath. "I have the rest of my life to show you that you won't."

"And I have the rest of my life to show you how much I love you."

She gave his lower lip a gentle nip that made a sound of satisfaction roll out of him. She raised a brow. "Then let's get started, shall we?"

Grosset trotted near, gave them a look as if to say, *Oh, no, not again*, then retreated to the kitchen where a soft bed and juicy bone awaited him.

A devilish smile curled over Theo's full lips. He yanked her down a degree on the couch, toward him, and pulled her pants off, exposing her panties. His thumbs slid under the elastic and rested on the tender part of her leg, where her thigh met her inner hip.

Theo's pupils grew larger and darker. His head lowered,

and his lips brushed lightly over hers. Her body quickened for him, falling into that now familiar feeling of erotic anticipation.

"I love this place on your body," he murmured. "Every time I bite it, it makes you moan."

"R-really?" Her tongue had gone dry.

His fingers found the hem of her sweatshirt and pulled it over her head, revealing her lacy black demi bra. At least she'd done something right that morning. "And your breasts. Did you know you make the most adorable little whimpering sound when I suck your nipples?"

"I do?" Her heart was beating faster now.

He nodded slightly, his finger tracing the plump of her cleavage and delving within her bra cup to rasp over one hard nipple. Pleasure shot straight to her sex.

"Uh-huh." He pulled her bra down so that one breast popped out and then leaned in to demonstrate. His hot mouth closed around her nipple and she squirmed a little on the couch, a small sound escaping her.

Oh, yeah, so she did.

Sarafina reached for his jeans. Just the sound of the button coming free and the zipper sliding down was enough to make her sex grow slick. She worked his cock out and stroked it, pushing a guttural groan of pleasure from his throat.

He pulled her off the couch and onto the floor, rolling her beneath him. His fingers found her clit beneath the silky material of her panties and stroked until it grew plump and needy against her hand. All the while he sucked on her nipple, making tendrils of pure want curl through her.

Her hands found the waist of his jeans and pushed them down, totally freeing his cock from its confines. While he hastily kicked his boots off, she pushed his shirt up. Her lips trailed over the dusky, muscled body she revealed, kissing and nipping at his skin.

When they were both finally nude, Theo pressed his warm, hard body down on hers, kneeing her thighs apart and settling between them. "I love you," he murmured, his teeth dragging her lower lip and his fingers trailing through her hair.

He spoke those three little words with more emotion than she'd ever heard from him. He spoke them like she was the dearest and most precious thing he'd ever touched.

Sarafina knew that her life with Theo wouldn't be all roses. Like any relationship, they would have ups and downs they would have to work through. Like any relationship, they would have to put forth effort to keep their love blooming.

But Theo was wrong when he said love wasn't enough. Love was the bedrock. Love was the glue. Everything else was built on that foundation.

Sarafina knew without question they would always have that most forceful of emotions tying them together and getting them through.

"I love you, too," she answered, tears filling her eyes. "So much, Theo. More than I can say."

He moved his hips, pressing against the core of her body, then slipping inside. One long thrust and he was within her—to the root of his cock. Her breath hissed out of her and she bit her lower lip, closing her eyes on a low moan. Having him inside her was beyond heaven. It was right, completely and totally.

Perfect.

He pulled out to the crown and then thrust back in slowly, letting her feel every single inch of him. His gaze found hers and held as he filled her, became a part of her, body and soul.

Nothing. No warlock, no demon, would ever part them again. They were free to be together.

"Theo . . ." A tear slipped from her eyes and meandered down the side of her face to drop to the carpet. "I'm so happy you came back to me."

"And I'll never leave you, Sarafina. You're mine. Just like how all my instincts have been screaming since the day I first saw you."

"They have?"

He pulled out and thrust slowly back in. "Mine, Sarafina. Every last inch of you. Mine to make love to, mine to cherish, mine to protect." He paused. "As I am yours."

"Promise?"

"I promise."

He rose up then and hooked her thighs over his, leveraging his body on hers in a way that suddenly swept all thoughts from her mind but the carnal ones. Her breath hitched in her throat as he pulled out and pushed back in again, forcing the muscles of her sex to stretch under the heavy veined width of his cock. Still he held her gaze, intensifying the intimacy of their joining.

She barely had enough breath left to speak. "And we'll do this on a regular basis, right?"

"Oh, yeah, honey. I like to make you come."

"I like it, too."

His thumb found her clit and rubbed as he thrust in and out of her. Warm, intoxicating pleasure filled her body and tingled through her sex.

"Are you going to come now?" he asked with a slow, devilish smile. He stroked her clit methodically—with just the right amount of pressure and at just the right pace.

"Uh-huh," she murmured. Her eyes closed and her breathing caught. The energy of her impending climax gathered in her body, made her feel replete. Closer and closer she grew to the precipice, until the weight of the sensation growing in her body grew too large for her to contain.

The wave of her climax crashed down over her, sweeping her away into a place where she couldn't think. All she could do was cry out under the force of it, her spine bowing.

Her sex pulsed around the pistoning length of his cock, her inner muscles milking him. On the heels of her orgasm, Theo tipped over the edge of his pleasure threshold as well, crying out her name as his cock moved deep within her body.

When it was over, he came down on top of her, rolling over and pulling her along with him. He kissed her lips and then fell to nuzzling her neck and inhaling the scent of her freshly shampooed hair.

"Live with me," he murmured.

"What?" The query came slowly. Her whole body was heavy and sluggish with satisfaction and contentment.

"Live with me." His lips bussed hers. "I want you to move in with me. I don't think I can handle another night without waking up beside you."

Sarafina paused for a moment, forcing her synapses to fire a little faster. "I would love to live with you, but can we live here instead of at the Coven?"

"Here?"

She supposed it was an alien request to a man who'd grown up connected to the Coven, knowing from childhood he was a witch. Why would anyone want to live separately from the people who were like them?

"It's just that I have friends who aren't witches, you know? Maria and many others. I don't want to lose them. I know I can't reveal every facet of the true me, but I don't want to completely walk away from the life I've been living, either. They mean too much to me."

"I would be happy to move in here with you, Sarafina. Do you plan to take the job Thomas offered you?"

She considered for a moment, tracing a line with her fingertip over his luscious bicep. All she had to do was touch this man, and she wanted him.

Okay, that was a lie. All she had to do was think about him or be within five feet of him to want him.

"In this case, yes. I'll find some cover to use with my friends to explain the job change. That way I can spend the day at the Coven and my evenings with my friends." She paused, smiling. "And all the time with you."

"Sounds good to me."

She drew a breath, realizing something. "Only . . ." She lifted her head, studying him.

"What?"

"I wonder if you'll be able to handle my social calendar." The blood drained from her face. "Do you think you can stomach Maria?"

He laughed. "If I can battle demons, I can take Maria. I think a bouquet of flowers and showing how I care about you will go a long way to taming that beast. Trust me, I don't have a problem with any friends of yours who are so protective. I think she and I can find some common ground."

She snuggled down against his chest and sighed happily. "But perhaps keeping your apartment at the Coven isn't such a bad idea. We can stay there sometimes, too."

Sarafina still felt torn between two worlds, especially now that the crisis with Bai was over. She had no doubt she would find equilibrium eventually, though. She could face anything as long as she had Theo by her side.

Theo chuckled. "Grosset will have to learn to ride a Harley."

"We can get him a Pomeranian-sized helmet."

He reached over and pulled a small box from the pocket of his jeans. "I'm glad you said yes to the first question, because I have another to ask." He opened the box and set it on the carpet between them.

It was a diamond engagement ring.

Her breath caught in her throat. "Theo?"

He said nothing, only watched her face.

"*Theo.*" She picked up the ring and slid it onto her finger.

It was a perfect fit.

THIRTY-FOUR

❧

"WE NEED TO GO DOWN."

Sarafina rolled over lazily in bed and gazed at Theo.

The Coven was hosting a party to celebrate the defeat of the Duskoff and the *Atrika*. Although apparently, the primary purpose of the party was some mysterious announcement.

The celebration came on the heels of twenty-nine days of mourning. One day for every slain witch—twenty-two witches had perished. The extra seven days were the official Coven mourning period for the thirty-two witches who had lost their magick in the battle.

For the last month the Coven had been a somber place as they all grieved and repaired what had been so badly damaged, both physically and nonphysically.

During the time since Sarafina had accepted Theo's proposal, Theo had moved into her apartment and made peace with Maria. As she'd requested, he'd kept his apartment, too—a solid tie to the Coven—and they'd spent the previous couple of nights there.

"I don't know. I'd rather stay here in bed with you." She laid a kiss to his chest.

Sarafina had an announcement of her own to make, but the thought of it made butterflies rise in her stomach, so she put the thought away for the moment.

"We've got the rest of our lives to spend in bed together, baby." He chuckled low. "I'm really looking forward to that."

She stretched, enjoying her satisfied lethargy and the soreness that came from being well loved. There were some types of pains that were more like pleasure. "What should I wear?"

He slipped the sheet off her, exposing her bare breasts and stomach. His heated gaze took her in for a moment, a familiar lust turning his eyes even darker. He lowered his head and sucked one nipple into his mouth and then the other, taking time with each.

It was odd how there seemed to be a direct line from her breasts to her sex when Theo touched them.

"I would prefer nothing at all, but I guess you should go down in a dress," he murmured.

"A dress," she answered in the breathless voice that Theo seemed to so often produce in her. "I can manage that, I think."

He rolled off the bed and stood. Sarafina sat up, admiring the bare rear view of him—the long, strong legs and back, and the most perfect male derrière she'd ever seen in her life.

He glanced out the window at the darkening twilight. These days they didn't have to worry about Bai popping in on them, or Stefan threatening them, so they could do self-indulgent and absolutely exquisite things like spend the whole day in bed. That was exactly what they'd done.

"I guess we should get ready," she said.

"The party will be starting soon." Theo reached out a hand and pulled her to her feet. He raised a brow. "Shower?"

She smiled. "If you're in it, sure."

After they'd showered and . . . other things, Sarafina pulled on a light gray spaghetti-strap dress and a matching pair of dove gray heels. She added a strand of pearls and pearl earrings, then did her hair in a tumble of boisterous curls and put on makeup.

She finished touching up her lipstick and walked out into the bedroom. Theo stopped in his tracks and stared. "Wow."

"Thank you." She smiled. "You don't look too bad yourself."

He was dressed in a charcoal gray shirt and a pair of black pants. His hair, still just a little damp, hung loose over his shoulders and his tattoos peeked from the neckline of the shirt. He held out his hand. "Should we go?"

She nodded and took his hand.

Grosset was lying on the couch. When they entered the room, he lifted his head and wagged his tail. After patting him on the head and promising him a walk later, they left the apartment.

On the way down to the ballroom, they ran into Mira and Jack. Mira wore a beautiful red gown and Jack was dressed in all black. Both of them were practically running to get downstairs.

Adam and Claire came around the corner just as Sarafina and Theo did.

"Hey, what's your hurry?" called Adam. "I'm sure Thomas ordered enough alcohol to last the whole night. No need to rush."

Jack called over his shoulder. "They just called to let us know that Helen is back with Eva!" They hurried on out of view.

That explained it. They hadn't seen their daughter for over two months. They'd waited to have her brought back just in case the warlocks had something else up their sleeves.

Now the family would never have to be separated again. Jack and Mira would never have to worry about their very rare little air witch daughter being abducted or used in a *daaeman* circle. They were safe.

Theo, Sarafina, Adam, and Claire reached the ballroom just in time to see the reunion.

Eva toddled from Helen's arms to her mother's, a huge smile on her cherubic face, dark curls tangled around her chubby cheeks. Mira scooped her up and held her, her eyes closed and tears streaming down her face as she rocked her back and forth and whispered over and over how much she'd missed her. Jack wrapped his arms around both of them and nestled his nose in Eva's hair.

Sarafina wiped away a tear of her own at the touching scene of a family reunited.

All around them stood the witches of the Coven, all talking and laughing. Waiters and waitresses circulated with appetizers and glasses of champagne and other drinks.

Theo wrapped his arms around her. "Are you all right?"

"I'm just happy and anticipatory and, well, hormonal."

"Hormonal?"

She turned toward him and looked up into his eyes. "You said once that you hoped you could have kids one day, after all the mess with the warlocks was cleaned up."

"Yes," he said slowly, his expression one of dawning— *stunned*—realization. "I want them one day."

"That's a good answer." She let out the breath she hadn't realized she'd been holding. "How about in two hundred and seventy-nine days, give or take?"

"What are you talking about, Sarafina?" From the tone of his voice, he knew, but it hadn't really hit him yet.

Butterflies flapped in her stomach at his reaction.

Theo stared down at her, his face going blank and then white. A second later he smiled and shouted, lifting her up and swinging her around. He set her to her feet and kissed her. "Finally, some good news."

"I can't tell you how relieved I am you think so."

He spread his hand on her stomach. "Sarafina, you've already given me love, hope, and joy. Now you're giving me even more. Of course I'm happy about this." He dragged her up against his chest and kissed her again. "I love you," he murmured against her mouth.

"Hey, what's going on?" asked Adam near them. Claire gazed at them curiously.

Theo answered before she could even get a word out. "I'm going to be a dad."

Adam smiled. "That's just about the best news I've heard all day. One day Claire and I plan to have kids, too. Only we're leaning toward adoption instead. There are little elemental witches out there caught in the non-magickal foster care system. We're going to—"

Sarafina pulled from Theo and launched herself into

Adam's arms. "Kids like I was," she whispered huskily, once again on the edge of tears.

Adam laughed. "Yes."

She detached herself from Adam and gave Claire a hug, too. "That is just so, so . . . awesome," she finished lamely, at a loss for any words to express her emotion. She looked at Theo. "Maybe we can do that, too."

Theo blanched again, then chuckled. "Yeah, maybe. Uh, let's handle the one on the way first."

"I think Theo is still in shock," said Claire with a grin.

"Speaking of kids, have you heard Thomas and Isabelle's news yet?" asked Adam.

"No," answered Claire with a smile. "You're kidding, right? Are they pregnant, too?"

"No, not yet. But Micah's been messing with some earth magick. Found a spell that might help with witchy infertility problems. Something might come out of it." Adam shrugged.

"Wow," Sarafina replied. "Micah is a genius."

Adam nodded. "He is. He using some of the *daaeman* spells he got from a book given to him by the *Syari* when he came over to Eudae with me and Claire." He paused, glancing at Micah across the room. "The loss of his magick is just brutal."

"Yes, how is he cooking up the earth magick?"

"He can brew a lot of it, and research all of it. It's just that someone else has to store and wield the charms and spells. He's using a magickal surrogate, basically."

Sarafina looked over at Micah. He was speaking with Thomas. "He seems to be coping okay with it all."

Claire glanced in Micah's direction. "His first love is research. I think he'll be fine. He just needs someone as geeky as he is to test his spells. A permanent research and testing partner." She looked pointedly at a tall, attractive brown-haired earth witch who was sipping a glass of wine across the room.

"*Oh*, she's very pretty," Sarafina answered. "Have you been meddling, Claire?"

She pinched her thumb and forefinger together. "Just a little. I think Emily and Micah will get along really well.

She's just as interested in history and magickal theory as he is. Micah just needs a little . . . push, is all." Claire grinned. "They're going to be working very closely together in the future. Plus, Emily's been smitten with Micah forever. Micah has just never noticed before. He's so oblivious to anything but his work."

Sarafina watched Micah glance at Emily across the room, then look again and stare at her a bit.

Uh-huh. Magick in the making.

"He's not oblivious anymore," Sarafina murmured, raising her eyebrow and taking a sip of her sweet tea.

Claire laughed. "Nope. The seed has been planted. It has nothing to do now but bloom."

"Good for Micah." Sarafina sighed. "All this good news after so much bad, it's heartwarming. We'll all be raising a whole new generation of witches soon."

"The Coven's future is bright," answered Theo. He pulled her against his side. "Like ours."

"Okay," said Thomas loudly. "It's almost time for our announcement."

All the heads in the ballroom swiveled toward Thomas and the conversation hushed. Sarafina felt in the know, figuring his announcement would be Micah's fertility tinkering. But when the large screen descended from the ceiling, Sarafina realized that perhaps that wasn't what they planned to announce, after all.

"For your viewing pleasure," Thomas announced to the hushed crowd. He smiled vibrantly, Isabelle and Micah on either side of him, also smiling. "I think you'll enjoy this." He hit a button on the remote control he held.

The evening news popped on.

And in business news this evening, millionaire Thomas Monahan has purchased a controlling stake in Duskoff International. Duskoff International has been in the news lately because of the mysterious disappearance of celebrity CEO Stefan Faucheux. Faucheux took the company public only last spring. The police are actively

*investigating his disappearance. But perhaps for now,
the rudderless company has found a new man to help
lead it.*

The video cut to a smiling Thomas.

*"Now that I have a stake in the future of Duskoff International, I intend to take an active hand in shaping the
company's future."*
In other news . . .

Everyone in the ballroom cheered.

The video stopped and the screen went back up. All
around them people cheered and clapped.

Thomas hushed the excited murmuring of the crowd once
again and raised his glass. "To the future of the Coven." He
paused. "To us!"

Everyone raised their glasses and repeated the toast.

Magick flickered and flared all around them, the crackle
and spark of all four elements in harmony and proximity,
rising and falling, blending and twisting again. Up and up it
all went to the ceiling of the ballroom and beyond—a combined expression of the Coven's current shared state of mind
and emotion.

Lightness and joy filled Sarafina. Smiling, she reached
out and took Theo's hand in hers. Fire sparked from Sarafina's chest and curled downward to twine around their hands
and wrists in licks of harmless but pretty blue fire.

Theo looked down at her with love lighting his dark eyes
instead of the coldness that had filled them the first time
they'd met. He lowered his head and caught her lips with his.
"You're so beautiful, Sarafina," he murmured against her
mouth.

She glanced down at her dress. "Thanks. It's new."

He tipped her face up to his. "I didn't mean the dress. I
didn't even notice the dress. You're just beautiful, everywhere.
Inside and out. Up and down. Every single inch of your body
and your soul."

She tipped her head to the side a little and smiled. "Theo, is that you? Where'd the poetry come from?"

He took a long moment to answer. "It comes from you, Sarafina." He kissed her. "You gave it all to me."

Turn the page for a preview of the next
exciting paranormal romance from Anya Bast

WICKED
ENCHANTMENT

Coming soon from Berkley Sensation!

"Sex incarnate," the women and men around her whispered. "Half incubus."

Aislinn didn't know if it was true, but she did know the man was Unseelie in a Seelie Court. That didn't happen very often, so she stared just like everyone else as he passed down the corridor.

Dressed head to toe in black, wearing heavy boots and a long coat over a thin crew neck sweater that defined his muscular chest, he seemed to possess every inch of the hallway he tread. He walked with such confidence it gave the illusion he took up more space than was physically possible. Seelie nobles shrank in his wake, though they tried to stand firm and proud. Not even the most powerful ones were immune. Others postured and drew up straighter, offering challenge to some imaginary threat in their midst. Not even the gold and rose bedecked Imperial Guard was immune to his passing. It was as if they sensed a marauder in their midst.

Maybe this man was a marauder.

No one knew anything about him other than that the dark magick running through his Unseelie veins was both lethal and sexual in nature. The court buzzed with the news of his arrival and of his meeting with the Summer Queen, High Royal of the Seelie Tuatha Dé Danann.

According to gossip, Gabriel Cionaodh Marcus Mac Braire had been welcomed past the threshold of the gleaming rose quartz tower of the Seelie Court because he was petitioning the Summer Queen for permanent residence, a subject that had received a huge amount of attention from Seelie nobles. Predictably, most of the people against it were men.

Gabriel, it was said, held Seelie blood in his veins, but the incubus Unseelie part of him overshadowed it. The rumors went that he was catnip to females and—when his special brand of magick was wielded at full force between the sheets—he possessed the power to enslave a woman. The afflicted female would become addicted to him. She'd stop eating and sleeping, wanting nothing more than his touch, until she finally died from longing and self-neglect.

Just the thought made Aislinn shudder, yet it didn't seem to deter his female admirers. Maybe that was because no one had ever met a woman who'd suffered that fate. If this man could use sex like a deadly weapon, apparently he never did.

Yet some kind of sexual magick did seem to pour from him. Something intangible, subtle, and seductive.

Watching him now, so self-assured and beautiful, Aislinn could see the allure. His long black coat melded with his shoulder-length dark hair until she wasn't sure where one began and the other ended. A gorgeous fallen angel whose every movement promised a night filled with the darkest, most dangerous erotic pleasure? There was nothing to find uninteresting. Even she, jaded and disillusioned by "love" as she currently was, could see the attraction.

That attraction, of course, was the stock and trade of an incubus, and Gabriel was at least half, if court gossip was to be believed. But for all his dark beauty and lethal charm, and despite that odd but subtle magick, he didn't entice Aislinn. To her, he screamed danger. Perhaps that was because of the very humbling, public breakup she'd just endured. All men, *especially* attractive ones, looked like trouble to her now.

"Wow," said her friend Carina, coming to stand beside her. "I see what everyone was talking about. He's really . . ." she trailed off, her eyebrows rising into her ebony hairline.

"He's really what?" Carina's husband growled, coming up from behind them to twine his arms around his wife's waist.

"Really potent," Carina answered. "That man's magick is so strong that even standing in his wake, a woman feels a little intoxicated, but it's false." She turned and embraced Drem. "My attraction to you is completely real." Her voice, low and honey soft, convinced everyone within hearing range of her honesty.

"Do you think he's *potent*, Aislinn?" Drem asked, curving his thin lips into a teasing smile.

She watched the man disappear through the ornate gold and rose double doors leading into the throne room at the end of the hallway. The last thing she saw was the edge of his coat. Behind him scurried a cameraman and a slick, well-heeled commentator from Faemous, the annoying twenty-four-hour human "news" channel with coverage of the Seelie Court that the Summer Queen found so amusing. "A woman would have to be dead not to see his virility, but if he's got any special sex magick, it's not affecting me."

Drem shifted his green eyes from her to stare at the end of the hallway where the man had disappeared. "So detached and cool, Aislinn?"

She shrugged. "He doesn't make me hot."

"You're the only one," Carina muttered. Her husband gave her a playful swat on her butt for punishment. She gasped in surprise and then laughed. "Look over there. He's the reason no men are making you hot right now."

Aislinn followed Carina's gaze to see Kendal in all his glittering blond glory. He stood with a couple friends— people who used to be *her* friends—in the meet-and-greet area just outside the court doors.

Ugh.

Kendal locked gazes with her, but Aislinn merely looked away as though she hadn't noticed him. She'd wasted too much time on him already. She could hardly believe she'd ever thought she'd loved him. Kendal was a social climber, nothing more. He'd used her to further his position at court, for the prestige of dating one of the queen's favorites, and then tossed her aside.

"I have nothing to say to him," Aislinn said in the coolest tone she could manage.

Carina stared at him, her jaw set. "Well, I do." She began to walk across the corridor toward him.

Aislinn caught her hand and squeezed. "No, please don't. Thank you for being furious with him on my account, but Kendal isn't deserving of the attention. Anyway, that's what he wants. It feeds his ego."

"I can tell you what that weasel *is* deserving of."

Aislinn laughed. "You're a good friend, Carina."

The doors at the end of the corridor opened and a male hobgoblin court attendant stepped out dressed in the gold and rose livery of the Rose Tower. "The Queen requests the presence of Aislinn Christiana Guinevere Finvarra."

Aislinn frowned and stilled, looking toward the doors at the end of the corridor through which Gabriel had recently disappeared. Why would the queen wish to see her?

Carina pushed her forward, breaking her momentary paralysis. Aislinn moved down the corridor surrounded by silence. She'd grown used to being the topic of court gossip lately. The Seelie nobles didn't have much to do besides get into each other's business. Magick wasn't a valuable commodity here, like it was in the Unseelie Court.

She entered the throne room, and the heavy double doors closed behind her with a loud thump. Caoilainn Elspeth Muirgheal, the High Queen of the Seelie Tuatha Dé Danann, sat on her throne. Gabriel stood before her, his back to Aislinn. The Imperial Guard, men and women of less pure Seelie Tuatha Dé blood, lined the room, all standing at attention in their gleaming gold and rose helms and hauberks.

It always gave her shivers to stand in the throne room before the queen. Arched ceilings hand painted with frescoes of *Cath Maige Tuired*, depicting the fae taking over Ireland from the Firbolg, humans in their less-evolved and more-animalistic form, instilled a sense of awe in all who entered. Gold-veined marble floors stretched under her shoes, reaching to rose quartz pillars and walls. It was a cold place despite the warm colors, full of power and designed to intimidate and control.

The Unseelie, Gabriel, seemed utterly unaffected. In fact, the way he stood—feet slightly apart, head held high, and a small, secretive smile playing over his lips—made him seem almost insolent.

The Faemous film crew stood near a far wall, the light of the camera trained on the Summer Queen and Gabriel. Though now the camera turned to record Aislinn's entrance. The silver-haired female commentator—Aislinn thought her name was Holly something—whispered into her mike, describing the goings-on.

Ignoring the film crew, as she always did, she halted near the incubus, yet kept a good distance away. The last thing she was going to do was fawn like most women. Out of the corner of her eye, she saw him do a slow upward appraisal of her, the kind men do when they're clearly wondering what a woman looks like without her clothes. He wasn't even trying to hide it. Maybe he was so arrogant that he felt he didn't have to hide it.

Aislinn was seriously beginning to dislike this man.

She curtsied deeply to the queen, difficult in her tight Rock & Republic jeans. If she had known she was going to be called into court, she would have worn something a little looser . . . and a bit more formal. Today she was wearing a gray V-neck sweater and wedge-heeled black boots with her jeans. She'd twisted her hair up and only dashed on makeup. This was not an event she'd planned for.

The queen, as always, was dressed in heavy brocade, silk, and lace. Today her color theme was a rich burgundy and cream, her skirts pooling at her feet like a bloody ocean. The Royal's long pale hair was done up in a series of intricate braids, and heavy ruby jewelry glittered at her ears and nestled at the base of her slender, pale throat. She wore no makeup because she didn't need it. Her beauty was flawless and chilly.

Caoilainn Elspeth Muirgheal gestured with a slim hand, the light catching on her many rings. "Aislinn, please meet Gabriel Mac Braire. He is petitioning the Seelie Court for residency, in case you hadn't already heard. It seems word has spread through court about it. I am still considering his case. As you know, we don't often grant such requests."

Yes, but there were precedents. Take Ronan Quinn, for

example. He was part blood druid and part Unseelie mage. He'd successfully petitioned the Summer Queen for residency in the Rose Tower over thirty years ago because he'd fallen in love with Bella, Aislinn's best friend. Ronan had lost Bella, fallen into a state of reckless despondency, and pulled some mysterious job for the Phaendir that had nearly gotten him beheaded by the Summer Queen. In the end, Ronan had retained his life and won Bella back—but both had been banished from the Rose Tower as punishment for Ronan's transgressions. Aislinn didn't know where they were now.

She missed Bella every single day. Bella had been the only one to know her deepest and darkest secrets. Without Bella's presence, she felt utterly alone.

That entire story aside, Ronan Quinn was one example of an Unseelie male who'd managed to find a place in the Rose. Ronan, like Gabriel, was exceedingly good-looking. That would weigh heavily in Gabriel's favor. The queen couldn't resist a virile, highly magicked man.

"He'll be staying here for the next week, and I have decided you shall be his guide and general helpmeet while he's here."

"Me?" Aislinn blinked. "Why me?" The question came out of her mouth before she could think it through, and she instantly regretted it. One did not question Caoilainn Elspeth Muirgheal; one simply obeyed.

The Summer Queen lifted one pale, perfectly arched brow. "Why *not* you?"

"With all respect due you, my queen, I think—"

"Do you have a problem with my judgment?"

Oh, this was getting more and more dangerous with every word the queen uttered. The room had chilled a bit, too, a result of the Seelie Royal's mood affecting her magick. Aislinn shivered. "N-no, my queen."

Gabriel glanced over at her with a mocking smile playing on his sensual, luscious lips.

Nope, she didn't like him one bit, even if he did have sensual, luscious lips.

"That's a good answer, Aislinn. Do you have a problem with Gabriel? Most women would kill to spend time with him." The queen gestured airily with one hand. "I thought I was doing you a favor after your . . . unfortunate incident with Kendal."

Oh, sweet lady Danu. Aislinn gritted her teeth before answering. "I don't have a problem with him, my queen."

The queen clapped her hands together, making Aislinn jump. "Good, that's all settled then. You're both dismissed."

Aislinn turned immediately and walked out of the throne room, Gabriel following. Aislinn didn't like having him behind her. It made her feel like a gazelle being stalked by a lion. He'd soon find out this gazelle had fight. There was no way she was going to lay down and show him her vulnerable, soft stomach . . . or any other part of her body.

The corridor was thronged with curious onlookers as they exited. Carina, partway down the hall with Drem, made a move to walk to Aislinn, but Aislinn held up a hand to stop her. All eyes were on her and Gabriel. She didn't want to linger here, and she really didn't want anyone listening in on their conversation and using it to weave rumor. They could watch Faemous for the juicy details, just like everyone else.

Gabriel surveyed the scene and ran a hand over his stubble-dusted, clefted chin. "Is it always like this over here?" His voice was deep and low, and reminded her of dark chocolate.

"Like what?" she snapped in annoyance.

He encompassed the thronged corridor with a sweep of his hand as they made their way down. "Is this all the Seelie nobles have to do? Stand around and gossip?" He glanced at her stern expression and sobered. "Never mind. Forget I said that."

"Insulting my home is not a good way to start things off, Mac Braire."

"Call me Gabriel, and I wasn't insulting it. I was making an observation. I want to make this my home, remember? That's why I'm here."

"Sounded like an insult to me," she muttered, hightailing

it away from the clumps of Seelie nobles doing exactly what he'd just accused them of. She had to fight to keep up with the strides of his longer legs.

"I apologize."

"How does the Shadow King feel about your defection from the Black? He can't be very happy."

Gabriel gave a low laugh. "He's not. I'm taking a huge gamble. If the Summer Queen rejects me and I lose the protection of the Seelie Court, I may lose my head, too."

"You don't seem all that nervous about it."

"Life is too short to spend in fear. Anyway, I've lived so long that I'm a thrill seeker. Anything to break up the monotony. Anything for change, Aislinn."

The way he pronounced her name sent a shiver down her spine. He rolled it on his tongue like a French kiss, smooth and sweet as melting candy.

It made her miss a step and deepened her annoyance.

She picked up her pace and matched his strides once more. "Listen, I don't know why the queen selected me for this job, but the last thing I want to do right now is babysit you."

Ouch. That had been harsh.

She winced as the words echoed through her head. He hadn't done anything to her, and she wasn't sure why she was feeling so hostile. It had to be because of her recent breakup with Kendal. Gabriel reminded her of him.

Every man reminded her of him.

She still felt so raw and vulnerable. She needed time alone to lick her wounds and heal. The last thing she wanted was to be forced into spending time with an obvious womanizer who could wield sex as a weapon. Literally. Perhaps she was using this man as a scapegoat for her wounded pride and broken heart. If so, that was wrong . . . yet she couldn't seem to help herself.

"Whoa. Look, Aislinn, if you feel so strongly about it, I'm sure I can find someone else to *babysit* me."

She winced again. She was being a bitch and needed to rein it in. Maybe she'd misjudged him, and he was a great guy. After all, he bore nothing but a passing resemblance to

Kendal. That wasn't his fault. Regret pinched her, and she opened her mouth to apologize.

"It's too bad you don't want to spend time with me, though, since I have news of Bella and Ronan. They've been anxious to get back into contact with you."

Danu. She nearly tripped and fell. Bella and Ronan? So they were at the Unseelie Court, after all. Aislinn had assumed they'd gone there but wasn't sure whether or not the Shadow King had allowed them to stay in the Black Tower.

The Seelie Court was called the Rose Tower because it was constructed of rose quartz. The Unseelie Court was referred to as the Black Tower because—never to be outdone— it was made from black quartz. The delivery of large quantities of each had been allowed by human society and the Phaendir, and magick had been employed to make it useable as a construction material.

Gabriel walked ahead of her, intending to leave her in the dust. Damn the man! He'd tossed that last bit out and then left to punish her. He knew she'd chase him. Clearly her first impulse to dislike the man had been dead on.

"Hey." She took a couple running steps to catch up with him. "I'm sorry. I've been unfair to you. You're all alone and could clearly use a friend"—although she was sure he'd end up with plenty of "friends" here soon enough— "and someone to show you around. Let's start over."

He stopped, turned toward her, and lifted a dark brow. "Ah, so you do want word of Bella and Ronan."

"No." She shook her head. "I mean, yes, but I didn't say that just to have news of them. This is about me being fair and giving you the benefit of the doubt."

"Benefit of the doubt? What movie about me have you made in your head, sweet Aislinn? And without even knowing me."

"That you're a dangerous, arrogant, superficial man with piles of discarded, heartbroken female bodies to each side of the path you tread."

They'd stopped in a large open area with a huge fountain in the shape of a swan. There were less people here. For a moment all was silent except for the sound of running water and the clicking heels of the few passers-by.

He studied her with hard, glittering dark blue eyes. "Your honesty is very refreshing. I'm sorry that's your first impression of me. Perhaps I can change it."

"Maybe you can."

"A little too honest, that's my first impression of you." He narrowed his eyes. "And perhaps a bit jaded about men at the moment." He loosely shrugged one shoulder. "Just a guess."

Good guess. Time to change the subject. "Why do you wish to change courts anyway?"

"I'm surprised a pure-blood Seelie Tuatha Dé would ask such a question. I thought everyone here believed the Rose Tower superior in all ways. There should be no question why I wish to defect from the Black."

Aislinn didn't understand the twist to his words. It was almost—but not quite—mockery. An odd attitude to have when he seemed to want to join those he mocked for the rest of his very long life.

"Apparently Bella and Ronan have gone to the Unseelie Court. It can't be that bad."

Gabriel smiled. "Well, there's no Faemous film crew there." No. Apparently the film crew the Shadow King had allowed in years ago had been eaten. "And the nobles aren't as . . . prissy."

She raised her eyebrows. "Prissy?"

He nodded. "The Unseelie Court is darker, and you have to watch your step."

"So I've heard. Magick cast; blood spilled."

"Sometimes. The magick is stronger, more violent, and held in higher regard. You know that. The laws are different there, and you must be careful. You don't want to make enemies of some of them."

Fear niggled. "How are Bella and Ronan?"

"Very well. They've adjusted to life in the Black. They said to tell you they're fine, but Bella misses you. They say to tell you they're happy."

She studied him for lies. It was what she wanted to hear,

of course, and Gabriel seemed the type to tell you what you wanted to hear. But she *so* wanted to believe what he'd said. She'd lost more than one night's sleep worrying about her friends. The memory of watching them walk away into Piefferburg Square on Yule Eve, forever banished from Seelie by the Summer Queen, still made her heart ache.

Though the crime that Ronan had committed—taking work from the Phaendir—normally would have held the punishment of death. He'd been lucky. They both had. The Phaendir, a guild of powerful immortal druids, were the sworn enemy of the fae—Seelie and Unseelie alike.

There was good reason.

The Phaendir, with the full support of the humans, had created and controlled the borders of Piefferburg with powerful warding. They called it a "resettlement area."

Piefferburg's inhabitants called it prison.

If one wanted to be philosophical about it, the fate of the fae was poetic punishment for the horrible fae race wars of the early 1600s that had decimated their population and left them easy prey to their common enemy, the Phaendir. The wars had forced the fae from the underground, and the humans had panicked in the face of the truth—the fae were real.

On top of the wars, a mysterious sickness called Watt Syndrome had also befallen the fae. Some thought the illness had been created by the Phaendir. However it had come about, the result was the same—it had further weakened them.

The two events had been a perfect storm of misfortune, leading to their downfall. When the fae had been at their most vulnerable, the Phaendir had allied with the humans to imprison them in an area of what had then been the New World, founded by a human named Jules Piefferburg.

These days the sects of fae who'd warred in the 1600s had reached an uneasy peace. They were united against the Phaendir because the old human saying was true—the enemy of my enemy is my friend.

Aislinn cleared her throat against a sudden rush of emotion. Bella had been the only one in the court who'd carried the weight of Aislinn's secret. Really, Bella had been more of a sister than a friend. "Come with me. I'll give you a tour before dinner."

"Sounds good."

They walked the length and breadth of the Rose Tower, which was enormous and completely self-sufficient. She showed him all the floors and how they were graduated in terms of court ranking. The higher floors, the floors closest to the Queen's penthouse apartment, were where the Seelie Tuatha Dé with the purest blood resided. She showed him the courtyard in the solarium where the families with children lived so they could have yards to play in. The school. The restaurants on premise where the nobles dined. The ballroom. The numerous gathering areas and the banquet halls.

Most of the residents never really left the building for much beyond shopping or to have a night of dining out. Some of the more adventurous slummed it at a few of Pief-ferburg's nightclubs, but the Summer Queen discouraged the Seelie Tuatha Dé from mixing with the trooping fae—those fae who didn't belong to either court and weren't wild-ings or water-dwelling.

While social contact with the trooping fae was discouraged, unchaperoned and unapproved contact with the Un-seelie Tuatha Dé was strictly forbidden. Aislinn suspected more of the illicit sort went on than was widely known. After all, she suspected her own mother of it. There was no other way to explain away certain . . . oddities . . . in Aislinn's magickal abilities.

She and Gabriel ended up at her front door. A good thing since she wanted her slippers, a cup of hot cocoa, and her own company for the rest of the evening.

Gabriel grabbed her hand before she could snatch it away. "Thank you for spending time with me today," he murmured in Old Maejian, the words rolling soft and smooth like good whiskey from his tongue. He bent to kiss her hand in the old custom, his gaze fastened on hers. At the last moment, he flipped her hand palm up and laid his lips to her wrist. All the while his thumb stroked her palm back and forth.

That calloused rasp in conjunction with his warm, silky

lips sent shivers through her. Made her think about his hands and lips on other parts of her body, which made her think of his long, muscled length naked against her between the sheets of her bed.

In a sweaty tangle.

Limbs entwined . . .

Bad incubus. She snatched her hand back.

He stood for a moment, bent over, hand still in kissing position. Then he grinned in a half-mocking, half-mischievous way, straightened, and walked down the corridor. Pure sex wrapped in black and adorned with a swagger.

She supposed the Summer Queen thought spending time with Gabriel would be good for Aislinn after her break up with Kendal. A little meaningless fling to get her back on the dating horse? But Aislinn did not do meaningless flings.

And she was definitely unappreciative of being saddled with a man like Gabriel Mac Braire.

Sweet Danu, what had the queen thrown her into?